*My GreatGrandfather
Was Stonewall Jackson*

My Great-Grandfather Was Stonewall Jackson

Stonewalling in the Shadow of a Legend

Volume II

David Jonathan Sawyer

Jonathan Publishing Company ● Baltimore, Maryland

Copyright©1994 by David Jonathan Sawyer

All rights reserved. No part of this book may be reproduced or transmitted in any form by any means, electronic or mechanical, including photocopying and recording, or by any information storage or retrieval system, without permission in writing from the publisher.

Published by Jonathan Publishing Company
David Jonathan Sawyer, Publisher
P.O. Box 3324, Baltimore MD 21213
410-563-4431

ISBN 0-9634206-1-5
Library of Congress Catalog Number 92-074120

Manufactured in the United States of America
First Printing: Second Volume: August, 1995

This book is dedicated

to my wife, Carolyn, who was amazed at my candor, but with tongue in cheek is always there for me. It is also dedicated to the memory of my late parents, Noah and Mary Jackson Sawyer, and my other Sawyer and Jackson relatives; to my daughter, Lois; to my stepdaughter, Sherri; to my stepson, David; to my parents-in-law, Lois and Furman Quick; to my granddaughter, Richelle; to my step granddaughter, Kellanda; to my great-granddaughter, Alishia and Nehemiah; to my nieces Wanda and Sylvia; and to my sister and brother-in-law, Katie and George King. The book is also dedicated to the other black descendants of General Thomas Jonathan "Stonewall" Jackson.

Cedat Fortuna Peritis

"Let fortune yield to experience"

Motto of
General Thomas "Stonewall" Jackson

Contents

Homeward Bound 13
That's about the Size of It 21
Marlena 33
The Train 45
Home Again 53
Miz Hannah's Lament 57
Grandpa's Family 67
Papa's New Beginning 79
A Mule And Other Stuff 93
Abstinence Rewarded 107
Returning Home 119
Little Ed's Homecoming 137
Square Business 147
Ducking the Law 161
The White Woman 173
What to Do on a Rainy Day 185
Jailhouse Blues 197
Preparation for Redemption 213

Contents

Baptism, Wet Devil, Dry Devil 223
Jimmy's Back 241
Jimmy's Blues 253
Rice with or without Gravy 271
Physical Education 279
Papa, a Squirrel And I 291
Appendix 303

Prologue

The fact that Thomas Jonathan Jackson had a brief affair with a slave girl in the Summer of 1857 in Mecklenburg County, North Carolina did nothing to change the course of history. The only consequence of the little known event was a child born to Mary Walker, the mulatto slave girl. She named the boy Isaiah Jackson. Jackson was in North Carolina to be married to Mary Anna Morrison, the daughter of a prominent doctor in the country. Jackson's quick detour on his way to the alter caused concern to no one. What he did was not unusual, white men of that era had no compunction about leaving their reproductive juices in the bodies of female slaves. Besides, it lightened the tarbrush and a mulatto offspring was a boon in that time of barter in human flesh. I make no apology for being a direct descendent of Thomas Jonathan "Stonewall" Jackson. It was not my doing. It was more than a hundred years ago when he had an affair with my great-grandmother, Mary Walker. My maternal grandfather, Isaiah Jackson, was the immediate result of Jackson's dalliance with the pretty slave girl.

This story is not about degrees of blackness or whiteness or ethnicity. Nor is it about cultural images revived by the beat of African drums. It is not intended to resurrect the broken dreams of racial equality, and it has nothing to do with unfulfilled promises to Indians, who were the first Americans. Neither is it an attempt to prove my kinship to the famous Civil War hero. The first volume of this trilogy explains the legacy with telling accuracy. I can vouch for my kinship to the Southern officer with more conviction than any person alive. This book is a true account of how I inherited the strange personality traits of the wily Confederate general and the effect it had on my life. The facial resemblance certainly exists, but it does not scratch the surface, or give any hint of the forces raging inside of me. The physical side of Jackson is a story in itself. I know because I am cursed with the same peculiarities that troubled my great-grandfather. I shuddered at the thought of sharing our dark secret, but then I decided it must be told. Let me assure you, I know first-hand about the physical and every other facet of the woefully eccentric military genius known as "Stonewall Jackson."

The general's known hypochondria, his inability to get along with fellow human beings and his religiosity was passed down to me. I also received a generous helping of his little-known affinity for sexual misconduct. His every whim and fantasy are a part of me, and his well-known foolhardiness asserts itself without any prior warning. The much touted bravery of the fabled hero comes and goes, but the cunning was always there for me. For the love of heaven, do not consider it trivial, or play down the importance of heredity. You are a product of those who came before you. To deal constantly with near madness is a frightening thing. Living in the shadow of such a monumental legend was a ride on a roller coaster headed downhill with the nether regions in plain sight. I'm David Jonathan Sawyer, the great-grandson of the mighty "Stonewall Jackson". Go with me, if you dare!

1

Homeward Bound

It was January 1, 1947, and I was somewhere in the Midwest aboard a Western Flyer that belched smoke and steam as it sped and thundered on the iron highway. The train's big driving wheels showered sparks along the roadbed as it roared due East toward its destination. After a brief dawn, which had hurriedly swept the darkness from the shiny steel ribbons of the tracks, the morning sun was free to stretch with abandon in any direction it pleased. It shone brightly and made the slim shadows of telephone poles and the few trees beside the tracks dance awry. With complete disdain, the brightness filtered through the dirty windows and rippled across the faces of the passengers seated quietly in the colored people's Pullman car.

The arrival of morning did nothing to bolster my flagging spirits. The blaze of sunlight was simply a mocking reminder of the reason for my being on the train in the first place.

I was in full uniform. My artillery and good conduct medals were pinned correctly across my chest. The Technician Fifth Grade corporal's stripes on my sleeves, of which I was so proud, meant nothing to me now. The fact that I had forfeited my heritage was uppermost in my mind. At this juncture, it was about the only thing that still mattered to me. All of my life, I had considered myself to be a special individual. My

Homeward Bound

great-grandfather was the world-acclaimed Civil War general known as "Stonewall" Jackson. My whole life had been geared to emulate his greatness. Now the Stonewall dream was shattered into a million pieces. It was the end of a quest, one destined not to be fulfilled. Sadly, it dawned on me that I could never be like my hero. I was no longer a member of the United States Army. I was simply David Jonathan Sawyer, colored civilian. It was a sobering time for me.

With the culmination of the second big war and the end of all hostile acts, the powers that be found it difficult to find duty for the Negro soldier. A few of the colored troops were sent to Germany and Japan to act as constabulary police. The bulk of the colored soldiers, now no longer needed, floated aimlessly in limbo.

I was a member of Company A of the First Infantry Battalion formerly of Fort McClellan, Alabama. Now at Fort Sill, Oklahoma, we were reactivated as the 969th Field Artillery Battalion. There was some discussion in high places about using the whole battalion to build a golf course for the white officers, but for some reason it never happened. The whole company was fuming with rage. The young troopers were a proud bunch. We had been trained as top-rated fighting men and that was what we wanted to do. The recent war had proven over and over again that the Negro's patriotism and love of country were never in doubt.

The company's outrage slowly subsided. The original plan to use the battalion as school troops to train friendly forces from France, England and the other Allied nations was quickly put into action. The artillery pieces to be used were the 105 howitzer and the 155 millimeter big gun, which was often called the "Long Tom." Both guns were awesome in their range and firepower.

It was an ideal situation for me because Great-grandfather Jackson had been a master of artillery warfare. I had been totally fascinated by the battles in which he fought, using all of the deadly firepower at his disposal. I had been obsessed since childhood by Stonewall's daring exploits. His motto, "Cedat Fortuna Peritis," "Let fortune yield to experience," was my motto too.

Even aboard the train, I still carried a small, tattered book that was given to me by my grandmother. It chronicled Stonewall's battles and adversaries with the times, dates, places, personalities and events involved.

Throughout my life, the book had been my constant companion, giving solace when solace was desperately needed. I had used it as a cripple uses a crutch. As the train sped through the American heartland, I reached inside the pocket of my Ike jacket and took out the tattered book. The edges were ragged with years of ingrained dirt, and the back of the book hung by a single thread.

Just then, my attention was diverted by the train's whistle that screamed mournfully as it rounded a curve and slowed to cross a trestle, one that stretched across a deep gorge filled with rushing water. The depths of the gorge were terrifying, but it was all right with me. I was safe because the spirit of Stonewall was still with me. As the train left the trestle, I thumbed quickly through the book until I found a familiar passage. I began to read, slowly scanning the tattered pages.

Sunday, July 21, 1861. The battle of Manassas gave a man a chance, and the man responded. As a result Thomas J. Jackson won a reputation and a nickname that lasts until today. When there is talk in war rooms, command posts or oval offices about great commanders and military leaders, Stonewall's name invariably comes to mind. As Manassas's furious fighting raged back and forth, Jackson was called on to reinforce other troops. His strict discipline and training paid off. The men fought superbly. In the midst of the action, General Bee called out to his troops, "Look. There's Jackson standing like a stonewall! Rally behind the Virginians!" I smiled and whispered, "Go, Ol' Jack! Go!" After a few moments, my thoughts turned again to my present predicament.

Fort Sill, the 969th Field Artillery Battalion and everything connected to the United States Army were things of the past. It had taken the company commander, along with the urging of the first sergeant, about a week to start the process that culminated in my dismissal from service. It had been brazenly unfair. Bad blood between First Sergeant Hosea Walker and myself was something that I had not wanted, but it had happened, and it was probably my fault. Hindsight was an exercise in futility. Maybe I shouldn't have gotten as friendly as I had with Sergeant Walker. Captain George Lewis, the battery commander, had been quite affable toward me until he was influenced by Sergeant Walker.

To someone who grew up watching movies about cowboys and Indians of the Wild West, Fort Sill was an exciting place to be. It had

Homeward Bound

begun as a remount station, and for a short period it was Civil War hero General Phil Sheridan's stomping grounds. This was where countless legends of daring-do had originated. The post museum was formerly the old guardhouse where Geronimo, the mighty Apache chief, was imprisoned for 20 years. However, he was allowed to roam the reservation at will, limited only by his love of strong drink.

Near the entrance to Fort Sill was the grave of Quanah Parker, the half-breed chief, who was the son of a white woman named Cynthia Ann Parker and Peta Nakoni, a Comanche chief. Cynthia had been kidnapped by the Comanches when she was nine years old and had lived among the tribe and bore children the Comanche way. White settlers had forcefully repatriated her against her will. She died of a broken heart.

Even then in 1946, there were still signs of the Old West. Negro cowboys in full regalia wearing chaps, spurs and usually carrying a lariat could be seen walking the streets of nearby Lawton. The town of Lawton was established in August, 1901, just after three million acres of the Kiowa-Comanche reservation were opened by lottery to white settlers. Ten percent of the present-day Lawton citizens were Negroes; the rest were whites and Indians.

Great day in the morning. This was a perfect place for me, made to measure for the final grooming that was needed for the black great-grandson of the mighty "Stonewall" Jackson. It was no wonder that I was keyed up and fine-tuned for the grueling task ahead of me.

Perhaps that's why I was ripe and more than ready for the peculiar machinations of Sergeant Hosea Walker. He was originally from Tupelo, Mississippi. During the war, the sergeant had been in the thick of the fighting and had seen action with the 92nd Infantry Division in Europe. He had been badly wounded and could certainly have been discharged.

Sergeant Walker returned to Tupelo after the end of the war, only to discover that the owner of the farm on which his family sharecropped had taken his Palomino horse and sold it. Walker had raised the pure-bred Palomino from a colt. It took an awful lot of persuasion from the sergeant's father to keep him from killing the unrepentant farmer. Walker swore never to set foot on Mississippi soil again. Latent animosity fostered the feelings that boiled and seethed inside him, and hatred had made him rigid, an unbending taskmaster with whom to deal. His stern face below kinky black hair sported a hawkbill of a nose. His face was the color and texture of old leather. He stood as straight and as tall as a Comanche warrior's spear. In Sergeant Walker's battery, rules were not made to be broken.

I had been acting corporal in my infantry training company at Fort McClellan, so it was only natural that the taste of leadership was still sweet in my mouth. Unfortunately, the only job opening in the newly-formed battalion was radio operator for the 155 howitzer Battery "A." I jumped at the chance. Once training was completed, the position carried the rank of technician fifth grade, which was the same as corporal. So, it was a step in the right direction. Sergeant Walker watched my frantic efforts with a jaundiced eye. I had made no secret of the fact that I wanted to advance to become a gunnery sergeant, squad leader or even a chance at officers' candidate school.

I was firm in my commitment to be like the mighty Stonewall. I did everything by the book and some things that were above and beyond the call of duty. In service lingo, it was called bucking for rank. I did it unashamedly, unconcerned by the sneers and derisive taunts of the other troopers. Sergeant Walker said nothing pro or con, but he continued shrewdly to watch my every move.

I could have gone directly to Captain Lewis, but that was not a wise move. The captain was a twenty-year-man and was about to be discharged. The stage was set. Pretty soon Sergeant Walker would have to come to me, if only to tell me that my bucking for promotion was all in vain.

He did come to me but not in the manner that I had anticipated. In my eagerness to get ahead of everybody, I had devised a scheme to be up and ready for reveille before any of the others. The night before, I would always make up my bunk in perfect military fashion complete with neat hospital creases. Then, I would sleep on top of the covers covered only by the comforter. Doing it like that would give me a few extra minutes to take my morning shower. It would also give me a degree of privacy that I would not normally have had. For reasons of my own, I was quite self-conscious about bathing in front of the group.

What prompted my shyness had happened on Friday morning. Sergeant Walker had done his own personal bed check the night before,

Homeward Bound

which he did occasionally. In the course of his rounds, he saw me asleep on my bunk in a way that certainly did not fit into his idea of military correctness. He raised holy hell with me and threatened to take away the single stripe that I did have. For a while, there was no mention of a promotion. Two weeks later, he informed me that I had gotten the job as radio operator for the 155 millimeter guns of A Battery. My star was ascending. There were no limits to what I would do.

It was the beginning of April, and the green of prairie grass was spreading quickly across flat plain of the gunnery range. The Wichita Mountains made a towering backdrop, lightly shielding the towns of Lawton and Anadarko from the noise of the big guns. It was early Monday morning, and there would be no more dry runs. All was in readiness. Soon the big guns would spit and belch their 105 pounds of instant death, sending the projectile whistling through the clear skies to a target miles away. It was going to be a wonderful moment, and I would be a part of it. It would be my first fire mission. Look out Stonewall! Here I come!

"Battery adjust! Shell, high explosive! Charge five! Fuse, quick!"

Those words were music to my ears, as I relayed them from the small spotter plane to Lieutenant Barnes, the executive officer. Seconds later, an earsplitting boom would send the glistening shell zooming down range toward the target. Quick eyes could follow the path of the projectile until it was out of sight. I could understand why Great-grandfather Jackson had gloried in the sights, sounds and the smell of gunpowder. He had relished the bloody business of artillery warfare.

The days hurried by as we learned the basic facts of field artillery and the many uses of the big guns on the field of battle. It was rewarding to know that at the end of the day firing the field pieces was no longer a haphazard operation but a test of skill.

On a Friday afternoon, the squad of men from our gun was exuberant. The chief of section was Sergeant Joe Wilkes, an intense light-skinned Negro, who was not much older than myself.

"Well, troopers y'all did a pretty good job today," he dismissed us good-naturedly when we arrived at the barracks. "I don't know what you guys are going to do, but I'm going out to Lawton View and try to get laid before the sun goes down. I'll see y'all later. Don't take no wooden Indians."

We scrambled for the barracks. A hot shower and change of clothes was the next order of business. The mess hall would be all but empty this evening. The troopers would eat at various clubs and restaurants around Lawton and Lawton View.

I undressed slowly as everybody headed for the shower at the end of the barrack. Dick Texeria, the gunner, was the first man to reach the shower. Then came Big John Sykes, the tractor driver. Pfc. Jimmy Wooten and Pfc. Jimmy Scott were the ones who rammed the projectile home, and Carl Jones was an expert in setting the fuses for the huge shells. Privates Asa Carter and Carney Jones were the pit men, and I was the best radio operator in the whole outfit.

I was still a little leery about taking a shower in front of the rest of the guys, but we had worked together so well until there was a sense of camaraderie among us, and my shyness began to abate. I grabbed my towel, walked to the end of the barrack and stepped gingerly into the shower. There were four faucets against the rear wall and two at each end of the shower. I removed the towel from my waist and hung it on the rack by the door. I moved quickly to the shower, adjusted the faucet and began soaping myself. My mouth felt dry, and my throat felt funny. I looked slowly around the shower, glancing covertly at each of the men. My worst fears were realized. It was something that had bothered me ever since I was a boy.

There were seven men, including myself in the shower. I had looked them over carefully, and there was no doubt in my mind. My penis was the smallest of the lot. I had tried for years to figure out why it was so small. I could find no valid reason, and it was a frightening thing with which to live. I felt that large genitals were a sure sign of being a man, and I was solely lacking in that regard. I didn't know what to do.

2

That's about the Size of It

No one seemed to have paid any attention to my discomfort in the shower. As time went by, it occurred to me that it was my own actions that caused the men to start taking a long look at me.

Soon the barracks were completely empty. The ancient bus that left for Lawton had been packed with troopers. The Busy Bee Cab Company was doing a booming business taking the troopers to town that Friday evening.

I sat alone on my bunk relieved by the sounds of silence around me, knowing full well that my eyes were not playing tricks. I looked down at the the area of my fly. The imprint of my manhood was barely visible. Haphazard thinking ran rampant about my brain, like the senseless wanderings of a rabid dog. As always, depression followed on cue. There was no obvious reason for the sweat that trickled from my armpits and darkened my drab olive undershirt. It was happening again, and there was nothing that I could do to prepare for it. I steeled myself and waited. Suddenly, a feeling of inferiority swept over me with such intensity that I grabbed the edge of the bunk for support.

It was not the first time that it had happened, nor would it be the last. A leopard cannot change its spots, and neither could I change the feelings that haunted me. I felt a quick surge in my bladder, an urge to urinate. This too was a part of the phenomena. I hurried toward the toilet at the opposite end of the barracks. Once inside, I left the urinal and walked into one of the stalls. I undid my shorts and looked down at the source of my problem. My penis was just too small. Inspecting it closely as I stood there, it seemed quite vulnerable and smaller than ever. The limp organ was not a pretty sight, but genitals are not supposed to be pretty. The same was especially true of women's genitals, but the miracles accomplished by that orifice more than made up for its ugliness. It would be years later before understanding corrected my assumption. I would come to know a woman's vagina has its own special appearance, possessing a delicate one-of-a-kind elegance that is uniquely beauteous and forever joyous. My preoccupation with that part of a woman's body would cause me all kinds of trouble.

Dammit! For a youngster approaching maturity, who was trying hard to make his mark in the world, my sex was a pitiful offering. I was almost twenty, and the growth cycle was complete. I was looking at the sum of my sexual existence. What you see is what you get. Members of the opposite sex would not stampede and tear down fences to get to me.

Who was to blame for this awful thing that had screwed me up for life? In terms of heredity, it couldn't have been Papa or Grandpa. They were both better than average in that department. And if heredity were a factor, it couldn't have been Grandfather Isaiah Jackson. Grandma used to brag all the time about Grandpa's virility. Then, could it possibly have been his father, the mighty "Stonewall"?

The more I thought about it, the more plausible such an explanation became. It would grieve me no end to think that the famous hero of the Confederacy had been cursed with a penis as small as mine. Maybe Stonewall had big balls. From what I had heard from Uncle Joe, big balls and bravery went hand in hand. If that were true, then the general's balls must have been huge. His daring and resourcefulness were the stuff of which legends were made. It looked as if heritage had damned me with one of the worst peculiarities of the famous Southern hero. It was a terrible legacy to bequeath. There were times when I wished that Stonewall Jackson would rot in hell.

I wasn't concerned about the size of my own testicles. They were round, firm and average. The act of sex was not totally foreign to me. I had had my first sexual encounter the year before I was drafted. I would always be eternally grateful for the unique way that I lost my innocence.

It had happened in an old Ford as I rode on a country road that ran past our little shack. I was on the way to revival at the nearby church. The willing recipient of my virginity was a hot, sweaty and overly eager young girl named Cissy. It was over much too quickly, as she sat on my lap in the back seat of her father's car. She squirmed frantically and was completely oblivious of her two brothers seated on either side of us. By manipulating her hips in quick short strokes, it was easy for her to take away something I had wanted to be rid of for a long time. Her parents sitting placidly in the front seat were totally unaware of our lewd behavior. In the midst of a driving rain storm, the two of us found paradise on a bumpy road to church.

We had seized the moment recklessly while filled to the brim with a wanton spirit that had nothing to do with the Holy Ghost. The covert act had been thrilling, fulfilling and something to cherish forever. I never got a chance to ask Cissy how she rated my performance. I got the idea that she thought it less than spectacular. At least I had gotten my first piece of tail. I had been afraid that her father and mother would somehow find out what was going on. Luckily, the whole family was singing, and the noise from the old Ford drowned out any noises we were making. It was something that I would always remember.

Thoughts of home flooded my mind as I stood there in the tiny cubicle. Sorrow came to me as I thought about my mother. She had been dead for almost a year. Lucille, my younger sister, had gotten married and lived in downtown Fayetteville. The oldest of us, Katie, was with her paratrooper husband at Fort Campbell. My brother, Jimmy, was working on a farm in Sampson County, and I was at Fort Sill Oklahoma trying to make a name for myself.

I walked out of the toilet and looked around. There was no one in sight. The barracks were still empty. I was wallowed in self-pity as I made my way back to my bunk. I sat and quickly unbuttoned my shorts. I took a small ruler from my footlocker. Retrieving my penis, I fumbled a bit and grasped it between my thumb and forefinger. Measuring it had become a routine that I followed religiously. I had used the ruler over and over again through the years. I pressed one end of the ruler to the base and ran it along the length of my penis. It was the same length that it had been for longer than I cared to remember. It was all of three and a half inches long. With a full erection and filled to the hilt with blood, it was five and one-eighth inches long.

Because of my inadequacy, I was less than enthusiastic about the act of sex. Hearsay, coupled with sleeping directly across from Mama and Papa in the little shack while growing up, had left me with little knowledge about the act of love. I knew that foreplay was appreciated and that fingers were used to compliment the act. But, it was a sad state of affairs when I could offer little more than a finger. Regardless of the effect of touching, petting or kissing, nothing could take the place of the real thing. Nature demanded that the act of procreation be pure and simple. In such a well-ordered scheme of things, what could I do? What part would I play? I was a misfit, and I felt like crying.

It was something with which I had to put up. There were many times when I ignored the problem and concentrated on trying to be like Stonewall. The irony of the situation was that I was too much like Stonewall. I was convinced that I was heir to his quirks, peculiarities and worst of all his sexual smallness. Quite often I would find myself thinking about my strange predicament. I knew that when aging begins the penis shrinks, leaving a snout that is both empty and ugly. There was never any thought of my getting circumcised. In my condition there was nothing to lose. I needed everything available.

It terrified me to think that my maleness would be almost nonexistent if I lived to be old. I could expect ridicule, and the woman of my dreams would be the five fingers of my left hand. The Stonewall curse was alive and well. I would go through life on a fruitless search. Old woe-be-Dick looking for the right piece of tail.

I wondered if somewhere there were a member of the opposite sex with a problem similar to mine. If so, we desperately needed to find each other.

I thought about Papa. He was a small-time preacher, but one of the things that he taught us was that prayer heals the wounded spirit. I fell quickly to my knees and prayed to the Lord for strength and guidance. I felt better. Papa was usually right, but once or twice he had given me some bad advice.

That's about the Size of It

I would never forget the day that he caught me playing with myself in the corn crib. Papa was full of fun at times, but that day he was dead serious. I believed him. He was shouting above the noise of the rain storm as we hurried out of the crib and up the path toward the house.

"Dave boy, don't ever play with yourself. It ain't healthy. It'll drain your strength and make you weak as a kitten." We were about to go into the house when he grabbed my arm.

"I'm telling you for a fact son. Don't pull and jerk on your worm because the more you pull on the blame thing, the more it will grow. Leave it alone, you hear?"

Papa saying that to me was just like urging Brer Rabbit to jump into the briar patch. I pulled and jerked furiously every time an opportunity presented itself. I waited and watched anxiously, expecting new growth. Nothing happened. I was highly upset with Papa. He must have been pulling my leg. It was a cruel joke and certainly not funny to me. He had led me to believe something that was simply not true. I was even more troubled and confused. Worrying about things I couldn't change would get me nowhere.

It was late afternoon, and the sun was about to set. I walked over to the window and looked out at the road that led into town. The 969th was based along the railroad. The all-Negro barracks were well away from any contact with the white soldiers. However, the outfit did have its own service club, post exchange, theater and swimming pool. The army had achieved a near miracle in keeping the white and colored troops firmly segregated. Even in battle, the same had held true. If it came to pass that white and Negro soldiers did die together in battle, it was a fluke, entirely unexpected and certainly not the fault of the army. We had mostly white officers of course, but it had always been like that since before the Civil War. The policy had nothing to do with bravery. The Negro soldier had always given a good account of himself.

I had to do something to shake the doldrums that surrounded me. I could walk over to the PX and get a beer, but I really didn't like beer. Hard liquor was out of the question. Because of the Indian population, no strong drink was sold in Oklahoma.

The railroad was a little ways from the barracks, and there was a small group of shanties just past the spot where the road crossed the railroad. Lawton was the last of the Oklahoma cities to be born overnight out of the dust and clamor of an Indian reservation opening. The shanties were the final remnants of the reservation, mute testimony to the demise of a proud people.

There were a few indigent families left. Among them were two women who had gained a certain notoriety as ladies of easy virtue. One of them was a tall Comanche with striking good looks. She was called "Proud Mary" because of her regal bearing and royal demeanor. The other one was also a Comanche, but she was short, fat and ugly. She was appropriately called "Sitting Butt" and had the dubious distinction of single-handedly servicing, with the exclusion of myself, most of the troopers of the 969th on one payday weekend. The only ones not included were the troopers on KP and the CQ.

As I watched, a trooper came out of one of the shanties, stood at the door for a moment, and a woman that I recognized as Proud Mary suddenly appeared at his side. He spoke with her for a moment and then started walking purposely down the road to Lawton.

I was puzzled as all get out because I recognized the trooper. It was Sergeant Walker. I was sure of it. The squared shoulders and ramrod straight posture could belong to no one else. But, I was still a trifle confused.

It was common knowledge that he was engaged to a very beautiful and sophisticated lady in Lawton named Marlena Wrigley. She was the director of the colored USO club and had a daughter named Lila who was a younger version of herself. I had met Lila at the service club swimming pool. She often came there with her friends. I liked her because she reminded me of a girl in my class at school.

I had to put these crazy thoughts behind me, forget about women and get back to the real business at hand. The Stonewall legacy was not all bad. I could not let it languish. I had to fulfill my heritage. Because of my concern about my sex organ, I knew that I would be walking a slippery tightrope stretched high above a river of anxiety. A fall of any sort would dash my hopes and dreams and send me tumbling into an abyss of doubt and despair.

The comfort of darkness came suddenly. It was getting late, and the barracks were still a quiet empty place. I looked around to ensure that there was no one in sight. Then I quickly fell to my knees. I was going to say another prayer and hope fervently that it made its way to heaven. According to Papa, a man couldn't pray too much. At that point in time, I probably should have sent up prayers in five-minute intervals.

Doldrums come, and doldrums go, but they simply cannot compete with the rarified air above the broad flat plain of a gunnery range. It was the first of May, and the doldrums had left with speed akin to a 105-pound projectile hurtling toward its down-range target. I was exuberant, and so were the others troopers of the 969th. We were handling our jobs with precision and flair. We were getting accolades for our ability to hit whatever targets that were assigned to the battery. There was even talk of a unit citation.

There was one slight problem. Colonel Bradbury, a tall, lean Southerner and our commanding officer, who was the highest ranking white officer in the battery, insisted on calling us "You people!" He was fond of saying things like this to his subordinates: "Captain Lewis, bring your people over here." The Negro soldiers resented being singled out as "You people." But, in lieu of all of the praise being heaped upon them, they decided not to make an issue of it. Captain Lewis was from Cleveland. He was short, fat and could easily pass for white. He acted white so it really didn't make any difference.

Things were also going quite well for me in other areas. Lawton had a population of 18,000, a mixture of white, Indian and Negroes, with the Negroes comprising about ten percent of the total. Ten percent was fine with me because I knew exactly where to find my kind of folk. Besides, I was seeing the precocious Lila and being with her was really special. We usually met downtown or at the USO where her mother worked or maybe at the swimming pool on post. Lila's mother was not overjoyed about me seeing her daughter, but her worry soon diminished because I usually saw Lila only in her presence.

Lila's mother was a classic beauty, possibly of Negro and Indian heritage. She was tall, black-haired, full-breasted with high cheekbones and bold, sensuous lips. She had been a widow since her husband had drowned on a Liberty ship in 1942. The other non-com's who frequented the USO were quite envious because she had chosen Sergeant Walker as the next man in her life.

Lila was a delicate image of her mother, small-breasted, tiny-waisted with small but well-formed legs. Her fragile looks heightened the childlike quality of her beauty. She looked as if she needed protection and that was exactly what was on my mind. I felt that way from the first day that we met.

She was standing beside the ping pong table in the USO recreation room. I walked up to her, totally fascinated by her sloe eyes and her heart-shaped face. Her eyes looked into mine, and the long lashes fluttered prettily.

"Do you want to play a game of ping pong soldier?"

I nodded my head quickly. I was caught like an eager fish, dangling helplessly and hooked for life by the strange enchanting beauty of Lila.

We exchanged names as I picked up a paddle and walked to the opposite end of the table, with what I hoped was a debonair smile on my face.

"Lila, honey, I am going to be easy on you. You just play as hard as you can, and I won't beat you too badly. Okay?"

As I spoke, I gently lobbed the ball across the net. Without a moment's hesitation, she backhanded it, smashing it across the net as I stood open-mouthed.

We played seven games, and she won every one of them. Placing the paddle on the edge of the table, she smiled and leaned toward me. Her pink tongue raced playfully about her full lips and then pointed straight at me.

"You wear your hair way too long for a soldier, and you play ping pong worse than I've ever seen it played." She was almost to the door before she turned and called out, "I'll be here just about the same time tomorrow."

The more that I learned about Lila, the more I became hopelessly in love with her. She was just sixteen, and I haven't mentioned it, but I was sure that she was a virgin. That assumption alone made me love her all the more. I was in no hurry to find out. In fact I had considered loving her in a platonic sort of way.

As the days went by, I began to feel really good about our relationship. It became crystal clear to me that Lila did not intend to remain a virgin. I was in a delicate situation. I was aghast at the thought of anyone else but me relieving her of her innocence. My main concern was the fact that if she were intimate with anyone other than me, if and when we became lovers, she would immediately know the difference. In that case she might begin to compare the two of us, and I might wind up on the short end of the stick.

Everything was moving right along, and I had returned to my old habit of showering alone and at odd hours.

Things were going quite well on the gunnery range. I was seeing Lila every chance I could. The following Saturday I was going to take her to see a new movie at the post theater. The name of the movie was "Gilda," and it was a tempestuous tale of love starring Rita Hayworth and Glenn Ford. Lila had been calling me all week raving about the movie, and when I saw her on Saturday evening, anticipation had made her face a thing of pure beauty. I was peacock proud to be in the company of the vivacious Lila and extremely happy to have her on my arm.

The movie was pretty good as movies go, but for Lila, it was a revelation, something akin to Paul's vision on the road to Damascus. The transformation began even as we left the movies. "Gilda's" mannerisms appeared immediately. The toss of her head and the impish smile, coupled with a sloe-eyed look simmering with passion, made me know for sure that I was madly in love with Lila, "Gilda" or whomever she claimed to be. It was only natural that we would see the movie another three times in the coming days.

On that last night, we came out of the movies into a warm Summer night that was made for lovers. On such a special night, there was no hint of segregation at Fort Sill. The evening air and the moon's rays were distributed equally, shining bright on the white, Indian and colored populations. The western sky was a panorama of low-hanging stars, and a waxing moon silvered the Summer night.

The wraith-like specter of "Gilda" hovered about us as we gloried in this paradise for two. As we stood outside the darkened theater waiting for a cab, I looked down at this child-woman of my dreams. Her full lips puckered like the delicate petals of a flower closing at sundown. I bent and kissed them tenderly, just as a flower should be kissed. Suddenly, her mouth became glued to mine, and her agile tongue wormed its way between my teeth and roamed about my mouth. A delicious hurt

That's about the Size of It

came over me as her hips suddenly began to grind sensuously against my own. The spell was broken when a Busy Bee cab came to a stop beside us. The driver leaned over and yelled, "Taxi?"

We left the cab on "B" Street and decided to walk the six blocks to Lila's house. She and her mother lived in a quiet colored neighborhood on "C" Street around the corner from the USO. We walked slowly, stopping to kiss every few feet. The streets were deserted, and the quiet friendly darkness gave our passion a gentle push as we strained toward each other.

I was totally fascinated and helplessly in love. We reached a grassy knoll between two houses. In the center of the vacant lot, a small tree stood forlornly. The two of us paused for a moment, and as her hungry lips sought mine, she whispered fiercely, "David, I'm hot, hotter than 'Gilda' was just now. Take me! Take me now, David, right now!" She was begging fiercely, "Do it to me David, please! Please!"

I wanted her as badly as she wanted me, more than I had ever wanted anything in my life. But she was my princess, and I did not want to cheapen her on a grassy knoll in downtown Lawton. Besides, Stonewall Jackson had always been the soul of courtesy and proper behavior toward women. The innocent but willful Lila deserved better than that.

I kissed her gently, and mumbled, "Not here Lila, we can't do it right out here in the open. I love you and respect you way too much to ask you to do anything like that. Don't worry, we can be together real soon." I tried to kiss her again, but she turned away. Her body stiffened, and the air around us became freezing cold. Her voice was aloof and distant.

"I'm going home now. I don't need you with me. I don't ever want to see you again!"

The heels of her tiny slippers played taps for me, as she turned and hurried angrily up the street. Later, I decided that I was probably the biggest fool in the world, but I just couldn't ask her to lie on the grass. She was too much of a lady for that. I knew that whatever we had between us was over. I would never have Lila or "Gilda" again.

The next time I saw Lila was a couple of weeks later at the service club's swimming pool. She was dressed in a red skintight bathing suit that showed every voluptuous curve of her budding young body. She was with Big John Sykes, who was the tractor driver of our gun crew. He was big, with a bullet head, big lips and the hard tight build of a professional wrestler. He had been one of the seven troopers in the shower that day. Where size was concerned, he was just as big as I was small, firmly entrenched at the other end of the spectrum. I don't know how long it had been going on, but he and Lila seemed quite fond of each other. I couldn't understand her attraction for Big John. He was crude, uneducated, ugly and straight from a corn field.

Lila was standing in the center of the pool watching Big John's showing off on the diving board. From his perch on the board, he shouted, "Hey 'Gilda,' watch this dive! Open your legs. I'm gonna swim between them!" He laughed crudely. "I might even stay between them for a while!"

When they came out of the pool, their arms were entwined, and they were laughing. I was burning up with jealously. She did not even give me the courtesy of a look. I tried not to watch them, but I couldn't help it. I had to look.

As they walked away, his huge hand was casually cupped around her buttocks. He was kneading them crudely, first one and then the other. It was an obscene gesture of intimacy, and she didn't seem to mind. In fact, she smiled up at him as if she liked it immensely.

The next time I saw the two of them was after midnight in downtown Lawton. I had left the USO and was going to walk past her house in the vain hope that I might see her or maybe even get a chance to talk. Suddenly, I heard noises just ahead of me. I went closer. It was Big John and Lila or "Gilda." I didn't know which. They were leaning against the small tree on the same grassy knoll that I had refused to share. As I watched, her arms tightened around his neck. Her legs opened wide as she climbed up and scissored them around his broad back. Sykes braced himself, adjusted her hips. Suddenly, she cried out in pain. A moment later, she groaned and murmured a huge sigh. Her thin body began to move sensuously, and her hips strained against him. Lila's arms tightened around his neck, and the branches of the small tree began to shake, waving furiously as if in total agreement with the ragged beating of my heart. I knew that I would never go out with Lila again. It was obvious to me that she preferred the crude fondling and uncouth love-making of Big John Sykes. Sadly, I turned and walked slowly up the darkened street.

The neighborhood was deserted. There was no traffic, and no cabs available at that time of night. I trudged forlornly through the darkness, dodging the ghosts of settlers in covered wagons and the spirits of long-dead Indian braves. Silently the wraiths accompanied me, riding easily on the gentle night wind. I didn't bother them, and they didn't bother me. The dawn greeted my return to camp.

3

Marlena

The caissons kept rolling along, and I scrambled to keep up with them. I was one serious Technician Fifth Grade. I had never envisioned trouble on a disciplinary level, and at that point there were no problems on the field. In fact, nothing would have happened at all if I hadn't accosted Big John Sykes about his ongoing affair with Lila Wrigley. It was mid-September in the not so wild West, and once again I was suffering from the pangs of unrequited love.

I had begun to wonder just how much more I could take. I had a big problem with Big John. He was not a gentleman. He was boorish and country to the core. He would tell anyone who would listen about the sordid affair between himself and the young girl. I was angry that he did not respect Lila. Besides, I couldn't forget the memory of the night I saw them flagrantly making out on the grassy knoll. I was burning with jealously. The confrontation between Big John and me happened one afternoon as we were coming in from the range. He was about to go into the barrack when I pulled him aside.

"Hey John, can I talk to you? It won't take but a minute."

"What the hell do you want Sawyer?" He looked pissed off to begin with, probably because he knew my feelings about Lila. The feeling was mutual. I hated the uncouth bastard.

Marlena

"I just wanted to talk to you about Lila. It's no skin off my back, but you ought to treat her with a little respect. You talk about her like she was a whore or something. She ain't trashy. If y'all are doing stuff together, you ought to keep it to yourself. Anyhow, she's way too young for you."

I was looking straight into his eyes. I wanted to be sure that he got the message. He was grinning, and the sardonic sneer on his face was making me madder and madder.

"You kiss my ass, bitch! She's my woman, and I'll say any damn thing I please. Why don't you mind your fuckin' business and leave mine alone?"

His little pig eyes twinkled crazily. He was enjoying my discomfort. "I put a fixin' on that pretty girl night before last."

I was furious, and he knew it. His big lips twisted with scorn.

"I tell you for a fact Sawyer she is one sweet babycake. It took me half an hour to pick the hair out of my teeth."

I hit him flush in the mouth with all of the strength that I could muster. He barely blinked. In fact, he just stood there as if nothing had happened. The sneer never left his face as he moved toward me.

"Awright pretty boy. You want it here and now, or do you want to settle it in the gym with boxing gloves?"

"It don't matter a damn with me, you black motherfucker! We can do it anytime, anywhere. Your ass ain't got no fence around it. You scare some people, but you don't scare me!"

"Awright bitch, tomorrow evening at five o' clock in the gym. You kin get ready for your hospital stay. I'll tell my woman about it after I kick your ass."

I had lied again. I was scared to death of Big John. I couldn't understand what motivated me to challenge him. It must have been Stonewall Jackson's misguided bravery surfacing at the wrong time. I certainly didn't want people to think of Lila as easy. I kept hoping that her fascination with the Gilda character would end. I knew that underneath she was just a passionate young girl who had gotten ahead of herself. I still wanted her more than ever. And, somewhere in the back of my mind, the nagging feeling of inadequacy remained. Try as I might, I could not forget the disparity of size between myself and John Sykes.

The next day on the gunnery range, during a lull in the firing, Dick Texeria, a tall, thin, good-looking, extremely dark trooper from Boston, came over to where I was seated. We were friends of a sort because we worked together closely as gunner and radio operator. There was a note of concern in his voice.

"Sawyer, are you sure that you want to go through with this? He's bigger than you, and he's always getting into fights and stuff. To me, it looks like a no-win situation. Nobody would blame you if you backed out of this one. You're lucky if you don't get killed. I wouldn't want to be in your shoes for a ton of money."

I tried to keep my voice calm, but it still wavered a bit.

"I know exactly what you mean Texeria, but I just can't. It's the principle of the thing. I've got to fight him."

I would not destroy my heritage. I was the great-grandson of Thomas Jonathan Jackson. I wondered if my heritage were responsible for my reckless actions. Why would I do a crazy thing like that? Regardless of the consequences, I had to go forward.

Texeria looked directly into my eyes. "You're my friend, and I know you're making a mistake. It's not just the fight. Why don't you forget about Lila? She's young and pretty, but she's not worth all of the grief you're going through. What you need is to get laid. You could try Proud Mary or Sitting Butt. Sergeant Walker hangs out with Mary most of the time. It must be a pretty good piece." He thought for a minute.

"Of course, I could take you out to Lawton View. I know a couple of girls out there who work together. Between the two of them, they could fix you up good."

Aw man, I had been nervous and on edge all afternoon, and when it was time to go to the gym, I was terrified. I put it off as long as I could and then walked slowly toward the building.

Sergeant Walker was standing at the door to the gym. Unbelief was written all over his face.

"Sawyer, what the fuck is going on here? What in the name of all that's holy possessed you to agree to fight John Sykes?"

He was really puzzled. He shook his head slowly.

"This hasn't got anything to do with you and Marlena's daughter, has it? According to her mom, she's been running like crazy here lately." When I didn't answer, he shook his head again.

"Well, you made your bed, and I'm sure John Sykes will put you in it." He walked away, still shaking his head.

I was in for another shock when I entered the gym. I thought the fight would be a private matter between Big John and myself. The whole battery was there, plus some people that I didn't even know. Dick Texeria and Jimmy Wooten had agreed to be my seconds. Jimmy Scott and Asa Carter were seconds for John Sykes.

It was not really a fight. According to Texeria, it was a slaughter. When I leaned down and stepped through the ropes, I had but one prayer: that the fight would be over quickly.

It only lasted two rounds, but it seemed like two years. My puny blows bounced of the rock hard body of John Sykes like water from a duck's back. He could have easily knocked me out from the first moment if he had wanted to. His evil grin grew wider as he inflicted more and more punishment. He was methodical, content to deliver numbing blows to my head, kidneys and midsection. My right eye was swollen shut. My front teeth were loose, and my nose was bleeding badly after the first round. Texeria wanted to throw in the towel at the end of the first round.

"Awright Sawyer, enough is enough. Let's stop it right here."

I shook my head and staggered back out into the ring. I couldn't stop then. When Sergeant Walker finally stopped the fight in the middle of the second round, my left eye was also swollen, and my face was a bloody mess. The stubborn spirit of Stonewall Jackson had goaded me to continue fighting Sykes. There was one small feeling of consolation. They had to make me get out of the ring. In the face of all of that bruising abuse, I hadn't quit.

A wounded lion seeks a quiet place where solitude enables him to lick his wounds in peace. It was not so with me. In the confines of the barrack, my shame was there for all the world to see. It was a miserable time for me. I was on sick call for three days, and it was another three days before the bandages came off. It was a few days before I began to feel better. I had expected all kinds of hazing and ridicule about the fight. I was more than a little surprised when it didn't happen. In fact, a lot of the troopers acted very sympathetic toward me.

I did not get any sort of apology from John Sykes. I didn't expect one. As it turned out, he was having problems of his own. He was acting funny, kind of sad and morose. I found out the reason for his behavior from Sergeant Walker. He casually mentioned that Lila's mother had tired of the controversy concerning her daughter and had dispatched her to Oklahoma City to live with her sister, Martha, who was Lila's aunt.

On the next weekend, curiosity got the better of me, so I went into town to the USO. It was Saturday night around ten o' clock when I arrived. It was also the middle of the month, so there were just one or two troopers hanging around. I fooled around at the pool table until it was almost closing time. Finally, I put the balls away and walked over to Marlena's desk.

"Good evening Miss Marlena. How have you been?"

God, she was beautiful! I could see why she had caught the roving eye of Sergeant Walker. Her big brown eyes narrowed. It seemed like a full minute before she spoke. Her lilting voice was as cool as ice. "You're Sawyer. Right?" I nodded, and her eyes softened a trifle.

"You're the first soldier that Lila was involved with." She eyed me shrewdly. "You don't look like much of a soldier. You're just a boy." She spoke absently, as if to herself. "I wonder why she didn't like you?"

"No ma'am. I'm a full-grown soldier. I just got my corporal's stripes a few weeks ago. I was just wondering when will Lila be back? I heard she was out of town, and I was wondering when she would be back. I kind of miss her. We were friends."

"She won't be back," said Marlena flatly. "She'll be staying in Oklahoma City until she finishes high school." With that, Marlena abruptly changed the subject.

"I heard that you got beat up. Walker said that Sykes almost killed you. What were you supposed to be some sort of savior for Lila?"

"No ma'am. It was just something I had to do."

It suddenly dawned on me that she knew more than she was telling about Lila and me. We made small talk for a time, and then she stood from the desk.

"It's time to close. Do you want to help me to get out of here?"

Quickly, she went about the business of closing. I helped kill the lights and made sure that all of the doors were bolted. When we stepped outside of the double doors, I looked down at her.

"Could I walk you home Miss Marlena? It's kind of late. I want to make sure that you get home safely. I can leave your house and get a cab."

Her voice was a breath of laughter in the darkness.

"Sure Sawyer. You can walk me home. Why not? I don't see Old Faithful waiting in the wings." Her voice suddenly hardened. "I'd bet a $100 in gold that Walker, the dirty son of a bitch, is bedded down with his Indian whore. All men are lousy bastards. All of them."

We walked down the steps and onto the sidewalk. The streets were deserted at this hour. There was no need to hurry; it was only a few blocks to her place. As we walked, the smell of her tantalizing fragrance wafted around us, and the sound of her voice in the darkness was like night music.

"How do you like it here in the West? I take it you're from the East?"

"No ma'am, I'm from North Carolina. I do like it out here. I've never seen so much flat land before. My draftee time is almost up, so I am going to re-enlist in the regular army. Maybe I can stay out here another year at least."

In the last few days I had given a lot of thought about re-enlisting. I'd have to get my papers in order pretty soon, or my time would be up.

Marlena laughed softly. I was laughing too but for a different reason. I was thinking of Lila.

We crossed the street, and suddenly we were at the door of Marlena's neat little cottage. I stood quietly as she fumbled for her keys. She put the key in the lock and looked back at me.

"Sawyer, do you want to come in? We could talk for a bit. Maybe it would help me to unwind. It's been a long day. You could have a beer." She paused.

"And stop calling me ma'am. My name is Marlena. It's a pretty name, and I like it."

"Yes ma'am. I mean Marlena. I would appreciate a cold beer and some conversation."

She flicked the light switch, and we went inside. My mouth opened wide as I stood there. I had never seen such luxury. For someone who had been born and reared in a three-room shack, her living room was the height of elegance and good taste. She motioned for me to sit on the overstuffed maroon sofa. I squeezed past the shiny oval mahogany coffee table and sank gingerly down into the comfort of the expensive settee. She walked into the kitchen and returned shortly with a frosty quart of Falstaff beer and a tall glass.

She placed the beer and the glass on a doily and said airily, "Just

Marlena

make yourself comfortable. I've got to get out of this dress, and then I'm going to freshen up a little bit."

Marlena was carrying a full bottle of Scotch and two glasses when she returned. Her face was devoid of makeup, and the long black hair was no longer tied. Now it billowed down around her shoulders. She had changed into a short Mandarin robe that hugged her lithe body like a jealous lover. The robe was bright orange and shimmered like pure silk. Now, the musky fragrance that floated about the room was more pronounced. It almost took my breath away.

As she sat beside me, I looked deep into her eyes. Immediately, I thought about Stonewall during the Mexican war and his fascination with the beautiful senoritas of Mexico City. Marlena's beauty would rival any of them. The Jackson lust burned inside me. I didn't know how to handle the situation, but I was going to stay with it come hell or high water. Marlena's voice was soft and soothing.

"Why don't you pour yourself a shot of whiskey Sawyer? I'm going to have a double. I need to unwind."

I didn't care too much for hard liquor. However, in the quiet of Marlena's plush living room, I found myself drinking shot for shot with this exciting woman. As she talked, I came to feel less in awe at her candid remarks. It was easy to see that Sergeant Walker meant an awful lot to her. At the very sound of his name, her spirits would soar to dizzying heights. I had nothing to do with her excitement. It was generated by her memories of Walker. As we talked, her inhibitions melted away, and I began to see more and more of her long tan legs. When she realized that I was watching, her legs began to do all sorts of strange exciting things. They were opening wide, hiking the short robe high above her thighs and leaving nothing to chance. I wasn't handling her startling display of heated womanhood in the right manner. I wasn't handling it well at all. My throat was dry, and my groin ached like a toothache.

The expensive Scotch was having its effect on the two of us. Marlena's voice was slurred and thick with passion. Her brown eyes were slits of lust. Suddenly she was standing above me. Her scent was overpowering, and her slinky body was almost touching my face. Casually, she opened the robe, held my face in her hands and pressed it gently against her belly. The heat from her body sent crazy shivers down my spine. Desire widened the brown eyes as she looked down at me.

"Sawyer," her voice was a husky groan, "do you like what you see?"

Her hands left my face and traveled upward until they cupped her full breasts. I was in shock. Marlena kneaded her breasts for a moment, and then her hands moved slowly down until her tapered fingers laced the soft darkness below her navel. At that point, I lost all remnants of sanity and self-control. She stood grinning wickedly as I scrambled out of my clothes. I hesitated a split second before we fell helter-skelter on the sofa.

Even in the heat of passion, the nagging question of size would not go away. I knew that I could not match the phallic virility that she was accustomed to from Sergeant Walker. But, there was no time to think about things of that sort. Stonewall Jackson was in full control, and like it or not, my actions were not my own. Marlena jerked me roughly between her legs and locked them around my back. I was trapped in a moist vacuum of such intensity that it made me gasp for breath. She gritted her teeth fiercely, and her hungry body shook with want. A second later, I was trembling violently. It was unavoidable and over before it really began. I couldn't stop the dam that suddenly burst, leaving me breathless and drained. Marlena was furious. The veins in her neck stood out like a woman possessed. Her fingers clawed viciously at my back.

"C'mon damn you! Give it to me!"

Urgency was never far away, and I complied to her request as soon as I was able. And almost immediately, it happened again. She screamed aloud in anger and frustration.

"Don't do that to me! For God's sake. Let me finish! Dammit! You can't leave me like this!"

Her hands were trembling as she moved quickly, trying to get me back inside of her. I simply couldn't do it. It was too hot in there. Disgust made her voice loud and shrill. She screamed.

"Get the fuck out of my house. I mean it! Get out of here right now!"

I dressed as quickly as I could and got out of there. The door slammed behind me, making a noise that should have awakened every soul on that street. I walked out to the sidewalk and then trudged slowly down the quiet street. It was the second time in the last few months that I had walked the whole distance from Lawton back to Fort Sill.

Marlena

It was Tuesday morning, a few days after the incident with Marlena. My re-enlistment papers were at battalion headquarters courtesy of Sergeant Walker. It was a good thing that I had turned the papers in because the United States Army was discharging servicemen left and right. The reason stated was the convenience of the government. Draftees were allowed the option to re-enlist, but they had to be fully qualified to meet the tough standards of the regular army. It was only natural that the colored soldiers would be the first to be affected by the ruling. White soldiers were being discharged too but not on such a grand scale.

I was on sick call again. I had awakened with a terrible headache, even worse than the one inflicted by John Sykes. I had other problems too. When I went to the toilet to urinate, there was pain and itching. The burning was like the devil. The pain soon became unbearable. There were times when I had to grab the pipes of the urinal and hold on for dear life. I decided to go to the dispensary. The sergeant in charge of sick call was brusque, no nonsense and all business.

"Awright soldier, lemme see whatcha got."

Reluctantly, I dropped my pants and began to explain.

"I don't know Sarge. I've been having trouble urinating. It burns something awful and when I stop it's even worse. The sergeant leaned over and peered closely for a moment. He then left abruptly to confer with the doctor. Returning within a few minutes, the sergeant carried a small piece of rectangular glass. There was a smirk on his face as he approached.

"I've got to get a smear to see if we can find out what's going on here." He was grinning nastily.

"From the looks of things and judging from past experience, my guess is that the love bug done bit you for sure."

It was more than an hour later before the doctor came in and beckoned.

"Sawyer, come on back to my office." I followed him back into the small cubicle. "Sit down Sawyer. I'm Captain Jacobs." I squeezed into the chair beside his desk and waited expectantly. He was short, red-haired, and he had a slight paunch. He wore horn-rimmed glasses and had a slight tic under his left eye. His voice was a guttural rasp.

"Well Sawyer, you do have a venereal disease, probably gonorrhea. Don't worry, it's something that we can cure. There is a new drug called penicillin. It usually takes about four shots to cure the infection. It seems to work especially well in these cases." He paused for a moment. "You're not out of the woods yet. We have to do a blood test to see if you have contracted syphilis."

It was unbelievable. How in the world could I have caught something like that? Except for Marlena, I had had no contact with anybody since I had been at Fort Sill. Good grief! Suddenly it dawned on me. I knew what had happened. Sergeant Hosea Walker was the real culprit. It had to have been his fault. His fooling around with Proud Mary was the reason that Marlena had become infected with the disease. How could he have done that to his bride-to-be? It was a terrible situation, and I was caught right in the middle of it. Captain Jacobs must have seen the look on my face.

"It's a little worse than you might have imagined," Captain Jacobs said. "I keep having to lecture you guys about the dangers of catching venereal disease. The army really frowns on this sort of thing. In fact, a directive just came down. It states that personnel who have three incidents of venereal disease can be discharged immediately." He was pensive for a moment.

"One other thing Sawyer, you are going to have to talk to the CID. You're going to have to tell them whom you contracted the disease from and whether you might have transmitted it to anybody else. The CID, with the help of the civilian authorities, will pick up the woman and treat her whether she agrees or not." He thought for a moment and then stood up abruptly.

"Awright Sawyer. Bend over and drop your pants."

He started getting the needle ready. A minute later, I felt a sharp stab of pain. "It's a whole lot better to use a condom or prophylaxis than to go naked into a loose woman," the captain lectured. I agreed with him. It was a terrible ordeal.

It was the beginning of the end for me. My entire future came crashing down like a house of cards. The word was out. All of the members of Battery A knew the whole story. The hatred that Sergeant Walker felt toward me fouled the very air around the barracks. He could barely keep his anger in check. I had not mentioned the incident to anyone, and I was ashamed that I was a part of it.

I had been honest with the CID. Its staffers questioned me extensively. I had to tell them the truth. I mentioned the connection among Proud Mary, Sergeant Walker and Marlena Wrigley. I related that Proud Mary was probably the source of the infection. I tried to stress the fact that Marlena was unaware that Walker had infected her and that she probably still didn't know that she was infected.

The tangled mess continued to unfold. Proud Mary and Marlena were picked up and forcibly treated for being carriers of a venereal disease. Sergeant Walker was also examined and questioned for his role in the affair. I was ignored, ostracized and generally treated like a persona non grata. On that Monday morning Sergeant Walker spoke to me for the first time in days.

"Sawyer, the captain wants to see you at 0900 hours in the orderly room. You will wear your Class A uniform. Be there!"

I dressed slowly and carefully. I had no idea what it was about, but I knew that it wasn't anything good. I braced myself as I entered the orderly room. Lem Tooter, the battery clerk, looked up and nodded toward the closed door.

"Go ahead back, Sawyer. They're waiting for you."

They were all there. Colonel John Bradbury, the battalion commander, Captain George Lewis, our battery commander, Lieutenant Ezra Barnes, the executive officer and First Sergeant Walker, who was the only one standing. The rest of them were seated around the large desk. I knew then that I was looking at the awesome power of the United States government. Too soon I realized that the full force of it was directed against me.

Captain Lewis was the first to speak. His face was florid, and his little pig eyes were as cold as ice.

"Corporal Sawyer, good morning!" He didn't waste time but went directly for my throat.

"This isn't a formal type hearing or anything like that. Papers concerning you just came down from battalion headquarters. Under the Articles of Convenience of the government, your draftee status ends on the 28th of January. You will be given an honorable discharge. Is there anything that you would like to say regarding the action taken?" I said nothing. Colonel Bradbury cleared his throat to speak.

"Ahem, Sawyer, there is one other thing. Because of your propensity for catching venereal diseases, the army is no longer interested in you as a candidate for the regular army."

I stood there numb with shock. I wasn't expecting anything of that sort. It took me a full minute to get myself under control, and then the words came tumbling out.

"Captain Lewis, sir! There's got to be a big mistake of some sort. I turned in my re-enlistment papers weeks ago. Sergeant Walker said that if I didn't hear anything to the contrary, everything would be okay. I've got a good record sir. I haven't been gigged more than once!"

I was trembling with anxiety. It didn't bother the executioners one bit. Captain Lewis was right. It wasn't a hearing per se. It was a lynching by the United States government designed solely to get me out of the military. And, to make sure that I had as little dignity left as possible.

"I turned your papers in for processing, Sawyer," said Sergeant Walker. "They must have been misplaced. Battalion headquarters said that it had no record of them," he said flatly. "It looks like you're up shit creek. I tried to help you Sawyer, but no dice."

The officers stood up from the desk. The steely eyes of Captain Lewis were boring into mine.

"That will be all Corporal Sawyer. You will hear from Sergeant Walker when your discharge papers are ready. This meeting is over! You are dismissed!"

"Yes sir, captain, sir!"

I came to attention, saluted smartly, did an about-face and walked slowly out of the orderly room. My world had crumbled to dust. The Stonewall dream was no more, and my ambitions littered the floor of the orderly room. The final engagement was over. There were no goodbyes. Nobody gave a damn about what had happened to me. Soon, I would be David Jonathan Sawyer, ex-Technician Fifth Grade, formerly a member of the 969th Field Artillery Battalion. I was a broken man. In a world rigidly divided into black and white, where would I go, and what would I do? The army had been the only place that made me feel like a man. All hope for the future vanished, leaving a cloud of despair.

4

The Train

The lonesome wail of the train's whistle was somehow comforting to me. It interrupted my thoughts about my present state of being, which was a good thing. The clickety clack of the Pullman car's wheels reminded me that every revolution was taking me farther and farther away from the origin of my Summer of discontent.

My mind was still dwelling on the events of the past few months. I immediately tried to put them out of my mind. The whole scenario would surely be back to haunt me over and over. Maybe the colored Pullman car with its strange array of occupants would wean my thoughts away from things that I didn't want to remember.

The car was crowded with people from all walks of Negro life: cowboys, farmers, oilfield workers, two women with babies and several women who looked like domestics. Seated just across from me was a shapely, bushy-haired young Negro girl. She was dressed in a dirty pink dress, and her luggage was a greasy paper bag and another cheap cotton dress that was rolled around a pair of soiled white pumps. The girl's cheekbones were prominent, and her mouth was big and moist with yellowed buck teeth. Her body was as loose and ripe as tropical fruit. Her striking figure more than made up for the angular ugliness of her sullen face. She smelled to high heaven of Dixie Peach hair grease, stale Talcum

The Train

Powder, sweat and the earthiness of womanhood. Her raunchy odor should have been offensive, but to me it was tantalizing as hell. I was suddenly wide awake.

The noises in the car were hauntingly familiar, and so were the other odors that wafted around it. There was the smell of stinking feet removed from shoes for comfort. Rank perspiration mingled with the acrid smell of soiled diapers lying on the floor beneath the seat of the two women with babies. The odor of cigars, cigarette smoke and fried chicken permeated the car, and the smell stale collard greens lingered in the air. There would be no takers for the dry, moldy sandwiches that the porter would soon bring through the car. Negroes always carried their own food.

The tiny cubicle in the corner of the dining car was seldom, if ever, used. Besides, the dining car was really for white folks. I was used to going along with whatever the program. It was almost like being at home.

To add insult to injury, the train rounded a curve, and the door to the toilet at the far end of the car swung open. The door slammed shut with a loud bang, and a minute later it opened again. A brand-new odor suddenly surfaced in the car. I got up quickly, hurried to the end of the car and shut the door. After checking to make sure that the toilet door was secure, I walked slowly back to my seat. Enough was enough. So much for brand-new odors caused by the opening of a swinging door. The car was already lit up like a pinball machine.

I had casually glanced down at the bushy-haired girl when I strolled past her seat. She had certainly gotten my attention. Her firm legs were carelessly spread apart, and the flimsy dress was still fighting a losing battle trying to cover her thighs. Her eyes, with their incredibly long lashes, were half closed. Her tongue kept darting out to lick the loose lips. It was fascinating to watch the pinkness disappear behind the haven of her large teeth. Sitting there, it occurred to me that she would be more than open for anything pertaining to the act of sex. She would probably welcome any sort of encounter, regardless of the length of time or the effort required. Of course, it might be just supposition on my part, or maybe it was all in my mind. I could imagine whatever I wanted, and I was having a great time just thinking about the girl. She was still in my thoughts as the train moved slower and slower and finally screeched to a stop.

We were at a small isolated station somewhere between Lawton and

The Train

Oklahoma City. A field of corn with wilted leaves almost hid the two outdoor toilets that stood directly behind the station. The older of the two women with babies gathered her things and her share of dirty diapers from under the seat, carelessly picked up her baby and headed for the front of the car. As soon as the woman was off the car, the train eased forward and soon was off and running. Its lonesome whistle cried in the morning air. Something bothered me for a moment. I hadn't heard the conductor call out the station. So, that was the meaning of whistle stop.

For no apparent reason, I was depressed, sliding deeper and deeper into a familiar state of mind. Thinking about the bushy-haired girl had once again triggered my concern about the Stonewall inadequacy. I reached into my jacket and took out the small grey book that chronicled the heroic deeds of my great-grandfather. The story of his daring and bravery had helped me at other times in my life. I needed help from the spirit of the mighty Stonewall Jackson. Once again I needed assurance. I thumbed through the book until I saw a passage that I felt would help me.

During the height of the seven days' battle, Jackson, chewing his lemon, forgot weariness, confusion and the necessity of strictly obeying orders. He caught fire. Every one of his commanders received a message.

In a voice that rang like the deadly crack of a rifle, he shouted to his staff officers: "Tell them that this affair must hang in suspense no longer. Sweep the field with the bayonet!" It made me feel good to know that there was no inadequacy where his daring and bravery were concerned.

I should have been elated. My spirits usually soared after reading about the exploits of my great-grandfather. I felt nothing, nothing at all. Mercifully, sleep came.

I dreamed that I was at home, and Mama was cooking collard greens. When I awakened, it was early afternoon. The train had discharged passengers, taken passengers on board and was pulling out of the Oklahoma City station. My eyes widened, and for a moment I thought I was still asleep and dreaming because standing beside my seat was Dick Texeria.

"Good grief! How did you get here?"

Texeria was grinning widely, and as I watched, he burst into laughter.

"I came by covered wagon, fool! I just missed the last stagecoach."

I was glad to see Texeria. He was the nearest thing to a friend that I had at Fort Sill.

"Where are you going, man? I couldn't see you leaving Fort Sill for anything. What's up?"

"My papers came down the same day that you got discharged. Unlike you, I'm glad to be getting out of that shit. I'm going to New York and then on to Boston to see my mother. She runs a dry cleaning business. I'm going to help her." He was serious for a moment.

"Since you ain't playing soldier no more, do you want to go with me?" The car swayed a bit and then righted itself. He grabbed the back of the empty seat in front of me, then sat down and turned to me. His deep voice was sympathetic.

"I figure you got a rotten deal. Everybody was talking about the way you got railroaded. It was probably for the best though. You never would have made it as long as Walker was first sergeant. He would have kept leaning on you until you would have ended up with a bad discharge or doing time in the stockade."

I was about to answer when I noticed a wide grin on his face. He thought for a minute.

"But Sawyer old buddy, you didn't hear the latest. Marlena dumped Sergeant Walker. Then Proud Mary dumped him, and the last thing that I heard was that he can't buy, beg or steal a piece of ass in Lawton, Lawton View or the Witchita Mountains."

"Well, I'll be damned, that is good news. I hope all of them, including Colonel Bradbury, rot in hell and that's too good for them! They're a bunch of cutthroat sons of bitches!"

"I know how you feel," said Texeria. "Oh, there is one other thing," he continued, "Lila Wrigley is back in Lawton, but she's not living with her mother. Big John got her a room above the Busy Bee cab stand. It seems that she just couldn't stay away from John." He mused, half under his breath.

"It's a wonder that he didn't bust her wide open with that thing." He looked at me, and a sheepish look crossed his face.

"Aw man, I'm sorry as shit. I had clean forgotten how you felt about the girl. Don't pay any attention to that."

My face felt hot. Memories of Lila came flooding back, but they receded slowly when I was reminded that I would never see her again. There was no point in beating a dead horse. I didn't feel like talking any more about it. Anyway when the bushy-haired girl had gotten Texeria's attention simply by just being there. I dozed off again, and when I awakened, Texeria had moved across the aisle and was seated beside the long-legged gal. The two of them were laughing and talking as if they had known each other for years.

The train's whistle mourned twice. The big engine was gathering speed as it roared through a stretch of dry prairie. The sun's afternoon journey was coming to an end, and the soft shadows of impending darkness waited quietly in the wings. I looked toward Texeria and the girl. They were talking softly now, and his arm rested casually around her shoulders. A half smile was on his handsome face. I watched them, wondering, why couldn't I talk to girls like that? Texeria made it look easy.

The bushy-haired girl yawned and stretched sensuously. She had given up completely on trying to keep the dress down. Texeria spoke from across the aisle. "Hey Sawyer. This is Ella, my new girlfriend. How do you like her?"

He was laughing good-naturedly as he gave her a quick hug.

"She's a mess, I tell you." He looked down at her. "Ain'tcha babycake?"

Her big brown eyes flirted crazily upward, and her pretty pink tongue came out and kissed the big lips before she answered.

"Sawyer, that's right, ain't it?"

I smiled and nodded my head. It was fascinating to watch as her big mouth opened.

"I tell you for a fact, Sawyer. You have got one crazy-ass friend here! And he's pushy as hell." Smiling affectionately, she looked up at Texeria,

"I like your nerve pretty boy, but you're one pushy fool." I was grinning as I looked at her.

"Girl, you're right as rain. He is a pain in the ass. I don't see why you want to be bothered with him."

"She was going to Memphis," Texeria informed me, "but now she wants me to take her to Boston. That's her problem. Ain't that right, baby?"

"Yes!" She laughed like a true coquette, and it worked beautifully. The banter continued for a few minutes. I turned away and looked out into the darkness. The odor of food became prevalent in the air around me. It was suppertime, a tradition that was honored even on the speeding train. As the passengers began to open bags and parcels of food, the buzz of conversation slowly died. Ella opened her greasy paper bag,

The Train

gave Texeria a piece of chicken and offered to share with me. I accepted gratefully.

I looked around the car. After eating, sleep came naturally to most of the passengers. In the dim light, figures lolled in various awkward positions of disarray. My eyes were drawn to Texeria and his new girlfriend. They were definitely not asleep. They were kissing avidly, as if they had known each other for years.

As I watched, Texeria's hand moved ever so slightly until it came to rest on Ella's inner thigh. She placed her hand on his, lifted it and put it exactly where she wanted it to be. She sighed breathlessly as she snuggled closer to Texeria.

I could hardly stand it. Desire rolled over me in sickening waves, and I felt sweat dripping from my armpits. It was getting worse. The two were frantic for each other. I was beginning to wonder how they were going to carry out this frenzied search to satisfy their passion for each other. Suddenly, they stood up, and Texeria moved to the seat next to the window. Ella did not take the seat that he vacated, instead she stood quickly, lifted her right leg and then arranged herself squarely on Texeria's lap. He leaned around her and whispered hoarsely.

"Hey Sawyer, sit over here in this seat, so that nobody will see us. Hurry now! C'mon dammit!"

I did as he asked. Soon, the three of us were squeezed into the two seats. My senses reeled as I joined their agitated state. There were no high morals or lofty principles inherited from Stonewall Jackson. If there were, they went flying out the window and into the darkness. I began to ache. The Stonewall curse quit its smallness and grew bold and stretched tightly against my fly. I avidly watched the two of them quietly engage. Triple lust crowded the two seats of the Pullman car. It was a tight situation filled with danger and intrigue.

I sat there with sweat dripping from every pore as Texeria and the girl continued their mating game. I had never played the role of voyeur but watching the two of them made feelings surface that I had never felt before. I was an amorous Stonewall watching primeval coupling being consummated in its most graphic sense. On the worn seat beside me was an erotic puzzle. As I watched, each piece of seduction and fulfillment came together with painstaking clarity.

What about me? I was aroused and goaded by lust, prodded by

imagined wrongs and watching a scenario that had me at the breaking point. My whole body was an aching bundle of want. As I watched their faces, Texeria shuddered and his thin frame went limp. It wasn't hard to figure out. His problem was the same one that I had been troubled with at Marlena's place. It was not so with the volatile Ella. Her brown eyes were closed, and she kept biting her bottom lip. When her eyes finally opened, they rolled back into her head until only the whites were visible. Her problem was just the opposite of Texeria. She began to cry, softly. And as I watched, frustration twisted her face into an ugly mask. She kept whining, and a drop of blood appeared on her bottom lip. Texeria's voice came out of the darkness.

"Sorry baby, I couldn't help it. That mess was just too good. That's all for now."

I could feel Ella trembling uncontrollably beside me. Texeria's voice was suddenly sardonic.

"It ain't the end of the world, baby." He winked broadly at me.

"You could get Sawyer to straighten you out."

Texeria turned away to avoid looking at her tortured face. He spoke softly.

"How about it baby doll?"

My voice was a ragged whisper.

"Yeah, Ella baby," I whispered hoarsely. "I know just how you feel. How about letting me fix you up? I'll be glad to take care of you."

Ella's teeth began to chatter, and she was shaking as if she had the ague.

"Lordy me! I can't stand this! I've got to finish! Somebody do something quick!"

I stood up, crazy with anticipation. I had to act quickly, or the mood would be lost.

"Gimme a hot minute honey. I got to go to the bathroom. Wait just one second, and everything will be fine, you hear?"

With my left hand in my pocket, I hurried down the aisle to the toilet. Stonewall Jackson was always a prudent man. It was only going to take a second to protect myself. I was not going naked into that stormy night. I was in for a terrible shock and was certainly ill-prepared for what I saw when I came out of the toilet. The big burly conductor was standing at the other end of the car counting tickets with exacting slowness.

The Train

Texeria and Ella had regained their composure and were seated side by side. Texeria sat silently, and Ella somehow managed to look quiet and demure. I walked back to my seat and sat. It was going to be a long ride.

5

Going Home

Darkness was here to stay. The train's whistle sounded twice, eerily screaming its determination to be in a certain place at a certain time. It was not so with Stonewall's great-grandson. I was to meet my destiny in no special place, and I would be there at no particular time. For the people beyond the world of the speeding train, it was a simple matter of a train passing. For the people aboard, it wouldn't be as long as it had been, and for me it made no difference. Time was of no concern.

Time did make a difference to Ella. It was of great importance. She asked Texeria to take her to Boston with him. Ella had been pleading plaintively, child-like with a hint of desperation in her voice. Texeria had trouble keeping a smile on his handsome face. He was putting her off with all kind of vague promises that even she found hard to believe. The desire that I felt for her ebbed as the chances of fulfillment lessened. It disappeared completely when I noticed some sort of commotion at the opposite end of the car.

There was a wizened little white man, with a sallow, pockmarked face standing in the aisle. He was carrying a pasteboard box, and it was obvious that he was selling something, food perhaps. From the responses of the cowboys and oil field workers, he was definitely making sales.

Going Home

His ferret eyes were darting everywhere as he moved quickly down the aisle. When he neared my seat, I glanced at the box. Inside were books neatly enclosed in brown wrapping paper. The bloodshot eyes bored into mine. His voice was a rasping whisper. "I got dirty books here, boy, real nasty books. Get one now! I ain't got much time. Hurry now. You want one boy? They cost a dollar and a half."

I thought for a second. Why would I need the help of a book filled with lurid photographs and sordid innuendo when pornography raw and dirty was seated just across the aisle? What the heck. I fumbled in my pocket and found the right amount of change. I gave the money to the little man and waited until he left the car. I tore off the wrapping and looked at the book. It was an old Reader's Digest, smudged and soiled. And like the little man said, it was quite dirty.

It is said that lightning does not strike twice in the same place. I found nothing to dispute the assumption. The next event happened in another place and time. The train was entering the town of Little Rock in Arkansas. It was a short stop for whatever necessities the train needed for its journey north. I was hungry. The small piece of chicken that Ella gave me was gone and forgotten. As the train slowed to a stop, I noticed a young Negro boy standing beside the track. I wondered why he was out so late at night. Suddenly, I realized that it might be a chance for me to get something to eat. The boy's eyes widened as I called out to him.

"Hey Sonny!" His oval face was a question mark.

"Do you think you can find a ham and cheese sandwich and bring it to me real quick?" A wide smile flitted across his face.

"Sure thing soldier. There's a place right around the corner. It'll cost you a buck." I leaned out the open window and handed him two one dollar bills.

"Get one for yourself kid but hurry back because the train's not going to be here but a few minutes."

The boy was gone for a while. The train was slowly moving forward when he suddenly appeared, running alongside the car. He was eating a sandwich in one hand and holding out a dollar bill in the other hand.

"Here's your money," said the boy. "They were getting ready to close, and they only had one sandwich left." I turned away from the window as the train picked up speed. I was one trusting soul.

Going Home

When the train had regained its speed, Texeria got up and walked down the aisle to the toilet. As soon as he left, Ella leaned over and tugged at my sleeve.

"Sawyer, Texeria said something about taking me to Boston with him." She was insistent.

"Please talk to him. He likes me. I know he does." Her voice broke.

"Please Sawyer. I don't really have any place to go." She was getting incoherent. "I left the farm and walked all the way to Oklahoma City. After Mama died, there was nobody left but Papa and I. Things weren't so bad until he started raping me. I jist got tired of having my own daddy do it to me all of the time. The last time he did it to me, I hit him in the head with an axe." She stopped and licked her lips tentatively.

"I sure hope that I didn't kill him. He had $34.20 hidden in a Prince Albert tobacco can. I took every cent of it, and when I got to Oklahoma City, I caught the first thing smoking." She shook her head slowly.

"It's a damn shame. Everybody said that I looked just like him. I reckon that's what made it really bad. It was as if he was doing it to himself." She was crying openly then.

"Please tell Texeria to take me with him, you hear? Please David."

Ella's story was something that I was not dying to hear. The personal attraction that I felt for her slowly dissolved into pity. I knew that Texeria was not going to take her to Boston or anywhere else. Her ticket was valid until she reached Memphis. I figured she would be okay as long as she didn't end up on the wrong side of Memphis. I decided to be honest with her. She deserved that much.

"Girl, I ain't got no influence on Texeria. I don't know how he feels about you." I paused and shook my head.

"Maybe he will take you. I just don't know."

At that moment Texeria returned from the toilet. Ella was still crying softly. He seemed a bit concerned and put his arm around her shoulders. He looked at me and shrugged.

Ella stood up, squeezed by Texeria and hurried up the aisle to the toilet. He heaved a sigh of relief.

"Aw man, she's still talking about me taking her to Boston. The girl just can't seem to realize that Boston is just not her kind of town. She just wouldn't fit in. She don't know it, but a quick piece of ass won't get her

55

Going Home

nowhere near the state of Massachusetts. Boston is a special sort of place. It wouldn't work."

6

Miz Hannah's Lament

Ella's problem was uppermost in Texeria's mind. It also topped my thinking for the moment. For Ella, it was to be a turning point in her life. With Texeria's help, she could become an independent woman of the world.

When the train pulled into the station at Memphis, Texeria solved Ella's problem in a fashion that did not adhere to her aspirations. He simply disappeared. She looked everywhere: inside the station, at a nearby colored restaurant and a shoeshine parlor. She enlisted my help, but I couldn't find him either. I knew of course that we would not find him. She looked small and helpless as she stood watching the train move slowly forward. I looked at the forlorn figure standing beside the pillar at track No. 5. She bit back the tears that welled from her eyes, and with her small pink tongue she caught the ones that got away.

I was saddened by her predicament. There were some things that even Stonewall could not change. That was the way of the world, some coming and some going, some watching and some waiting and some crying.

Contrary to popular thinking, the train had not lost its way. It was just traveling slower and making more stops once it left Memphis. Atlanta had been the last stop. Birmingham would be next.

Three nondescript Negroes in ragged overalls came aboard. One of

Miz Hannah's Lament

them, a small wiry black man with gold-rimmed glasses and his hat on backwards, was evidently the leader. The men were talking loudly and bragging about how well they could play cards. In a few minutes, several of the farmers, a couple of servicemen and I were introduced to "Three Card Monte," a wonderful new game played with three cards.

Our teacher was the little man with the hat on backwards. He was good-natured, fun to listen to and a genius at his craft. In less than half and hour, he had relieved everybody in the game of most of their money. He accomplished it with such ease that nobody could get really angry. I was $120 lighter, and he had offered to cash a $100 check, which was the last of my mustering-out pay.

As the three Negroes left the car, I changed my mind and decided to let the little man cash my check. I followed them to the rear of the car and was surprised to see the three of them jump from the slow-moving train. On my way back to my seat, the fat porter stopped me.

"I'll swear to God," the porter declared. "Y'all is some stupid niggers. I thought sho' y'all had more sense than to lose yo' money like that. Those three slickers work this section of track every day in the week."

I just looked at him and kept walking. I was beginning to harbor an intense dislike for trains. The next time I would take a bus.

It was the middle of the day. The sun was as bright as it dared for this time of year. We were traveling somewhere in South Carolina. A two-horse wagon, pulled by mules, was making its way along a dirt road that ran beside the railroad. Nostalgia was my silent companion, and we watched the wagon until it faded from sight. With every mile, the countryside began to look more and more like home. The large white houses overlooking the acres and acres of farmland were a pleasant sight. Even the dilapidated shacks of the sharecroppers in the background seemed to welcome me. The wood smoke that drifted up from the chimneys was quickly snatched away by the late Winter breezes, and the smell of corn bread cooking tickled my nostrils.

A huge sign came into sight as the train rounded a curve. It was a large billboard on a hill above the tracks. The rays of the early afternoon sun shone directly on the impressive sign. It was a knight in full regalia, riding a snow-white horse with lance and shield at ready and a shiny sword at his side. The caption's fiery letters burned across the top of the sign. "Keep America Pure! Join The United Klans Of America!" Yessir, there was no doubt about it. I was home. That fact was blazoned on the highest hill in the neighborhood.

A little later, the train eased into the station at Fayetteville, North Carolina. It was no longer a village-town as it had been in the 1930's. Now, it was metropolitan to the core.

It was Friday. Soldiers, sailors and farmers were everywhere around the city. Nearby, Fort Bragg was still the largest artillery fort in the nation, and it was bursting at the seams with returning servicemen. Each returning hero had a tale to tell. I would keep my mouth shut. Nobody would hear my story or learn about the depths of my humiliation. Fayetteville could welcome the other heroes.

The train screeched to a stop at the small depot located at the corner of Hay and Hillsboro streets. It had been an unusual journey, and now I was exactly three miles from home. I decided to leave my duffel bag at the station and walk. Besides, I didn't have bus fare.

I left the station and began to walk briskly up Hillsboro Street. In a few minutes, I was out of the business section and passing the little shotgun houses of the Negro city dwellers. From that point, it was uphill.

Hillsboro Street ran parallel to Ramsey Street and was the main highway heading north to Raleigh. The two streets met at a junction about a mile from town. There was a little white church on a slight knoll on the right side of the road overlooking the junction. It was a Methodist church called "Mood's Temple." I had attended Sunday School and church services there for as far back as I could remember.

On the other side of the road was a much-traveled dirt road. It was called the Rose Hill road because of the mountain roses that grew abundantly along the ditch banks. This was home. The woods, trees and swamp beside the road were considered by me to be my personal property. Besides, for the next two miles, everyone who lived along the road was my kin, either uncles, aunts or cousins. Home for me was wherever I chose to hang my hat.

Rose Hill Road was as curvaceous as a woman and as bitchy and as willful. It was only a few miles from Fort Bragg and was used as a lover's lane by the soldiers and their women of easy virtue. The ribbon of dirt and dust conjured up lustful thoughts, as it meandered through thick

Miz Hannah's Lament

underbrush laced comfortably with tall pine and oak. The road was also sandy in part with fringes of Carolina mud lying lazily along the ditch bank. It was an ideal place, a playground for dalliance.

I had been walking faster than I had realized. I rounded a curve and neared a wooden bridge that straddled a small creek called Rocky Ford. When I reached the bridge, I paused for a moment and stared down into the narrow chasm. I was amazed at the speed of the swirling water. As a boy, I had fished for minnows in this very spot, using a bent pin and Mama's sewing thread. What better place than this to try to figure out how to cope with the Stonewall curse. My whole life was ahead of me. Was there some sort of middle ground with which I could be comfortable? Somehow I had to work it out.

The little stream was criss-crossed with trash, reeds and debris. The water was stained black from the roots of poplar trees as it raced through the tangled mess. Suddenly, out of nowhere, I felt a quick surge in my bladder, an immediate urge to urinate. This too was a part of the phenomena. I looked both ways to make certain that no one was watching and moved to the railing of the bridge and quickly relieved myself.

Depression weighed heavily, like an anvil, around my neck. As I watched the amber stream disappear into the murky depths of the stream, I became even more depressed. I was looking directly at the source of my problem. There was one indisputable fact. I was back home, and the problem was still with me. I was miserable.

I regained my composure. My footsteps quickened and sanity returned. I left the bridge and walked up the road until I came to a path that led off to the left and up a long hill. I looked up at the sun, surprised that there was still about three hours of sunlight. My spirits lifted, and my depression took a back seat. I knew exactly what I was going to do.

Our little shack was about a quarter of a mile up the road. I was in no hurry to get home. Uncle Joe's little cabin was just up the path and over the hill. I would ask his advice. Uncle Joe knew a lot about everything. He would be glad to help me. From my early childhood, his advice had been invaluable to me over the years. I almost ran up the hill.

After reaching the top of the hill, there was a clear view of the little valley. Grandpa's modest house nestled in the middle of the mottled browns and greens of the fertile valley. He had acted early. Already the

Miz Hannah's Lament 5

acreage around the house had been plowed into neat rows for the next planting season. The house was surrounded by a barn, a chicken coop, an outhouse and the remains of a small smokehouse. It was a peaceful sight, but my immediate interest was in the little log cabin just down the path to my left. It was hunkered down behind a small clump of trees. There was smoke coming from the chimney, so I hurried down the path toward the cabin. The path split the cultivated rows of rich earth that would soon be Miz Hannah's garden. The door creaked open just as I reached the steps, and Miz Hannah Blue stood there.

Miz Hannah was taller and heavier than I remembered, but the wide hips and the strange disparity of her uneven breasts were the same. Her big placid face was a question mark until she recognized me. A broad grin pushed the lines of worry away. "Little David, when did you come home? I wuz jist thinking about you the other day!" She seemed delighted to see me.

"Are you still in the army?" I was grinning too.

"I just got in Miz Hannah. No ma'am, I've been discharged. I'm out of the army for good."

My eyes strayed a bit and then focused on her bosom, reluctant to leave the fascinating sight of one bulging breast and one slightly larger than an apple.

"How have you been, and where is Uncle Joe?" I was still grinning.

"You ain't got to tell me, Miz Hannah. I betcha he's still sleeping off last night's moonshine. His head is probably busting wide open."

I was looking forward to seeing Uncle Joe. Anger tinged with sorrow suddenly clouded Miz Hannah's face. I could see wetness around her eyes. Something was wrong. Miz Hannah's voice sounded as tired as her eyes.

"C'mon in David. Joe ain't here. He's been gone for more than three weeks." Tears trickled down her cheeks.

"He left me for Rose. You know that trashy gal from Jones Street who used to hang up here all of the time."

Despair slumped her shoulders as she turned from the door. I walked up the steps and followed her into the semi darkness of the little shack. She opened the makeshift shutters, and late sunlight flooded the one-room shack. Miz Hannah walked past the wood stove and over to the lone bed against the wall. The bedsprings creaked loudly as she

Miz Hannah's Lament

sat down and began to cry. I stood there, not knowing what to do. I knew that Uncle Joe was a rounder and liked women immensely, but this was completely out of character for him. Besides, he was almost totally blind. Rose was a tramp at heart and incredibly easy. She cared about no one, not even herself.

I looked around the little cabin, nothing had changed. Neatness was everywhere. Uncle Joe would never again find the caring and concern that Miz Hannah had exhibited in these last few years. Sobs racked her body, and the wrenching sounds filled the small room. I sat down beside her and put my arms around her shoulders.

"Please stop crying Miz Hannah. Tomorrow I'll go down on Jones Street and see if I can find him. It won't be hard to find out where they're shacking up. Maybe he'll listen to me."

Her crying ripped my composure to shreds. I rubbed her shoulders gently and pulled her tear-stained face closer until it pressed against my own. I was in a quandary. This kind of thing was entirely new to me. I had always been the recipient. Mama had comforted me in a like manner for everything from skinned knees to a bruised ego. Mama could always make the world a brighter place to be. I wished that I could do the same for Miz Hannah.

Her face moved until it was buried between my neck and shoulder. Her body was still shaking, and the acrid smell of Railroad Mills sweet Scotch snuff stung my nostrils. Tears and snuff spit ran slowly down my shirt. The stain spread quickly, darkening my shirt, and making it slick and clammy. I sat motionless.

Minutes passed, and her trembling subsided, except for an occasional hiccup like the waning noises of a small child crying. My hand came up and slowly caressed her head. Her mixed grey hair was in tight corn rows that covered her head like a skull cap. Gently, I began to rub her head, hoping that it would be a calming gesture.

Miz Hannah moved a bit, and her muffled voice came from somewhere beneath my chin.

"Lord have mercy, David. What am I going to do? Joe's got almost twelve gallons of liquor stashed in the swamp. When he git's ready for a drink, all he has to do is tell her which bush or log to look under. She'll either come and get it or or send one of that Jones Street crowd to get it. He kin stay drunk for months." She started to cry again. "Lord have mercy! I'm so afraid that something will happen to him."

I was bewildered. There had to be something I could do to help. I put one arm around her shoulders and the other one around her broad waist. I nuzzled her hairy cheek, unmindful of the brownish stains around her mouth. She relaxed a little and put her arms around me. I don't know how long we sat holding each other, but when she stopped crying, sunlight seemed to flood the little cabin. I was getting cramped from sitting motionless, and I wanted to move, but I was afraid. She would start crying again. I nuzzled her cheek again and was about to stand up when she squeezed me again. She turned her face until it was almost touching mine. A wan smile appeared briefly.

"David honey, thank you for paying attention to a whining old woman. The good Lord must have sent you to me."

I was about to say "Yes ma'am" when her arms tightened around me. My eyes widened in disbelief as her half-opened mouth complete with snuff moved swiftly toward me. She kissed me squarely on the mouth. She forced her tongue between my teeth, and it began moving hungrily deep inside my mouth. The Stonewall lust stirred and was suddenly wide awake. The level of its intensity was equal or more to Miz Hannah's starved feelings.

She began to grunt loudly. Her snuff-stained mouth was no problem, and her ragged teeth didn't bother me at all. Her hands began a feverish assault, caressing my body and hungrily searching for anything to soften the pain caused by the absence of hard-rolling Joe Sawyer.

Miz Hannah would be sorely disappointed. Uncle Joe's sexual exploits were well-known. There was no way that I could wear his shoes or fill the bill. I would be a poor substitute for his vaunted virility. She needed to know the truth.

Miz Hannah was still tugging at my clothing. Her voice was hoarse. It quivered anxiously.

"David, take off your clothes, quick! Hurry now! I don't owe Joe a blame thing! I got to have a piece. I ain't had nary a drop for over a month!"

She jumped up from the bed and hastily began to undress. Buttons flew everywhere as she tore herself out of the dress. She had the dress off and was trying to pull the ragged shift over her head before I started to undress.

Because of the Stonewall curse, arousal had never been a problem for me. I felt a tinge of guilt, but the feeling passed. I could get excited by looking at the curves of a tree. Miz Hannah's urgency and state of disarray only served to increase my excitement. But, there was no need for me to raise her expectations. I simply had to tell her about me. It was the right thing to do.

I slipped out of my shoes and was about to take off my pants when I looked over at the bed. Miz Hannah had removed the shift, and the upper part of her body was naked. Her skin was smooth, unblemished, and the unique sight of her breasts made me want her even more. She began to take off a huge pair of pink bloomers. As she wriggled free of them, a tin snuff box fell from somewhere and clanged to the floor.

For a moment, our nakedness was the only sound in the little cabin. Suddenly ashamed, I turned away. She grabbed my arm and pulled me onto the bed. I tried to cover my crotch with my hand and started to stutter.

"Wait a minute Miz Hannah. There's something I've got to tell you."

She paid no attention to me. She was fumbling awkwardly, trying to force my hands out of the way. I reluctantly let them fall away.

"Miz Hannah, I was trying to tell you, before we started doing anything. I'm built kinda small. It ain't real big or long like Uncle Joe. I just wanted you to know before we got started. I hope you won't be badly disappointed." Anxiously I watched her face, afraid of what I would see there.

She paused for a moment and then looked down at me. It seemed like forever, and as her eyes focused on me, a half smile played about her face. Her eyes searched my face as she grabbed me firmly and began to caress me. She started to laugh, but it was good laughter. She knew I was getting upset.

"You don't have to laugh and giggle at me, Miz Hannah. I told you it was kind of small, but it ain't nothing for you to make fun about." Anger rose in my throat. I got up to leave.

"I'm going home. I don't have time for this mess. I got other stuff to do."

Still laughing, Miz Hannah pushed me back down on the bed and threw one leg across my hips. I couldn't move. She was strong as a bull.

"Jist hold still for a minute David and listen. I was funning you a little bit. You are a teeny bit small, but don't worry about it." Her eyes narrowed, and she whistled softly.

"Good gracious, Davy boy! Look at it," she crooned softly. "The 'lil feller ain't very big, but he's hard as a rock." A second later disgust tightened her face. "I get so tired of having to fool with limp do-nothing peckers. That sorry uncle of yours is a good example."

Miz Hannah's leg relaxed, and she pulled me gently to her side.

"Come closer David, and let me show you something."

I glanced down at the salt and pepper mound. When she spoke again, her voice was low and insistent.

"Jist do like I tell you, Davy boy." I followed her instructions to the letter.

Miz Hannah's arms cuddled around me, and her hips spread wide underneath me. Her work-hardened fingers guided me into a vortex that hurled me to and fro like a leaf tossed by an angry wind. The rickety bed with its loud springs, groaned, creaked and swayed to the sound of our grunts and groans. The burning heat from Miz Hannah's body seemed to rise and meld with my own body. Never had I encountered such a feeling. I rose to heights that I never dreamed of as I was carried away by the ferocity of her movements. The storm of our coupling increased to hurricane strength. The wild ride abruptly ended against our wishes. Miz Hannah screamed. "David, put it back, quick!"

The loss of a split second meant nothing in that race. There was absolutely no danger of making the same mistake twice. Perish the thought. The vise-like grip of Miz Hannah's legs scissored across my back would not let it happen again. The explosion came again and again. I was caught like a rabbit in a snare. Every time I tried to pull away, Miz Hannah would make the right move, and her hips would swivel me into more torment. It was lucky for me that skill and ingenuity were not needed. It was simply a matter of holding on for dear life. Miz Hannah's expertise transformed the old bed into a learning tree. Slowly and surely, she led me through a maze of erotic behavior. It was designed as much to ease her frustration at Uncle Joe's infidelity as it was to calm my fears.

The sweaty interlude did not end in a blaze of glory. Thirst was

Miz Hannah's Lament

slaked, and that was the immediate goal. When it was finally over, I lay there on the rumpled bed with doubt and worries running through my head. The uncontrolled tremors and orgasms that had shaken Miz Hannah's body could not have been faked, or could they? Did I make it happen? Maybe she was just trying to make me feel better. Was it my own uncertainty about my sexuality that gave me pause? I should have felt honored that Miz Hannah had let me into her bed. It was a privilege because Uncle Joe had sworn that the legendary Fast Fanny, who was the undisputed queen of Jones Street, was a slowpoke compared to Miz Hannah. To get acclaim like that from a rounder like Uncle Joe was high praise indeed.

Fast Fanny was known far and wide for the speed with which she took care of soldiers, sailors and ordinary folk in her little shotgun house on Jones Street. The customers were in and out of her bed in minutes flat. Fanny was good, but this good-natured lady, Miz Hannah Blue, was the very best. I was a better person because of her.

What a day it had been. What a strange unusual day. Miz Hannah was standing in the door as I walked slowly out of the yard. Her shrill voice floated out behind me.

"David, I'd sure 'preciate it if you'd try to talk some sense into that fool uncle of yours. Tell Joe I said that it's all right for him to come home." She paused for a moment. "And David, don't worry too much about size, you'll be fine." There was a grin on her face. "It worked pretty good for you just now, didn't it?"

7

Grandpa's Family

The path to Grandpa's was well-worn. It was used constantly by family members and visitors. Ever since the girls, Esther and Ruth, my cousins, started courting, the traffic had increased considerably.

Over on the other side of the valley was a wagon road used by the few automobiles that ventured up the steep hill, which led from the Rose Hill Road to the Sawyer homestead. For me, this was hallowed ground. I had roamed every inch of Grandpa's little valley. Just like the sparrows and other small birds, I knew exactly where to find briar berries, honeysuckle vines and juicy black grapes. The snakes, frogs and small game had all been my traveling companions. It was good to be back in familiar surroundings. I walked slowly and savored the tiredness. I felt drained, squeezed as limp as a dish cloth. It was a good feeling.

When I reached the bottom of the hill, I paused at the edge of a small stream that meandered between the two hills that comprised the little valley. Stagnant water stood in small pools beside the little stream. The sun's rays would soon cause the water to evaporate.

Stale water standing in puddles always reminded me of the 1945 flooding of Fayetteville. It had happened the year that I was graduated from high school. Grandpa's little place was comfortably north of the

Grandpa's Family

floodline. Water would never leave the banks of the Cape Fear River and travel this far north. There had also been a big flood in 1908. It had flooded the whole of Fayetteville but had come nowhere near the communities and farms on the Rose Hill Road. Floods, hurricanes and killer storms always avoided Grandpa's little valley.

I stood by the little stream, still remembering the flood. Wild water on the loose is a frightening thing. The recent flood that I had witnessed splashed a grim picture of havoc wreaked by rushing waters that heeded no one, rising fitfully at the bidding of capricious nature. Do not hesitate. Go quickly to the high ground. Downtown was ground zero, the focal point, and as usual I had been right in the thick of things. I had felt no guilt or remorse, as I left the comfort of dry land to spend time downtown with the hapless flood victims. Was it concern for the victims, or the fact that the army fed and clothed the bedraggled tent dwellers? Army chow was free. Bologna and cheese were plentiful, so I too was a victim. My mind returned to the present. I jumped across the little stream and hurried up the hill.

The coolness of the evening air reminded me that it was still late Winter. I could see that all of the family members, except for Grandma, were seated on the porch. Aunt Sarah, Papa's sister, was seated in the swing located on the left side of the porch near some rose bushes. Seated beside her, was Cousin Esther, Aunt Sarah's youngest daughter, whom we called "Baby." Seated near the window in a cane-bottomed chair, and securely tied with a length of plow line, was Cousin Ruth, Aunt Sarah's oldest daughter. I wasn't upset or alarmed at the sight of Ruth tied to a chair. It simply meant that her mind was acting up again. Grandpa was sitting in his favorite position on the steps. When he recognized me, a big smile brightened the copper hue of his face.

"Praise be to God!" He sounded genuinely glad to see me.

"It's Little David! When did you get back, son? Are you still in the army?" I was grinning too. Respectfully, my eyes sought Grandpa's.

"I just got in today Grandpa. I'm out of the army for good and back to being a civilian. It's a good feeling Grandpa. I'm really glad to be back home."

Everybody started talking at once. Aunt Sarah's firm soprano won hands down. "David, son, you're a sight for sore eyes. Come here and give your old aunt a hug!" She held out her arms. I bounded up the steps, past Grandpa and into her open arms. She hugged me tightly and then held my face in her hands.

"Boy, it's good to see you. Have you been behaving yourself?"

Her popping eyes seemed ready to leave her face. The protruding eyes were the result of a large goiter on her neck that she refused to have removed. Before the goiter, when she was younger and quite good-looking, she had been a flapper and belle of the ball. She, too, had frequented Aunt Lizzie's bootleg house and had also been partial to the ill repute of Jones Street.

During World War I, Aunt Sarah had married a hometown soldier named Jack McNeill. He had fathered two daughters before he was drafted and later killed in the trenches of France. Aunt Sarah's only son, my cousin Bill Jr., was the offspring of a slick rounder from Philadelphia. The elder Bill had deserted Aunt Sarah during a violent mid-Winter snow storm. She had returned to Fayetteville to rear her children in the safety of Grandpa's house. Bill Jr. was killed in a truck accident at Fort Bragg in 1942. Such sorry circumstances had forced Aunt Sarah to give up her wicked ways. Now, she was a confirmed Christian washed squeaky clean in the blood of the Lamb. Her eyes were searching my face.

"Have you been up to the house to see your daddy? Noah's kind of changed, if you know what I mean."

I was going to ask Aunt Sarah what she meant about Papa when my cousin Baby came up and put her arms around my neck. She was full-breasted and pretty as Aunt Sarah had been. Baby had short bobbed hair above an elfin face. She, too, was without a husband at the moment. Baby was urbane and sophisticated. She had spent some time in New York's Harlem. And, there had been a brief marriage to a Panamanian national. The only thing unusual about their short, fiery relationship was that the Panamanian had big lips, kinky hair and was as black as the ace of spades. However, his passport listed him as a Caucasian businessman. After the failed marriage, Baby also sought the comforting shelter of Grandpa's place.

"C'mon David, give me a kiss. Act like you're glad to see me," Baby cajoled.

I put my arms around her and kissed her soundly on the cheek. Her

Grandpa's Family

smile widened as she nodded toward Ruth, who had been watching the two of us with a look of vague curiosity in her eyes.

"Why don't you speak to Ruth, David, and give her a kiss? She's glad to see you too."

I walked over and bent to take Ruth in my arms.

"Y'all give me time. I was just fixing to give Cousin Ruth a big hug." I reached for Ruth.

"C'mon Ruth, honey. I want to give you a big hug."

Her face was blank. There wasn't a sign of recognition in the restless dark eyes. The delicate beauty of her face gave no inkling of her tortured state of mind. I was appalled that she didn't have the slightest idea about who I was. I held her shoulders and looked directly into her dark brown eyes.

"C'mon Ruth, stop playing with me. You know me, don't you? I'm Little David," I said plaintively. Her voice was flat, without a trace of emotion.

"You got a cigarette? I sure do want me a cigarette."

It was no use. Ruth's mind was still shrouded in the veil of lunacy that had suddenly destroyed her brilliant career as an elementary schoolteacher.

Ruth and Esther had been graduated from Fayetteville State Teachers College in the Summer of 1941. Unable to find jobs in the local elementary schools, they were overjoyed to find work in a small community just outside Macon in Georgia. They were both fortunate because they were employed by the same school. The family was pleased and proud of them.

Uncle Mike, Papa's younger brother, was especially proud. He had been in President Roosevelt's Civilian Conservation Corps. Until Uncle Mike joined the CCC, he had been a bootlegger, gambler and ne'er-do-well. Guilt and remorse were probably his reasons for donating money to educate the girls. His explanation was that he didn't want Ruth and Esther to grow up as maids or cotton pickers.

Once they commenced their teaching assignments, the girls' letters to Aunt Sarah were full of praise about their new jobs and the fact that they were getting along so well with the children's parents and the school principal. Suddenly, without any warning or apparent reason,

Grandpa's Family

Ruth's mind snapped completely. It was right at Christmas, and there was nothing Esther could do but bring her home. They arrived in Fayetteville the day after New Year's. Nobody knew exactly what had happened down in Georgia. There were two schools of thought about Ruth's nervous breakdown. Aunt Sarah and Grandma firmly believed that somebody, a conjure woman or a witch doctor, had put a spell on Ruth. She had always been nervous and high-strung, even when she was a child.

Grandpa felt that it was worry and stress that had caused the breakdown. However, they all did agree on one thing: the extremely smart and intelligent girl that they had once known was no more. Ruth's mind was completely gone.

Aunt Sarah was the first to try to find a remedy for the terrible spell that had been cast on her eldest daughter. My aunt began to hire every root doctor, conjure woman, fire talker and spell-caster in Fayetteville and the surrounding county to see if any of them could lift the potent spell that held Ruth in its grasp. Into Grandpa's house came a lot of strange, unusual folk, who muttered incantations, waved wands and chicken feathers, while either dancing around the poor girl or rubbing her head with foul-smelling concoctions. Nothing worked.

Grandpa and Esther were of different generations, but they banded together to try a different approach. Grandpa was the soul of religion; he did not believe in roots or spells. There was an eminent doctor among Grandpa's white friends, who assisted him in trying to get medical help for Ruth. After consulting doctors from all over North Carolina, the family decided to take the doctors' suggestion that Ruth be given shock treatments at a hospital in Durham. The suggestion was not well-received by others in the family. However, nothing else had worked, and at this point the family was willing to try anything that would help Ruth regain her senses.

The shock treatments did nothing for Ruth. The busy hands, the quick involuntary movements and the restless darting of her dark eyes continued unabated. She was not violent. Her constant chattering of unintelligible words and half syllables, coupled with her restless habit of walking to and fro, was irritating but not dangerous. Uncle Joe made matters worse when he introduced Ruth to cigarettes. She would leave lighted cigarettes anywhere, on her bed, the sofa and all over the house. The fire

Grandpa's Family

hazard lessened when Aunt Sarah stopped buying cigarettes for Ruth. Aunt Sarah tried to get Ruth to use snuff, but she wouldn't touch it.

The family was at wits' end when a big, husky, incredibly black man named Theodore Jones came calling. He had been a classmate of Ruth's and had courting on his mind. Theodore had always cared for Ruth. He had tried courting her before, but he had been an unwanted suitor. The family had considered him to be too black and too ugly for the pretty mulatto girl. Now things were different. In fact, the family decided that the reason for Ruth's problem was due to her cloistered upbringing. Her chastity was not questioned, and the family could rest assured that Ruth was still a virgin. Now the family believed that her sexual nature had gone to her head and created an awful disturbance. Theodore was deeply concerned about what had happened to Ruth. He was happy that he was now accepted by the family.

The courtship of Ruth passed strangely. Theodore would come dutifully Sunday and Wednesday nights. The former classmates would have the living room to themselves. Theodore would hold her hand as she babbled incoherently, with her eyes darting everywhere, never looking directly into his face. After the strange courtship had lasted for a few weeks, Theodore asked Ruth if she would consent to be his wife. "Hot damn!" she replied. "I'm dying for a smoke. Do you have a cigarette? I sure could use a nicotine weed."

The wedding was at Mood's Temple Church. The service was brief and to the point.

"Do you take this man to be your wedded husband?" the minister asked Ruth. Her answer rang out clearly in the small church.

"Excuse me Mr. Pistol. I didn't know you was loaded." Ruth's answer to the minister was quickly accepted. The bouquet was tossed; rice was thrown. The marriage was a done deed.

The happy bride and groom were to leave Fayetteville and make their home in Harrisburg, Pennsylvania. Theodore had gotten a job in a steel mill that suited his size and his ambition. His letters were bright and encouraging at first. Later, they turned into whining missives, loaded with hopelessness and despair. Ruth had not changed one iota. It was impossible for him to work in his job at the mill, not knowing whether Ruth would be in the small apartment or wandering somewhere in the streets.

She had no sense of time. Nor could she concentrate on any one thing. She could not cook and would not eat unless he personally held the spoon. Besides, the constant wandering off into the streets grew progressively worse.

The only solution for Theodore was to keep her locked in the apartment when he was at work. There were times when even that did not work. The straw that broke the camel's back also broke Theodore's heart. Ruth escaped several times. The last time Theodore found her, she was at the police station in a bedraggled state. When he walked into the station, there was no sign of recognition. Ruth just stared blankly. "Please, mister. Do you have a cigarette? I sure do want me a cigarette." Theodore was at the end of his rope. He had no choice but to take Ruth back to Aunt Sarah's. It just wouldn't work.

The giant Theodore was a pathetic sight as he lamely tried to explain to Aunt Sarah why he had to return her daughter. Aunt Sarah accepted Ruth's return and Theodore's halting apology with grace, gently dismissing his excuses with a shrug of her shoulders. A few months later, to the complete surprise of everyone, Ruth gave birth to a baby girl. Nobody had any inkling that Ruth was pregnant, least of all Aunt Sarah.

Old Aunt Easter, the neighborhood midwife, was even drunker than usual when she delivered the tiny bundle. The child was born dead, which may have been the will of Divine Providence. There was no way that Ruth in her state of mind could do all that was necessary to rear the little girl.

A scuffling noise behind me got my attention. It was Grandma. She was standing just inside the screen door fumbling for the latch. Her dull eyes with their clouded irises were staring straight ahead. The bluish tinge of her eyes was a clear indication of her total blindness. As I opened the door, her thin arms reached out for me. Her voice trembled with age.

"I thought I heard Little David talking out here." Her hands came up and tentatively searched my face, and her mouth slowly widened into a toothless grin. "Praise the Lord! It is David! When did you get back, son? We all missed you, especially your Grandpa."

"I got back awhile ago Grandma." Her gnarled hands touched my face carefully. She cackled as she tickled me under my chin.

Grandpa's Family

"Aw Grandma, that's real hair. I been shaving for almost a year. I'm a full grown man, Grandma."

"Well, you always did try to act older than you really were," she mused. "I guess we've got your Uncle Joseph to thank for that." She shuffled outside the door, tapping her cane on the uneven floor of the porch.

"There is one thing you can be sure of. Your Grandpa's certainly glad you're back. He ain't had a decent shave since you left." She thought for a moment. "Come to think of it, he ain't had a good bath either. At least not the kind he used to take when you would tote the water from the spring. These girls won't tote no more water than they have to."

Grandpa shifted his weight and leaned forward from his comfortable perch on the steps. At eighty-six, his wiry body could still move wherever he willed it to go. A big smile lit up his face.

"You've got that right Mary! Nobody knows how to shave me the way that Little David shaves me." He shook his head.

"I keep telling everybody that you have to pull the skin tight, so that the razor will cut smoothly. They just won't do it, and I end up with my face cut to pieces." He smiled up at me.

"Yessiree boy. You're a sight for sore eyes. I'm glad you're home!"

Everybody was laughing good-naturedly. I was too.

"I'm glad to be home too, Grandpa. Besides, I kinda like shaving you, and I don't mind toting your bath water. I don't mind it one bit."

I looked across the field at the trees at the edge of the swamp. The sun was blood red, sinking slowly as it pulled the cover of night about its head.

"I tell you what, Grandpa. I'll make two quick trips down to the spring. That will be enough water to give you a good bath."

I started toward the kitchen then turned to Aunt Sarah.

"Are the buckets in the usual place?" She nodded, and I hurried through the house and back into the kitchen. Nostalgia came with the smells that wafted about the kitchen. The faint smell of fatback, collard greens and that morning's smoked sausage made my homecoming a tangible thing.

The job of bathing Grandpa had been passed down to me. Aunt Esther, Papa's sister, who had died before I was born, had a son named Ed. He had helped to bathe Grandpa until he was drafted in 1941. Cousin

Bill took over the job until he was killed in a truck accident at Fort Bragg.

The buckets were in their usual place on a small table beside the stove. I emptied the buckets into a large dish pan on the kitchen table. I hurried out the door, ran across the yard, passed the big hickory tree and ran down the crooked path to the spring. It was in a little grotto, not unlike the spring that was down in the swamp from our own little shack. I started skipping down the path like old times. Aw man! Life couldn't get much better than this.

It was pitch dark when I emptied the last two buckets into the big washtub that Grandpa always used for bathing. We were in Grandpa and Grandma's bedroom. The rest of the family was in the living room listening to the battery radio. The fireplace in my grandparents' bedroom was the largest in the house. In earlier years, it had been used for cooking. The blaze had dwindled to ashes and a few coals. That was no problem. Grandpa never worried about heat when he was bathing. I had never known him to use hot water in Summer or Winter.

He had peeled off the stiff undergarments and stepped quickly into the tub of cold spring water before he turned to me. "David, son, I sure appreciate you helping me to clean up a little bit. It's been a good while since I had a good bath." He rubbed the bar of strong Octagon soap until it lathered and then began to briskly rub his chest. I waited patiently. The ritual had been established way back when I first started helping Grandpa to bathe. He would always wash in front, soaping himself over the entire length of his body. Then, I would lather the back of his body and rinse the the soapsuds away. Grandpa would step out of the tub and dry himself.

That night was no different. Grandpa was emitting small contented grunts of satisfaction as I briskly rubbed his back. His body was thin and wiry. Age had not bent or twisted his compact frame. His skin was fairly smooth, the color and texture of old leather. His hands were huge for such a small man. The chin was hard as a rock, always held high, and he stood as straight as an arrow. There were few men left like Grandpa.

I had finished washing Grandpa's back and was rinsing away when I happened to look down at Grandpa's front. The cool water had washed away the suds and wow! What in the world! I couldn't believe my eyes. Grandpa was standing there with a powerful erection, one that would

Grandpa's Family

have made a man half his age extremely proud.

It was mind-boggling because Grandpa was at least 86 years old. I had always heard that potency decreased with age. What I saw before me was reason enough for me to check my sources carefully in the future. Grandpa was still making contented noises, humming to himself snatches of his favorite hymn. He seemed totally unaware of the strange new development. I backed away quickly, still looking at Grandpa's unusual problem.

I handed him a towel as he stepped out of the tub.

"Well, that's about it Grandpa. There's nothing like a good bath to make you feel better."

I looked at him again. It was the first time I had seen anything like that happen to him. The problem did not go quietly. I thought about Grandma and wondered if she would be caught unawares. If so, she was in for a grand surprise. I was certain that Grandpa would not waste such a stroke of good fortune. I shook my head. It was an amazing occurrence. It certainly did not jibe with the facts as I knew them.

I decided that it was time for me to go. I went back to the living room and said goodnight to the family. I walked down the steps and into the yard. Gingerly, I felt my way along the once-familiar path. Stumbling occasionally, I hurried through the trees and up the hill toward our own little shack. My spirits were sagging, and I knew why.

Depression crushed my resolve. I wondered, with my origins, why had it happened to me? Grandpa's father had been a full-blooded Cherokee Indian. His wife, Martha, had been half Indian and half Negro. Grandma Sawyer was a full-blooded Negro, but she came from hardy stock. There just wasn't a valid reason for the curse of smallness. It was the same with my mother's family, even more so because her grandfather was Thomas Jonathan Jackson, hero of the Confederacy and the idol of millions of Southerners. My smallness was inherited, and Stonewall had to be the culprit. It was a cruel twist of fate to be descended from greatness and have such a crazy thing happen. My mind wavered in disbelief. Jackson my idol, whom I had worshipped for years, had feet of clay. Heredity be damned.

I had completely forgotten about the afternoon spent with Miz Hannah and her words of comfort. I was back to constantly worrying about something that I couldn't change. Over and over, I tried to put the Stonewall heritage out of my mind. Why me? Worry was a dull ache within me as I came out of the trees and walked past Mama's empty chicken coop. I veered around the smelly toilet and walked into the yard. There was no feeling of relief at being home. Papa was probably asleep. I paused for a moment and knocked loudly on the door.

"Papa! It's me, David! I'm home Papa! C'mon Papa. Get up! It's cold out here!"

8

Papa's New Beginning

It was early morning, and we were eating grits, fatback and eggs. Papa's culinary skills definitely left something to be desired, but it had been a long time since I had eaten fatback and eggs. We had talked since the wee hours of the morning. I had done most of the talking. Aunt Sarah was right. Papa had changed a lot since Mama's death. It had only been a year, but he seemed much older and acted distant and withdrawn. The only way I could get him to perk up a little bit was if I talked about old times. If I happened to mention Mama, he would talk about her as if she were still alive. That morning, he seemed a little like his old self. At first I couldn't understand it, but as he kept talking, I began to see what was on his mind. Papa was withering on the vine. He needed something to do.

Old Miz Hamm had died about two months after Mama's death. She had few relatives or legitimate heirs. Her little shack and ten acres were sold by the county to satisfy taxes. The land was purchased by the Reverend Lonnie Pierce, a colored minister, who was pastor of the rather large Mount Zion A.M.E. Church. It was located in the colored neighborhood near the train depot.

Reverend Pierce knew little about the business of farming. Since he and Papa were friends and members of the same general conference, it

Papa's New Beginning

was only natural that he would ask Papa to run the farm on a sharecropping basis. The minister would put up the money for expenses, and Papa would furnish the expertise and the labor. My daddy seemed quite enthusiastic about the venture. He would be doing something that he liked to do. It was the first time since Mama's death that he had shown any interest in anything.

I had no problem with Papa's new venture, as long as I wasn't included in the work force. Farming was not for me. I had been too far and seen too much to be saddled with such drudgery. Besides, I considered myself much too cool for manual labor.

The war years had changed Fayetteville from a small courthouse village to a fast-growing metropolis. As a result of the influx of soldiers at Fort Bragg, prostitution, illegal gambling, bootlegging and something entirely new called the numbers game was rampant, even in the suburbs. The criminal element flourished in and around Fayetteville. The military police, the sheriff's department and the local law were up to their necks trying to curb the lawlessness. I had no intention of going to jail either.

From my experiences caddying at the golf course, I knew exactly how to operate on the fringe, and besides, I had other things in mind.

"The preacher and me are going to work old lady Hamm's place," Papa said. "We're jist gonna plant a little cotton, corn and tobacco. We might even plant some taters." He looked shrewdly at me. "You're welcome to work with us if you want to. We could use a young buck."

"No thanks, Papa. I ain't got nothing like that in mind. I don't ever intend to even go near a farm, let alone work on one."

At that moment, I really didn't know what I was going to do. I was going down to the main unemployment office and apply for the $20 a week that veterans were eligible to draw for a period of 52 weeks. I didn't want to caddy or work at the golf course. Besides, I needed time to do something about my personal problem.

"Don't worry Papa, I'll find something to do that will keep me out of trouble. Just do the best you can with that sharecropping thing. Maybe you can get along with Reverend Pierce. I heard that he's kinda finicky and hard to please."

"I kin git along with any white man in this county. I know I kin git along with a nigger, especially a nigger like Lonnie Pierce. He ain't nothing but a blow-hard. I kin out preach him any day of the week." Papa pushed back the chair and got up from the table.

"I got to git on up to the farm. Lonnie and me has got some talking to do. We're 'sposed to see old man Dowden about buying a mule."

Papa grabbed his old straw hat and headed for the door. He glanced back over his shoulder.

"By the way boy, Janey Smith's little gal has been asking about you. I forgit her name. She and her mama still live down on Jones Street jist behind the church." He thought for a minute.

"Ain't that the same little gal that your mama didn't want you to mess with?" he grinned. "I jist thought I'd mention it. She's a pretty little thing."

With Papa gone, the little house was quiet except for the muted whispers of half-forgotten memories. It was all right. I needed the solitude. But, solitude per se was not mine for the taking.

There was a loud knock at the door followed by a shrill voice.

"Noah, open the door! I got something for you. C'mon now. It's hot off the stove!"

I opened the door quickly. I backed up in surprise and bewilderment. It was one of our neighbors, Miz Snoog Malloy. She was decked out in a big red and blue-flowered dress as large as a tent. The dress had to be big because it housed 350 pounds of bold womanhood.

Miz Snoog's hair was in cornrows, and her mouth was a big crimson tulip. Her ebony cheeks had red circles on either side, and there was an impish grin on her face.

"Stop looking at me as if you're crazy, boy," Miz Snoog said. Her eyes fluttered girlishly.

"You don't hafta tell me. I know I look good. Where's your Pa? I got somepin for him." I stuttered.

"Yes ma'am. You kind of startled me for a minute. You just missed Papa. He went up to Miz Hamm's old place."

I was confused. Why was Miz Malloy dressed like that? She had always looked nondescript, quiet and subdued, always wearing dirty dresses and dingy aprons. She had been like that ever since Mr. Malloy took off for parts unknown. Then it dawned on me. Miz Malloy had come courting, and Papa was the object of her affection.

Papa's New Beginning

"Don't jist keep staring at me boy. You might git to liking what you see. I'm already spoken for." She held out a greasy paper bag.

"This is a tater pie for your daddy. It's nice and fresh. I jist cooked it this morning. Put it up for him, you hear? I got it wrapped real good so the flies can't git at it." Her little pig eyes were watching me closely.

"You finally growed up, didn't you? You're almost as big as my Freddie."

"Yes ma'am I'm full grown now."

I reached for the pie.

"I'll be sure and give the pie to Papa as soon as he comes home."

Without another word, Miz Snoog waddled around the corner of the house and went down the path that led down the hill to her little place. It seemed as if I could hear her labored breathing even after I had closed the door.

Over the next few days, Papa became more and more engrossed in preparing Miz Hamm's place for planting the crops. He fixed up the old house for storage and rebuilt the sagging barn. A tobacco barn had to be built from scratch, but that was no problem. Papa was as good a carpenter as anybody in the neighborhood. Besides, he had the moral support of Miz Snoog Malloy and her delicious tater pies. She began going up to Miz Hamm's place almost every day.

She always wore the big brightly-colored dresses. Her face was always plastered with rouge, and her mouth was smeared with lipstick. I considered her a nuisance, but Papa and Reverend Pierce didn't think so. Both of them vied for her attention. Miz Snoog was ecstatic to be wanted by two ardent suitors. She took full advantage of the situation and played it to the hilt.

I was surprised at Papa. He had shown no interest in women since Mama's death. This was not like Papa at all. To see him gladly accept the flirtatious actions and come-hither looks from Miz Snoog was a bit out of character for him.

Miz Snoog loved the attention showered on her by Papa and Reverend Pierce. They could hardly get the job done because of preening and posturing for her benefit. Miz Snoog's rouged cheeks and crimson lips got redder still, and all 350 pounds of her buxom body tripped the light fantastic, especially when she knew that the two men were watching. She was a gadfly flitting coyly between the two men and causing all sorts of trouble. I began to wish that she would hurry up and give in to one or the other. The suspense was beginning to bother me. I knew Papa and the preacher were upset with me. They wanted me to help rebuild the farm, but all I did was sit around and watch.

That morning when I reached the farm, Papa and the preacher were squared off like game cocks. It was kind of funny because Papa was small and wiry like Grandpa. He only weighed about 150 pounds. Reverend Pierce was short also, but he weighed almost as much as Miz Snoog. The two men weren't actually fighting, just arguing as usual, but the arguments were becoming more and more frequent.

I did have a couple of idle thoughts about what would happen if the preacher happened to win. I tried to imagine Miz Snoog and the preacher locked in a fond embrace. It would be 650 pounds of lust, straining and grunting toward mutual satisfaction. It was an exciting scenario, but I didn't see how it could possibly work. I left the whole business alone. It was time to address my problems.

I had to try to give some direction to my life. I had been in the military, but now it was time to go back to the world of cool.

It was Friday night, and the coolest place in town belonged to a lean, hungry-looking black man called Pegleg Pete. His joint was located down the Rose Hill Road, just past the bridge. There was a small, wooded road almost hidden by brush and vines. A few yards down the road was an old two-story house. The ground floor had been gutted to form a dance floor. It was a juke joint in the classic sense, complete with piano, juke box, a kitchen and small rooms in the back that cost $2 to rent for half an hour. The law enforcement agencies were always paid promptly, and there hadn't been a killing in three years. Like I said, it was the coolest place in town, and I was the very essence of cool.

I dressed carefully. There was a certain look that I wanted to achieve. I put on my best pair of olive drab pants and a good gabardine shirt open at the neck. The shirt still had my stripes sewn on the sleeves. I bloused the pants over a pair of shiny combat boots, airborne-style like the ones worn by paratroopers. My Ike jacket was complete with stripes and shiny field artillery buttons. And, last, but not least, was an overseas cap cocked to one side, giving a good view of my curly hair. I could wear it longer now that I was no longer in the military. I wanted to look as if

I had just gotten out of the army. That look in itself gave an illusion of having funds: travel pay, mustering out pay, gambling wins or just money period. If my uniform had been wrinkled and old, it would mean that I was broke. I also made sure that I had my discharge papers with me. I had no intention of spending the night in the guardhouse at Fort Bragg. Now, it was time for the Cool Kid to pimp-walk on down to Pegleg Pete's.

The joint was jumping. The varied clientele were doing the nasty boogie. Killer Joe was an unskilled novice compared to those dancing fools. Wyonie Harris's big blues band was blasting from the jukebox. His big voice was wailing and full of questions for the patrons on the floor. He needed to know "Who Threw the Whiskey in the Well?"

I stood at the door for a moment, looked over the crowd carefully and then did a jive-time walk to the center of the dance floor. I gave a pimp's salute and then shouted, "Hey y'all, the Kid is back!"

All the old gang was there: Big Dan, with whom I had fought off and on ever since grade school, Eddie and Jeff Malloy, who were Miz Snoog's nephews, Retha Jane, the pretty girl that Papa mentioned, Slick Willie B, a hustler from downtown and Fast Fanny, the queen of Jones Street. There were several others that I didn't know, including three bitchy-looking girls from little Harlem, located down near the train station.

The music blared as they crowded around me. Big Dan was the first to speak.

"Hey Dave, when did you get back?" He looked shrewdly at me.

"Are you ready for me to kick your ass some more? Are you still talking that bull shit about you being so tough because you're kin to somebody named Stonewall Jackson?"

I wasn't afraid of him, and I had to let the rest of the crowd know how I felt. "Look, you sawed off bastard, you got to bring ass to get ass. We can get it on right now! You want to carry this mess outside?" He stood for a moment, sizing me up.

"Nah, I've got plenty of time to kick your ass. Tonight, I want me some liquor, some reefer and some hot meat, in that order."

With a final wail of his trumpet, Wyonie Harris finished his piece. Big Dan walked over and put a nickel in the jukebox. He hit the select button, and the hard-hitting sounds of Louis Jordan and his "Tympany

Five" filled the smoky room. Louis and his saxophone were full of questions. The song was about "Caldonia," and he was wondering about the hardness of her head. By this time, Pegleg Pete's patrons were dripping with sweat as they rocked to the driving beat of the down-home music. Some were jitterbugging, and some were trucking, and some were doing a new dance called "The Hucklebuck."

Pegleg Pete did his number. He put his hands at his waist and prissy-walked, snake-hipping crazily across the floor. The noise was wild, and the partying was hot and heavy. Folk were getting down. It was Friday night. Time to let it all hang out. The crowd went plum fool.

I moved slowly through the milling throng of hep cats. When I reached the wall by the door, I paused and carefully checked out the dance floor. Retha Jane was in the center of the floor jiving and posturing with Slick Willie B. She was gorgeous. I hadn't seen a girl with a build like that since school days with Cissy Jones. Retha Jane was fat and pretty as a government mule. I knew that she liked me, but I had never pursued or tried to have a relationship with her. Eddie Malloy caught my eye, and he moved through the crowd toward me. He had once been quite good-looking, appealing to all of the girls. Now his face was criss-crossed with scars, traces of the beating given him by Cissy's brother, Lucius.

The whole thing started because Eddie tried to court Cissy two years ago. I had barely missed getting beat up by Lucius for the same reason. It was only after the incident in the back seat of her father's old Ford that I found out that young Lucius was sexually involved with his sister. He was in love with Cissy and would kill anyone who tried to be with her. When Eddie found out about it, he gave the two of them a wide berth. Eddie seemed genuinely glad to see me. He was smiling as he walked toward me.

"Well, if it ain't old bull shitting Dave Sawyer! How you been cut buddy?" His eyes twinkled.

"Are you still hung up on that Stonewall bullshit? When did you get back, and what have you been up to?"

"Ain't nothing changed hoss. I'm a bad motherfucker. I ain't been doing nothing unusual, just tearing down windows and knocking down doors, drinking sweet wine and knocking up whores. I'm so damn bad until I scare myself."

I waited grinning. It was an old dodge, something we used to do all the time. I had just slipped him in the dirty dozens, and I wanted to see how he would respond. I waited a few seconds; he was grinning too, but he didn't take the bait. Eddie shouted above the noise.

"You still think you're half slick, don't you old buddy?" The smile faded. "You're still bull shitting yourself. I'll have you know that I got me a real job working at the dairy. I ain't bull shitting around, talking slick and doing nothing. Except for that bullshit uniform, I'll bet you ain't got a pot to piss in, a window to throw it out of, nor a ground to catch it. And, I bet you ain't had a piece of ass in a month of Sundays. A good piece of tail and a glass of ice water would kill you deader than hell." He was shaking his head. "I tell you old buddy, it's a wide world, and you better get with it."

I was irritated, but I didn't let it show.

"Aw man, you're crazier than a June bug. I just hit this bullshit town a few days ago. I bust Miz Hannah Blue down the first day that I got back." I paused to see his reaction. He looked at me kind of funny, but he didn't say anything.

"Uncle Joe split and left her in the cabin by herself. She was crying her ass off because he's hanging on Jones Street with Rose. I don't know what's wrong with him. Rose is about as sleazy as they come." I shook my head. "I tell you for a fact, Eddie, it was a piece out of this world. I did a bang-up job on the old soul. She loved it to death."

The noise was deafening. We had been talking loudly to each other over the sound of the music. The music stopped suddenly, and so did our conversation. Someone jostled my elbow. It was Retha Jane. Her pixie face and dark mischievous eyes were as alluring as ever. Her small, puckered lips looked quite ready to be kissed, touched and loved. Her small tongue caressed her white even teeth. She looked up at me.

"David, when did you get back? Honey, I missed you something awful. You think we can get together now that you're home for good?"

As she spoke, I looked across the dance floor. I knew that Slick Willie B would be watching the two of us. His lean frame was coiled like a steel spring. There was no mistaking the deadly malice in his eyes. But, like I told Big Dan, he would have to bring ass to get ass.

My gaze was drawn back to the charming creature in front of me.

Aw man, her eyes were really something. I would have cheerfully drowned in the deep pools. At that point, they were laughing at me. I smiled down at her.

"I don't know baby. You're definitely on my schedule." I nodded toward the dance floor.

"It all depends on whether or not you can dump the big ape you're messing around with now."

Retha Jane was about to answer when the music started up again. I looked up to see Willie B making his way toward us. Instinctively, my hand slipped into my right hand pocket. There was a scowl on Willie's ugly face. I didn't want trouble if I could avoid it. If memory served me right, he always carried a straight razor and a .32 owlhead revolver. He glared at me and then turned to Retha Jane.

"C'mon bitch before I have to fuck up you and pretty boy!" He grabbed her arm and roughly pulled her back out on the dance floor. I took my hand out of my pocket. There was nothing in the pocket but lint.

We had gotten the crowd's attention. It liked this sort of action. In a little while, the murmuring stopped, and the music started again. This time the music was haunting and slow. It was the syrupy sweet voice of Billy Eckstine. He was singing a romantic ballad called "I Cover the Water Front."

The rowdy noises subsided, but the smokey heated atmosphere remained. The mood changed abruptly, and the dancers sweated and strained to get as close as possible to each other. Steamy bodies searching for a good feeling were aided by the smell of corn liquor, reefer and the acrid odor of chitlins and pig's feet. The overall scent was so bad until it smelled good. I was getting irritated as hell. I didn't like the way that Willie B was dancing with Retha Jane. I didn't like it at all.

In the first place, she had no business dancing with Willie B when she could clearly see the shape that he was in. As she swayed against him, I knew Retha Jane couldn't help but feel his obvious excitement. Her face was flushed, and she seemed to be enjoying it. I looked into her eyes. They were slits of passion as she moved lockstep about the floor with Willie B. His equipment was a bulging pylon, and her pelvic region was a reckless stunt pilot, who cavorted around it, loving the feel and smell of danger. Her ecstasy was there for everyone to see. I watched with my mouth open as her eyes rolled back into her head, and her tongue played loosely around her lips.

Eddie came through the crowd grinning evilly. He knew exactly how I felt.

"Boy, your would-be girlfriend is sure rubbing pussy all over Slick Willie B. Whatcha gonna do about that Stonewall? He's raising hell in your valley. You better call in some artillery." Eddie was getting a kick out of mocking me.

"I guess you know that Willie B is one mean dude. It don't pay to fuck with him." Now Eddie was laughing out loud.

"But you're Stonewall Jackson, right?"

Eddie knew that I was boiling mad. I started to slip him in the dozens again. This time I was going to talk about his mama. I changed my mind. There was no need to take it out on him.

I looked across the floor at Retha Jane and Willie, and I knew exactly what I was going to do. The music stopped again, and the dance floor patrons began milling aimlessly around. It was time to make my move. I was going to turn Pegleg's place clean out. I had to do it quickly because every time the music played Retha Jane would be rubbing it all over Willie B. If I didn't move fast, they might get off right there on the dance floor.

My plan was simple, and it would work. Most folk would call it signifying, and it was considered worse than stealing. I was good at what I was about to do. Persuasion and sincerity were the keys.

The whole idea was to create as much animosity as possible in the loaded confines of the juke joint. I decided to begin with the three girls from Little Harlem. All three looked tough as whitleather. I sidled up to the ugliest one of the group.

"Hey babycake, what's happening? What's going down?" Her mouth twisted into a snarl.

"What do you mean what's happening, bitch? Have you got any money? That's what's happening." She put her hands on her hips and shook her butt suggestively. She was ready for business, but I wasn't having any.

"Nah, girl, I don't want no messing around. I just wanted to tell you that the other girls been talking about y'all something terrible. One of them said something about beating y'all up. They claim y'all ain't got no business in their territory. I don't want to see anybody get hurt, so I just thought I'd warn y'all to kinda watch yourselves. I'm just trying to be helpful."

I moved slowly about the dance floor, whispering to the dancers and pointing out who was pissed off at whom. By the time I had made my way about the dance floor, the animosity and ill feeling that I had created was so thick that you could cut it with a knife. I stood by the door patiently waiting for the shit to hit the fan. It didn't take long. The ugly girl from downtown was the one that started the whole mess. She slapped Fast Fanny. That was the worst mistake she could have made. I braced myself near the door. It wasn't long before the whole place was bedlam.

Pegleg was screaming at the top of his lungs, trying to restore order. Willie B was standing in the middle of the floor with his razor in one hand and the old pistol in the other. Retha Jane pulled away from him and ran for the door. I grabbed her arm and pushed her out into the darkness. We ran up the little wood's road and out onto the Rose Hill Road. It was pitch black as we made our way up the hill past Courtney's dairy.

The sky was overcast, and a few big drops of rain started to fall. Storm clouds were shoving each other about, and sheet lightning flared again and again. I started to walk faster, pulling Retha Jane along with me. Suddenly, I heard voices behind us. It was Willie B, and he wasn't alone. Some of the others had figured out that I had caused the disturbance. There was no telling how many were after me. I was beginning to worry. I turned to Retha Jane. "C'mon girl! We can't let them catch us. C'mon now!"

We ran as fast as we could until we reached the junction of the Rose Hill Road and the Raleigh Road. We stopped gasping for breath. Across the road, sheet lightning illuminated the stark whiteness of Mood's Temple Church. There was no traffic at this time of night, so we hurried across the road into the churchyard. We could hear Willie B and the others approaching the crossroads. He was cursing loudly.

"You just wait until I catch that half slick bastard. I'm gonna cut him too thick to boil and too thin to fry! Nobody pulls that shit on Willie B!"

Papa's New Beginning

We had to do something quick. Beneath the steps of the church was an opening for a storage bin of sorts. The pillars of the church were walled in with cinder block. Lying around the opening were huge stones and more cinder block. I was about to crawl under the steps.

"I ain't going under there! It's wet, and there's probably snakes under there," Retha Jane declared.

The grumbling noises from the crowd were nearer and coming closer. It sounded as if Willie B and the gang were about to cross the road. I grabbed Retha Jane's arm and ran up the steps of the church. I jerked at the door. It creaked open. We stumbled inside and closed the door. We stood quietly in the darkness of the vestibule panting for breath. We were safe for the moment.

Later, we heard voices and scraping noises outside the church. Willie B's voice sounded above the noise.

"This ought to fix the both of them, Retha Jane and that sorry Sawyer nigger. I know they are in there. Pile them rocks up real good so they can't get out. We'll keep them under there all night. If they do get out, I'm gonna fuck them up real good."

Aw man, it was a break of sorts. Willie B and the others thought we were hiding under the church. All we had to do was to remain quiet until they left. I was sure they would give up after a while. A few minutes later, we heard curses, and a bit later we heard them leave.

It was pitch dark in the little church. The only brightness was an occasional flash of sheet lightning. We stood in the middle of the aisle holding each other, thankful that we were not caught by Willie B and his friends. The storm worsened, and we held each other tighter. Retha stirred against me, and her warmth kindled a quick fire in the bottom of my stomach. She easily matched the intensity of my feelings. I knew she was hot because Willie B had already started her fire. It didn't matter how or why the fire burned within her supple body. I was glad to share the warmth. Speaking in whispers, we moved slowly down the aisle until we bumped against the offering table. Somehow I knew that both of us were frightened.

Lightning flashed, and the thunder boomed as I lifted and sat her on the table. Her armpits were wet with perspiration, and for some reason the wetness raised my level of excitement to feverish heights. The lightning flashed again. It was a terrifying moment, and I was scared silly. I lost nothing because lust took over. I was greedy for the feel of her body. Regardless of where we were, and the ferocity of the storm outside, Retha Jane wanted me as much as I wanted her.

From that point on, we were not responsible. Desire ran the show. Retha Jane shifted her bottom until she sat on the very edge of the offering table. Quickly, she slipped out of the left leg of her panties, squeezed closer to me, and a brand-new world opened up. What happened next was worst than blasphemy, but we couldn't stop. Our feelings grew as the storm grew, raging in its intensity. Outside, the Lord was doing His holy work, and inside, we were desecrating His holy temple, worse yet fornicating on the very place where his tithes and offerings were laid. It was sacrilege, an act that was truly profane. There was no shame. That would come later.

Two bolts of lightning struck at once, one somewhere outside the church, and the other on the sacred offering table inside the church. Rolling thunder sounded after each bolt. Retha Jane tried desperately to hold me. I was trembling as I backed away from her anxious legs. Retha Jane was not happy about my sudden departure. Since we were doing wrong, she wanted to enjoy it to the fullest. I knew she was steaming, but it was over. The unholy sin had been committed by the two of us. Now all I wanted to do was to get out of there. God was surely going to punish us for what we had done. I could only hope that it was not an unpardonable sin.

It was a week later, and I was still feeling guilty. Time had not healed my worries, but I felt a little better. I was down on Jones Street. I still hadn't found Uncle Joe. Retha Jane and Fast Fanny were sitting on the porch at her mother's little shotgun house. Fanny looked up as I approached.

"I do declare Retha Jane, here comes that cute little David. I tell you for a fact that's one good-looking young boy. No wonder you're so crazy about him." Retha Jane looked daggers at me.

"Well, you got that right about him being little. He is certainly that. And, I'll tell you something else, he can't screw from diddly. And, if he kin do any humpin' at all, my hiney kin pick a bale of cotton. I ain't joking. David Jonathan Sawyer ain't about nothing, nothing at all."

I stood there for an instant, watching the two of them. Then, I turned and slowly retraced my steps back out to the main road. My eyes blurred, and feelings of disgust and self-loathing overwhelmed me. I didn't know what to do.

9

A Mule And Other Stuff

Papa and the preacher were at it again. Their arguments had intensified, and it was nowhere harvest time. Miz Snoog's continued presence did not help the situation. It simply threw coals on an already volatile relationship. They were an odd threesome, somehow bound together in that balmy mid-April of 1947.

For farmers and sharecroppers alike, it was a time of complete cooperation. Every effort had to be made to nurture the tender cotton, corn and tobacco plants to maturity. I wished the tender shoots well, but that was as far as I was prepared to go with the business of farming. The only reason that I had walked up the road that morning was because Papa asked me to bring him some lunch. Fatback and eggs made sense any time of the day.

As I walked up the road toward the farm, there were a couple of things that I couldn't get out of my mind. I had been keeping to myself, staying pretty close to the little shack. There were two things that bothered me: my ongoing problem and the fact that Uncle Joe finally came back home.

I should have been glad, but my meeting with him was anything but sociable. He had heard from several people down on Jones Street that I had been going around bragging about the incident with Miz Hannah.

A Mule And Other Stuff

The trouble started as soon as I walked into the yard of the little cabin. I had simply stopped by to chat with Miz Hannah. I had no idea that Uncle Joe was home.

He opened the door. He hadn't changed at all. He was still the same short, pudgy black man with failing eyes and bad teeth that I had known most of my life. I could tell that he was angry because the good eye and the bad eye were jumping around like crazy. What I didn't know was that his anger was directed at me.

"David, jist what in hell's the matter with you? Why did you tell everybody and his brother that you had been to bed with Hannah? You have got to be the dumbest nigger in the world! There wasn't a durn thing wrong with what you did. It didn't matter a hill of beans to me. But, to put her business in the street the way you did was the worst thing in the world that you could have done. All of those years I spent trying to teach you stuff didn't mean shit! Boy, you is one dumb nigger!"

I stood silent taking the full brunt of Uncle Joe's verbal abuse. Miz Hannah's eyes dimmed with tears as she looked reproachfully over his shoulder at me. There was nothing that I could say. I was guilty as hell. I turned and walked slowly out of the yard. I knew then the senseless pain that my big mouth had caused Miz Hannah to endure. I hadn't meant to hurt Miz Hannah. I was just blowing smoke to improve my image.

In the coming weeks, my image had another startling jolt. Retha Jane announced to the whole world that she was pregnant. Stranger still, she declared that I was the father. It was difficult for me to believe because she never stopped seeing Willie B, and she had told me in no uncertain terms about my limited sexual expertise. It was no small wonder that there were a lot of things on my mind.

A noise just ahead in the brush caught my attention. Miz Snoog waddled along the path that led up the hill from the swamp. She came out of the brush just ahead of me. There was a funny look on her rouged face. The ruby red lips smirked as she waited for me to come abreast. The smirk turned into a nasty grin as I approached.

"I been hearing a lot of bad things about you, boy." Her lips tightened.

"You ought to be ashamed of yourself diddling old lady Hannah and then spreading the news all over the neighborhood."

"Yes ma'am Miz Snoog. I don't know how all of that mess got started, or how it got around. I might have mentioned a little something to Eddie, but that's all,"

"You are one trashy nigger," Miz Snoog said. She shook her head slowly.

"Well, Joe had flew the coop, and I guess old Hannah needed a little tetching up." She looked slyly at me.

"Everybody needs a little tetching up at one time or another. I thought one time about letting you tetch me up. It's a good thing I thought better of it because you would have told everybody and his brother. Your Daddy or Lonnie would have kicked your butt for sure."

She was still watching me with a strange look in her eyes. I thought I detected a hint of admiration in her voice.

"Somebody was saying that you got some little gal down on Jones Street knocked up. Boy, I tell you, they ain't nothing you won't do."

"Yes ma'am Miz Snoog. I know what you mean. I'm sure glad you didn't let me tetch you up. I got to go now. Papa's waiting for his lunch."

I moved quickly aside and hurried up the path. When I got to the barn, Papa and the preacher were nowhere in sight. I looked at the new planting around me. The farm was coming along nicely. The tobacco patch was over near the new barn. The young plants were growing rapidly. Already the young leaves were fanning out. Beside the tobacco patch was the sweet potato patch. The brand-new vines were stretching green and lovely. The vines cuddled, protectively shielding the lightly buried yams from the harsh sunlight. It was a time of expansion. The power and the glory of Spring was everywhere. Beyond the potato patch on a small sloping hill were rows and rows of young corn plants standing tall, pointing their leaves toward the sun. Farming was a glorious venture, especially if you didn't have to participate. It was a labor of love for some folk. I admired Papa and the preacher.

My thoughts were interrupted by a loud braying followed by a harsh shout. There was some sort of commotion on the other side of the barn. I hurried around the corner of the barn. Jumping Jehosaphat! What a sight to behold! It was the biggest mule that I had ever seen. His coat was burnished copper, tightly covering rippling muscles that fit his huge

A Mule And Other Stuff

frame like a silken glove. His large head was reared back in defiance, as he looked sideways at Papa and the preacher. The preacher was standing with his mouth agape, watching Papa, who was trying to quiet the the mule. Papa was holding a brand-new set of plow lines hooked to the new leather bridle that the mule wore.

As I watched in awe, the mule reared up and pawed the air, trying desperately to rid his mouth of the big brass bit. There was foam around his mouth, and ropes of saliva hung down on either side of his mouth. His eyes rolled furiously, and his ears had been pointing in opposite directions. Now they were flattened against his head. I didn't know much about mules, but I could see that the big mule was certainly having a problem with what he was supposed to be doing. I could see right off that he had been gelded. For a gelding, he sure was raising cain, and from the belligerent way that he was acting, the operation hadn't worked. If the gelding had been meant to alter his demeanor, it was a total failure.

Suddenly, the mule quit pawing the air. His eyes were still rolling, but for the moment he was standing stock still. Papa stood quietly too. I guess the two of them were taking a breather.

Reverend Pierce tentatively moved a little closer to Papa and the mule. He had been standing well out of the way giving lip service. Now, the three of them stood quietly eyeballing each other. The mule was hooked up to a sweep plow. Papa was holding the plow lines that were also looped around the plow handles. The thin blades of the sweep plow served a double purpose. They were used to cut the grass and weeds from around the young plants and to push up the rich earth and around the roots of the plants. It was a ticklish operation, which required skill and precision on the part of the plowman. A skilled plowman and a good mule could cover a lot of ground in a day. But the big red mule was not a good mule. And besides, somebody had the unmitigated gall to name the mule "Tootie." Maybe that was the crux of the problem.

Reverend Pierce turned to me. His face was shiny with sweat, and he was breathing hard. You would have thought that he was the one wrestling with the mule.

"Son, your daddy is kind of bull-headed. I tried to tell him how to handle that mule, but he won't listen. He's a young mule, and you have to be firm with him." Papa was scowling. The reverend looked balefully at Papa.

"I keep telling Noah that he's a young mule, jerking on the lines just makes him unruly."

Everybody was mad except me. The mule, the preacher and Papa were about to boil over. I looked at the two men. Reverend Pierce looked like a little fat monkey in an ill-fitting suit. The blue serge suit was in sharp contrast to Papa's old overalls, denim shirt and sweat-stained straw hat. Papa looked straight at the preacher.

"I told you in front, before you bought that fool mule, that you should have bought the other mule from old man Dowden. Any fool knows that you can't run rows, side cotton or do nothing else with a young, inexperienced mule. This one ain't good for nothing but breaking up new ground."

I had completely forgotten about Miz Snoog. She had been watching the whole thing from the corner of the barn. Papa and the preacher were about to argue again. Miz Snoog knew it too. Her bright red lips were moist with anticipation. It was my move. I had to stop another confrontation between Papa and the preacher. I walked over and took the plow lines from Papa. My voice was gruff with confidence.

"Gimme that crazy-ass mule Papa! I'll show y'all exactly how to handle a balky mule." I grinned at the two of them. "Y'all ought to be ashamed of yourselves. Both of y'all are 'sposed to be ministers of the Gospel, and here you are fighting like cats and dogs. Y'all stand back and watch an expert in motion. When I get through with this fool mule, he'll purr like a kitten."

The mule turned his head and looked at me. He acted like he didn't like what he saw. I didn't care whether he liked it or not. I was the great-grandson of Stonewall Jackson, and I knew exactly how to handle a stubborn mule.

Papa, Miz Snoog and the preacher watched with bated breath as I gently righted the plow and tightened the plow lines. "Awright Tootie, get on up there!"

The big mule didn't budge. I was going to be firm. The plow lines whistled through the air as I slammed both of them squarely down on the mule's backside.

A Mule And Other Stuff

"Git up there fool!"

All hell broke loose. The big mule reared with his hooves flailing frantically in the air. He began to dance, ruining the tender shoots on several of the rows. I was holding both lines and shouting.

"Whoa fool! Whoa! You dumb-ass mule!" Papa ran toward us.

"Hold him boy! Don't let him run!"

That was exactly what I was trying to do. The mule was pulling me, the plow and a whole lot of the young plants up as he danced around in a circle. Papa was still shouting.

"Dave, drop one line, and jerk the other one as tight as you can. He can't run if you hold it tight enough."

I dropped the line, dug my heels into the dirt and held on to the other line. It was a moment before I realized that Papa had misinformed me again. The mule reared again, and this time when he came down, I was spreadeagled among the rows. I still had a grip on one plow line, but I was being dragged across the field toward the Rose Hill Road. After doing a lot of grandstanding about my prowess with mules, I couldn't very well turn the plow line loose. I would look awful silly letting the mule get away. I wanted to get out of the situation with some degree of grace, but the mule had other plans. I have yet to figure out how I got over the barbed wire fence that separated Mr. Dowden's farm from the Rose Hill Road. The mule dragged me helter-skelter across the newly plowed ground of Mr. Dowden's south forty.

The mule headed straight for a tobacco patch down near the woods that were at the back of the field. Jesse Potts, the Dowden field hand, was out working, using the older mule that Papa had mentioned. Mr. Dowden walked up just as Tootie slowed to a walk. I watched as the mule sidled up to Jesse, nudged him gently and then stood as docile as a lamb. There was a wide grin on Jesse's dark face, and Mr. Dowden's thin frame was shaking with laughter as he called out.

"Old Tootie shore took you for a ride, didn't he, boy?"

"I figured he'd come home first chance he got," laughed Jesse. "I didn't know he was bringing company, though."

"Tell you what David," said Mr. Dowden, as he looked at my torn shirt and dirt-stained pants.

"Since you had a slight problem with Tootie, and the trip was unexpected, I'll git Jessie to take Tootie back down to the preacher's place." He laughed again. "You're a real mule skinner, boy. You're almost an expert."

"Yessir Mr. Dowden. You got that right." I turned abruptly and started walking back across the field. I was smarting all over. The excruciating pain from the barbed wire, briars and being dragged across two farms was burned into my memory forever. I did not go near the preacher's place again. For the next few days, I avoided Papa like he had the plague. I didn't even want to think about the farm or the mule or the preacher or Miz Snoog and the crazy game that she was playing. The heck with all of it.

Miz Snoog came to my attention again much sooner than I had expected. I had completely forgotten about the strange lovers' triangle. I was more than a little surprised to come home on a Friday afternoon and hear funny noises coming from inside the little shack. I rushed up the steps and into the kitchen. There was a half-eaten sweet potato pie lying on the table. That should have made me aware that something was up. The funny noises were coming from the bedroom. I pulled aside the ragged curtain and peered into the semi-darkness.

Great day in the morning! At first glance I knew that Papa had won the hand of the flirtatious Miz Snoog. In fact, Papa had won all 350 pounds of the late blooming coquette. She was sitting squarely on Papa's middle in the most awkward position that you could imagine.

As I moved closer, I realized what had happened. The slats of the bed had broken under the combined weight of Miz Snoog and Papa. The springs sagged in the middle, and Miz Snoog's right leg was caught down between the railing and the bedsprings. Miz Snoog still had the big bloomers hanging from her left leg, so it must have been a spur of the moment thing. Papa's head was jammed against the head board, and his body was trapped beneath Miz Snoog. They were screaming and hollering to high heaven.

"Thank God, boy," said Papa as he peered over Miz Snoog's shoulder. His lean face was a study in pain and frustration.

"Help us to git outta here! The blame bed broke down! Please git her offa me, boy! She's mashing the shit outta me! Hurry up before she squashes me to pieces!"

"For God's sake help us, David!" Miz Snoog begged. "Please see if you kin git us loose. My leg is killing me! Oh Lawdy me!"

My first thought was to wish for an army truck, a six by six complete with a winch. I stood there trying to figure out what to do. I walked closer to the bed and almost tripped over Miz Snoog's big flowered dress. Miz Snoog was buck naked. I had never seen such a bulging expanse of flesh. The whole thing had been a really bad idea on Papa's part. He should have stayed with the missionary position, at least he could have backed away when trouble started. I hurried around to the end of the bed, grabbed Miz Snoog by the shoulders and pulled as hard as I could. She didn't budge an inch. Then, I squeezed my way around behind the bed and tried to untangle her leg from between the bedsprings and the railing. Still no luck. I grabbed the railing at the foot of the bed and jerked furiously. The railing suddenly came apart, and the mattress and springs fell from the bed, banging loudly as they hit the floor.

Miz Snoog gingerly moved her leg from between the springs and the railing. Papa heaved a huge sigh of relief as Miz Snoog rolled away and tried to stand. With considerable effort, I managed to get her on her feet. Papa avoided my eyes. There was a sheepish look on his face. I was embarrassed for the two of them so I quickly made myself scarce. I walked away thinking that any sort of relationship with Miz Snoog could be a dangerous business. Papa had better be really careful. He could get crushed or maimed for sure.

It was early Saturday evening. Jones Street was ready to rock. There was the usual crap game going on down in the bushes at the dead end of the street. The soldiers from Fort Bragg and the prostitutes from downtown had not arrived. Jones Street was almost like any other street: unpaved, with rows of shotgun houses on either side and toilets out back. The big difference was that you could buy anything that was available in the world right there on Jones Street. I had discarded my uniform and was dressed Jody-sharp, maybe even a little ahead of the times. I was decked out in a gray flannel suit, black silk shirt, white tie and black shoes shined to perfection. It was time to get down.

As I crossed the junction of Rose Hill Road and the main road to Raleigh, I glanced up at the little church perched on the hill. Remorse washed over me as I remembered the quick sordid moments of desecration and desire in the willing arms of Retha Jane. I quickly erased the images from my mind. By the time I left the hard surface of the highway and walked onto the well-traveled dirt of Jones Street, guilt was gone, and I was the very essence of cool.

I did an exaggerated slouch and then eased my body into the half-slick style of a pimp's walk. I walked toward the end of the street where the crap game was in progress. On Saturday, a crap game was always in progress. I checked my pockets to make sure that I had my dice with me. I would cheat only as a last resort. My mind was primed, and my instincts were fully cocked. They could get the word out. The Kid was on the street and ready for some action.

The little houses were not far apart. Fast Fanny's little place was the third house from the corner, and Retha Jane and her mother lived right across the street. As usual, Fanny was sitting on the porch business-like with her dress hiked up and her legs open. I appreciated the sight because Fanny had a shape like nobody else on Jones Street. She had huge breasts, a small waist and a big behind that had a mind of its own. From her big mouth to her small feet, everything about Fanny blatantly advertised her true calling. She relished her nickname. It gave her a sense of style. Brazenly flaunting her body was a part of her job.

There was one drawback in being with Fanny. It was something completely beyond her control. She would scream at the top of her lungs during the sex act. The longer it went on, the louder her screams would become. The screaming was exciting to some of her customers, but it would completely unnerve some of her patrons. Everybody on Jones Street would know each stage of the game and exactly what was happening. Curiosity seekers would wait with bated breath, watching the door to see the condition of her latest customer. Because of her loud cries and vocal outbursts, she did lose some of her patrons. Fanny's bubbling enthusiasm, speed and expertise would override the concerns of most of her customers. They would cheerfully bite the bullet and endure the screaming.

When I reached Fanny's little place, I walked over to the porch and smiled up at her.

"Hey Fanny, girl you sure look spiffy today! Whatcha putting down babycake? What's happening honeybunch? You look good enough to eat."

"You got that right, slicker. That's what a lot of them say. Just what do you want to happen pretty boy? I kin let you have it wholesale. You kin git a bale of this good stuff if you got any money." She grinned lasciviously.

"I got a few minutes before business picks up. I'll lay some tail on you so quick it'll make your head swim." Her eyes narrowed. "Gimme four dollars."

"I got the money, but I ain't got the time." A little grandstanding was needed. "Anytime you see me with my pants on, I got money. Nah Fanny, some other time, I'm on business." A thought crossed my mind. "Tell you what though. I do have a small favor that I'd like to get you to do for me. It's like this. I walked in on old lady Snoog and Papa the other day. She was pushing a piece of tail off on Papa, and she sat on him. The old biddy weighs over 300 pounds. I believe she hurt Papa pretty bad. He may never want another piece of tail. If you could lay a little bit on him, it might straighten him out. I'd sure appreciate it to the highest." I added quickly, "I'll be glad to pay whatever you charge." She licked her lips.

"Sure thing, I'll be glad to take care of him, anytime you say." She thought for a minute.

"Send him on down here, but tell him that any funny business will cost him extra. I ain't doing this for charity."

"Okay Fanny, I'll see if I can get him down here pretty soon." I turned to leave. "I'll see you later. I might take you up on your offer. I'd love to bust you down."

I walked to the end of the street where the crap game was in full swing.

The usual crowd was there: Slick Willie B, Eddie and Jeff Malloy, Big Dan and three other guys from downtown whom I didn't know. Willie scowled as I walked up.

"I still owe you an ass-kicking for the other night. I ought to take my razor and carve my initials on that pretty face of yours," he threatened. Warily, I watched his face to see if he were serious or trying to bullshit me.

"Like I told you Willie, you got to bring ass to get ass. I ain't here to fight. I'm here to take your money."

The dice were lying idle. I picked them up, held them to my ear and shook them for a moment. Satisfied, I looked around at the group.

"Awright, who want's to take the Kid's money? I'm betting a dollar. If you ain't got a dollar, gang up on me. A penny apiece for poor folk. C'mon y'all! Fade me fast. It's time to shake rattle and roll. Take a shot at the Kid's bankroll!" Willie had me faded before I finished speaking.

The first roll of the dice came up an eight.

"Jump on it y'all!" I made the eight on the second roll of the dice.

"Eight skating and donating! y'all!" Ten minutes later, I had a stash of $190. I didn't even have to introduce my dice. It was too early to use the busters. I might get caught, and besides I had already won some money. It was my policy to take some and leave some. Willie had been covering all of my main bets, and he was really pissed. I didn't want to goad him into a fight. It was time to go.

Willie B put his hand in his pocket and glared at me.

"Listen, you half-slick bastard. Turn them dice loose, and let them git a full roll. Quit trying to choke 'em up, and stop trying to spin them. Nigger, if you keep trying to cheat me, I'm gonna cut your dick string loose. Do you understand what I'm saying to you?" I looked him in the eye and then decided that he wasn't going to do anything.

"The hell with you nigger! C'mon. I want your money!"

I shook the dice and threw snake eyes twice in succession. I crapped out on the next roll. I stood up, brushed off my pants and checked my shoes for dirt.

"Y'all don't go nowhere. I promised Fanny a half pint of corn liquor for doing me a favor. Keep the dice hot. I'll be right back, y'all."

The gamblers were muttering angrily, especially Willie B. They also knew that what I was about to do was a constructive thing. Fast Fanny was like good corn liquor. She got better after a few drinks. Whomever was lucky enough to end up in her bed at that point would reap the benefits of my generosity. It happened just as I hoped it would. After a few implied threats, they didn't hinder me, and I was free to go.

I walked away, nonchalantly at first and then hurried back up the street. I glanced over my shoulder. The players had not resumed the game. They were standing at the end of the street watching me. Fanny was still sitting on the porch. I stopped right in front of where she was sitting, reached into my pocket and began to count my money. I made a

A Mule And Other Stuff

big show of counting the rumpled bills. There were mostly ones, and it amounted to $190. From where Fanny sat. It looked like more than it actually was. Fanny walked over to the edge of the porch. "C'mon up here for a minute. We need to talk."

I crawled out of Fast Fanny's bed about 30 seconds after she started to scream. She sounded as if I were committing bloody murder. It didn't matter. I was glad to get away from the burning heat of her body and the noise of her screaming. Doors had opened all along the street, and neighbors were craning their necks to see Fanny's latest customer. Eyes followed me as I hurried up the street. I was walking with my head down and almost bumped into Retha Jane. I had never seen her as angry as she appeared to be. She acted as if I had hurt her feelings, or worse.

"Damn you to hell David Sawyer," Retha said loudly.

"What were you trying to do sneak past me or something? You listen to me! Don't act as if you don't know what I'm talking about!" I shook my head.

"I ain't got the slightest idea of what you're talking about. Girl, you had to be bullshitting when you said you were knocked up, right?" She looked me straight in the eye and with a defiant look.

"I am pregnant, and it's your baby. What are you going to do?"

I was puzzled. In the first place, she was certainly hooked up with Willie B. And secondly, she had already told me that I wasn't worth a damn. Why did she want to hang a bad rap like that on me? I was getting highly upset.

"Retha Jane, you might as well stop that jive-ass claim right now. The baby belongs to Willie B. You know it, and I know it. You might as well forget that shit. I've already got something else lined up. I'm gonna get me something new." She was as mad as I had been. Her lips curled.

"Something new! Is that what you said? Ain't that some shit? If you had had a couple of more inches the other night, you could have got something new, nigger. It was right there. You just couldn't reach it!"

I didn't have to take that mess. I didn't owe her a thing. I walked away as she stood there giving me hell. Her tirade continued until I was across the road and out of earshot. I walked slowly up the road. I had put Retha Jane out of my mind and was thinking about the scorching heat of Fast Fanny's body. She was exceptional in spite of her screaming. I had never felt such fire.

Suddenly, I remembered something. I had felt such heat at another time and another place. It was something that I should have always remembered. The quick session that I had with Fanny was similar to the time spent with Marlena. Great day in the morning! I could only hope that I wasn't going to experience the second kick of a mule.

It was exactly nine days later, and I was seated in the small waiting room at the Cumberland County Health Department. After an hour or so, the doctor came to the door. He looked around the room and then called out, "Sawyer. David J Sawyer!" I stood up. "Yessir, I'm right here doctor!"

He looked as mean as any redneck that I had ever seen. I followed him into the examination room and took off my clothes. The examination was brief, and he did not touch me except when it absolutely necessary. The doctor left, and a few minutes later he walked briskly back into the room. There was a smirk on his face as he studied some forms for a second. Then he looked at me.

"You're a hep cat, aren't you boy?" he grinned nastily. "Boy, you've got the damnest case of the bull head clap that I've ever seen. You're going to have to take shots, boy, and you're going to have to give a rundown on all the people whom you have had contact with. We have to keep this disease from spreading." He looked at me sharply.

"I mean every contact that you've had or even heard about. This is serious business, boy."

The doctor was right. I was a fool for not having been doubly careful. Left alone, the disease could cause all sorts of damage to the community. Like other towns near army posts, Fayetteville had been extremely active in preventing the spread of communicable diseases ever since the devastating flu epidemic of 1918.

The flu had caused so many deaths that the town fathers said, "Never again!" They enacted strict laws to prevent the spread of any infectious diseases. They were particularly concerned about venereal disease and tuberculosis. The clinic doctor was only following the law.

It was my civic duty to act as soon as possible. I gave the doctor the names and addresses of everyone who lived on Jones Street, including the names of a few occasional visitors. These people would be contacted by the health department and asked to come in for an examination. If they did not agree, the sheriff would pick them up and escort them to the clinic. I had no qualms about turning in the whole of Jones Street. It was the right thing to do. Before many days had passed, the street would be the cleanest street in Fayetteville. I was proud to have done my duty. I also warned Papa about the perils of Jones Street.

It was much later when I heard that the sheriff had forcibly taken the Reverend Lonnie Pierce to the health clinic. I never did find out how he got caught in the net. I guess he was just lucky.

10

Abstinence Rewarded

I was through with women. Because of everything that had happened to me in recent months, I had decided to become asexual, neither here nor there. I was tired of being ridiculed and rebuffed, recklessly placing myself in harm's way at risk of catching infectious diseases. Preventive measures were one size fits all, but I preferred the Biblical flesh to flesh. It was man and his mischief that had forced improvisation. For me, it was all or nothing. At less than age 21, it was a big decision to make. Common sense dictated that if you're not able to do something well, it should be left alone. I was trying put aside my feelings and be brutally honest with myself.

There were other things in life, things aesthetic and spiritual. I would concern myself with the beauty of Spring flowers, the smell of plum blossoms and honeysuckle vines. I would concentrate on the finer things of life. But first, I had a lot of praying to do. I had to come to terms with the Lord and ask His forgiveness for my scandalous behavior in His house of worship. I expected to be beaten with many stripes, so I decided to begin my atonement as soon as possible and get it over with. I knew that if I were truly repentant, the good Lord would forgive me. The only problem that confronted me was that the good folk of Jones Street did not know of my decision to change my life. In fact, most of the folk

Abstinence Rewarded

on the street were thinking of ways to end my life.

I had planned on going to church every Sunday as a sign of my commitment to the Lord, but I was forced to change my plans because the church was too close to Jones Street. It wasn't that I was afraid. Staunch bravery was one of the things that I had inherited from Stonewall Jackson. Just as he liked living life on the edge, so did I. But, right now Jones Street was simply too close to the edge.

The list of people that might have been infected through casual sex was quite long. And, the list of people who were infuriated with me for turning their names over to the health authorities was also quite long. For safety's sake and my own well being, it was time for me to put some distance between myself and Jones Street. Fortune smiled upon me in the person of Charles Williams, my old shop teacher from high school. History was about to repeat itself. The spirit of Stonewall Jackson was on the move again.

Fayetteville, in the forefront as always, had just established a colored employment office down below the Old Market House on Person Street. Mr. Williams was the head of the department. The claims adjuster at the white employment office had already refused to honor my claim as a veteran who was eligible for $20 a week for 52 weeks. He argued that my father was sharecropping a farm on Rose Hill Road, and I should be working on the farm. There was no need for the government to waste money on me when I could be gainfully employed.

Due to the lack of jobs for Negroes around Fayetteville, Mr. Williams was riding high, living in the best of all possible worlds. All that he had to do was to look really important and brag about the fact that he was the first Negro to hold such a job as head of an employment office.

However, the war's end also brought an end to the fevered prosperity that both whites and Negroes had enjoyed during the heat of the hostilities. Sugar and gasoline were no longer rationed, and stamps were no longer needed to purchase government-controlled liquor. The concerted effort of the powers-that-be was to seek new horizons and help the returning servicemen to adjust to civilian life. Also, included within that concerted effort would be plans to make doubly sure that Negro servicemen were a safe distance behind.

The lengths that the white folk would go to maintain the status quo

Abstinence Rewarded

were amazing. It was back to the sharecroppers farm for the colored soldiers, some of whom had enjoyed the fine wines of war-torn Europe and had slept with white women who once had been the toast of French and German cities. It was a galling experience and a bitter pill indeed to have to revert to saying "Yassuh boss!" and to know that the former Negro soldiers' very survival depended on how quickly they averted their eyes in the presence of the white man's woman.

I had no problem with the racial aspect of the situation. My own experiences had given me a clear picture of exactly what to do and what not to do. Besides, Papa and Uncle Joe had taught me well. Shuffling and fawning played a major part, but Grandpa somehow managed to get along with the white folk and retain a certain amount of dignity in the process.

As for myself, trial and error had taught me that the less contact with white folk, the better my chances for the good life. I was secure in the knowledge that just as my great-grandfather had done, I could make my own way. Now was the time for me to light a shuck and go smoking to greener pastures. Mr. Williams was anxious and willing to help me achieve my goal. Salvation was two Trailway buses that would be leaving Fayetteville in a few days for a small town in Delaware called Houston.

On a Thursday morning, the little hall of the colored employment office was crowded with job seekers. All of them had heard about the giant canning conglomerate that was hiring workers to unload vegetables at the canning docks and to run the canning and labeling machines. Mr. Williams looked taller and thinner than ever, as he peered over his gold-rimmed glasses at the applicants. He cleared his throat, removed the glasses and muttered, "Good mawning y'all. The purpose of this meeting is to sign y'all up for jobs in Houston, Delaware."

His thin face was beaming as he continued.

"There are 61 jobs. So, that's all of the folk that I'm sending up there. The pay is 75 cents an hour, but the company will take ten cents of every hour for your living quarters. The ones who are hired will have to carry a blanket, a frying pan and whatever money you can scrape up. Y'all got any questions?"

Abstinence Rewarded

There were no questions. The 60-odd job seekers were glad to be considered for jobs, any kind of jobs and especially jobs that would take them north of Fayetteville. All of the applicants were not hired. An angry Willie B was told that because of a criminal record he would not be considered. Eddie and Jeff Malloy were hired. So were Big Dan, another acquaintance named Harry Ray and Paul Hamilton, a kind of slow-moving introvert, who was the son of one of Papa's deacon friends. Paul was chubby, dark-skinned and about my own age. He could neither read nor write. The only reason that he was hired was because I filled out his application and faked his Social Security number. For some reason, I kind of liked Paul. When the countdown was finished, there were 54 potential workers going to Delaware.

I did not get a lecture from Papa when I told him of my decision to go to Delaware. In fact, he did not seem overly concerned.

"Dave boy, you take care of yourself as best you can. I used to do a little traveling when I was a boy. Anyhow, they tell me that the white folk treat niggers a little better up yonder. Lemme know how it is when you get back, you, hear?"

It was on a Monday afternoon. We had gathered at the employment for a final briefing. Some of the workers carried their blankets and frying pans in burlap bags. Some bags were tied and wrapped with twine. A few workers carried traveling bags. My blanket, frying pan, a few clothes and my Stonewall book were in my duffel bag. After the meeting, we milled around on Person Street. There was still time because the buses were not due to leave until seven p.m.

It was only a short walk up past the Old Market House to the bus station. Person Street was filled with pedestrian and automobile traffic: soldiers, farmers and ordinary people, a duke's mixture of whites, Negroes and a few Croatan Indians. Everybody was hurrying up and down the street, rushing madly to get from one place to another. It was a thing of beauty to watch how adroitly the Negroes moved to get out of the way of the white folks. It was a classic example of yielding to the white of way.

The two Trailway buses pulled out of the station at exactly 7:15 p.m. The mood in the buses was jovial and light-hearted. After all, we were headed for God's country. Highway 301 North was the Jacob's ladder that led to heaven. The shepherds were a tall skinny redneck, who drove the lead bus, and a short, fat pasty-faced Jew, who drove the second bus. The sky was clear. The full moon was yellow, and the stars were hanging especially low, peering down to see what brand of fools these black mortals be. I made myself comfortable in the rear of the second bus. I was a seasoned traveler and wanted no truck with folk that did not know how to travel. Traffic was light except for big tractor trailers that squeezed past us, as they screamed down the narrow roadway going south. The headlights of the buses illuminated the dark green of the Carolina roadside and seemed to shine even brighter as the buses roared into the Commonwealth of Virginia. As I looked out of the window into the darkness, my thoughts were the thoughts of the long-dead Southern general. Stonewall Jackson, primed and spoiling for a fight, was in his old stomping grounds. That night the wily fox was on the move again.

Most of the passengers were fast asleep when the buses rolled over the Potomac River bridge. A few miles past the bridge, as the buses entered a deep swamp with steep ravines on either side, the little Jewish driver began to honk the horn furiously. Startled, the passengers awakened, wondering what was happening. The driver yelled.

"Good God Almighty! That fool Jimson is done gone to sleep! He's gonna wreck that damn bus, sure as shit!"

We craned our necks to see what was going on. The lead bus was careening from one side of the road to the other, weaving dangerously close to first one ravine and then the other. The driver must have finally awakened because the bus abruptly righted itself, pulled over to the side of the road and stopped. The red neck and face of the bus driver were white as a sheet. He walked unsteadily back along the roadside to talk with the little Jew. Stonewall Jackson was still in charge, but he was sweating like crazy. Somehow, a catastrophe had been avoided. I heaved a huge sigh of relief because Eddie and Jeff Malloy were in the lead bus.

There were no more incidents to speak of. When the buses reached Annapolis, the boys from down south were amazed that the ferry boat could accommodate the two large buses and automobiles and passengers also. Soon, the ferry boat moved quietly along the huge expanse of the Chesapeake Bay, headed upstream to the shores of Delaware. The night

Abstinence Rewarded

was still clear. The moon was still yellow, and the stars were still watching to see what the black mortals would do next. I was quiet. The general was always quiet when things were going well.

It was four o' clock in the morning when the two buses rolled into the compound at the giant canning conglomerate.

The firm of Billings, O'Neill and Billings had created a small village of cinderblock huts for its workers. Narrow dirt streets ran between the shanties, and at the far end was a commissary that sold meats and other bare necessities. Vegetables were free from the plant refuse dump. Credit was immediately extended if you were hired at the plant. The straw boss was waiting as the buses pulled into the compound. He was a big burly Negro in a soiled felt hat, with a billy club at his belt.

"Awright y'all, shut up and listen," said the strawboss. "You people were brought up here to work because the company's found out that niggers from down south work pretty good in the fields and in the canning factory."

He paused for a moment. His face looked malicious and grim in the light of the single bulb hanging from the pole behind us.

"Don't git your ass on your shoulder. You're not hired yet. You still have to be approved at the company employment office in the morning."

A man and a young girl suddenly appeared with a stack of mattress ticks. They placed the ticks on the ground in front and waited silently. The strawboss pointed at the mattress ticks.

"There's enough ticks here for each one of y'all, and the oat straw is out back. Y'all will sleep two men to a shack."

He gazed sternly at the group.

"Y'all don't look like you're worth a damn, but we'll find out. That's it. I'll come and git y'all in the mawning."

The morning came and went with everybody getting hired but Paul. We were called into the employment office one at a time. I wasn't able to be with Paul to help with his application. He couldn't work, and there was no way he could get back home, so I arranged to have him share a hut with me. We were only going to be in Delaware for several weeks, until the end of the tomato and bean canning season.

Eddie, Jeff and Harry Ray were given jobs unloading tomatoes at the dock. The tomatoes were dumped into troughs and carried by water past a row of women, who quickly stemmed the tomatoes and picked out the leaves and debris. The tomatoes were then dropped into huge vats to be cooked. Big Dan and myself were to run the labeling machines. It was harrowing work because once the complicated machines were started, the operator had to remain with the machine until the run was completed.

Running the machines was much harder than farm work. This job was certainly not in my plans for the future. However, my feelings were not the same as the others. It was surprising how quickly the down home boys adjusted to the utter sophistication of Northern living. The women of the camp were both easy and sleazy, fitting companionship for the rough and tumble environment of cannery row. The nights were filled with revelry, loose men and looser women loosely enjoying themselves. Despite the sight of cannery women brazenly showing their breasts and thighs, I saw no reason to break my vow of celibacy. I would sooner stick my head in a hornet's nest.

Living next to one or another is an integral part of any society. Neighbors are not only necessary but unavoidable. There were two women who lived next door, and there were two more who lived just across the street. Neighbors will be neighbors, and Lacy and Choo Choo from next door came calling. A minute later Minnie and Janey sauntered across the street. It had to be a fad of some sort because none of them were wearing brassieres. Their faces were obscure, an indistinct blur because they flaunted breasts, hips and funky behinds. Regardless of my vows, it got my attention. Lacy placed her left foot on the stoop, and knocked loudly on the half-open door. "Hey, down home nigger, c'mon out. I wanna talk to you!" I walked to the door with Paul right behind me.

"What do y'all want? I ain't got a drop of sugar. Is this a social call, or do y'all have something to sell?"

"Nigger, it's the middle of the week," said Lacy. "I know damn well y'all ain't got no money. If you could go all the way around the world for a nickel, you couldn't even git outta sight." Her big lips curled. "I jist wanted to know if you had any reefer papers. I got ahold of some good shit outta South Philly, and I thought y'all might want a tote."

Paul was craning his neck, watching avidly. The girls were sniggling loudly as they eyed the two of us.

Abstinence Rewarded

"Aw man," said Choo Choo, "let's leave these sorry niggers alone. They ain't worth a quarter." She grinned evilly. "Unless you wanna credit them a piece of ass til payday." I was grinning too.

"Nah, I don't smoke reefer, and Paul don't either. As for a piece of tail, I'm on the wagon. I got a girl back home."

I was still smiling as I looked at these women of the world. The four of them were covertly watching Paul.

"Y'all needn't be eyeing Paul, here. He ain't even thought about doing nothing like that." I turned to Paul.

"You don't want no tail, do you Paul? If you just have to have it, I'll buy you a piece and pay for it on Saturday."

Paul was blushing or doing whatever black people do instead. His lips were moving furiously, but no sound came from his mouth. Finally, he blurted:

"I can so git tail. I jist don't want none right now! Y'all quit funning me. I'm a grown man!"

The incident was of no consequence, so it was quickly forgotten. Hard back-breaking work made Saturday night a welcome sight for the down home boys. I welcomed it also but for different reasons. I was dog-tired. It was the end of a work week, and the cannery row workers were celebrating. I heard a loud bang just outside the door.

"My goodness, they've even got firecrackers, was my first thought."

It was a little later that I learned that the noise came from a big .44-caliber revolver. The girls were in the middle of the street arguing and yelling. Lacy was holding the gun. It dwarfed her small fist as she waved it in the air. She had fired the big gun into the air, and she was also fired up on reefer or booze, for reasons of which I wanted no part.

Farther down the street, somebody was playing a washboard, accompanied by a steel guitar. Rowdy good times were breaking out all up and down the row. Soon, the Delaware police would make their regular Saturday night visit to the compound. I wanted no part of that scene. Jail was one of the things that Papa had taught me to avoid at all costs. Besides, Delaware's principal method of punishment for lesser crimes was the whipping post. And, I did not want to be in a position to compare whippings or take notes. I still remembered the whippings that Papa had given me when I was a boy. I closed the door tightly, glanced over at the sleeping Paul and then went to sleep.

Sunday morning was just the beginning of another day in the cannery compound. A few of the late bloomers were still on the street, searching for a taste of reefer, wine or whatever they had been using the night before. Every now and then stray preachers would enter the row of ramshackle huts with the intention of spreading the Gospel. After they found out what was really going on, they tarried not. Most preachers left in frantic haste and took their spiritual aspirations with them. There was no room for church on Sunday in cannery row because the party was still going on. I looked over at Paul's cot. It was his chore to cook breakfast. His bunk was empty, and he was nowhere in sight.

I wasn't too alarmed, but I felt that Paul was my responsibility. I put on my clothes and walked to the doorway. I looked up and down the street. There were a few people out, but no sign of Paul. I walked several doors down the street to the hut where Eddie and Jeff Malloy lived. At my third knock, Jeff came to the door.

"Hey Dave, whatcha doing up so early in the mawning?" He rubbed his eyes. "I was sleeping my ass off. What's going on?"

"Nah Jeff, ain't nothing shaking but the leaves on the trees, and they wouldn't be shaking if the wind wasn't blowing." Eddie's face suddenly appeared behind Jeff. There was a question on his thin face.

"Hey Eddie, I was just about to tell Jeff, here, that I can't find Paul. He wandered off somewhere. I ain't got the slightest idea where to find him. It ain't like him at all. You know, he's kind of simple, and I sure as hell don't want anything to happen to him."

"I wouldn't worry about him too much if I was you," said Eddie. "You ought to check with Lacy or them two ugly bitches across the street. While you're working, he's been bullskating around with all of them. I believe he likes one of them. I don't know which, but either one is a piss-poor choice. It's like an even-Steven swap between the devil and the witch."

Just then, Big Dan and Harry Ray came to the door of their hut down at the end of the street. They saw us and hurried up the street to where we were standing.

"What's going on?" said Dan.

"Probably nothing at all," said Eddie. "Dave, here, jist woke up, and Paul wasn't in the hut," Eddie said. "I told him that he might be with them sorry broads from Philadelphia," he grinned.

"Y'all c'mon on. Let's go find Dave's baby." He was still grinning. "He can't sleep without little Paul."

We walked back up the street. All of us were a little concerned. Paul was one of our own.

"There's something that you don't know," said Harry Ray.

"Paul's been doing shit that you don't know nothing about. I believe those women have got him smoking reefer and drinking wine too. He's getting to be a regular sport."

Big Dan was grumbling as the five of us walked up the street.

"Boy, I tell you for a fact, that's why I travel by myself. I don't have to take responsibility for nobody but me. As long as I keep my ass in line, everything goes along just fine." He looked sideways at me.

"You kin barely take care of your own ass. You should have left Paul at home with his daddy. You know he ain't right. Bringing him up here was a big ass mistake."

I had been thinking the same thing, but hindsight was no good. I just had to find Paul. I was walking faster and faster when we came abreast of the hut where Lacy and Choo Choo lived. The door opened, and Paul stumbled out into the street. His face was ashen, and his eyes were darting in every direction. He was shaking as if he had the ague. I was mad as a March hare.

"Paul, what in the world's the matter with you? I've been looking like hell for you all morning. I'm supposed to be looking after you, and you go and pull some mess like that."

A child-like look flitted briefly across his moon face. His lips moved, but no sound came out of his mouth. Finally he spoke. "I wasn't lost. I was just over at Lacy and Choo Choo's. I would have come home last night, but after Minnie and Janey came over, they just wouldn't let me go."

He was silent. I knew he was thinking and remembering. He mumbled ashamedly. "They kept making me do stuff. All of them just kept on making me do it."

The group was all ears. The guys crowded around Paul and me. Eddie leaned forward grinning maliciously.

Abstinence Rewarded

"Do what, Paul? Jist what in the world did they make you do?" Paul gulped.

"They kept making me kiss them. I didn't really want to do it, but Lacy had a straight razor, and she said that she would cut my throat if I didn't kiss them."

"Don't git so upset," said Harry Ray, speaking for the first time. "Ain't nothing wrong with kissing a woman, and kissing four of them is even better."

"But, Lacy didn't want me to kiss them on the mouth," said Paul. "She wanted me to kiss them in a whole lot of different places." Once again he thought for a minute.

"It was kind of warm, and it tasted salty. They didn't hurt me, though." Big Dan guffawed. "Hey Paul, tell us how you handled that particular situation?" Then, Big Dan turned to the others.

"What do y'all think? What do you think old lover boy did? Those trashy bitches schooled little Paul. I'll tell you what they did. They turned him into a pine rooter from way back." They were all laughing including myself.

"Take a real good look at homeboy," said Eddie. "Take a look at his throat. It ain't cut, is it?"

That episode ended as it had begun, with no great fuss. I was sure that everything would blow over. I had not expected an aftermath. But somehow, Paul could not leave alone the group of women. Lacy, Choo Choo, Minnie and Janey seemed determined to sink Paul deep into their own quagmire of disappointment and broken dreams. As time went by, the women took complete charge of Paul. His oral assignations were not confined to the four women. Soon, Lacy and Choo Choo began to lend Paul to other women in the camp. It was similar to a consignment except that he always came back. However, the two were loud and boisterous in making it plain that he was their exclusive property. Paul actually bloomed as he continued to be well-fed and well-rewarded. After all, in that strange arena he was getting a fair exchange and that was certainly no robbery. The slow, doddering Paul was slow no more. He was anxious to fulfill his strange calling.

I didn't know what to do. I couldn't just pick up Paul and bodily prevent him from carousing with the women. They made it easy for him to do their bidding. Paul seemed happy that he was completely under their control. Part of the plan was to always keep Paul as high as a kite. He would stumble across the street from one hut to the other with a silly grin on his moon face. It was a game to Lacy and Cho Choo, a sickening game that I knew would mean no good for the plain and simple country boy. Once again I was weighed down by guilt. Remorse was my constant companion.

The canning season for beans and tomatoes was over at Billings, McNeill and Billings. It was time for us to seek new horizons. Harry Ray was not going home. He was going to look up relatives in Philadelphia. Big Dan was off to New York to look up kinfolk. Eddie and Jeff were to leave later. They had been offered a couple of weeks of clean-up work at the plant. Paul was completely adamant about staying with the women. His feelings were like those of Ruth in the Old Testament. I kept asking him to come home with me. "Dave, don't worry about me," he said. "Lacy, Choo Choo, Minnie and Janey are my best friends. I've got new friends too. Now that the season is over, I'm going wherever they go. They follow the seasons and go lots of places. They already told me. Their folk will be jist like my folk. I'll be okay. Don't worry, you hear?"

Well, my Summer endeavor was over. I had learned little, gained nothing, and my celibacy was still continuing. It had been a long drawn out Summer. Celibacy be damned. With every fiber of my being, I wanted a woman. Lust was a persistent ache in my groin. I wanted to touch, feel, smell and make love to a woman.

It was time for Stonewall Jackson to make another move. I didn't even look back at the cannery. A chicken factory in Milford, Delaware was my next stop. The pungent odor of dead chicken changed my mind in a hurry about seeking employment. In downtown Milford, I purchased a J.C. Penny suit, a black silk shirt, a snap brim fedora by Adam Hat Corporation and a pair of Thom McCann shoes. After paying for a bus ticket to Fayetteville, I had 61 dollar bills, a twenty, two tens and three fives. On the street, they called it a "Philadelphia roll." The general was in fine fettle, armed and ready to do battle.

11

Returning Home

Well, I was back in good old Fayetteville, North Carolina, and all of the folk on the Rose Hill Road and Jones Street were talking about me. Fast Fanny should have hated me, but she was one of my ardent supporters. She was telling everybody who would listen:

"Did y'all hear the latest? Little David Sawyer is back in town. That slick rascal's been up North all Summer. He's got an ass pocket full of money. I saw it with my own eyes. Yessirree Bob! That pretty nigger went up yonder and came back with enough money to burn a wet mule! I'm gonna lay some tail on him. I got to git me some of that money!"

I still wanted a woman with every fiber of my being, especially on cold, rainy nights. My smallness in no way hindered my sexual desires. If anything, it heightened and intensified them. My mind sought peace, but uneasy hormones would not let me be. The Stonewall curse was alive and well. Relief was not forthcoming, so I usually did the only thing left to do and then drifted fitfully off to sleep. I wasn't ready to dive headlong into Fanny's questionable embrace.

Somehow, I had to be sure that the mandatory treatment administered by the health authorities had worked. Celibacy was still the rule for the time being. Besides, my life was at a standstill. In this instance, I was not as fortunate as my great-grandfather Jackson. Stonewall had his friend and map maker, Jed Hotchkiss, to plot the terrain and plan routes of easy access that led to high ground from where the enemy could be soundly defeated. I had no one, but it was a challenge to figure out my next move in the intricate game of life.

Stonewall Jackson would ford rivers, climb mountains and gallop across arid plains to meet a challenge. Because he had been my kin, I could win this game. I was a chip off the old block. The Rose Hill Road was my staging ground. From that winding strip of Carolina mud, dirt and sand, I would plot my next endeavor.

The junction of the Rose Hill Road and the main road to Raleigh was a busy place. Services at Mood's Temple Church on Sundays and three nights a week, plus the rowdy nights and weekends of the Jones Street crowd, kept traffic at a grueling pace. There was a service station across the street called "The Brown Derby" that sold gasoline, beer and groceries. It was run by an old white man named William Brown. He was what the Negroes called a decent white man.

The first house passed was a small clapboard cottage on the left, as the road dipped sharply downhill. A family of Croatan Indians lived there, completely ignoring the traffic around them. The Indians were close-knit, closed mouth, with a quiet dignity. There were two grown daughters, quite good-looking but aloof. The family bothered no one, and no one bothered it.

From that point on, for the next mile and a half, the road was peopled with family members of the Sawyer and Elliot clans. On that particular stretch of the road, home was anywhere I decided to hang my hat. The Sawyers and the Elliots really liked me. There were few of the younger Sawyers left and less members of the younger Elliot clan. The elders felt that I was the hope of the future. Boy, were they in for a surprise.

Aunt Lizzie Elliot, Grandma's sister, lived in the next little house on the left. There were two Chinaberry trees in the yard and rosebushes at each corner of the porch. Neatness was an integral part of Aunt Lizzie. She was also a bootlegger, who sold the best crystal clear moonshine whiskey on the Rose Hill Road. She was also a staunch member and deaconess of Mood's Temple Church.

Whites and Negroes bought whiskey from Aunt Lizzie on every day except Sunday. On the Lord's day, rain or shine, she was always in church. Derb Coulter, the county sheriff, was one of Aunt Lizzie's best customers. He had long since recognized the futility of trying to arrest Aunt Lizzie for selling untaxed whiskey. He would always stop by and warn her of any impending raids. It was a wonderful arrangement.

Aunt Lizzie's house was in an open field about a 100 yards from the road. There were two other houses in the little field.

In one house lived Grandma's brother, Noah. He was a retired minister, who dabbled in voodoo and herbs. He was also supposed to be clairvoyant and able to perform acts of levitation. Most of the family gave him a wide berth.

Papa's brother, Uncle David, whom I was named for, and his wife, Aunt Mary, lived in the next house. He was also a minister, and unlike Papa, he was quite well known around Fayetteville.

Across the road, on the crest of a small hill, were several houses where white prostitutes lived and worked. The area was called "Sugar Hill" and was run by a florid-faced white man called "Mr. Randy." There was a small stand of pines on either side of the road, and then more open field and more houses staggered on both sides of the road.

Uncle Mike Sawyer, Papa's brother, lived in the first of a group of three houses on the left. The second house belonged to Little Ed Sawyer and his wife, Louise. She had four children: three by a first marriage and one that was born while Ed was overseas. Ed was still overseas. I was hoping that he would come home soon. Little Ed was almost as much a hero to me as Stonewall.

More dwellings filled with Sawyers and Elliots dotted the curves of the Rose Hill Road. After the houses was Mr. Courtney's dairy. His big house sat on the crest of a hill, and a long line of fence posts stretched along the road in front of the swamp.

Just past the little bridge was Lovers' Lane. Then came Grandpa's place. Like I said, home was anywhere that I chose to hang my hat.

The Rose Hill Road was a tranquil place at that time of year. In Winter, bluish smoke from each of the chimneys rose gracefully above the trees, each spiral meeting other tendrils of smoke like old friends shaking hands in the clear skies above the road.

It was Monday morning during the first week of November, and I was walking downtown to see about a job at the Lafayette Hotel on Hay Street. I wanted to get out of the house because Papa had been abrupt and short-tempered for the past several weeks.

For one thing, he had been expecting my brother, Jimmy, to come home from the Pitt farm up near the Sampson County line. Papa had not heard hide nor hair from Jimmy. The second thing that really bothered him was the farming venture with Reverend Lonnie Pierce turned out to be a real bust. In fact, they made very little money, and according to Papa Reverend Pierce owed him $60. They had had a real blowup at settlement time.

In a violent rage, Papa had borrowed Grandpa's crippled mule, loaded the sweet potatoes on an old wagon, and hauled them about town. There were 40 bushels of potatoes. The ones that Papa didn't sell, he gave away to everybody up and down the Rose Hill Road. Potato pie was indeed plentiful all of that Winter and most of the Spring.

Miz Snoog's torrid romance petered out on all counts. After the ill-fated episode in the little shack, Papa completely lost his taste for sweet potato pie with meat. If he saw Miz Snoog coming, he high-tailed it the opposite way.

Somehow, Miz Snoog found out about Reverend Pierce's forced appointment with the city health authorities. She immediately lost interest in any sort of liaison with the fat little preacher. She discarded the big, flowered dresses, stopped painting her face and lips and began to dress sensibly. Her dreams of love and romance sagged, like a half-empty sack of potatoes. Quietly, she gave up any thought of courting and resigned herself to being a grass widow.

I was having none of that sort of living. Fayetteville was becoming a cosmopolitan city, and I was going to be a part of it. The job in which I was interested was as a bellhop at the Lafayette Hotel.

There were two hotels in Fayetteville. Both were located near the center of town on Hay Street.

The Prince Charles Hotel catered to the well-to-do clientele that came to town for one reason or another. The Lafayette hotel was for the less well-heeled, the traveling salesmen and people of low estate.

Returning Home

As quiet as it was kept, the Lafayette Hotel was also a thriving brothel. Prostitutes rented rooms at the hotel by the month and sold their favors to the soldiers from Fort Bragg. The bellhops, along with their other duties, arranged the sales, sneaked the women into the soldiers' rooms, protected the women from questionable customers and were paid a percentage of the profits.

The hotel clerk, a sweet, elderly Southern lady named Mrs. Judy Dowling, had absolutely no inkling of the sordid doings that went on in the upstairs rooms of the staid hotel. It was exactly the kind of setting that I needed. I could do well in an atmosphere that required a maroon jacket, white shirt, dark pants and a bow tie.

If I got the job, I would still be wearing a uniform of sorts. It was going to be a good feeling. Being polite and deferential to white folk would get me a continuous flow of tips. I wasn't sure about whether or not I wanted to be a peddler of flesh. Peddling flesh, especially white flesh, could be a dangerous business.

Fayetteville was a busy place on that Monday morning when I arrived for the job interview at the hotel. The streets were teeming with soldiers, farmers and shoppers of all races.

The Negroes walking the streets were still playing the game of artful dodger, managing to safely stay out of the way of white folk. The Negro women shopping the department stores were slightly perturbed when the white clerks would not let them try on hats, gloves and shoes. Dresses, too, were sometimes made a part of the guessing game. The items were taken home and altered to fit. A women's style shop on Bow Street would not even allow Negro women to enter.

It was the accepted way of doing things. Most of the Negroes were small enough to bend with the wind, cope with the times and roll with the reality of what had to be. Limited liberty and certain injustices were standard fare.

I paused for a moment, took a deep breath and entered the big double doors of the Lafayette Hotel. Mrs. Judy Dowling was a small, fluttery woman who always spoke in a high breathless voice. Her gold-rimmed glasses were sometimes perched on her forehead or dangled from a small gold chain. That morning, they were placed firmly on her beaked nose. Her brown hair was mixed with grey, and her pinched face was devoid of make up except for traces of lipstick on the thin slash of her mouth. There was annoyance on her face, and her voice was as cold as ice water.

"What can I do for you, boy?"

If it had been anything but a hotel, I would have been at the back door with my hat in my hand. I wasn't wearing a hat, and I was determined. Besides, I knew how to talk to white folks.

"Yes ma'am Mrs. Dowling. I'm David J. Sawyer. Julian Smith said that I might be able to talk to you about the bellhop job that you have open."

I didn't give her a chance to answer. The words tumbled out.

"Julian will vouch for me ma'am. I'm a good worker. I wouldn't lose any time, and I finished high school." Her stern face softened a bit.

"Well, I do need a boy for the night shift. If Julian recommended you, I might consider hiring you. Can you work from 8 o'clock at night till 8 o'clock in the morning? I'll pay you a dollar a night, and you will have to scrub the lobby every morning, but you'll make pretty good in tips." She said as an afterthought. "That's providing you're prompt and polite. Nobody likes uppity Negroes." Her lips pursed.

"Here's what we'll do. You can come in tonight at 8 o'clock. Julian will be here, and he can show you how we do things. If you work out, okay, if not, it's up the road for sure."

"Yes ma'am, Mrs. Dowling."

I drooled politeness, giving her my best smile.

"I'll prove myself to be one of the best bellhops that you've ever had. Thank you again ma'am. I sure appreciate you giving me this chance. I won't mess up."

The lobby of the hotel was real old-fashioned elegance. The elevator and the stairs were off to the far left of the clerk's desk. Potted flowers ringed the large lobby, placed correctly about the well-worn furniture. I stood quietly by the elevator and waited.

Julian was late. It was five minutes after eight when he walked through the door. He had been graduated from high school with honors the year before I was. Julian was about my complexion, short, bespectacled, with a serious look on his face, which disappeared completely when he smiled. There was a slight hump in his back, not enough to be called a deformity, but it gave him a look of being much older than his real age. His face lit up as he walked toward me.

"Hey Dave! You got the job! I was sure that she would hire you. I'll show you around in a minute."

"Yeah man, no problem. She hired me right away."

Julian smiled as I looked around the sedate lobby of the old hotel. Aw man, I was picking in high cotton for sure. I could see why the transformation from field Negro to house Negro made such a difference. It was a sign of progress for the ones who achieved that coveted status.

"C'mon, I'll show you around," said Julian. "We'll start with the lobby, and then I'll show you the rest of the hotel. It has four floors." He pointed toward a closet against the wall.

"Here's where we keep the brooms, mops and cleaning supplies."

It was early, and things were slow, so we had plenty of time. As we toured the building, Julian explained the complexities of the bellhop's part in this peculiar operation.

The tips meant little to Julian. They were chicken feed. The real money came from the varied customers via the prostitutes in the rooms upstairs. The central idea behind the whole operation was to first recognize the prospective customer. Then, get to the soldier, businessman or whomever before he reached the desk. Otherwise, he might accost Mrs. Dowling and ask her about the services of a prostitute and that could cause a calamity of major proportions. The more Julian talked about the job, the more I began to like the idea.

The arrangements with the eager customers were usually made in the elevator during the trip upstairs. The fee was usually $10, unless some special activity was required. Whiskey that sold at the state store for a $1.85 was resold for $4.50. That profit was strictly for the bellhop as was $3 of the $10 service fee. The Colonial Restaurant was right next door. It was a separate entity. The bellhops would buy breakfast, lunch or dinner from the restaurant and sell to the patrons of the hotel, making another small profit in the bargain.

Soon, the tour ended, and patrons began to trickle into the hotel. Under the watchful eye of Julian, I began to assist the customers with their luggage, deliver ice and make sure that everything in the rooms was satisfactory. I made $8 in tips on that first night, and Mrs. Dowling's face wore a pleasant smile that morning when she paid me a dollar for cleaning the lobby. I was on my way to becoming one of the best bellhops ever to work the Lafayette Hotel.

For the first few weeks things went well on my new job. My ready smile and quick responses to all requests gave me an edge in the amount of tips that I received. I did not get involved with the several prostitutes

Returning Home

who lived on the second and third floors of the hotel. One of the main reasons was that they figured that I was too green and might end up getting them and me in trouble with the local law. The Fayetteville and Fort Bragg authorities were not entirely oblivious to what was going on in the hotel.

In fact, both the Hotel Lafayette and the Prince Charles Hotel had been raided several times during the war years. General James Gavin's crack paratroopers were also famous for jumping out of the second floor windows of both of the hotels. Their line of work was ideal, enabling them to avoid arrest for aiding and abetting prostitution.

There was also another way to make money. Hustling whiskey carried little risk, and the profits were greater than 100 percent. I decided to try it. The operation was a huge success. I simply hid the pint bottles of Old Grandad, Three Feathers and Jack Daniels behind the dumpster in the back of the motel.

My first major problem came about when a veterans advisor named John Dunlap from Greensboro approached me. He was short, stocky, and wearing thick glasses. He wore his blond hair in a crew cut and had a slight limp. I was seated in my usual place near the elevator when he finished signing in and walked slowly toward me.

"Say, bellhop, bring me up some ice," he said. The door opened, and he stepped into the elevator.

"I'm in 204, and hurry up, will you?"

"Yessir, I'll bring it right up sir."

I turned just as Julian was coming through the door with an elderly fat man. The man went to the desk, and Julian walked over to me. Force of habit made me speak softly.

"Hey Julian did you know the dude who just went up in the elevator?"

"Sure, I know him. He comes here two or three times a month," Julian chuckled. "He's gonna want a couple of pints of Jack Daniels, and he's probably gonna ask you about me." For some reason he was still giggling.

"If he does ask for me, tell him I'll see him later."

When I carried the ice up to Mr. Dunlap's room, I also carried two pints of Jack Daniels. I set them down beside the door and knocked softly. The door opened quickly. I handed him the ice and waited. He reached in his pocket and gave me two quarters.

"Thanks boy. C'mon in for a minute. You don't happen to have any liquor, do you?" I was grinning.

"Yessir, I do. Julian told me about you. I've got two pints just outside the door, Jack Daniels Black Label. Julian told me that you were a veterans advisor."

I said proudly, "I'm a veteran too, sir, I was with the 969th field artillery at Fort Sill."

After I gave him the whiskey, he poured a big double shot and then gave me the exact change. Suddenly, he put his arm around my shoulder in a chummy fashion. "So you're a veteran, are you? What's your name?"

He drank the whiskey in one gulp and wiped his mouth on his sleeve.

"Well, boy, it might be that we can help each other. I need a small favor from you, and then it might be that I can help you with school or buying a house that sort of thing."

"I'm David J. Sawyer, sir. And, yessiree, I would sure appreciate any help that I could get. I've been thinking about going back to school."

I was elated. This was real honest to goodness help from the government.

"I'm certainly interested Mr. Dunlap. What is it that you want me to do?"

His face was suddenly flushed, and a sheepish grin appeared.

"You see David, it's like this. I don't care much for women. The thing that I really enjoy is a hard piece of meat." He was staring directly into my eyes.

"All you have to do David is drop your pants for a minute."

I came out from under his arm and began backing hurriedly toward the door. I lost my cool completely.

"No sir, Mr. Dunlap! My Daddy is a preacher." I began to sweat.

"I'm sorry, but he taught us that we would burn in hell's fire if we ever done anything like that!"

"Hold on David," said Mr. Dunlap. "It's all right. Don't get yourself into a dither. I didn't know you felt that way. Julian usually straightens me out. Have you seen him tonight?"

"Yessir, he's downstairs. I'll tell him that you want to see him as soon as I go back downstairs."

I almost ran back to the elevator. I needed some time to think about what had just happened. I had completely forgotten that there were people like that. I didn't see Julian for almost an hour. When I told him what had happened, he laughed himself silly.

"Boy, I know that he got to your natural ass. Why didn't you take care of him?"

"Aw man, I had no idea that he was screwed up. We were talking about stuff like school, government loans and stuff." I was still shocked.

"I tell you for a fact. He surprised the shit out of me with that mess."

"Well, I ain't got time to mess with him right now," Julian said. "I got too much going on. I got all three of those whores on the third floor working like crazy. I'll probably check him out later tonight." He grinned again. "However, you could take care of him yourself."

I was busy for the next hour or so. A jewelry salesman, a fur coat salesman and an elderly couple from Texas kept me running for ice, beverages and food. Finally, I got a chance to sit down on the little stool beside the elevator. I was still thinking about Mr. Dunlap. Why would a personable young man like him have the urge to be with his own kind? I was still mulling it over in my mind when the door to the elevator opened. I couldn't believe my eyes. Standing in the door of the elevator was Mr. Dunlap, wearing a white shirt, tie and not a stitch of clothing below his waist. His face was red as a beet, and he was gesticulating wildly at me. I looked down at his nakedness. The hugeness of his genitalia was an amazing sight. He whispered loudly.

"Where's Julian? I got to have me some dick, right now!"

I stood up, horrified. Mr. Dunlap had a terrible problem, and there was no telling how he planned on getting it solved. I tried to keep my voice down.

"Mr. Dunlap, you can't come down here with no clothes on! You better get back upstairs before Mrs. Dowling sees you. She'll call the law on you for sure. I'll get Julian to come up to your place as soon as I can. You better hurry, now, before she comes over here." He turned reluctantly and started to push the button.

"Tell Julian to hurry and come up as soon as he can. I got to have it. I just got to."

Returning Home

Aw man, I just couldn't comprehend Mr. Dunlap's actions. Here was a man blessed with God-given equipment, totally designed to satisfy the most finicky of women, and he was desperately trying to solicit satisfaction of some sort from his own kind. Because of my problem with smallness, I had harbored a fascination for huge genitalia. It was not sexual in nature or for gratification of any sort. It was simply wishful thinking. I was wishing that my own was as big and as bold.

It was sometime during that night that Julian came to the rescue and saved the day. Mr. Dunlap went about his business, a happy man, cheerful to the extent that as he was leaving, he spoke to me.

"David, the next time I'm in town I'll be glad to talk with you about your rights as a veteran. Y'all take it easy, you hear?"

Within the next few weeks, I was sucked deeper and deeper into the hush-hush world of pimping and prostitution. I was making good money, and I had no problems with things that I could not change. The chicken sandwich that I got from the back door of the restaurant next door tasted just as good as the chicken that was served to the patrons seated at the tables. Equality and things like civil rights were not due for Negroes. Only an idiot would expect such outlandish things to occur. And, I was anything but an idiot.

I soon became an old hand at the business of bellhopping. I made enough money to be able to save quite a bit. No bank or savings account was needed. I did it the old-fashioned way. My stash was a half gallon jar hidden in a hole in back of the little shack.

Only one thing bothered me. I was still celibate. Even though it was by choice, it was still a hard pill to swallow. It would have been an easy matter to be with one of the white prostitutes. In fact, there were times during the month when the women would gladly grant their favors in exchange for loans to pay their rent until the first of the month. There was a catch though. I was still making most of my money from the sale of whiskey and tips. None of the seven women in the hotel would let me work as their pimp. All of them were afraid that I was too green and might get them arrested. There was just one of the girls who seemed to really like me. She was a thin, exceptionally good-looking little blonde from Georgia. Her name was Peggy Moon.

Returning Home

For a few weeks, I had been running errands and doing inconsequential things for Peggy. On a rainy night in February, she left a message for me with Julian. It was the beginning of the shift when he stopped me in the lobby.

"Hey Dave, if you get around to it, Peggy said for you to stop by for a few minutes. She wants to talk to you." I was less than enthusiastic.

"Aw man, I wonder what she wants with me? I ain't all heated up about going out in that rain. I got some things on my mind. I need a quiet night like this to figure them out." Julian looked at me for a moment.

"I don't know what it's about, Dave. But if I were you, I'd check it out. She could be talking money." He smirked. "You know how you are about money."

It was a slow night. Out in the street, the blustery wind was blowing the rain sideways, making it hammer on the plate glass windows of the stores adjoining the hotel. There was nothing doing in the lobby, so I decided to go up to the second floor and find out what Peggy wanted to see me about. When I knocked on the door, I heard a woman's muffled voice.

"All right, c'mon in. The door's unlocked."

I barged in and quickly closed the door behind me. It was force of habit when visiting the women for any reason. It was a good idea to open the door and get inside as quickly as possible. I looked at the bed and instinctively backed up.

"Ohh ohh, I didn't know y'all were busy!"

They were busy indeed. A big, burly bald-headed man with his back covered with hair and freckles was grunting and grinding furiously on top of the lithe body of Peggy Moon. My entrance into the room had not distracted either of them from their frantic pace. Her legs remained firmly scissored across his broad back. They simply ignored me completely and concentrated on doing what they were doing. I turned and placed my hand on the door knob.

"Excuse me, y'all. I sure didn't mean to disturb y'all. I'll come back later when you're not busy, Miss Peggy."

Without missing a twist, Miss Peggy peeped around the burly man's shoulders. "It's all right Dave. This is my husband Pete. You just wait there for a bit. This will only take a minute, you hear?"

Miss Peggy was absolutely right. Her husband was really working out. In fact, he hadn't missed a single stroke. As I watched, my faith in human nature was reaffirmed. There's nothing, absolutely nothing, that can compare with true love between a husband and wife. Fifty-eight seconds later, the agile Pete heaved a huge sigh and rolled away to the far side of the bed. His face was flushed, and he was still breathing hard. His watery eyes looked into mine.

"How you doing boy? Peggy told me about you. I think she's gonna give you a shot." He must have seen the expression on my face. He laughed out loud.

"Aw shit, boy! I didn't mean she was gonna give you a shot of tail. I was saying that she might let you do a little pimping."

The arrangement between Miss Peggy and myself worked out fine. I would always screen her clients, weeding out the ones that I thought she might have trouble with. I had accomplished a miracle of sorts. After being around a white woman in her most disarming and intimate moments, I still hadn't succumbed to my own desires. Upstairs, Julian and the women had their hands full. The spillover trickled down to Peggy and myself. She was a real trooper, eagerly taking on members of the 82nd Airborne, Field Artillery and raw recruits who were training at Fort Bragg. Every dogface on the base knew about the good times to be had at the Lafayette Hotel. Good old Pete, Peggy's faithful and adoring husband, was as pleased as punch. He would be especially happy when she would turn ten to 12 tricks a night.

One of the problems with members of the 82nd Airborne was keeping them quiet. General Gavin's "devils in baggy pants" would start to yell "Geronimo!" at the most inopportune moments. There were a few real Indians in the airborne, recruited because they were brave enough to be in one of the toughest outfits in the army. As for the assignations, it was essential that quiet be kept in this type of operation. There were ticklish times that kept my nerves teetering, as I walked the tightest of ropes. I should have known that at some point something would go awry, but I had no idea of the depth and magnitude.

It all happened on a Friday night when a big Indian paratrooper with a "Screaming Eagle" patch on his shoulder and a buck sergeant's stripes on his sleeves staggered into the hotel.

Returning Home

"Ohh ohh!"

If the trooper had been a big jovial white man, I wouldn't have worried too much. However, this was a Plains Indian, and he looked as if he had already had too much firewater. Julian wasn't around, so it was my immediate problem. I had to get to him before he reached the desk and Mrs. Dowling. I would urge him to go ahead and pay for his room and get him on the elevator and upstairs. Once that was done, I could notify Peggy that she had a prospective customer. I rushed over and met the trooper at the door. I whispered softly.

"Hey Sarge, just pay for your room. I'll fix you up with a woman when we get upstairs. "For Christ's sake, don't say anything to the clerk, just pay her. I'll be right up," I said fiercely.

After the paratrooper had registered, I carried him upstairs, sold him a pint of Three Feathers blend and then knocked on Peggy's door. When she opened the door, I could tell that she was ready for the night's work. She was beautiful as only a blue-eyed blonde in a red peekaboo negligee can be. I didn't waste any time.

"Listen Peggy, I got a customer for you. He's a paratrooper, and he's got plenty of money. You don't have to give him any liquor, he's high as a kite already." She nodded agreement.

"By the way, I don't suppose it makes any difference, but he's an Indian or maybe a Mexican. You don't mind do you?"

"No, I don't mind a bit," said Peggy. "I need some money. Pete blew every cent that I had at the stock car races in Darlington last week. Bring the sucker on in here. I'll fix him up."

I went down the hall to the trooper's room and knocked softly on the door. When he opened the door, I stepped inside. He was standing, rocking from side to side, much drunker than he had been before. He was gruff and to the point.

"I'm ready for a woman. You got a woman for me?"

I had misgivings for a second, and then I thought, "What the heck. He'll probably go to sleep."

"Sure Sarge. Just follow me, and I'll fix you right up. Aw man, this one's pretty as hell."

I led the way down to Peggy's room, knocked softly and when the door opened, I pushed him gently inside the room and closed the door.

Returning Home

When I got back downstairs, Julian was seated by the elevator. He had a disgusted look on his face.

"I could have stayed home tonight," he said. "I ain't made shit. That brunette and the redhead turned one trick apiece." He looked up at me. "What about you? You doing any good."

"Nah man, nothing doing here either. Peggy's doing a trick with a drunk Indian right now. It looks as if that's gonna be all for tonight."

Just then, a loud noise reverberated and something crashed into the street, landing right in front of the hotel. Julian and I hurried through the lobby and out into the street. There was glass lying everywhere. A screen and one half of a shutter were also lying in the street.

"Damn, Dave, it came from Peggy's room," said Julian. He looked looked up at the open window. "Good grief, what in the world do you have going on up there?"

"Man, I don't know. It looks like that Indian is raising holy hell in Peggy's room. I guess I better see what's going on up there."

I ran back inside, took the steps of the stairway next to the elevator two at a time and hurried down the hall to Peggy's room. I didn't knock. I just pushed the door open and went inside the room. The big Indian was buck-naked as he stood poised with one foot on the window sill. Peggy was cowed and huddled in the center of the bed. She looked as if she had been on the losing end of a ruckus with ten Indians and a medicine man. I looked around the room. The sparse hotel furniture was in shambles. Peggy screamed at me.

"Don't let him jump Dave! Get him out of here, quick, before the police come!"

"Awright dammit, but you've got to help me, Peggy. I can't do it by myself!"

The big man was beating his chest and babbling in some sort of Plains English. I didn't understand a word of it. I tried with Peggy's help to calm him. It took a superhuman effort by both of us to persuade the big man to come away from the window, put his clothes on and leave by the back stairs. Just then, a siren wailed in the street at the front of the hotel.

When I got back to the lobby, two policemen were questioning Mrs. Dowling about the broken window. She beckoned for me to come to the desk.

Returning Home

"What do you know about that broken window David? Did something happen upstairs?" I had to handle this very carefully.

"Yes ma'am Mrs. Dowling, something did happen. That lady in 204 claims that she has hay fever or some sort of allergy. She asked me to raise the window a little bit. I put a coke bottle under the sill."

I paused to see how she was taking my explanation.

"I had clean forgot to tell you that the window was loose and needed fixing. I guess it must have come loose and let go. I'm sorry ma'am. I plum forgot to tell you about it." Mrs. Dowling was a bit peeved. "David, I hired you to take care of things like that. I could have had the window fixed if I had known about it. Don't let it happen again, you hear?"

She turned to the two policeman and said sweetly, "I appreciate y'all stopping by, but everything seems to be all right. I'll be sure and get in touch if I need you."

The incident of the broken window had been a close call indeed. The bellhop's job was suddenly less appealing to me. Peggy, too, was highly upset. She had been traumatized by her bout with the angry warrior. She refused all comers, except the regulars that she knew. My personal income dropped dramatically.

"David," Peggy said. "For God's sake, don't bring me any more Indians, Orientals, or anybody that ain't jist plain white folk. That son of a gun almost killed me! He jist kept on doing it to me. It looked as if he would never finish. My behind is so sore that I can barely move."

It was not so with Julian. His business was booming. He was getting cocky and sure of himself. He began to refer to the prostitutes as his "mules." The constant flow of money to his pockets had made him what the colored folk called "nigger rich." It was inevitable that something would happen. Fate intervened on a Saturday night and changed Julian's life forever.

The Fayetteville law enforcement agencies worked closely with the army to curb prostitution, gambling and the use of drugs, which was a brand-new problem. The Lafayette Hotel had long been suspected as a haven for illegal activity. The raid was meticulously planned and well-executed.

In one fell swoop, the minions of the law descended upon the hotel. With warrants in hand, they opened doors and surprised the bewildered patrons. They did not find a single soldier or John in any of the rooms in the hotel. Julian was on a well-deserved retreat at the time. He had been holed up with the redhead and the brunette for the last couple of days in the brunette's room. When the authorities barged into the room, they found Julian lying cozily in bed between the two women. The minions of the law were dumbfounded.

Julian's audacity knew no bounds. He had always declared that two pieces of tail were better than one, and if they happened to be white, it was better still. Rumor had it that Julian and the two women were lying heads up and heads down, an odd but not unheard of position. The white lawmen were angry at what they considered to be a terrible affront to everything that they held dear. They beat Julian half to death before they locked him up.

Julian's bail was set as high as the law would allow. He was charged with white slavery, aiding and abetting prostitution and whatever else the judge could think of. If Fayetteville had not been such a cosmopolitan city, the probability that Julian would have been lynched would have become a certainty. The trial was a speedy affair, and there was certainly no doubt about Julian's guilt. The judge gave him 40 years, without benefit of a parole, at the state prison in Raleigh.

I quit my job at the hotel immediately. With the cunning of Stonewall Jackson, I had arrived at the decision to shun the very appearance of evil. The very thought of doing any more bellhopping at the hotel made me ill. The possibility of a jail sentence in the penitentiary no longer loomed above my head. I would do the right thing. It was time for the general to move on. There were other battles to fight.

12

Little Ed's Homecoming

Regardless of what had happened at the hotel, downtown was still a wonderful place to be. First-run movies at the three theaters were still okay, even if viewed from a segregated balcony designated "colored only." I also frequented the colored poolroom on Person Street. One of the larger furniture stores on Hay Street had a truly scientific marvel displayed in its window. It was something called a television set. I would stand at the window and the grainy screen for hours. I was always one for keeping up with the times. It was an integral part of the Jackson personna. Progress in Fayetteville was speeding along at a breakneck pace.

Julian's arrest and conviction made an interesting bit of news. It made the front page of the local paper and was also mentioned in several papers around the state. His case was ideal. It sent a stern message to other Negroes. It would let the younger Negro men understand and know without a doubt the pure folly of fooling around with white women. Well, it certainly made a believer out of me. I had read about the legal problems of the Scottsboro boys. It was nothing unusual to listen to the radio and hear about outrages done to Negroes or to pick up the newspaper and read about a lynching. The vehemence exhibited by the whites toward Negro men rose to a new level if white women were

Little Ed's Homecoming

involved. It was amazing. There was always an element of danger lurking wherever white women were concerned. I could understand being with a white woman in a closed environment like the Lafayette Hotel. I was glad that I had refused when offered the same exotic fare that got Julian into big trouble.

But, according to Uncle Joe and Julian's first-hand account, there was absolutely no difference between going to bed with a white woman and going to bed with a Negro woman. Both of them declared emphatically that the women smelled alike, and the end result was the same. But regardless of how you look at it, 40 years is a mighty long time to serve in jail for getting a single piece of tail. It was a terrible price to pay for a feeling that was over in seconds, an exorbitant fee for simply trying to scratch an itch.

Besides, at that moment I was too busy watching Fayetteville grow. The city was taking giant strides into the future, but even I was in no way prepared for what the city fathers did next. Another near-miracle occurred. The police department hired not one but two colored policemen to combat the burgeoning crime rate. It was a boon to everyone concerned. However, there were certain limitations. The colored policemen could only arrest the colored doers of misdeeds. That was okay because it gave the white lawmen more leeway to arrest both black and white. It was still a step in the right direction, reaffirming the fact that Fayetteville was ahead of its time.

The chief of police warned the new recruits. "Y'all know that you're not to arrest white folks, and don't arrest any white whores either. Leave them to the white officers. There's enough niggers breaking the law to keep y'all plenty busy."

I was proud of what the city had done, but I was a country boy at heart, and it was time to see what was happening on the Rose Hill Road. It was a long slow walk from the junction to our little shack, which assured me that life along the road was still traveling at its own pace.

The road and its inhabitants were going about their everyday business. However, there was an air of expectation, as if everyone were waiting with bated breath for something extraordinary to come about. Even the greenery of Spring sensed that something was about to happen, bursting forth in all of its glory, way ahead of schedule. The gardens grew rapidly. Their vegetables ripened overnight, astounded at the fresh new world that welcomed their birth. The bare trees budded immediately, putting the all-year evergreen trees to shame with their verdant brightness. There were a number of reasons for this strange phenomena. I thought of one, but I wasn't sure, and I wondered idly, could it be that it was because Little Ed Sawyer was coming home?

Little Ed was born in 1911 to Papa's younger sister, Esther. She had been the first of Grandpa's children to graduate from the state normal school for Negroes. It was the forerunner of the state teachers' college over on the Murchison Road. After Aunt Esther's disastrous affair with an older man named John Carter, the boy was born. Marriage between Aunt Esther and John Carter did not happen because Esther died of pneumonia shortly after Little Ed was born. Grandpa and Grandma reared him as best they could. There was no reason for Ed to grow up to be a bootlegger, rounder and a woman chaser. He was an accomplished self-taught trumpet player, who had traveled and played with colored bands all over the South. Little Ed had done that sort of thing ever since I had known him. In my opinion, he was second only to Stonewall Jackson. I had always admired him.

Little Ed was certainly due to come home. The war had been over for a year, and he had plenty of points to be eligible for discharge from the army. I could understand Ed's reasoning. He had talked about it just before he went overseas. Ed had wanted to stay in the army long enough to make enough money to build a decent home for his wife, Louise, and their children. Louise was the mother of four children, and only one of the children, a little girl, also named Louise, was conceived by Ed. The rest of the children were the product of his wife's previous marriage.

Neither the Sawyer family nor the Elliot family was brimming over with pleasure because of Ed and Louise's decision to marry. The Sawyers felt that Ed should not be taking on the burden of trying to take care of four children that were not his own. The Elliots were upset because Ed and Louise were actually third cousins, and according to them, that was too close for a comfortable marriage. But, both Ed and Louise firmly believed in the old adage, "The closer kin, the deeper in," and they practiced it diligently.

Louise was a beautiful woman. Nobody that ever looked at her

Little Ed's Homecoming

could deny that. Her skin was burnt olive, seared by the smoldering heat of quiet passion that lay just beneath the surface. Her eyes were grey-green, and her patrician nose was sculptured just right above a lush full mouth. Having four children had done nothing but enhance her beauty. She wore her curly hair in a stylish bob, and her stunning figure was as perfect as the rest of her, an equal and exciting match for the amorous and doting Ed. However, it was not a match made in heaven because heaven would not allow such mess. Neither the kingdom, the power nor the glory would condone the burning lust that smoldered and flared, blazing red hot between the two lovers.

Louise's color was fair enough. Even so, she could not pass for white, but the blood of the white men who looked upon her boiled at the sight of that sensuous woman.

Our family was completely blind to Louise's exotic beauty. It could see nothing but an opportunistic tramp bent on quickly getting her problems solved, a twice married woman of easy virtue, who took advantage of Ed's gullibility simply so that he could take care of her children.

Ed had been gone for three years, and for a woman like Louise, three years could be a lifetime. Nobody that knew Louise expected her to be the prim and proper soldier's wife, waiting patiently for her man to return from the wars. Even Ed did not think along such lines. In a close-knit community like the Rose Hill Road, there were no secrets.

Louise had not been carelessly open about her affairs. In fact, there had only been one serious relationship and that was not based on love and affection. It was primarily to satisfy the urgent needs that all but consumed the love-starved Louise, and besides, the man always came by way of the back door.

Jody Peet was the back door man. He lived with his own wife and children farther up the Rose Hill Road. He was a burly, good-looking black man, who made his living with his mule. In the Spring, Jody would break ground and run rows for the folk who had gardens along the road and and around the rural community. His ease in seducing the women whose gardens he plowed made him well-known for his plowing ability in their gardens as well as in their beds.

Jody Peet was well-suited to do the intimate plowing that Louise needed so badly. He obliged her often. There was no need to worry

Little Ed's Homecoming

about Jody's wife, Maria. She knew about his infidelities and loved him all the more in spite of his wayward ways.

When Louise heard that Little Ed was coming home, she blossomed boldly, blooming openly, slightly time-worn, but blooming nevertheless. She felt renewed and full of joy, just like the trees, shrubbery and flowers that surrounded the countryside. Louise sent Jody Peet packing. After all, he couldn't take it with him, and Ed certainly wouldn't miss something that he hadn't had for three years. Maybe memory would serve him well. Ed came home on a Saturday evening, and Louise's life suddenly changed for better or for worse. It was all according to how you looked at it.

I had been down on Jones Street, minding my own business, and I had just crossed the highway and was walking slowly down the brick-red dust of the Rose Hill Road. A car horn honked loudly, and an old Dodge touring car pulled up beside me. It was Charlie Jones at the wheel of his taxicab, and Little Ed was seated beside him grinning as only he could grin.

"Hot damn, if it ain't Little David Sawyer!" Ed cried. "Git in the car, boy! I ain't seen you in a month of Sundays." He was still grinning. "What's this shit that I heard about you being in the army? Whose army were they talking about?"

I was grinning too. I knew exactly what Ed was talking about. He knew that I had spent only a limited time in the army and did not go overseas. He was a hero of sorts, especially to Negroes who had followed the course of the war. Ed had been in the European theater of operations. He had driven the big quartermaster supply trucks that had brought food and munitions to the Allied soldiers at the front. When the trucks returned, they were often loaded with bodies of the soldiers who were killed.

The colored soldiers were proud of themselves and of their outfits. They were a race of dare devils, racing along the devilish route to hell. They drove quartermaster supply trucks and were known as members of "The Redball Express." The treacherous roads were dangerous enough, carved through narrow mountain passes and stretched across deep ravines. The presence of German machine guns and artillery fire that often raked the roads was a constant hazard. The black soldiers gunned

Little Ed's Homecoming

their engines, laughed at death and lived each day with gusto as if there were no tomorrow.

I was still grinning as I climbed quickly into the old touring car. I smacked Ed on the chin and hugged him at the same time. I looked him over carefully. There were a few grey hairs in his mustache, but basically Ed hadn't changed a bit. It was good to see him again.

"Yessir old buddy," I said. "I know you're glad to be home. You're just like the rest of them fools. Every time one of you nigger soldiers comes home, you bullshit everybody, telling them how you won the war single-handedly." I winked at Mr. Jones. "Y'all ought to quit that shit, Ed. It won't get you nothing but your feelings hurt. You're back in the heart of Dixie old buddy, and it sure as shit ain't what you been used to. In fact, it's worse than ever."

I was grandstanding, but Ed knew I was telling the truth. My line of bullshit got me nothing but a sour look from him. There was no way that I could talk to him about the army because he had been halfway across the world, teetering on the cutting edge of real trouble and dealing night and day with death and dying. I had been nowhere and seen nothing, except for bullshitting and play-acting in Oklahoma.

However, there was one thing that we had in common. We could talk about women and tail in particular. Ed was an authority. It was one of his favorite subjects, but things like that could wait until later. Ed had more important things to do. I could always catch him at a later date. I needed plenty of time with him, so that I could ask his honest opinion about my problem. It might be that Ed could tell me what I should do. I was just hoping that he wouldn't laugh at me. I'd had enough of that.

We made small talk for a bit, but Ed really didn't want to be bothered. When the old Dodge pulled into the yard between Aunt Lizzie's house and Ed and Louise's little place, his eyes were shining with wetness, and his breathing was ragged with anticipation. He turned to me.

"I'm gonna have to check with you later, Dave. I got things to do."

Mr. Charlie got out to help Ed with his bags.

"Jist sit the stuff on the porch," Ed said to Mr. Charlie. Ed smiled and squeezed my shoulders.

"Listen, Dave, old buddy, we'll have plenty of time to talk later. I ain't seen my old lady for three years." He winked broadly.

Little Ed's Homecoming

"Don't knock on my door under any circumstances. I'm sending the kids over to Aunt Lizzie's place." A wide grin crossed his face.

"I'll talk to you sometime next week or later. I'm gonna be doing some heavy duty fucking for the next few days. I got a lot of catching up to do." He licked his lips, still grinning.

"I'm a long-fucking fool, but you knew that, didn't you, Dave?"

Louise was standing in the door. Ed was still grinning as he ran across the yard and took her in his arms.

I turned away and walked into Aunt Lizzie's yard. There were several of the Jones Street bunch milling about the yard. Fast Fanny and Willie B were engaged in a heated conversation over by the porch. Aunt Lizzie's house and Ed and Louise's house were only about 50 feet apart, separated only by a small grassy plot. I could hear the sound of subdued voices coming from inside Aunt Lizzie's. That in itself was unusual because Auntie's business was mostly buy and run. The only logical reason for the the influx of customers was that Jones Street was bone dry.

Everybody liked the quality of Aunt Lizzie's liquor, but nobody liked to hear her mouth. Her caustic wit and accurate observations about the patrons' behavior would usually send the customer packing. I stood for for a moment, debating whether or not to go inside for a drink. I wasn't particular about hearing my aunt's mouth either.

She seemed to derive a special pleasure from fussing at me. I got the feeling that she knew everything about me. I wondered if she knew about my sexual problem. I decided that there was no way that Aunt Lizzie could know about it, and besides, it was Saturday and being celibate on a Saturday night in early Spring was not a good thing. I had to have help, and I was going to get it.

A double shot of crystal clear moonshine would begin the night that would end my vaunted celibacy. The powerful potion would make me strong, virile and as hard as times were in 1932.

Fast Fanny and Willie B were still standing near the steps of the porch. I grinned nastily.

"Excuse me, y'all. I got to see Aunt Lizzie about some drinking liquor." I pushed past the two of them.

"The Kid is getting ready to get down. Do y'all wanna join me?"

They declined, and I was about to open the door when I looked

Little Ed's Homecoming

over at Ed and Louise's place. From the way that Ed had talked, I figured that by now the two of them would be in bed, mired deep down in the chummy mud of requited love. I had no idea about what was happening now.

When Louise first came to the door, she was wearing a simple print dress, but anything that Louise wore shouted the same message. Now, she was wearing a shiny fur coat over the dress. As I watched, she had began to pirouette, with her hands caressing her full hips. I looked at Ed's face. He should have been pleased, but his thin face was ashy with rage. Suddenly, Ed voiced his anger in no uncertain terms, and the shrillness of Louise's rebuttal rang out loudly in the evening air. The commotion immediately got the attention of Aunt Lizzie's patrons. They stormed out of her little place and into the yard. All eyes were focused on Ed and Louise. The crowd wasn't being boorish or rude. It was just that it didn't want to miss anything.

It wasn't hard to figure out why Louise and Ed were arguing. It was about money. I knew, and most of the Jones Street folk knew, that for the past couple of years Ed had been sending Louise money to build a new house. Then, they could stop paying the $3 a week to Aunt Lizzie for rent, and they could have a much nicer house on Ed's own little lot over in the field. They were still arguing fiercely.

"Dammit Ed," screamed the enraged Louise, "I keep telling you, dammit, there jist ain't no money left! Me and the chillun had to eat, and they sure as hell can't go to school without shoes!" Their faces were almost touching each other. "I'm telling you Ed, it wasn't easy with you being away for three years. The only money that I spent on myself was for this fur coat. It ain't even mink, it is jist rabbit fur."

Ed was crazy with rage. He looked as if he were going to have a stroke. He kept gesticulating and cursing. The crowd moved close in unison. The children had disappeared somewhere in the rear of the house.

"Fool woman," said Ed angrily. "I lied. I stole. I broke every law that the army had. Black market, blue market, it didn't make a damn bit of difference 'cause the money was to build us a house!" He stopped to get his breath. "Shit, woman, I sent you over $3,000, and now you're telling me that all you have to show for it is a rabbit fur coat!" Ed looked up toward the sky.

"I'll be a sack of motherfuckers," yelled Ed. "Good Lord, will you look at what this crazy ass woman's done gone and done? Now, we ain't got a pot to piss in!"

Louise was just as angry as Ed. She did not look at all like a repentant housewife. Her lips curled, and her arrogant face was as cold as ice.

"I'm telling you like it is," said Louise. "If you don't like the way that I tried to keep things together, you kin let the door hit you where the bad dog bit you. I ain't got time to listen to your load of crap!"

Ed grabbed the fur coat and jerked Louise to him until their faces were almost touching.

"I'll fix this mother jumper!"

The coat split at the seams as he yanked it from her body. Louise looked on as Ed tore the sleeves and threw the coat piece by piece into the yard. He looked at Louise and pointed to the ragged bundle of fur lying in the yard.

"There's my money. There's my three years of ducking 88 shells and mortars and not knowing whether I'd live from one day to another."

He stood there, shaking his head and looking down at the remnants of the coat. Ed was not prepared for the slashing attack of Louise's claws. A scream of pure malice came from deep in her throat, as she dug her nails deep into his face.

Ed grabbed the neck of the print dress and jerked downward. The dress ripped apart as he roughly pushed her away. Ed threw it on the pile as Louise came at him again with her claws cocked and ready. She was wearing nothing but a brassiere, pink bloomers and rolled up stockings, but that did not hinder her fighting ability in the least.

All was fairly quiet. The Jones Street crowd was breathing sensibly. The on-lookers did not want to do anything to spoil the fun. Louise hit Ed smack in the face with as much force as she could muster. He hit her back, and then the two of them fell to the ground.

Louise's silk-stockinged legs were flailing, glinting boldly in the late evening sunlight and sharing quick glimpses of shocking pink with the Jones Street crowd. Ed and Louise were fighting like cats and dogs. The silken legs were still flailing madly when the pink bloomers somehow joined the remnants of the fur coat and the dress. The transformation from fierce antagonists to lusty lovers happened with unbelievable speed. One minute they were biting and scratching in heated anger, and the next minute they were biting, scratching and making love with an abandon that surprised and titillated the hardened folk of Jones Street. The crowd "oohed and aahed" as the red sea parted again and again. Soon, the miracle was over.

The Jones Street gang watched avidly as Ed and Louise shuddered simultaneously. The ending was the best part of their performance. It was great. The audience loved it. I was a little embarrassed for the two of them. I wished that they would have stopped long enough to go inside where they could have had privacy. It would have been the decent thing to do, but decency was not at the top of the list for neither Ed nor Louise. They sat up sheepishly, noticing the crowd for the first time and scrambled to their feet and hurried into the house.

Fast Fanny was suddenly standing beside me. One look at her face, and I knew that the spectacle that she had just witnessed had upset her to no end. I could sympathize with her because I was beset with the same problem. The sight of Ed and Louise making love had affected all of the people who had had seen love in the great outdoors. Fanny's voice was low, husky and urgent. "David, honey, I'm as hot as a $2 pistol."

Her face was flushed, and she was gasping for breath. The big lips pursed, and her long pink tongue came out for some air. Knowing Fanny, I believed every word that she said.

"If you got any money, Davy boy, you kin git this cherry. It's ripe and ready!"

"What do you think Fanny? I got my pants on, ain't I?"

We walked out of the yard and headed up the Rose Hill Road. We were both in trouble. By the time we reached the junction, we were both running. When we reached her little house, she almost tore the door from its hinges trying to get in. I didn't have time to even think about my problem.

It didn't take long. She started screaming right after we got in bed. The only thing that marred the quick interlude was Fanny's remarks as I went out of the door.

"I really needed that," she said. "You did pretty good, with what little you had to work with. I'll see you around, little David, you hear?"

I knew that with Fanny it was all business, but her remarks still hurt.

13

Square Business

At nine o'clock on a Monday morning, it was the beginning of another marvelous day. I was walking slowly down the Rose Hill Road. It was the kind of a morning that made you cherish every moment. The sweetly quick showers of April were gone, and a beaming May ushered in the promise of a brand-new Summer with an entirely different point of view. Flowers of every shade bloomed, peeking impudently through the briars and reeds along the dusty roadside. The infant season squirmed impatiently as it waited in the bright sunlight for its turn at the gaming tables. Nature in all its glory stretched languidly, like a haughty princess after a night of love. The soft trills of birds in the trees beside the road were her gentle sighs of satisfaction. I was in complete accord with everything that was happening around me.

I stood at the junction of Rose Hill Road and Raleigh Road. My mind was at peace for the moment, thinking nothing but pure ethereal thoughts about the beauty of nature, the incredible journey of mankind to its present state of being and my role in the scheme of things. Suddenly, a big, bright-red Indian motorcycle roared up to the intersection and came to a screeching halt right beside me. Its dazzling chrome handlebars and the silver logo of an Indian chief in full head dress on the gas tank gleamed in the bright sunlight. I was pleasantly surprised to see that the driver of the motorcycle was a woman and a pretty white woman at that.

She was perfectly dressed for the dare devil role that the scene implied. Her long black hair flowed from beneath an aeroplane cap complete with goggles. A white silk scarf was wrapped carelessly around her neck. I watched idly as the wind waved her hair, moving it and the scarf gently to and fro in the morning breeze. Her large eyes, pouting red lips and her lightly rouged cheeks gave notice that she knew exactly what she was doing. Arrogance was an integral part of her manner, and self-confidence was evident in the way she glanced at me. Beneath the incredibly long lashes, her eyes were deep blue, a fascinating mixture of fire and ice. A brown aviator's jacket and jodhpurs stuffed down into shiny black boots gave her thin, well-formed body the look of a woman of the world. My throat was suddenly dry. I knew when a woman was beautiful, whether she was white or black. At that moment, I was staring at beauty that had all the qualities of a perfect diamond, including its hardness.

She twisted the throttle and looked again in my direction, not really seeing me. Not seeing Negroes was easy for white folk. They did it all of the time. The ethereal thoughts vanished, and lecherous thoughts clouded my mind. The muscles tightened below my navel as I wondered idly who would be the recipient of the feelings generated in her supple body by the subtle vibrations of the big engine. As the red-hot cylinders muttered and growled between her shapely legs, how did it feel to know that the awesome power that she sat astride was hers and hers alone to control? I suspected that her lover would not have an easy time if he ventured to match his love-making with the stirring effects of her wild ride on the motorcycle. The poor fellow would catch holy hell trying to top the runaway feelings kindled by the big machine. My mind wallowed in the dirt, drooling like a mongrel dog in heat. It grasped the carnal imagery of the situation and hungrily squeezed it dry. Riding horses would probably cause the same erotic feelings of power and naked want. I'd bet my last dollar that the beautiful white woman was also an accomplished horsewoman.

Lusting after a white woman could be a dangerous business, even in a private situation. I was glad when a harsh noise blasted me out of my reverie. The engine of the big motorcycle sputtered and backfired. I blinked back to reality. The guttural rumblings of the big engine were exactly what I needed to get my mind out of the gutter. The pretty white lady looked both ways and gunned the motorcycle. Her blue eyes narrowed as she looked right through me again. The long black hair waved in the morning breeze as she roared away. The huge bike quickly gained speed as it roared up the Raleigh highway. I watched as the figure grew smaller and smaller and then faded from sight.

I shook my head to clear it. There were much more important things to think about. My stash was almost gone, and I needed money to support myself in the style that I liked. Caddying wouldn't do it, and I was out of the pimping business. I had to think of a way to make money without dealing with white folk. It wasn't that I hated white folk or anything like that. It was something I had learned ever since I was a boy: the less involvement with white people, the better it was for all concerned, especially me.

I was thinking about several things as I walked slowly down the hill: limited options that would help me to replenish my dwindling resources. I had a couple of stops to make along the road. I needed to talk to Ed simply because we really hadn't had a chance to talk. I wanted to know his plans for the future.

When I got to Ed's little place, I didn't knock on the door because he was out working on the little plot of land that he had purchased from Mr. Courtney. When I walked up, he was busy with a shovel trying to level an area for his new house. The lot was between the house that he and lived in and Uncle David's two acres. Ed was using a block machine to build blocks for his new house. It was a slow process. The machine was designed to make cinder block, but Fred was using it for sand instead of cinders. Sand worked just as well, and there was plenty of sand all over the place.

Ed stood up as I approached. His thin handsome face was bathed in sweat. He pulled a red handkerchief from the hip pocket of his khakis and began wiping his face and neck. His thin, wiry body was Sawyer to the core. He looked exactly like the rest of us. I was a little taller of course, but that was because I had inherited my height from Stonewall. The angry rays of the mid-morning sun were blistering hot, and Ed was sweating profusely. His face lit up as he looked at me.

"Well, if it ain't the little soldier boy. How you doing soldier boy? You seen any short-timers lately or any bullshitting too-scared-to-fight enlisted men?" A huge smile stretched across Ed's face.

"Tell me Davy, boy, did you start fucking yet, or are you still beating your meat?" His eyes narrowed as he watched my face.

"Do you think you'll ever get up enough nerve to eat pussy? It ain't half bad once you get used to it. If you kin git past the smell, you got it made. Everybody's doing it but you."

I grinned. I had to stop his line of crap in a hurry. Ed was talking that old army bullshit, and he was much better at it than I.

"Damn, Ed, old buddy," I said slowly, "going overseas and being in the war certainly gave you a dirty-ass mind. You should be ashamed of yourself talking like that. I'm gonna tell Louise to kick your ass. You were hell when you were well, but now you stay sick all of the time. There ain't no difference. You and I are in the same boat, trying to keep from kissing the behinds of these crazy-ass white folks. Neither of us have jobs and nothing to look forward to. What did they tell you down at the unemployment office?"

"Aw man, them bastards handed me a whole line of bullshit," said Ed. He shook his head in amazement. "After all of that stuff they told us about when we were discharged, it didn't mean a blame thing. They kept me running from the white employment office to a bullshit colored employment office down on Person Street." Ed thought for a minute.

"The long yaller nigger in charge didn't know his ass from a hole in the ground. They kept me going for two or three days, and I still didn't get shit. No job and no money, jist a whole lot of talk."

"You're talking about Mr. Williams, my high school shop teacher. The old fool can't help his damn self. He jist does what the white folks tell him to do. Forget about that shit. Let's go over and sit under that shade tree. It's too hot to talk out here in the sun."

I pointed to a small apple tree at the lower end of Uncle David's garden. We walked through the garden and sat at the base of the tree.

"I know exactly how you feel Ed. There was one half-ass job that came through the colored office. Old man Williams sent a bunch of us up to a canning factory in Delaware. The pay was 75 cents an hour, with ten cents taken from each hour to pay for living quarters. I wasted a whole Summer screwing around up there."

I looked at Ed. He was still frowning. I was curious.

"Tell me, Ed, what are you going to do now?"

"I tell you exactly what I'm gonna do. I'm going back to dealing corn liquor."

He must have noted the surprise on my face. Ed was aware I knew that Uncle Mike, Uncle Joe and he had been run out of Fayetteville for making liquor. Drew Carter, the revenue officer who had almost caught the three of them, was still in charge of the bureau.

"No, Dave, I don't mean that I'm gonna make liquor in the swamp again. This time I'm gonna buy my moonshine from the Indians down in Pembroke or Lumberton. I'll get it from the same ones that sell to Aunt Lizzie. She gets her moonshine from Lumberton. Those Indians ain't worth a fuck. All they want to do is drink and fight, but they do make some pretty good moonshine."

"Why don't you buy your shine from Mr. Williams from up near Godwin? He's the old white man who sells liquor to Uncle Mike. It's cheap too. It's just $15 a case." Ed was laughing.

"I'll swear Dave. You don't know shit about what's going on. Old man Williams went to jail. The revenuers caught him awhile ago. He's the one who invented the automatic carbine that the army uses. Now, he's rich and famous. They call him 'Carbine Williams.' Boy, you're crazy as a June bug. Whatever army you were in, you had to have fired the damn thing, and you didn't know a blame thing about it." Ed was enjoying himself.

Uncle Mike, Papa's younger brother, had been selling moonshine on the sly ever since he got out of the CCC. Since Uncle Joe had to quit selling moonshine because of his eyesight, the field was open for new business. Pegleg Pete wouldn't be any competition because he sold the worst liquor on Rose Hill Road. Pete would buy muddy liquor cheap. Then he would add Clorox bleach. The bleach would make the moonshine crystal clear. In a really bad batch, you could smell the Clorox fumes. Folk would buy from Pegleg only if nothing else was available. Ed would be the fourth bootlegger within a radius of two and a half miles. I was already calculating the risks involved and the money to be made. A plan was slowly forming in my mind. I needed to know more about the bootleg business.

"Hey, Ed, when you gonna start this mess?"

"I'm hustling a little bit of liquor now," he said. "I got to be mighty careful though and keep a sharp lookout for the law. They won't treat me like they do Aunt Lizzie. If they catch me, they'll burn me a new ass hole." He paused for a moment. "And besides, Louise don't want them Jones Street niggers hanging around her house and messing with her chillun." Ed sighed. "Dave, I tell you for a fact, it ain't easy. I'm still playing catch up with Louise. Three years is a long time. I been doing it to her night after night and trying to build a house during the day. It's kinda hard, and it's putting a helluva strain on me." He sighed again and shook his head slowly. "Aw man she's good. The best I've ever seen, but I had no idea she'd want to fuck all the time. Louise's jist too hot to handle! I'll be glad when she settles down. I tell you for a fact Dave, she's putting a hurting on my ass."

Ooh ohh, he wasn't bragging, he was complaining. Ed needed help, an angel of mercy or a devil in disguise. I suspected that Jody Peet, angel or devil, was hovering in the background, willing and anxious to help. I had thought about discussing my sexual hangup with Ed, but he seemed to have his hands full at the moment. I would check with him later, but I didn't see his situation improving at all.

I was reflective. It was probably a good thing that Louise had had the services of a back door man in Ed's absence. Even with the help of Jody Peet in his absence, Ed was in trouble when he came home from the wars. Louise was slowly killing him with kindness. Her continued show of affection could possibly put Ed in the VA hospital. As it was, Ed didn't know a thing about what went on during his absence. Memory and the present served him in good stead. He was hopeful that he would soon catch up. Ed felt that he had it made, if he could just outlive it.

"I ain't got no more time to mess around," Ed declared. "I'm jist renting that block machine. It costs an arm and a leg. Your Daddy's 'spose to help me git some timbers from Grandpa's woods." He looked at the partially finished foundation.

"I'll swear David, if I had known that all of this hard ass work was involved in building a house, I never would have tried it."

"I know exactly what you mean, Ed." It was time for me to leave. I had a lot of thinking to do.

"Well, I got to move on." I looked slyly at Ed.

"You take it anyway you can get it, old buddy. I got to go and see what's on the limb for the lizard."

I left Ed's construction project and walked slowly back up the short distance to the road. I was still thinking about my new enterprise and analyzing just how the system worked.

Each bootlegger had his own particular customers. Some of them liked the conviviality of sharing a drink with Uncle Mike. White folk and others liked Aunt Lizzie's place. Her moonshine was superb, real easy-drinking liquor. Ed's business was fairly new, but for the ones who had seen Louise's body writhing buck-naked on the porch, Fred's bootleg operation was the one of choice. Louise's performance that evening on the porch definitely gave impetus to Ed's growing business.

Unlike Ed's bootlegging enterprise, Pegleg Pete's place was the last resort. There were times when he wouldn't drink his own liquor.

It was all settled in my mind. I was going to put my plan into action. There were other lucrative roads and streets around Fayetteville, but the Rose Hill Road's proximity to Fort Bragg made it an ideal place to sell moonshine and other skullduggery-like enterprises. I would make the road my own personal bootlegging joint. The doors, always open, would be any spaces between the tall pine and oak that lined the road. The thick canopy above the swamp would my ceiling, and my stash would be anywhere I wanted it to be. I was the wily General Stonewall Jackson, and once again I would be planning a course of action from the swamp, my favorite lair. From that vantage point, I could do battle with poverty and the racial vagaries of white folk, two powerful enemies indeed. It would take all of the cunning and resourcefulness of Stonewall, but I would certainly win. The swamp was my domain.

A few days later, I stopped by Uncle Mike's place. I was going to need his help to put my plan into operation. Uncle Mike's neat little house was in a small grove of pines just off the road. Flowers ringed the front of the little cottage, and a summer garden nestled on either side.

At the rear of the house were doghouses with a barbed wire fence stretched around them. Hunting was a passion with Uncle Mike. He raised rabbit and deer hounds to sell to hunters around the county. He also sold more moonshine liquor than anybody else on the Rose Hill Road.

His wife, Aunt Elma, was a short heavy-set mulatto woman with brown hair. She didn't like me at all, possibly because of the episode with Miz Hannah. I felt decidedly uncomfortable around her, so I usually tried to catch Uncle Mike outdoors. I was lucky. He was just coming out of the house.

Uncle Mike was short, heavy-set, but not as big as Uncle Joe. He was wearing a slouch hat, overalls and brogans suitable for his numerous trips to the swamp. His eyes twinkled, and there was a huge smile on his broad face.

"Well, knock me for a loop if it ain't Little David! How you doing fella? Ain't seen you but once or twice since you got out of the army." His eyes were still laughing.

"How's old lady Hannah doing? I heard that you've been trying to help Joe take care of business. I didn't know you had that kind of nerve."

"Aw, Uncle Mike, y'all ought to stop messing with me about that. Anybody can make a mistake."

His eyes were still twinkling merrily. I knew that he was having fun playing around with me. It suddenly occurred to me that I was talking to the smartest and shrewdest of the Sawyer brothers. I had considered asking Uncle Mike about his source for his operation, but that wouldn't have been very wise. It would be better for me to find my own source, and then let the news break gradually. Everybody would know soon enough.

"I'm just taking it easy for a while, doing exactly like you, Uncle Mike, walking slow and figuring out what to do next." He shook his head and frowned slightly.

"I don't know about you David," he said softly. "You need something to do. The white folk will quit watching you if you find yourself some gainful employment. You been bullshitting ever since you got outta the army." He paused for a moment.

"You kinda got a thing against honest work, ain'tcha?" he asked. Just then his wife appeared in the door.

"Nah, Mike," said Aunt Elma, as she looked down her nose at me. "All Little David wants to do is loaf up and down the Rose Hill Road and mess with other folks' women. He is one sorry cuss. Nobody with any sense would be common enough to be with somebody, especially somebody old enough to be his ma, and then put her business in the street like he did," she snarled nastily. "Ain't no getting around it, he's a piss-poor excuse for a man, sorry as all get-out."

"The boy's okay Elma," said Uncle Mike soothingly. "Give him some slack. He probably couldn't help himself. I keep telling you that a stiff dick ain't got no conscience. Little David's awright. He's jist got a lot to learn." There was a half smile on his broad face.

"Lemme know when you're ready, David. "I'll let you work with me at the sawmill. You'll like it. The hard work will toughen you up and do you good."

Uncle Mike was letting me off easy. If Aunt Elma hadn't been standing there, he would have lectured me in no uncertain terms. Uncle Mike knew the neighborhood, and he knew everything that happened in it, including the forced medication administered to me and the upstanding citizens of Jones Street.

I left Uncle Mike and Aunt Elma shaking their heads. I didn't have time for small talk. It was time to put my plan into action. The war and the fact that legal whiskey had been rationed had created an upsurge in the number of whiskey stills around the county. I would be careful and buy my moonshine from the Croatan Indians down around Lumberton or Pembroke. They were the best in the business when it came to making good liquor. The revenue officers were always looking for bootleg whiskey houses and raided them with alarming regularity. I figured that the smart thing to do would be to sell the moonshine from different locations along the Rose Hill Road. The plan was simple. All that was required was a good memory. Every tree stump, bush, tuft of grass or hollow log was a potential hiding place.

In order to convict, the revenue officers would first have to prove ownership and prove intent to sell, and unless you sold directly to the law, they couldn't prove a thing. The idea was to collect the money from the customer and then tell him where to look. The moonshine would not be on my property. The swamp, trees and bushes were mine in a sense, but they really belonged to the ages.

The plan worked just as I figured it would. My source was an old Indian from Pembroke named Henry Lowry. He had been named for a folk hero, who had been a Croatan tribal leader. Henry made the smoothest-drinking liquor that I had ever tasted. That fact alone helped my business tremendously. In a few weeks, I was a familiar sight along the road. I wore army camouflage fatigues, complete with cap and combat boots suitable for walking in the swamp. I knew how to stand or sit

Square Business

motionless and remain practically invisible, unless I wanted to be seen. Business was booming. The word was out.

"If you want good moonshine, see Little David Sawyer. That slick mammy-tamper will fix you up good."

The sun was mid-Summer hot on a Saturday evening, and I was sitting on the ditch bank, not too far from the bridge. I was counting my money. The wrinkled bills collected in a hurry was no longer a Philadelphia roll. I was getting accustomed to handling big money.

A white 1940 Ford, pulled over and stopped directly in front of where I was sitting. The driver was a big florid-faced white man, smoking a large cigar. I stood up, brushed my pants off and waited for him to speak. The cigar moved carelessly in his big mouth, and saliva dripped from the soaked tip, running from the corners of his mouth. It had been out for a while. He stumbled out of the car and stood beside it, rocking unsteadily. I knew that he was more than a little intoxicated. He was just plain drunk. His little pig eyes peered into mine.

"Listen boy, I need a pint of shine. Kin you git it for me? I want good liquor, none of that Clorox crap."

"Yessir, I might be able to help you, but it'll cost you $4 though."

I looked him over carefully to make sure he wasn't law.

"You'll have to wait here a couple of minutes. I'll be right back," I advised him.

I walked a little ways down into the swamp, reached behind a small poplar and pulled out a quart of moonshine. He was sitting on the bank when I returned.

"Look mister, the only thing I got left is a quart. I'll let you have it, but it'll cost you $8."

He fumbled in his pocket and came out with a large roll of bills. He peeled off a ten and handed it to me.

"Keep the change."

He leaned closer. His breath was the very essence of foulness. The acrid smell of stale alcohol and tobacco almost took my breath away. His hoarse voice fanned my face with a conspiratorial whisper. "Listen boy, do you think that you could fix me up with a colored gal? I ain't had me no colored meat in a month of Sundays." His face was close enough that

I could see the veins bulging in his neck.

"If you kin fix me up, I'll make it worth your while, boy. I need a piece of nigra tail to change my luck."

I was slow to answer. I had learned that you had to be really careful about what you said to white folks. It took a minute for me to give him the proper answer.

"I'd sure like to help you mister, but I'll swear I can't think of a single gal right this minute. But, if you come back a little later, I might can get you straightened out."

He took a long swig out of the jar and wiped his mouth with the back of his hand. "Awright boy, I jist might do jist that," said the befuddled redneck. Clumsily, he climbed back into the white Ford. It started on the second try, and he weaved from side to side, barely missing the ditches on either side of the road as he headed up the Road Hill Road.

I pulled out my roll and folded the ten around it. The day had been fairly lucrative, and there was still a couple of hours of daylight left. Everything was going as planned.

I was about to call it a day and walk down to Pegleg's place when I looked down the road and saw a figure coming toward me. I recognized her at once: that swaying seductive walk could only belong to Fast Fanny. She was the only person whom I knew who could take a simple walk and turn it into something nasty, suggestive and just plain wicked.

As she came near, I wondered what she was doing this far up the road. She had already passed Aunt Lizzie's, Ed's place, Uncle Mike's little house and Pegleg's place. She walked up to where I was seated and placed her hands on her ample hips. "What's happening sport? Have you got any liquor?"

I looked at her lush body. Lord have mercy! Her earthy smell tickled my nostrils. Suddenly my senses were alive and kicking. She was a tramp in every sense of the word.

"Sure I got liquor. I'm in the liquor business. What kind of business are you in, Fanny?" I thought for a minute, then looked directly into her eyes.

"Damn girl, you always show up at the wrong-ass time. I jist had a cracker here with a roll that was big enough to burn a wet mule. And guess what? He wanted to buy a piece of colored tail. You got some colored tail, ain't you Fanny?"

Square Business

"Where is the sucker?" asked Fanny. "I'll lay some tail on him quicker than a cat kin lick his lips."

She looked first one way and then the other. At that point, I looked up the road and saw the white Ford weaving from side to side coming slowly down the road.

"Get outta the way," said Fanny. "Here comes a fool!"

I grabbed her by the arm. "Listen Fanny, that's the cracker I was telling you about. I'm gonna get y'all together. Don't do it in his car. Take him down in the swamp. After you screw him, he'll probably go right to sleep."

I could tell by her face that she was beginning to understand.

"Listen, you clip him for that roll, and you clip him good. Don't try to bullshit me. I want my half, and I want it as soon as you come out of the swamp."

I had to talk fast because the white car was pulling up beside us. I whispered fiercely.

"One other thing, Fanny. Take him far enough down in the swamp so nobody can hear you screaming. You ought to quit that mess."

It was almost half an hour later when Fanny came out of the swamp. She hadn't even worked up a sweat. I hadn't heard any screams and that was unusual. Usually Fanny could be heard by anybody within a mile of the vicinity. She definitely needed to work on that part of her act. Her hips were swinging like always, and she was grinning slyly as she approached me.

"Aw man, that was too easy," she boasted. I watched as she moved her dress aside and began rubbing her inner thigh.

"I tell you for a fact, David, white folks are crazy as shit. That cracker didn't even try to fuck me. He jist bit me twice on my thigh and then went right to sleep. It took all of two minutes." She was grinning scornfully.

"I had to make sure he was asleep before I took his money. I declare. White folks can't do nothing at all." She paused. "You know you were dead wrong, or you can't see worth a shit. That cracker didn't have but $60. She fumbled inside her bosom. "Here, your half is $30."

I slapped her as hard as I could and grabbed both of her arms.

"Listen, you conniving slut. Gimme my money, and I do mean all of my money. I set you up so that you can get hold of some real money, and you try to put shit in the game! Drop my money out bitch!"

She leaned against me, suddenly as docile as a lamb. Her long lashes brushed her cheeks as she looked demurely into my eyes.

"David, honey, don't be mad. I was jist messing with you. That fool had $160. I got your half right here." The lashes fluttered prettily, and the full lips pouted.

"Unless, you wanna knock $10 off for a quick piece."

Her large brown eyes were pools of hunger. I knew that she was excited. The thrill of taking the white man for his money was the reason. She was as hot as a box of kitchen matches. The lashes fluttered again.

"That cracker didn't even git my motor running. If you got the money, honey, I got the time." She wiggled her butt suggestively.

"C'mon Dave, let's do the Honky Tonk!" I shook my head firmly.

"No Fanny. Not today girl. I'm a businessman. I ain't got time for no mess like that."

She reluctantly handed me the four crumpled $20 bills. She looked at me for a long moment, then turned away. I couldn't understand Fanny at all. I didn't know why she was forever belittling my sexual prowess, and yet she seemed to want to be around me.

Was it togetherness that she was seeking, or did she really want me? Somehow the question of sex always came up. I was going to have to give that a lot of thought. A tinge of regret came over me as I stood and watched her walk slowly back down the Rose Hill Road. The earthy artistry of her swaying strides was a wonder to watch. She really wasn't a bad person and would be even better if she could stop screaming like a banshee when folk were doing it to her. In her line of work, it was unnerving as hell and quite a distraction.

14

Ducking the Law

My bootleg business flourished. Aunt Lizzie, Ed, Uncle Mike and Pegleg Pete were a little surprised and perturbed by my success, but there was enough money to be made by everyone. With money comes power, respect, adulation and a sense of complete control. I wallowed in the feelings. The beauty of my operation was that I could move it anywhere along the Rose Hill Road. All I had to do was to inform Henry Lowry just where to unload the cases of moonshine. Later that night, his old Model A Ford would come roaring down the road. He would drop the cases of liquor in whatever part of the swamp that we decided on and take off, with the old Ford sputtering and popping as it disappeared from sight.

Uncle David, Papa's brother, who was a renowned minister, and his wife, Aunt Mary, would have been flabbergasted to know that on a recent weekend, I had hidden 16 pints of shine in the flowers that lined the path that led from the road to their little house. They did not know what caused the sudden surge of pedestrian traffic in front of the house or the rowdy language that accompanied it. My aunt and uncle's property was not alone. I had hidden pints and quarts of whiskey all up and down the road.

Like any smart businessman, I knew when to it was time to expand.

Ducking the Law

Venture capital was at my disposal, and besides, I had begun to handle merchandise other than cash. Typewriters, guns, watches and other moveable items were quickly accepted in trade for Henry Lowry's crystal clear moonshine. An old army tarpaulin hidden deep in the swamp covered a multitude of sinful contraband. Soon, regardless of the item in question, I could get it for my patrons wholesale.

A skinny black girl named Susie Q brought me stylish suits that had been shoplifted from Sears. I saw her once in the store on a busy Saturday. It was fascinating to watch her work. She always wore long-flared skirts and sensible shoes. I never did figure out how she managed to walk out of the store with a full-sized table model radio between her legs. I sold the radio as soon as I got it. Radios, pistols and shotguns went like hotcakes. It was a risky endeavor, but I was brave like Stonewall Jackson, and risk was a part of the game.

There was one thing that I had to do as soon as possible. I needed a flunky. All of the bootleggers along the road had someone to do their menial chores: run errands, help in the garden and deliver liquor to known customers. The person that I had in mind was a long, lanky good-natured, middle-aged man named Lengthy Walker. For a drink of whiskey, a few dollars and some conversation, he would do anything that he was asked. He could usually be found somewhere along the Rose Hill Road, especially in late afternoon. I did not have to look him up. He came to me. He was walking up the road past the dairy when I stepped out of the woods ahead of him.

His handsome face was a question mark as he looked at me.

"Hey Little David, I heard that you wanted to see me?" I waited a moment before answering him.

"Yeah Lengthy. I did kinda want to talk to you."

I was watching his face closely. Lengthy was nobody's fool. That was why I had picked him. He also had a reputation as a ladies' man. I had often wondered why. Maybe it was because of his name. Anyhow, he had no problem getting women. They flocked to his side, like birds hunting worms after an April downpour. His brow wrinkled.

"I was wondering if you would do a little hustling for me, nothing dangerous, just small time stuff. I'll pay you pretty good."

His eyes narrowed. He was definitely interested. I reached into my

Ducking the Law

pocket, pulled out a ten dollar bill and handed it to him.

"Here, this is on account. It'll get better as time marches on."

Greed immediately took a front seat in that airy theater of the deep swamp. Lengthy was hooked like a channel catfish. "Jist what did you have in mind Dave? I'm ready anytime."

I laid it out for him. Weekends would be the busiest times. I would have to get him a set of camouflage fatigues and combat boots for moving around in the swamp. He would be almost invisible too and that was necessary if my business were to thrive. I also had to replenish my stock of insect repellant. The mosquitoes in the swamp at that time of the year were as big as dragonflies.

In a couple of days, it was all settled. Lengthy would be working exclusively for me. The amount of alcohol that he could consume on any given day was unbelievable, but his astute way of dealing with the customers more than made up for his heavy consumption of booze. His manner was easy, and his demeanor was above reproach. The days flew by, and Lengthy was just as helpful as I thought he would be. With his camouflage fatigues, insect repellent and boots, he could maneuver in the swamp as well as I. I was careful never to let him know where my main stash was hidden. After all, there is a limit to blind trust. There was one other thing, which was more of an enigma than a problem. I knew that Lengthy was a ladies' man, but I had absolutely no idea of the extent of his involvement with scores of women.

On a Sunday morning in late June, I learned that Lengthy's women folk were not just the overripe women of Jones Street but also people of high regard.

A 1939 Ford pulled up just as Lengthy was coming out of the woods. I faded back into the woods as Lengthy walked nonchalantly up to the car. A light-skinned middle-aged woman with greying hair and gold-rimmed glasses stepped briskly from the car and walked around the front. She looked awfully familiar, and suddenly it dawned on me that I knew the woman only too well. It was my seventh grade teacher, Mrs. Wendy Jones. She was a tall, well-built woman, slightly on the heavy side with long shapely legs. In school, we had called her one cold fish. She was also strict, mean and arrogant, with all of the other qualities that make a mean teacher, including the use of a metal ruler for knuckles and

163

Ducking the Law

a paddle just in case.

Mrs. Jones and Lengthy were on equal footing as they stood beside the shiny Ford eyeing each other. She was looking directly into his eyes, and she did not look or sound overbearing. I had never seen her like that.

"Mr. Walker, could you come up to the house with me for a minute?" Mrs. Jones asked. "I've got something that I want you to do."

Her voice was hoarse. Whatever she wanted was decidedly urgent.

"Henry's away until tomorrow evening. Please Mr. Walker, will you come?"

Her lips were trembling. I couldn't figure out what was going on. Lengthy was his usual laconic self.

"I declare Mrs. Jones. I just can't make it right now. I've got a couple of things to do that just won't wait," Lengthy said smiling politely. "Maybe I can get over that way tomorrow evening. I could take care of it then." Mrs. Wendy Jones started to cry.

"Damn you to hell, Lengthy Walker!"

I watched in unbelief as she slapped the side of Lengthy's face as hard as she could.

"You just wait until I ask you again! You bastard!"

She ran around to the driver's side of the automobile, jumped in and a moment later the shiny Ford roared away.

Lengthy watched until the car disappeared, then turned with a slight smile on his face and walked across the ditch to where I was standing.

"I swear to God Dave. Sometimes women can be a pain in the ass. They want it when they want it, with no consideration for nobody else." He was shaking his head. "Sometimes I jist don't want to be bothered. Dave. if I screwed every time women wanted me to, I'd be deader than hell."

"Aw man, Lengthy, I guess I know what you mean."

I was lying in my teeth. I didn't know what he meant. Neither did I have the slightest idea how he could get a woman like Mrs. Wendy Jones. She was the soul of respectability, and I couldn't for the life of me see what Mrs. Jones saw in Lengthy.

The rest of the day went smoothly. The money flowed into my pockets from every source imaginable. The sun was dipping slowly behind the trees. Lengthy and I were sitting on the ditch bank counting

Ducking the Law

the day's take. A car was coming down the road toward us. I recognized it at once. The anxious Mrs. Jones was back. I stood up quickly and faded into the woods. I definitely did not want to be seen at that point. The black 1939 Ford suddenly screeched to a stop, and Mrs. Jones stepped out and walked over to the side of the road. Lengthy did not get up to greet her. In fact, he acted as if she weren't there. She stamped her feet.

"Lengthy, don't do this to me!" She was on the verge of crying again. "Please Lengthy, just give me a few minutes. I've got to see you!"

"Damn! You are a pain in the ass!" Lengthy told her. He pointed to the lovers' lane just up the road on the left.

"Listen Wendy, drive a little ways up that woods road and park. Wait for me. I'll be up there in a minute."

With a sigh of pure relief, she got back into the Ford and drove the few yards to Lovers' Lane. Lengthy watched until the tail end of the Ford disappeared into the brush. He stepped across the ditch and walked slowly up the road and turned in behind the Ford.

I stood there in the brush for a moment, still trying to figure out why Mrs. Jones was in such a dither about seeing Lengthy. It was not just simple curiosity on my part. I had to know the reasons why. I walked quietly through the woods until I was in some thick brush just a few feet from the Ford. I was on familiar ground. The reluctant voyeur was at it again, but this was important. I had my reasons for watching them. I also had a burning need to know. The shock was not as great as I had expected. But, seeing my grade schoolteacher in the back seat of the Ford, with her right leg hanging over the driver's seat, and her left leg jammed against the rear window of the Ford, and seeing Lengthy's angular body buried deep between her legs, did give me pause. Mrs. Jones's role as a grade schoolteacher was correctness always, and propriety itself forbade such actions. It was plain to see that she was not a stickler for the mores and restraints that governed the actions of common people.

Lengthy Walker was in his world, working diligently at what he did best. The slow rhythmic movement of his posterior left no doubt. He knew exactly what he was doing, and every thrust of his virile body elicited a delicious moan of pure pleasure from the pliable Mrs. Jones. As the thrusts became more pronounced, I had to reassess my opinion of Mrs. Jones. She was anything but a cold fish.

Ducking the Law

The women continued to come from up and down the Rose Hill Road to see and to be with Lengthy Walker. It was amazing. My business did not suffer, but it was quite distracting. Some of the women acted forcefully, and some were begging, almost in tears, but they all desperately wanted the undivided attention of Lengthy Walker. Even the wife of Reverend Lonnie Pierce came occasionally. I watched with a jaundiced eye as a constant parade of women converged on my domain, not for my liquor, or to enjoy the majestic beauty and quiet greenness of the swamp. They came for the same reason: to enjoy the smooth expertness of the sexual ministrations administered by the affable black man. All of the women wanted to see, feel and be touched in secret places by the irresistible magic of Lengthy Walker.

During the long hours spent together in the swamp, I formed a real friendship with Lengthy. After repeated tries, I finally got him to talk about himself. From the flawless diction of his measured speech, I knew that he was educated. The connection between Mrs. Jones and himself came about because the two of them had been with the same school system. His given name was Charles, and before his descent into the utter darkness and oblivion of an alcohol dependant, he had been a physical education teacher with a wife and two children, a boy and a girl. However, at that point he was perfectly satisfied with a life filled with plenty of women and the crystal clear, good-drinking moonshine delivered on request by Henry Lowry. In fact, life was especially good to both of us, until the law enforcement units of the Cumberland County ABC gave us their full attention.

The revenue officers began to patrol every inch of the Rose Hill Road, paying real close attention to the areas where liquor was sold. During peak hours, from Friday night until Sunday night, they buzzed like flies all up and down the road. Papa was quite surprised and a trifle upset when they raided the little shack on a Friday night. They searched the premises thoroughly, hoping to find any amount, large or small, of illegal liquor. After the raid at Papa's place, Ed, Uncle Mike and Pegleg became extra careful about how they handled liquor and to whom they sold it to. Aunt Lizzie had no problems. They would not bother her at all. I was not naive enough to think that they didn't know all about my methods and means of distribution. But, they would have to catch me and that was exactly what they set out to do.

It was on a Sunday in mid-afternoon when two carloads of officers came from opposite directions on the Rose Hill Road and met at the bridge. As soon as I saw them, Lengthy and I made a beeline for the deepest part of the swamp. We crossed the creek and went up a small hill and sat under the shade of a poplar tree. There was nothing else that we could do because the revenue officers might be searching the swamp for the rest of the day. The July sun was beaming down through the branches of the poplar. Big swamp mosquitoes were buzzing around us. They weren't biting because of the repellant, but they were worrisome as hell. Lengthy looked up at the sun.

"Damn Dave, we're going to fry sitting here in the sun." He stood up and began to remove his clothes.

"Let's beat the mosquitoes into the creek. I'm burning up! I've got to cool off."

"Aw man, you said a mouthful. Let's go!" I came out of my clothes in a hurry. We jumped into the creek, splashing water in every direction. The creek wasn't very deep, just waist high, and we had to sit in a hurry because the water washed away the insect repellant. We stayed in the creek for more than an hour. The water was cool, and we really had nothing else to do. I sat there in the little stream and tried to figure out exactly what I wanted to talk to Lengthy about. I was still curious about his prowess with women. I was about to speak when Lengthy looked up at the sun. "Dave. I'm kinda cooled off. I could use me a drink of liquor. What do you think?" He looked toward the road. "I wonder if those booze hounds are still out there?" I was ready too.

"I swear I don't know Lengthy." I moved toward the creek bank. "Let's get out of here and go see what's happening. That is if we can get by these flying buzzards."

Lengthy climbed out of the creek before I did. He grabbed his undershirt and began to dry himself. I was about to climb out of the creek when he turned toward me. I gasped and almost fell back into the creek. When I looked up, I was staring directly at the matted hair below his navel. What I saw was absolutely incredible. I couldn't believe my eyes. The celebrated Lengthy Walker, errant Casanova, renowned lover of scores of women, had a penis as small as my own.

Ducking the Law

To stare was rude. I stuttered badly, desperately trying to regain my composure. "Damn mosquitoes gonna eat me up if I don't hurry!"

I hurriedly began to dress. I looked over at Lengthy. He had almost finished dressing, and he was not the least bit uncomfortable. In fact, he had not even noticed that I was staring at him. Now, I was really puzzled. Because of all the women in his life, I had just assumed that Lengthy was more than well-endowed. Hence the nickname and his propensity for getting any woman that he chose. I was elated to find that I had been terribly wrong. Now, it was imperative. I had to know the secret of his charm and magnetism. There was hope for me yet if I could just learn how he performed the white magic that drew women to him like moths to a flickering flame.

A little learning is not necessarily a dangerous thing. I needed more knowledge as quickly as possible, and I would get it at the feet of the oracle himself. Slow-walking, easy-talking Lengthy Walker would be my learning tree. But, that would have to come later. Right then, Lengthy and I had to figure a way to get out of the swamp. The revenue officers were all up and down the road, and some were on the edge of the swamp. There was no way that we could account for our presence in the swamp. When we had finished dressing, sweat was pouring from our bodies.

"Hey Dave, which way are we going to get out of here?" Lengthy asked. He looked around nervously. "I sure as hell don't want to run into none of those suckers. They would lock both of us up just for the hell of it and throw away the key."

I thought for a minute. The little creek ran parallel to the Rose Hill Road. From where we were standing, it twisted and turned all the way up past Grandpa's place. Its origin was Slater's pond, which was down in the swamp behind Grandpa's little vegetable farm.

"I tell you what we're gonna do Lengthy." Wheels were still turning. "It don't make sense to go back across the creek and run right into the law. Let's go up the hill." I pointed to a small stand of scrub pine. "We'll be away from the mosquitoes, and we can follow the creek until we get up near Grandpa's place. Then, we'll cross the creek again and go past his house and on up the hill to Papa's."

Lengthy nodded his assent, and we hurried up the hill, slapping haphazardly at the big mosquitoes, which showed their displeasure at our leaving by trying to eat us alive. Well, we had gotten away from the lawmen. Even if they found us, there was no way that they could tie us to anything concerning the swamp. As we walked through the brush, I was still thinking about how to discuss my hang up with Lengthy. I had no qualms about telling him the source of my problem. After all, we had a little something in common. The time was not right at that moment. I would catch him later under more pleasant circumstances. Later, I would find a cool spot, sit a half gallon of Henry Lowry's best moonshine between us, and then we would talk.

Lengthy was no dummy. I had already decided to be completely honest with him. I was going to tell him everything.

It was the following Monday afternoon before we really had a chance to talk. We were sitting at the table in the kitchen of Papa's little shack. He had left early to do a chore for Mr. Dowden. Papa certainly wouldn't have approved of the jar of corn liquor that sat on the table. With all of the activity by the revenue officers in and around the swamp, the little shack was the safest place to be. Besides, the revenuers had raided it a couple of weeks before.

Lengthy and I had been talking since noon. The mason jar was full when we began talking. Now the jar was less than half full. Lengthy had just finished taking a huge swig of the potent moonshine. His speech was becoming garrulous, but I knew exactly what he meant.

"No David, let me stress this because it's damned important for you to know. When you are making love to a woman, it is not a question of the length or breadth of your sexual organ. Dr. Alfred Kinsey just covered that very subject in a book that just came out. Bigness, smallness, tightness or looseness has nothing to do with satisfying a woman." He was smiling to himself. "My son weighed nine and one half pounds when he was born. I used to tease my wife by telling her that the thing never did shrink back to its regular size."

He was silent for a moment. I said nothing. I was content to listen because what Lengthy was telling me was as important to me as life itself. I wanted to ask him about his marriage and why it had failed, but I figured that would be a little much.

"The whole thing centers around two things, David," he said. "It's a

Ducking the Law

matter of feelings and self-control." His brow furrowed. "You have to let the woman know that you care about how she feels and that her complete satisfaction is your first concern." He grinned slyly. "For Christ's sake David, don't get on a woman and do wham bam, thank you ma'am. You can get off anytime you choose if you practice self-control. Once you learn real self-control during the sex act, the sky is the limit. You can carry it to the end of the world." He laughed gleefully. The next time I looked at his face, the smile was gone, and I could tell that for now he was really serious.

"It's a state of mind, David," he said soberly. "When the woman begins to boil over with passion and starts to moan and whine about how good it is, think about something else, fishing or anything that will stop the abruptness of the moment. It takes a woman a bit longer, but if you are careful, desire will stay with you, and she will love you for waiting her turn."

His words were music to my ears. I clung to each syllable like a drowning man clinging to a lifeline. Lengthy was paying no attention to me. He was totally engrossed with his thoughts.

"Sometimes women tend to hang around together in groups, maybe five or six. All you have to do is to screw one of them really good, and the others will break their necks trying to give you a piece of tail. They'll roll over like bowling pins. You'll tire of women and fend them off just as I do." He leaned across the table toward me.

"One other thing David," said Lengthy. "Listen carefully. Nature or Divine Providence must have been looking out for people like us. The female counterpart that speeds the act of procreation is not hidden or deeply buried. It is right near the surface and accessible to a fault, waiting patiently for a partner. And when fully aroused, it stands bursting with readiness, proud and unafraid like the maid in the mist."

I was highly impressed, but there was one thing that bothered me. There was no need beating around the bush. It was something I had to know.

"Lengthy, there is one think I'd like to ask you. It's kind of personal, and I hope you don't mind."

"Ask away old buddy. I'll tell you anything you want to know."

"I was just wondering about something, Lengthy." I watched his face closely. I didn't want to miss anything.

"Do you eat pussy?" Still watching his face, I said quickly, "Don't get mad. I didn't mean any harm. I know a lot of people do that sort of thing, and I just wondered, is that one of the reasons you're so good with women?" He sat back and grinned.

"I ain't got a thing against eating pussy, Dave. It's jist according to how the drop falls."

I thought for a moment and tried to figure out exactly what Lengthy meant. Did he do it for his women or didn't he? Maybe Ed was right. Maybe everybody was doing it but me. I wasn't squeamish where women were concerned, but I decided to let that one ride, at least for now. I wouldn't do anything like that unless it was absolutely necessary. Good gracious! There were limits to what a man should do to satisfy a woman.

I knew Lengthy was proud of his knowledge and his wit. He had given me some much-needed information and had also turned a phrase that had captured my imagination. His soft-spoken words lulled my fears and blurred my concerns. I was smiling too. Our discussion had given me hope. If I followed Lengthy's advice to the letter, it would be possible for me to overcome the problems that had confounded me. I would no longer be the subject of scorn and ridicule. A new Stonewall Jackson, brimming with confidence, was seated at the kitchen table of the dingy little shack. This wily Casanova was girded and armed to the teeth, ready, willing and able to win the battle of the sexes. The key to his future encounters was a lesson well-taught by a former schoolteacher, who was a master player in the art of seduction. Lengthy's eyes closed, and he slumped forward on the table and began to snore.

15

The White Woman

The woods and fields up and down the Rose Hill Road were bloated with the fullness of Summer. I felt the same way. My spirits were soaring with new knowledge. I was chomping at the bit, anxious to test the validity of Lengthy Walker's lessons. I hadn't really decided just who would be the beneficiary of my schooling. Because of my self-imposed celibacy, I had not chosen anybody special. Somehow my thoughts kept returning to Fast Fanny. She seemed to like me a little bit, but because of her screaming our tryst would have to be far away from the common herd. Her little place on Jones Street wouldn't do. I was still a bit hesitant, and if I put into practice everything that Lengthy told me about, Fanny's screams would really be outrageous. It was an intriguing thought.

I did not want to be subjected to the ridicule that I had suffered before. I would have to use all of my skill and be careful not to let on what I was trying to do. My every move would have to be carefully planned. Before I could begin sexual experimentation, I had to figure out what to do about my business in the swamp. Bootlegging illegal liquor was getting risky, and as careful as I had been, the danger of getting caught and being sent to jail hung over me like a cloud. The revenue officers were becoming more aggressive. Now, they were patrolling the

The White Woman

Rose Hill Road and checking the swamp daily. Up until then, I had had no personal contact with any of the members of the Alcoholic Bureau of Control (ABC). I had merely watched them from the safety of the swamp. But, all of that would change and change drastically.

It all began on a Saturday morning in late July. It had been a disappointing morning. The sky looked as mean as a mad dog, and there were angry clouds moving about the horizon. The green of the swamp looked greener than usual, and thunder growled just above the tall trees. The sounds of thunder came closer and then moved away to gather momentum for the first assault. A sense of trouble was in the air, and the sudden quiet was signaling the start of the kind of storm that you wished had already happened.

It had been an uneventful morning. I had just one customer, Pegleg Pete, who bought a half gallon of shine at cost simply because his own liquor wasn't fit to drink. "Keep an eye out for the law this morning," he said. "They were watching Ed's place earlier, and I thought I saw a couple of them in the woods behind your Uncle Mike's garden."

"Don't worry Pegleg. I got them covered." A little grandstanding was needed just to stay in shape. "No sweat Peg. They'll catch hell trying to hook this kid. I'm way too slick for that mess."

I watched as Pegleg hobbled away, walking briskly for a man with one leg. I didn't feel half as brave as I sounded, and a loud roll of thunder didn't help. I looked up at the sky. The dark clouds were suddenly black, and now they were jockeying for the right position over the swamp.

It dawned on me that I didn't have a drop of liquor anywhere near the road. I couldn't be caught short, so I ran back down the hill into the swamp. I waved my arms to ward off the swarms of mosquitoes as I hurried through the brush. The surly insects seemed to be out in force waiting for the coming storm. When I got to the edge of the little stream, I reached into the hollow base of a large poplar and pulled out two half-gallon jars of moonshine.

I hurried back up the hill and was almost to the road before I realized that there was a black Ford parked almost directly in front of me. There were two men standing by the the car. I knew the tall one immediately. He was Derrick Carter, the chief of the ABC force. I didn't know the short fat man. He was probably a deputy. It was time for me to get lost. I faded back into the swamp and stashed the liquor under a log and then ran deeper into the swamp. The next time I came out of the swamp, I was near the road to Grandpa's place. The minute I stepped onto the road, the Ford pulled up beside me. Derrick Carter stepped out of the car, and suddenly there was a .38 revolver pointed at my middle.

"C'mere boy," he said. "Put your hands up! I want to talk to you!"

The pistol was black, and the barrel looked as big as a tunnel. I raised my hands carefully and turned to face Mr. Carter.

"Yessir," I said politely. "Just what did you want to see me about, sir?"

"You're David Sawyer, ain'tcha, boy," he said. I nodded my head. "The description that we have fits you to a T. You're one of them half-slick-ass niggers, and we know that you been selling liquor from the swamp for a couple of months." He shook his head in wonder. "Lemme tell you boy. I know Uncle Fred, your Grandaddy, and I know your Daddy, Noah. I also caught your Uncle Joe, your Uncle Mike and your cousin Ed for selling liquor. I put all of them in jail and on the county roads at one time or another. You wanna be next, I suppose? Jist where do you work, boy?" When I didn't answer immediately, he looked at me shrewdly. "Your ass is going to jail too, boy. You kin bet your last money on it."

"Let's go ahead and lock that nigger up," said the little fat man. His thin lips curled, and he aimed a big gob of tobacco spit directly at me. It landed smack on the toe of my shoe. He snarled. "Charge him with spitting on the road or walking too fast, anything that will put him behind bars. I believe we kin git him at least six months in the penitentiary at Raleigh."

"Nah," said Derrick Carter. He glanced over at the deputy. "I know old man Fred. He's a pretty good old darky. I jist might give this nigger one chance to git hisself out of the liquor business." He looked at me "What about it, boy?" I answered quickly.

"Yessir, Mr. Carter. You got me figured dead wrong. I ain't really messing with no bootleg liquor. I just do a lot of fishing in the swamp. If you say so, I'll be glad to stay out of the swamp."

I did a little customary bowing and backed away from the automobile. When it appeared that they weren't going to arrest me, I gave them

The White Woman

a broad smile.

"Yessir, if y'all are finished with me, I'll be getting on home. It looks like rain. I certainly appreciate y'all talking to me. Mr. Carter, I'll be sure and tell Grandpa that you spoke about him. I thank you both. Y'all be sure and have a nice day."

The two revenue officers climbed into the Ford, and a minute later they were gone. I just stood there. My hands were trembling, and sweat was pouring from my face. The lawmen were satisfied. They knew that they had put the fear of God in me. It was a good thing that Lengthy was somewhere downtown with one of his women. He wouldn't have liked a confrontation with the lawmen. He was deathly afraid of going to jail. I seldom drank, but the ordeal with Mr. Derrick Carter had left me nervous, and my whole body was shaking. I hurried back down into the belly of the swamp. When I reached the hollow log that housed my stash, I unearthed one of the jars and took a long drink. It didn't help fast enough, so I took another huge swallow. I was feeling pretty good, so I cradled the jar in my arms and walked slowly up the hill. By the time I reached the crest of the hill, I was as high as a Georgia pine. I looked around. I was still in the swamp and standing near the thick underbrush at the far end of Lovers' Lane. Suddenly, I heard sounds that were foreign to this neck of the swamp. I stopped and listened intently. There were people talking and occasional laughter somewhere in the woods ahead.

I walked slowly forward. Just ahead was an old blue Hudson Terraplane almost hidden in the bushes at the end of the lane. I moved quietly through the brush until I could see clearly. There were four white men and a woman seated in the car. They were all trying to talk at once, and they were all drunk.

As I watched, a short stocky white man with a florid face and a crew cut got out of the car. He walked toward me fumbling with the front of his trousers. He stopped almost in front of me and relieved himself. We were face to face when he finally looked through the brush and saw me. He appeared startled, but when he saw the jar of moonshine, he relaxed a bit. He didn't recognize me, but I had sold him liquor on several occasions. His voice was a gruff, whiskey-soaked whine.

"Whatcha doing out here in the bushes, boy? Are you selling shine?"

"Yessir mister, you got that right. I got almost a half gallon right here." Shrewdly, I watched his face. "It'll cost you $8 though, but it's good Lumberton drinking liquor. I got it from the Croatan Indians."

Another man got out of the car. This one was young and tow-headed with a pimply face. He staggered toward us, brandishing a $5 bill.

"Hey Al! John said to give you this." The florid-faced man took the five, added three ones from his pocket and handed them to me.

"Boy, these damn skeeters are about to eat me up," the pimply-faced boy complained as the mosquitoes began to make themselves known. The men were slapping furiously as they scrambled back into the Hudson. It was stifling hot outside. I could imagine what it was like inside the car.

I turned and walked a few feet back into the brush. I was still high, but it wasn't a good feeling. The liquor was bubbling in my stomach, and my head was starting to ache. Thunder rolled along the horizon, and sheet lightning occasionally lit the darkening sky. I sat down beside a small poplar and tried to get myself together. I looked at my watch. It was just past one in the afternoon.

The swamp was quiet, breathlessly waiting for the full fury of the storm. Raucous noises that grew louder began coming from the old Hudson. An occasional mosquito would disregard the insect repellant and bite me. I was used to that. It was just a friendly gesture on the mosquito's part. I had decided to sit there in the swamp until I felt better. I had nothing better to do, and I was still a little bit drunk. The noises from the blue Hudson wafted about the swamp. The commotion didn't bother me at all. I would be cool when the storm arrived.

My stomach had just begun to settle when an ear-splitting scream reverberated through the swamp. I knew instantly that it was the white woman. What in the world were they doing to her? I jumped up and hurried through the brush to the edge of the clearing, being extra careful to stay out of sight. The woman was kneeling a short distance from the car, and the red-faced man stood over her with his fist raised. It looked as if he had struck the woman once and was about to strike her again. The tow-headed boy was standing nearby fumbling with his fly. I got a good look at the woman. She wasn't pretty. She was kind of plump with a good shape and nice legs. At the moment she was crying, and there was a big bruise on her right cheek. Ruined mascara mixed with tears ran down her cheeks. Her long black hair hung dankly about her shoulders, and there was a look of terror on her face.

As I watched, the other two men got out of the car. They looked like soldiers, but I couldn't be sure. One was tall and thin, and the other was short with an average build. The big mosquitoes greeted the four men and the woman with ready beaks and open wings. They began to bite indiscriminately, focusing on everything within range. The furious assault did not deter the one called Al. He became even more aggressive.

"Give it up bitch," said the red-faced man, as his foul breath spewed past the wet cigar. He reached down and roughly positioned himself at the woman's rear. Smirking lasciviously, he winked and looked over at the tow-headed boy.

"Awright, Lou. you take the front end, and I'll take care of this big fat ass, okay?"

The mosquitoes buzzed eagerly as if agreeing with the strange arrangement. The sound of Al's labored breathing grew louder. His florid face turned redder still as he roughly hiked the woman's dress up and tore her underthings aside. He kneeled behind her, and a moment later she stiffened and uttered a sharp cry. Her head moved randomly, and she began to moan softly. The woman seemed terrified. "Listen, I don't mind giving it up. Y'all kin have it. Jist take it easy, and do it one at the time, please! Ow! Ohh Lordy me!" She began to whine pitifully. "Don't hurt me, please! Gimme time, y'all. Don't rush me! By Gawd, I'm giving it to you as fast as I can!"

The tow-headed boy fumbled with his trousers and quickly moved closer to her face. I couldn't make out the rest of what she was trying to say. The boy grabbed her hair, forcing her head toward his middle. His jerky movements quickened, and her voice suddenly became garbled. I could understand why it was difficult for her to talk.

The taller of the two men who were waiting moved closer. His mouth was open, and he was drooling with anticipation. "Y'all hurry up, now! We kin all git a piece if the damn mosquitoes don't git us first. C'mon y'all. I wanna fuck!"

His words were punctuated by a clap of thunder, followed by a bolt of lightning that zig-zagged across the suddenly dark sky. Unable to wait any longer, he pushed the tow-headed boy away from the woman and grabbed her head with both hands. At that moment the sky exploded. Rain came down in torrents, and thunder boomed as sheet lightning flashed at will about the swamp. Angry bolts of lightning followed, striking trees at random. It was as if the Lord himself were showing his anger at that sorry spectacle.

The red-faced man finally moved away from the woman, only to be replaced by the last of the four men. She was no longer moaning or crying. If the two men hadn't been holding her, she would have fallen into the dirt. Neither the rain, thunder, lightning or the swarms of mosquitoes seemed to deter the men. They were bent on degrading her to the fullest extent. The dark green of the swamp was a backdrop for terror. The men were using the poor woman in mean, despicable ways.

I had never seen such cruelty perpetrated by anyone. Grossly indecent things were happening to each end of her body. She moaned pitifully as the relentless assault continued. If they would do that to a white woman, there was absolutely no limit to what they would do to a Negro woman. I cowered against the trunk of a large poplar and peered through the storm at the unsettling sight of white men doing vile things to a helpless woman. I began to retch violently. It was a scene right out of Dante's vision of hell. The torment that the woman suffered would have been right at home in either of the nine circles of hell. The memory of her plea kept coming back to me whining pitifully through the blowing wind and rain.

"Gimme time y'all. Please don't rush me! By Gawd, I'm giving it to you as fast as I can!"

The fit of vomiting passed, and the next time I looked up the men were inside the car. The Hudson's wheels began to spin as the driver gunned the engine and backed out toward the road. The car was nearly out of the swamp before I realized that they had left the white woman lying in the mud and dirt of the roadway. The rain slowed a bit and soon was just a slow drizzle. I ran out of the brush and hurried over to where the woman was lying. She looked like an over-size rag doll lying there in the dirt. Mascara, mud and blood criss-crossed her pale face. Her hair was matted, and her head was half-buried in the mud. Her stockings, underwear and slippers were scattered around her body. At first I wasn't certain as to whether or not she was still alive. I kneeled in the mud beside her and placed my head on her breasts. Her chest rose and fell with agonizing slowness, and her breathing was shallow and ragged. Thank God she was alive. I knelt there for a minute, not knowing what to do.

Somehow, I had to help the white woman. I knew that if I helped

The White Woman

her I might be placing my very life in jeopardy. There was no telling what would happen to me if the police or any white person were to see me with the woman. The men and the woman had been drinking my liquor, and somehow the woman's plight had become my responsibility. I couldn't leave her there in the swamp. I had to stay with the woman and help her until she was able to leave the swamp of her own accord. I was in danger of the worst sort.

The storm grew in intensity, and the rain returned with a vengeance and began to come down in torrents. I was soaked to the skin and shaking as if I had the Saint Vitus dance. I grabbed a small sapling, clinging to it desperately for support. David Jonathan Sawyer, the great-grandson of Stonewall Jackson, was deep in the swamp, scared to death and at his wits' end.

I sat beside the woman in the mud of the little roadway, desperately trying to figure my way out of my dilemma. Time passed. I don't know how long I sat there with my head resting on my knees, trembling as the full fury of the storm unfurled around me. After a while I raised my head and looked around. A miracle had occurred. The swamp was flooded with sunlight, and the leaves and branches of the trees were no longer whipped by the raging wind. The storm was over, and the dark clouds had drifted away, leaving gentle cumulus clouds in their wake. The afternoon sun shone brilliantly, making the drops of rain clinging to the leaves of the trees shine like sparkling jewels. The wind became a gentle breeze whispering softly through the swamp, and as I looked at the woman, her eyes flickered and slowly opened.

She moaned and coughed, almost choking on her own saliva. After a couple of tries, she mumbled and looked up at me.

"By Gawd!" the woman moaned.

It was awhile before I could get some sense into her, and it was even longer until she began to fully realize what had happened to her in the swamp. She looked ruefully down at her dress as I helped her to a sitting position. I gathered up her stockings, slippers and underthings and handed them to her.

"By Gawd I'm a plum mess," she lamented. A few tears ran slowly down her discolored cheeks. I had been kind of hoping she wouldn't cry any more.

"It's my own fault though," said the woman bitterly. "The bastards gang-banged me! I didn't mind giving each one of them a separate piece. Al said he was gonna pay me right good if I took care of everybody." She sighed softly. "I sure as hell didn't want to take all of them on at the same time." She shook her head as she remembered the pain. A look of wonder crossed her face. "By Gawd, they almost killed me." She began to massage her neck, tenderly rubbing the area just beneath her chin, "By Gawd, my neck hurts something awful." She grimaced. "By the way, boy, I'm Clara Jimson. Who are you, and what's your name?"

"Yes ma'am," I said quickly. "I'm David Sawyer, and I just happened to be in the neighborhood. I was out at the road, and I thought I heard somebody scream." There was concern in my voice. "If you want me to ma'am, I'll try to help you get yourself together and show you the way out of the swamp." I thought for a minute. "I could walk you down to the creek, and you could rinse the mud out of your clothes. You could hang them on the bushes, and they would be dry in no time."

"I sho' appreciate your help, boy," said the woman. "I can't give you any money, though. Them bastards didn't give me a dime."

She struggled to her knees, wavered for a moment and then fell back into the mud. Her eyes clouded with consternation as she looked up at me.

"Gawd help me, boy! I'm so weak that I can't even stand up. Kin you give me a hand?"

"Yes ma'am. I'll be glad to help you. Just give me your hands."

She was heavier than I had thought. Finally, I managed to help her up and then maneuvered her feet far enough apart so that she could stand with my help.

"Easy now. I've got you."

Holding her tightly, I half dragged, half carried her down through the brush to the creek. As we walked, the mosquitoes began to swarm around the two of us. The miracle of returning sunlight and gentle breezes did not deter the ferocious insects. For them, it was business as usual. I stopped to take the repellant from my jacket pocket.

"Hold still for a minute, Miz Clara. I'm gonna rub a little bit of this repellant on your face and arms. It won't stop the mosquitoes, but it will kinda slow them down."

The White Woman

Rubbing any part of a white woman's body in a swamp filled with mosquitoes is not all fun and games. My vow of celibacy suddenly took an awkward turn. Regardless of the sickening events that had happened earlier, by the time I walked Miz Clara down to the edge of the creek, I was in real trouble. She laid her stockings, underthings and slippers on the creek bank as she slowly stepped into the water. Modesty was a moot question as Miz Clara slipped out of the soiled dress and began to rinse it in the clear water of the stream. Her long black hair hung almost into the water as she bent to rinse the dress. Her skin was unblemished except for the recent bruises.

The sunlight filtered through the trees and highlighted the fullness of her milky white body. I stood in awe of her beauty. It was a poet's dream. The diamond wetness of the leaves, the sunlight and even the mosquitoes paid homage. She was Juno of the swamp, a slightly tarnished goddess, and I had absolutely no business feeling the way that I did. Conscience took the same path as celibacy, and caution went away with the wind. Wanting something that I was forbidden to want in the first place became an irresistible urge that took a front row seat in this amphitheater of the absurd. Lust blurred the inherent danger of the moment. I wanted the white woman with every fiber of my being. I ached with longing.

At first I tried not to look at Miz Clara, but I couldn't help it. When she finished washing her things, she used her underpants to carefully sponge her body. My throat was dry, and there were all kinds of crazy emotions running through my mind. Blurred lust did not disguise the fact that there was deadly risk in this unusual encounter. What if someone saw me with the white woman? Suppose I got caught, or worse yet, suppose I caught something contagious from her? I was usually prepared for any opportunity that presented itself, but this time I had no protection with me. I watched unashamedly as Miz Clara finished washing and stepped gingerly out of the water. She drifted toward me like a true goddess. Her eyes twinkled a bit as she advanced. There was no doubt in my mind. Somehow she knew exactly how I felt. The brown eyes narrowed, and a slight smile played about her full lips. She was a true courtesan. It was written all over her face.

Miz Clara held the damp clothes in one hand and placed her other

The White Woman

hand on my arm to steady herself. Her brown eyes looked deep into mine.

"Listen David," said the woman. "I tole you that I ain't got no money to give you for helping me. I owe you something for helping me like you did. I'm still a little bit tender and as sore as a boil, but if you kin be right easy with me, I might be able to straighten you out."

Her lips pursed as she watched me quizzically. "You don't have to be afraid or anything, I ain't got no problem with you being a nigra. When I was a little girl, I was practically raised up by colored folks. I always did like nigras." She turned and carefully placed her clothing on the nearest bush. She smiled over her shoulder at me.

"It's gonna take a few minutes for my clothes to dry." She sounded impatient, as if she wanted to get it over with. "Well, do you want it or don't you?"

The dryness in my throat persisted. When I spoke, my voice sounded more like a croak.

"Yes ma'am, Miz Clara, I believe I do. I sure would appreciate it if it wouldn't be too much of a bother to you. I'd like it a whole lot."

She came to me, and we sank slowly down into the dark earth beside the creek. I held her close, careful not to hurt her bruised body. Ours was a gentle caring thing. Slowly she led me through a rite of passage that was nothing like what had happened earlier. She taught me tenderness, and I shared with her a quiet passion that rewarded us both.

Too soon, it was over. She had been more than true to her word and straightened me out just as she had promised. Clara Jimson had given me, Scot-free, a treasure worth more than silver or gold, a glorious feeling that I would cherish forever.

Afterward, oblivious of the mud and grime, we held each other tenderly for a while. Then, she smiled up at me.

"Well David, do you wanna go again?" she grinned. "That piece wasn't bad at all. In fact, it was pretty good. You kin have another shot if you want it."

"No thank you, Miz Clara. I got a plenty. I'm doing just fine."

I felt great. She hadn't said a thing about my size. I had the feeling that she liked me for what I was and that was the only reason. Later, she washed up again, and we dressed and slowly walked up the hill toward

The White Woman

the road. When we were almost to the Rose Hill Road, I grabbed her arm. "Miz Clara," I hesitated for a moment. "I can't walk down the road with you. The white folk would lynch me for sure if they saw us together."

I placed the $8 from the sale of the whiskey into her hand and closed her fingers around it.

"Here, take this money." She accepted it gratefully. "This is what we'll do. You walk along the road, and I'll walk here in the woods alongside to keep an eye on you. That way nobody will see the two of us together." She nodded.

"Where do you live ma'am?" I asked. "I'll walk along with you until it's safe. I don't want anything else to happen to you." She smiled.

"David, honey, don't worry, I'll be okay. I appreciate you helping me to the highest. I live right downtown, jist below the old Market House at the corner of Gillespie and Blount streets. You kin stop by if you want to. It's the first house on the corner." She thought for a minute. "One other thing, David. Make sure you come at night, you hear?"

I was feeling high and mighty, and it was for a perfectly good reason. In the leaves, mud and dirt of a hot steamy swamp, I had made love to a goddess. For a brief moment, Clara Jimson, the battered white woman, had been my Juno of the swamp and because of it I would never be the same.

I was feeling pretty good as I walked up the hill toward the house. I thought about what had happened in the swamp. I had just finished being with a white woman, doing the one thing that would certainly get a Negro lynched, tarred and feathered or hung from the nearest tree. Jail for a number of years would be the best of all possible worlds for someone accused of such folly. I had beaten the rap, gotten away without a scratch home free and paid no penalty at all. Would I do it again? Would I risk my life to lie between the warm sweetness of her lily white thighs? Would I try again for the feel of her pink nipples against my chest? I didn't think so.

16

What to Do on a Rainy Day

The days passed fitfully. I drank whiskey sparingly as I considered whether or not to curtail my bootlegging enterprise. My reasons were simple. I needed a clear head and my wits about me to cope with the ever-present danger of smart white folks who wanted to jail me. It was time for me to take a good look at the world around me. With the increased pressure that the law was exerting on bootlegging operations along the Rose Hill Road, it was only a matter of time before I was caught and sent to jail. Stonewall Jackson wouldn't have liked such trifling behavior, and I would do everything possible to avoid it.

It was early Fall, and the leaves of the forest were a blazing mix of color. It was a last hurrah before the trees shed their leaves and waited naked, braced to withstand the relentless cold of Winter. Soon, it would be difficult to hide moonshine in the swamp. The bare trees could not shield my activities. I walked slowly through the swamp carefully checking my inventory. When I had finished checking and double checking, I had 36 jars of clear easy-drinking liquor hidden about the swamp. I had considered selling my entire stash of illegal liquor to Uncle Mike or Ed at wholesale rates, but that wouldn't be profitable, and I had become accustomed to making money not swapping liquor.

I was seated at the kitchen table trying to decide what to do when

What to Do on a Rainy Day

Papa came out of the bedroom. He pulled up a chair and sat across from me. Papa was in unusually high spirits. I was glad because ever since the failed enterprise with Reverend Lonnie Pierce he had shrunk back into his shell. That morning he was jubilant.

"Fix me a bite to eat, boy," he demanded. "I'm in kind of a hurry. I've got to go over on the Raleigh Road this morning to see the Widow Nellie Smith. She and I are gonna raise us a crop come Spring planting season."

I sat a plate in front of him and shoveled a heaping helping of grits from the pot on the stove. It had always been easy to feed Papa, especially at breakfast time. I gave him two large slices of fatback and a link of smoked sausage. Then I smothered the whole business with grease from the frying pan. Since Mama's death Papa had refused to eat eggs. I never did figure out why. Maybe it was because of the special way that Mama had cooked them. I poured him a cup of coffee and set it beside the plate. I was puzzled as I looked over at Papa.

"I can't understand it, Papa. You're just getting out of trouble, and after the screwing that you took messing around with the preacher, why would you try farming again? It's got to be the worst way in the world to make a living."

"Preaching and farming is all that I know, boy," he said. "And besides I'm too old to do anything else. I ain't no good at selling liquor like my brother Mike, Ed and you. Papa raised all of us to be better folk than that." For a moment, a bit of the old fire came back. "I tried my best to raise you in a God-fearing manner, and now you're going from sugar to shit. You'll more than likely end up in jail. I tell you for a fact, boy, you ought to be ashamed. It's a crying shame to carry on like that."

I sat quietly because I suddenly felt guilty about my activities. I certainly didn't want to get into an argument with Papa, and besides I was still kinda scared of him. Whippings like the ones that he used to give me were not easily forgotten. I knew that there were a lot of things on Papa's mind.

For one thing, my brother, Jimmy, had not come back home from his job as a farm hand in Sampson County. Jimmy was the baby, and Papa was crazy about him. What Papa really needed was a woman friend. Since his failed attempt with Miz Snoog, I hadn't seen any evidence of Papa courting another woman. I had been much too busy to make any arrangements for him with women whom I knew. I didn't feel too good about his new alliance with the widow, Miz Nellie Smith. Concerning her sexual activities, she was loose as a goose.

Miz Nellie had been a hopeless alcoholic ever since the death of her husband, Henry Smith. I knew that Papa's interest in the widow stemmed from the fact that she was about the same age as Mama. In fact, she even looked a little like Mama. I hoped everything would work out for Papa. He was out of the door and going down the steps and into the yard before I spoke again. "Hey Papa, tell Miz Nellie that I asked about her, and I hope the deal works out." Papa looked at me, but he didn't say anything. I looked up at the sky. Storm clouds were brewing. It seemed as if a storm were always in the making. Something out of kilter always followed the dog days of Summer. It was November, and still the rains would come. Papa was almost out to the road before I yelled.

"Hey Papa, you'd better hurry. It's gonna rain!"

He kept walking as if he hadn't heard a word. I stood there watching until he disappeared around the curve. Papa was a lonely man.

I sat on the steps of the little shack and looked up at the patches of blue behind the gathering storm clouds. The trees were swaying gently, like a Baptist congregation moved by a solemn hymn praising the goodness of the Lord. Random thoughts that matched the troubled sky wandered aimlessly through my mind. Age did not have a monopoly on loneliness. I was lonely too. The new direction that I had decided to take regarding my approach to women was a road that I had to travel alone. Being with the white woman had bolstered my spirits for a time, but I was beginning to feel depressed again. I was hoping that I could remember all of the things that Lengthy Walker had told me about and not be subjected to rejection and ridicule. If that happened, I'd be back to square one.

Depression early in the morning is no good and neither was the persistent ache in the pit of my stomach. The solution to that problem was simple. I needed a woman. Childish fumbling would only worsen my agitation. A sure cure for my depression was in a half gallon fruit jar hidden behind a pillar at the corner of the house. I decided to take steps to alleviate both problems. I nestled the jar under my arm and walked out to the road. I was careful to stay in the bushes alongside the road.

What to Do on a Rainy Day

The fatigues that I wore would allow me to be almost invisible. I was almost down at the bottom of the hill when the rains came. This time it was not a thunderstorm, but a slow steady downpour of cold November rain. I would be soaking wet before I reached the bridge. Uncle Joe's little cabin was the closest shelter around. When I reached the path that led up the hill to his place, I left the road and hurried up the hill. I didn't see any smoke coming from the chimney as I approached the little cabin. I knocked several times and then decided that there was no one home. Finally, Uncle Joe's muffled voice came through the door. "Awright, awright, gimme a minute! Don't knock the damn thing down!"

The door creaked open, and a high whining voice said, "Hello Cousin David. C'mon in the house child before you get soaking wet."

I looked up in surprise. It wasn't Uncle Joe. It was Cousin Jamie June. It had been years since I had seen him. He had changed a lot. His teeth were gone, and he was bald, but he was still the same small wiry man that I remembered. The well-tailored dapper clothing that he always wore was dirty. He was desperately in need of a shave, and there was a silly grin on his dark face. His little eyes sparkled wickedly as he spied the fruit jar tucked under my arm.

"Good gracious Little David. I haven't seen you for a time." A loose grin widened his toothless mouth. "It's good to see you again, boy. You were about knee-high to a duck when I got sent up." His eyes were glued to the jar of moonshine. "Is that real drinking liquor you got under your arm?"

I held the jar up and shook it once. Beads danced and bubbled around the surface of the clear liquid.

"It ain't nothing but the truth Cousin Jamie, old buddy. This is the best shine in Cumberland County." I grinned. "You must be late out of shape and in the dark too. Somebody ought to have told you about me. I'm Little David Sawyer, the king of the bootleggers, and the biggest bullshitter on the Rose Hill Road."

"Git outta the door, Jamie June," said Uncle Joe. He leaned forward from the ragged cane-bottomed chair beside the little wood stove.

"Let the boy come in outta the rain before you start asking a lot of dumb-ass questions."

The wind slammed the door behind me as I stood there waiting for

What to Do on a Rainy Day

my eyes to get used to the semi-darkness of the little cabin. Uncle Joe's head turned in my direction. He was searching for the sound of my voice. "Dave, boy, look back in the corner," he motioned toward the bedroom. "See if there's a chair over by the bed and bring it in here. It's a mite warmer in here."

I walked into the bedroom, got the chair and placed it beside Uncle Joe's chair and sat the jar of corn between us. I looked first at Uncle Joe and then turned my eyes to Jamie June.

"Awright y'all, if y'all want to, we can get as drunk as a skunk."

I twisted the lid, opened the mason jar and handed it to Uncle Joe.

"Help yourself Unc. I was going to mosey down the road and get me a shot of tail, but it's raining like hell. The weather's bad, and I'm bad, too. This drink of good corn liquor is sponsored by the Kid. Drink up y'all. This one's on me!"

Jamie June's mouth was opened wide in a toothless grin. He was shaking his head and could hardly contain himself.

"It's a good thing that Miz Hannah's going to be over to Grandpa Fred's for most of the day. She's helping your Aunt Sarah shell some peas," he smirked. "From what I been hearing about you, Davey boy, kin don't mean a blame thing to you."

"Lay off the boy, Jamie," Uncle Joe said. "That shit is over and done with. Ain't no need to keep rehashing it." He sounded a bit peeved. "Suppose people kept talking about you like that. You done a lot worse things than Little David, here. All he did was to get a piece of tail." He paused. "Don't you forget, Jamie June. I've known you since day one. Everybody is still wondering how you could go to the penitentiary in Raleigh, leaving a wife and two chillun behind, and come back so fucked up until all you want is a dick. You completely forgot about your wife and chillun." He snorted. "I ain't never seen such shit in all my borned days."

I looked at Uncle Joe's face. The lines around his mouth tightened. This was serious business. I had no idea where this was leading. There were deeper issues here than met the eye. I looked over at Jamie June. He bit his bottom lip, and tears began rolling down his cheeks. His whole body was racked by sobs. He was crying audibly.

"Aw Jamie, shut the hell up," Uncle Joe demanded. "You didn't used to be a cry baby like that." Uncle Joe turned to me. "He wasn't like that until he went to jail. He jist had a streak of bad-ass luck. He was working up on old man Jim Smith's farm in Sampson County about six years ago when he got into trouble. It was the last of July, and he was siding cotton for the old man in a field right near the house. At lunchtime, Jamie June went up to the house to fill his water jar. The pump was on the back porch, and as he was walking past an open window beside the porch, he saw old lady Smith standing inside of the bedroom. She was naked as a Jay bird."

Jamie June wilted and sank slowly to the floor. He was still shaking, but the sobbing had subsided a little. Uncle Joe looked at me.

"Ain't that some shit? Look at him, David. He's the cryingest nigger I've ever seen. The fool should have bailed outta there. He had already gotten a good look at the white woman's behind. He jist couldn't leave well enough alone. Instead, he went behind a big oak in the yard and kept peeping around the trunk to get a better look at her old ass. I don't know why. She was ugly as shit. When old lady Smith saw Jamie June watching, she got right in front of the window and really began to show her naked rump. According to Jamie June, she was rubbing herself and carrying on something fierce. The two of them were having a good time until old man Jim Smith showed up. When the old bitch saw her husband coming across the field, she started screaming like a banshee. She told old man Smith and the sheriff that Jamie June had tried to rape her. The only thing that saved Jamie June's ass was that the jury didn't believe that he could have raped the white woman from a distance of 55 feet away. The charge was changed to aggravated assault, and they sentenced Jamie June to ten years in the state penitentiary in Raleigh."

A smile flitted across Uncle Joe's face. He was no longer perturbed. He leaned back in the chair and smiled.

"Awright y'all. Let's forget about that mess and drink some liquor." He listened for a moment. "Dave, boy, it's still raining like hell out there. You might as well forget about your craving for a piece of tail." He grinned sarcastically. "That is, unless you want to do it to Jamie June. He's been screwed up ever since he got outta jail, and he acts strange as shit. He really ain't got much use for women." Uncle Joe looked over at Jamie with disgust. "Try him and see. A quarter says that he'll do anything, anything at all," Uncle Joe snorted. "If he starts blubbering, jist smack the shit out of him. He likes that too." I shook my head.

"Nah, I ain't that hard up for a piece." The jar of moonshine shine passed quickly from hand to hand. A feeling of camaraderie came over the three of us. The effect of the strong liquor warmed our bodies and loosened our tongues.

It was a time to talk of many things, to tell stories about the vaunted prowess of the Negro. It was a practice that was as old as slavery itself.

The semi-darkness of the little cabin and the steady patter of rain on the tin roof made it the ideal place to tell tall tales. The stories would be meaningless bragging, but they did exactly what they were designed to do. In real life, the Negroes had caught hell from every conceivable direction. In the stories that touted the Negro's strength and sexual ability, the Negro always won. Whatever the adventure, he could not lose.

I didn't know how well Jamie played the game, but I would soon find out. I had heard Uncle Joe play the dozens on numerous occasions. I was anxious to get him started. When I spoke my voice was slightly slurred.

"C'mon, bad Joe Sawyer with your bullshitting self. Tell the Kid what's jumping. What's going down?" Uncle Joe was primed and ready.

"Nothing, you slow rollers, nothing at all. Ain't nothing jumping but the peas in the pot, and they wouldn't be jumping if the water wasn't hot."

Uncle Joe started to hum and then he began to chant:

"When John Henry was a baby boy sitting on his pappy's knee, he picked up a railroad spike and said, 'You're gonna be the death of me, Lord, Lord. You're gonna be the death of me!'"

Everybody knew that the mighty John Henry died with his hammer in his hand, but he lived again and again, and each resurrection regardless of the name made him more legendary and stronger still. In the sinking of the Titantic, his name was "Shine" and he was big, black and as powerful as ever. The awesome, unsinkable Titantic was sinking, and Shine was about to swim to shore when the rich white woman cried out, "Shine, Shine, please save poor me, and I'll make you as rich as any black nigger can be!"

"You're white to start with," said Shine with a grin, "and that's in your favor, but there's nigger women on the shore, and I like their flavor!"

"Shine, Shine," said the white woman, "I'm rich, and I'm pretty, and I hate to beg, but if you take me to shore, you can spend the rest of your life between my legs!"

"White woman, white woman," said Shine, "I sure hope you don't drown way out here, but I'm headed for shore and a dry atmosphere!"

Uncle Joe reared in the chair with a smug look on his face. The talk fest was about to heat up.

The bullshit meeting of men of color came to order. Jamie June's high whiney voice rose higher as he started to sing: "Ohh, the snake he wrapped his tail around the flagpole, around the flagpole. Ohh the snake he wrapped his tale around the flagpole. He slid down the pole and bust his asshole! His asshole!"

It was my turn. We were going into the realm of talking animals.

"Do y'all know the one about the signifying monkey?" I asked drunkenly.

It was as familiar to Negroes as the ballad of John Henry. I took a deep breath. "Awright y'all. It happened like this: Deep down in the jungle by the coconut trees lived the most signifying monkey that the world had ever seen. The signifying monkey told the lion on a bright sunny day. 'There's a bad motherfucker coming down your way. He couldn't have been your friend from the words that he said. He talked about your mama in a helluva way.' The lion jumped up in a big rage like a young cock knocker who had been blowing gage. He roared down through the jungle tearing up trees, making every living ass fall on their knees. He came upon the elephant who was minding his own business, eating grass and leaves.

"Mr. Lion swiped the elephant across his butt, and when the elephant raised his trunk, he hit him again right in the nuts. 'I heard you been talking about me,' said the lion. The elephant grunted once and then began to kick ass. They fought all that night and all the next day. I don't know how in hell that lion got away. The lion finally got away from that ass-kicking jive and came back up through jungle looking more dead than alive. That's when the monkey climbed a coconut tree and started his signifying.

"'Hey Mr. Lion, ain't you the one? You left huffing and bragging, and now you come back looking like you're damn near hung. I ought to jump down out of this tree and whup your ass some more!' The monkey was jumping up and down with glee. He hollered to the lion, 'Don't you

What to Do on a Rainy Day

dare fuck with me!' His foot slipped, and his ass hit the ground and like a flash of lightning and a ball of heat, the lion was on the monkey with all four feet. 'Please Mr. Lion, I apologize,' said the monkey. 'I won't do no more signifying.'

"'I know you won't,'" said the lion. 'I'm gonna bust your lips, with a helluva hit and that ought to stop you from talking that signifying shit!'"

The liquor flowed freely and so did the tall tales. There was a warm feeling in the pit of my stomach. Sexual desire was a turgid burden that heightened my inebriated state. I tried to stand and stumbled over Jamie's legs and almost fell into Uncle Joe's lap. Regaining my balance, I reached down and picked up the fruit jar. I took the lid off and waved it in front of Jamie. "Y'all wanna another taste? Ain't nothing left but a corner." Jamie shook his head drunkenly.

"Help yourself, Dave. I got a plenty. That shine went down so smooth, I didn't realize that it had a kick like a mean mule."

I turned to ask Uncle Joe if he wanted a taste, but his hat had fallen to the floor, and he was snoring, sound asleep with his head on his chest.

"It's all yours Dave," said Jamie. There was a peculiar look in his eyes, and a strange grin on his slack face. His eyes narrowed as I raised the jar to my lips. "Atta boy, sweetheart. Drink it down. Don't leave no corners for Johnny Law. Kill it, and you know it's dead. That's what I always say."

I downed the clear liquid in two big gulps. The room began to sway, and I had the sensation of falling. I grabbed the chair and tried to steady myself. Jamie struggled to his feet and grabbed my arm. I pushed his hand away.

"Nah, I'm okay."

Jamie seemed to be bobbing and weaving in and out of focus.

"Listen, I am kinda high. I'm gonna go back there." I pointed to the bedroom. "And I'm gonna take a nap. Be sure and wake me up before Miz Hannah comes back. She'll raise holy hell if she catches me in her bed." Jamie licked his delicate lips and stared directly at me.

"Don't worry sweetheart, I'll keep an eye out for Hannah. You jist go ahead and lie down for a while. Jamie will take care of you."

I stumbled through the door of the musty bedroom and fell across the lumpy mattress of the old bed. Lying on my back, I stared at the ceil-

What to Do on a Rainy Day

ing as the room seemed to spin dizzily around. As the room gathered momentum, I grabbed the bedspread and tried unsuccessfully to keep my eye focused in the semi-darkness. Finally, the room stopped spinning, and I drifted off into a drunken sleep.

Fragmented dreams drifted in and out of my subconscious, coming and going in a strange disjointed sequence. The dreams slowly welded and came together as one, filled with desire, peculiar overtones of lust and a sexual feeling that was as vividly acute as any that I had ever felt. My hips began coitus like movements, jerky and involuntarily. The feeling was much too real, and I awakened with a start. The sensation of having sex was still with me even after I was fully awake. It took a moment for me to realize that something awfully strange was happening to me. I couldn't understand it at all because I was still at Uncle Joe's place.

The acute feeling intensified. I sat up suddenly and was mortified to see Jamie June's bald head buried between my legs. His head was bobbing furiously, and he was making loud sucking noises. The feeling was exquisite, bordering on pain and almost unbearable. I had never felt anything like that before. My sexual identity was deep in his mouth, and he was wringing it like a hound dog with a juicy bone. Great day in the morning! This couldn't be. I was horrified.

I had never been party to anything like that in my life. I reached down with the full intention of pushing his head away. Instead, I found myself with an ear clutched in each hand. I lost all control in an orgy of self-helping, anxiously aiding and abetting the hungry mouth of Jamie June. My whole body jerked furiously, and too soon the race was over. Orgasm and relief were place and show, and revulsion came limping in at the last minute.

After it was over, I sat there still shaken from that unholy alliance. A nagging notion entered the corridors of my mind. I could not erase the anguished look on Jamie June's face.

I knew that what had just happened to me was sexual satisfaction, as raw and as real as being with a woman. But, I couldn't help but wonder, what feelings did Jamie June get from such a base act? Why was he driven to such lengths? Before the time spent in prison, he had been a confirmed family man with a devoted wife and children. Did prison completely kill his masculinity, leaving him with an out-of-kilter craving that drove him to seek satisfaction from the male gender when and where he could find it? Was there any chance that he could ever be normal again? How would it affect me? Was it catching? Would the single encounter screw me up for life?

I could not forget the tortured look in Jamie June's eyes as he looked up at me. I had been an active partner in that perversion. His depravity had been my depravity.

I could not lie to myself. It had been good, very good. I bounded out of the cabin and ran out into the rain. Maybe the cleansing rain would wash the guilt away. I was halfway up the hill to our little shack before I stopped running. I stopped and stood in the middle of the little path and held my face up to the blowing wind and rain. The cold November rain engulfed me, but it did not wash away the guilt. Nothing happened. The sky distanced itself from me, and the night was not in a forgiving mood.

I just got soaking wet as I stood there. I wondered if there were no limit to my sinful actions? What in the world had happened to my strict Christian upbringing? I had fornicated on the offering table in the Lord's house. My sinful behavior had become an everyday occurrence, and breaking the law was a fun occupation. Worse yet, I had just finished having a sexual encounter with a member of my own sex. I was as guilty as Jamie June. I stood there in the gathering darkness nursing the guilt like a mother suckling her child. The rain kept falling.

17

Jailhouse Blues

The fat, greasy jailer was grinning evilly as he walked slowly through the cell block. I was standing at the door of my small cell, which was at the end of the corridor on the left side. This was a holding cell. I was lucky in a sense because the authorities could have had me do my time on the county roads. The cells in this part of the Cumberland County jail were not dark dank or smelly. The walls were freshly painted, and the cells were fairly well-lighted.

In fact, the courthouse itself had been built to replace the 19th century structure that had stood on that same spot at Gillespie and Russell streets. The site was only a block south of the old Market House. Justice had been served in the old courthouse even as the auctioneers sold slaves from the balcony of the old slave market. The raucous sounds of barter in human flesh that wafted from the market and into the halls of reason did not tip the scales of justice one way or the other. Prime Negroes were always in great demand. But, this was a different time. Slavery was a thing of the past, and justice unrestrained was still the order of the day.

The system worked. I should know because I was about to do some hard time. The red-faced jailer was a study in benign dislike, as he shuffled up to where I stood at the cell door. Scowling, he spit a dollop of tobacco juice that landed on the floor of the cell, missing my feet by inches.

"You act like you got a problem, boy," the turnkey said nastily. "Your black ass jist got here. What's wrong with you?"

"I'm doing okay mister. I was just wondering if you had a cigarette?"

The jailer looked at me. His puffy cracked lips formed a grin.

"You betcha, boy, I sure do have a cigarette. I got a fresh pack of Camels right here in my shirt pocket." He pretended to be bewildered. "What business is it of yours? Tell me, boy, why did you want to know if I had cigarettes?"

His question didn't bother me. When I spoke, my voice was devoid of the longing that I felt.

"Yessir, boss man. I was wondering if maybe you could spare me a cigarette? I ran plumb out. I'd sure appreciate it if you could loan me one." The jailer grinned. "Boy, you got to be the craziest nigger in the world. If I gave you a cigarette, every coon in this cellblock would want one."

Still laughing, he turned and walked away. The noise of his footsteps echoed against the walls of the corridor. I walked over to the two bunk beds against the far wall of the cell and sat on the dirty mattress of the bottom bed. The odor from the discolored commode near the bed permeated my nostrils. The sink beside it was covered with grime. Claustrophobia ebbed and flowed as the walls of the cell seemed to be closing in around me. I had trouble breathing and sweat trickled from my armpits. The sensation was overpowering. Never in my life had I been in a situation where I couldn't walk away at my own discretion. It was a bad thing to happen to a young man.

Somehow I had to make the best of it. I guess I should have considered myself fortunate to be housed in such a structure. The new courthouse was a modern building of granite and marble, another fine example of progress in this fast-growing mecca that was Fayetteville, North Carolina.

The old jail had been Gothic in appearance, with a single spire and four clock faces like the old Market House. Its hanging well located in the center of the building had been the site of numerous hangings.

Papa had told us of a hanging in 1900 that followed the arrest, trial and conviction of a young Negro man named Louis Council. He had been charged with raping a young white woman on a farm up the Raleigh Road. There was widespread doubt about his guilt. Even the sheriff did not believe he was guilty and wanted to spare his life. The prisoner went to his hanging clutching a small wooden cross with both hands. He swore that he was innocent. It was said that at the hour of his execution a terrible storm came up. Papa told us that the sheriff, judge and everybody connected to the case died under strange circumstances.

According to Papa, the jail in the courthouse was a busy place that never lacked occupants. Both 1913 and 1914 were especially bad years. There were a lot of killings. In the space of two years, two police chiefs were gunned down. The killers, both of them Negroes, were quickly tried and hanged. One of the defendants was brought into the courtroom on a stretcher. He was in a coma from banging his head against the bars of his cell. Papa never said whether or not the Negro regained consciousness before he was hanged. He might have met his end without knowing when it happened or which direction he was headed.

There were several throat cuttings during that period and the brutal rape of a twelve-year-old girl. Embezzlement, pistol dueling, wife shooting, two axe murders, robbery and theft were just some of the crimes.

Grandpa also remembered the atrocities. He told me of a famous Negro short story writer who had been born and reared in Fayetteville. He had been quite critical of his hometown. He wrote in detail about the atrocities committed by whites against Negroes. His comments were written only after he had resigned as principal of the school that he had attended as a boy. From the safety of his new home in Cleveland, he mounted a scathing attack on the racial attitudes of the whites toward the Negro population of Fayetteville. He said that outwardly the little town seemed calm and serene, but beneath that lazy exterior was the coldest town that he had had the misfortune in which to reside. He swore that prejudice toward Negroes was more intense and uncompromising than at any time since since the Emancipation. It had never occurred to me to look at Fayetteville in that light. The white townspeople dubbed the novelist another "uppity nigger."

It was September, and the weather was warm. There was no reason for the chill that enveloped me as I stood in the center of the small enclosure. It took me a full minute to realize that the coldness was simply perceived, a product of my personal misery. After a moment, the thoughts of violence and the studied bigotry of yesterday faded, and my thoughts returned to my present predicament. After repeated admonitions from Papa and constant warnings from other kinfolk, I had finally ended up in the county jail.

Jailhouse Blues

It was ironic but fitting that my arrest came at the hands of the two newly-appointed colored policeman. They were Ed Naylor, the son of a black shoemaker, and Joe Banks, the son of the rector of Fayetteville's only Episcopal church.

The local papers gave them plenty of attention when they were selected to be the first colored police officers. I knew that they would go above and beyond the call of duty, and because of it, whether guilty or not, some colored folk were going to catch holy hell.

The new officers were instructed to patrol Person Street and Gillespie Street, an area where Negroes came to shop and pass the time of day. I didn't like either of the new officers, but I wasn't too concerned because the swamp was not in their jurisdiction. Besides, they would have enough problems on the downtown streets.

I was relatively safe because I was in the process of phasing out the bootleg operation. It was time to quit. ABC Chief Derrick Carter and his deputies had been unable to catch me in the swamp, and I had sense enough not to ever carry moonshine on my person.

The confrontation happened on a Saturday morning in late September during the season of torrential rains and deadly storms. The hurricanes that were born in the South Atlantic traveled north. They were nurtured to maturity by powerful winds. Such winds churned up huge tornadoes and held them in their grasp, shaking them like gigantic dice over huge waves before throwing them haphazardly along the vulnerable Carolina shoreline. The sound and the fury were not unexpected; it happened every year.

That day it was eleven o' clock, and the sky was blue, with big dark clouds roughly pushing the cumulus clouds aside. Above the disorder, an indifferent sun played hide and seek. The atmosphere was tense, electric, a day of risk and uncertainty. The old and new buildings took on a greyish hue. Even the lone skyscraper on Hay Street looked odd and different. The traffic lights that monitored the streets leading up to the circle around the old Market House were swinging like chimes tossed by the wind. On a day like this, anything could happen. The great-grandson of General Stonewall Jackson was ready for whatever came down the pike. I was cool.

I was standing on the corner of Person Street and Market Place,

Jailhouse Blues

checking things out and wondering if any would-be-pool-sharks were in the poolroom down the street. A growing breeze pressed the contours of my new tan gabardine suit against my body, lifting the wide lapels of the one-buttoned roll front. I loosened the russet tie from the pink collar of the expensive shirt and smiled as it gently caressed my face. I watched as the street came alive with farmers, soldiers, white and black folk who always came to town on Saturday. It was going to be an interesting day.

A sense of uneasiness came over me as I looked up at the sky. The feeling passed as quickly as the wind that swirled around me. I needed action. I turned and walked toward the poolroom. A few games of nine ball would be just the thing to start the day. The stakes didn't matter. I had enough money in my hip pocket to start a fire that could burn up a wet mule.

The poolroom was crowded. Cigarette smoke, stale beer, sweat and the smell of unwashed bodies floated about the oblong room. The scent of urine mixed with reefer came from the open door of the toilet in the corner. City slickers in overalls, zoot suits and worn khakis milled about the room. Pistol butts peeked from waist bands and occasionally the silhouette of a straight razor. I never carried a piece because Uncle Joe said that to carry a pistol was like asking for trouble. I moved through the crowd until I was facing the cue sticks that were lined in the rack against the wall. I smiled as I selected several cue sticks, held them up and sighted along the smooth length of the sticks. I picked a number 18. Size or configuration didn't matter. I could beat the socks off anybody in the poolroom, shooting with the butt end of a golf club, or maybe even a tobacco stick. I was brimming with confidence. But, it was not unusual. In battle, Stonewall Jackson had always been confident of victory. I felt the same way.

The few hustlers that knew me spoke or nodded briefly. Five minutes later, I was at the opposite end of the best table in the house, facing a tall ugly dude called "St. Paul Slim." I had never played him before, but from what I had seen he would be easy to beat. My thinking was as wrong as two left shoes. In little more than five minutes, I was playing against my own money. The game was eight ball, and I was losing steadily, so we changed the game to nine ball. Slim ran rack after rack with amazing accuracy. It took all of one hour and six minutes to be relieved of $204.80. I could not play the kind of pool or match the deadly precision of the long lanky nigger from St. Paul, North Carolina.

All eyes were upon me as I walked out of the door. I paused for a moment and looked around the busy street. The taste of humiliation was bitter as gall on my tongue. The Stonewall anger surfaced, and I reeled with rage and frustration. I had nobody to blame but myself. I reached inside my shirt pocket for a piece of gum. There were three in the pack. Tearing the wrappers from all three, I stuffed the gum in my mouth and threw the paper out into the traffic of Person Street. Suddenly, from out of nowhere, Fayetteville's newest and blackest policemen were on either side of me.

Ed Naylor, the smallest of the two, was on my left, and big burly Joe Banks was on my right. They twisted my arms behind my back and placed handcuffs on my wrists. They must have trained well because it only took a minute. I looked at the two of them and screamed in pain.

"Goddammit! What the fuck's wrong with you rookie motherfuckers? Let me go! I ain't done nothing!"

A crowd gathered quickly, surging around us, hungry for excitement and gawking at the sight of Negro policemen arresting a Negro. Joe Banks's slapjack came out of nowhere and slammed against the side of my head. He smiled wickedly, obviously enjoying himself.

"You're under arrest nigger!" He winked broadly at Ed Naylor. "We're charging you with littering a public place!"

The side of my head was smarting, and my ears were ringing. The policeman suddenly grabbed the waistband of my trousers and jerked roughly. He turned to his partner and pointed at the front of my trousers.

"Look at this, Ed. His fly is open. This common-ass nigger ain't got an ounce of decency in his whole body. If there's anything I hate, it's a nasty nigger. We're gonna have to charge this sucker with loitering and indecent exposure." The smirk was still on his face. "Awright Ed, I'll hold this slick-ass nigger while you call the wagon."

"If he gives you any shit, Joe, cold cock him with your slap jack," Ed, his partner, said. "I'll be back in no time."

A few minutes later, the police wagon screeched to a stop, and I was hustled inside by the two black policemen. There was no need for me to talk. It wouldn't do any good. My arrest had been a setup, engineered by the sheriff and the revenue officers. They hadn't been able to catch me in the swamp, so they figured out another way. The black policemen were only doing as they had been told. I knew for a certainty that I was going to jail, and how long I would be incarcerated would have to be determined by the judge. I couldn't think of a worse fate.

Monday morning justice was a swift affair in the crowded courtroom. Hiring a lawyer would have been a waste of money. I hadn't tried to get in touch with Papa. He would find out soon enough. Besides, he couldn't help me. I was booked to go.

The judge was a jovial free-hearted redneck who enjoyed giving lengthy sentences to Negroes. There were quite a few colored awaiting trial. The judge was full of goodwill—in a real giving mood. I got 30 days for littering a public street and 15 days for loitering and indecent exposure. I had never before been deprived of my freedom. Forty five days in jail would seem like an eternity.

If things weren't bad enough, on Tuesday morning the turnkey and a deputy brought a prisoner to share the cell. His name was Lobo Johnson, and he was a huge Negro, jet black, with broad shoulders and bulging muscles that rippled beneath his shirt. He had muddy red eyes and a moon face, and he smelled like a big man. His large nose flattened above big lips that covered uneven rows of bad teeth. Law enforcement officers usually avoided him like the plague. I wondered how many had it taken to bring him in. Lobo Johnson was well-known around Fayetteville, hated and feared as the meanest Negro in town.

He had killed three people that I knew about. It was said that he had more murders to his credit up in Sampson County from where he came. Few people called him Lobo Johnson. He preferred to be called by his nickname "Black Daddy." Most folk were glad to oblige because they got awfully uneasy just hearing his name. I was all eyes as the two deputies led him down the corridor and stopped at the door to my cell. When I recognized who he was, I panicked. My throat got dry and I began to tremble. "Ohh shit!" What a rotten piece of luck. I would be sharing a cell with the notorious Black Daddy. It was a horrible twist of fate, and it was the worst thing that could have happened to me. He was not just a killer. It was also rumored that he had a liking for young men. It had been said around town that Black Daddy would walk over ten naked women to get to one fully clothed young man. I suddenly remembered what had happened to Jamie June. There was nowhere to run. I didn't know what to do. My behind was in jeopardy the minute Black Daddy stepped through the door of the cell.

The door of the cell clanged shut. The two guards were laughing loudly as they walked slowly up the corridor.

"I sure do feel sorry for that young nigger," said the turnkey. "He's gonna catch hell tonight."

"Aw I don't know," said the deputy, "Black Daddy might let him slide for a day or two." His laughter filled the corridor. "But, I'll bet you a dollar to a donut, before that slick-ass young nigger gets out of that cell, he'll be holding a limp wrist and talking soft and sweet. Black Daddy will have his asshole reamed out so big until you kin drive a truck through it."

The footsteps of the deputy and the turnkey faded as the big man turned and faced me. He said nothing as his muddy eyes traveled the length of my body. Warily, I watched his big, ugly face as he sized me up. I backed up until I was touching the wall beside the bunk. There was no protection from the huge man. I knew that whatever I did meant nothing. I was as scared as I had ever been. My eyes never left his face. If he had licked his lips, I would have probably voided on the spot. At last he spoke. His gruff voice scared me even more.

"You're sleeping up top, ain'tcha sweetie?"

I moved quickly to the lower bunk and picked up the Gideon Bible that had been left by a former tenant.

"Yeah, Black Daddy," I said quickly. "The top bunk is just where I had planned to sleep." He grunted audibly, and his muddy eyes seemed to probe and feel every inch of my body. My mouth was bone dry, and cold sweat trickled from my armpits. Black Daddy said nothing else. I was to learn quite early that he was a man of a few words. I took solace in that revelation.

I looked down at the Gideon Bible. It looked brand-new. I squeezed it tightly against my chest and whispered, "Dear Jesus, please help me! Don't let this big nigger get ahold of me!" I knew that I needed the good Lord, His angels and anybody else who was willing to help.

When bedtime came, I was fearful that Black Daddy would grab my legs or try to hinder me. I picked my chance and scrambled up and into my bunk. I held the Gideon Bible and made a big production of saying my prayers. I spoke loud enough to make sure that he heard me. I started to mention Black Daddy in my prayers, but I thought better of it. I leaned over to get a quick look at him. His eyes bored up at me, but he said nothing. I was trembling, much too frightened to go to sleep. I lay awake all of that night tossing and turning, in a cold sweat and wondering if Black Daddy were going to try anything. It was like sleeping with the devil under your bed.

I was still a little perturbed the next morning. I grabbed my clothes, jumped down from the bunk and glanced at the lower bed where Black Daddy was lying. My eyes widened in amazement. He was lying on his back in nothing but his undershorts. The placket of the shorts was open, and I found myself looking at the biggest erection that I had ever seen. He began to twitch, and the huge organ moved jerkily to and fro. His small piggish eyes narrowed wickedly as he waited for a reaction from me. I glanced at the huge monstrosity and quickly looked away. If this were his idea of a scheme to hasten my seduction, he was out of luck. I wasn't going to give him any reason to come after me.

Black Daddy kept staring at me, and his eyes seemed to rake my body like hot coals. His huge lips were parted, showing his bad teeth, and there was an evil glint in his bloodshot eyes. I knew that it was a nasty scene staged especially for my benefit. He would use coercion or force, whichever worked to achieve his dirty aims. He might as well forget it. I was not going to buy into his line of conduct. The Stonewall heritage was alive and well. He continued to gloat as he watched my discomfort. I looked away in a hurry as instant fascination was replaced by fear. I went back to the berth, grabbed the Gideon Bible and walked over to the door of the cell and opened it quickly. The page happened to be the beginning of the eighth chapter of Romans. Thank God, I knew the chapter in its entirety. It was Grandpa's favorite chapter. As his sight grew dim, he had often asked me to read for him. Maybe the ruse would work.

I stood there at the door to the cell and began to read loudly, trying to sound like Grandpa. I was nowhere close, but as I began to read a strange thing happened. Black Daddy sat upright and began to listen. I glanced sideways to see how he was reacting. His sexual problem gradually went away as he listened intently to my voice. There was a puzzled frown on his face and a grudging look of respect. The intended violation of my body was on hold for the moment. It was a time to count my blessings, but I knew for a certainty that I was still a prime candidate to satisfy his lust. The threat to my posterior was real. Its innocence was in

Jailhouse Blues

imminent danger and hanging by a thread. My manhood was going to be put to a test, an unwilling captive, subject to the twisted whims and dark vagaries of the big evil man called Black Daddy.

During the next few days my situation did not improve. I always kept the Gideon Bible close at hand. I was convinced that Black Daddy's awe of religion and the Bible was the only thing that stopped an assault on either end of my body. He hardly ever spoke, but his eyes followed me everywhere, like a cat stalking a mouse. I finally decided that he wasn't going to use force except as a last resort. The Bible remained my rod and staff. Every time there was a hint of coercion, I would reach for the Bible. If it weren't within reach, I would solemnly begin to quote Old Testament Scriptures until I could get to it. There were times that I would hold it in front of me as if Black Daddy were a vampire, and I was holding a cross to keep him at bay. Somehow I managed, but each day it became harder to hold him off.

Mornings were the worst times. It was normal for a man to wake up with an erection, but it was not so with me. Because of my fear of Black Daddy, morning for me was an unruffled time of day. However, it was nerve-wracking to climb down from my berth and confront the lewdness that Black Daddy displayed like a badge of honor. I could not help but remember the tortured face of Jamie June and the perversion that I shared with him. I swore that nothing like that would ever happen to me again. I did not intend to be reduced to a sniveling fart who solicited male sex.

But now, I was caught in a perilous web, not of my own making, and it would take all of the strength and resourcefulness of the spirit of Stonewall to get me out of the madness that was seeking to be perpetrate on my soul and body. There was one consolation. I had completely stopped worrying about the size of my penis. There were other body parts to consider.

Several things happened within the next few days. Black Daddy was taken from the cell for questioning concerning the original charge of murder, and I came down with a bad cold. When they brought him back to the cell, he was in a foul mood. He began pacing the cell, and suddenly, without warning, he began to talk about it. "Aw man, them dumb-ass deputies are crazy as shit," Black Daddy began. "Jist 'cause they found Jim

Jailhouse Blues

Stewart's body in the ditch near my house, they think I killed him."

Jim Stewart was a known associate of Black Daddy, and his neck had been broken. One of the other men Black Daddy was accused of killing had also died of a broken neck. At that point, the law could not tie the recent killing to Black Daddy, but officials were working on the theory that he was responsible. The deadly pattern of bodies with broken necks certainly pointed the finger of guilt at him.

"Well," I said, carefully choosing my words. "There's one thing for sure, Black Daddy. If they can't prove you're guilty, they'll have to let you go."

It was Sunday, and we were eating a lunch of chicken, collard greens and potatoes with pumpkin pie for desert. I didn't like pumpkin pie, so I held out my piece to Black Daddy.

"Would you like my piece of pie? My belly is plum full. You're welcome to it." He nodded, then grabbed it eagerly. "Yeah, I'll eat it, but I ain't got no business with it 'cause I got a touch of sugar diabetes." He wolfed down the pie in seconds.

After that I would always offer him my desert or anything else that he wanted from my plate. Losing a few pounds was well worth the chance of a civil relationship with Black Daddy. There were times when I didn't have to worry about his advances because he would always drop off to sleep as soon as he had eaten. It was a ritual that never varied. Sometimes he would sleep for hours. However, during his waking hours, it was always the same. His eyes would be riveted to my backside, hungrily watching every move. There was no escape. The world outside and the prisoners in the other cells ceased to exist. It was just Black Daddy and I. I was in constant danger of being subjected to his warped desires and deviate behavior.

My nerves were ragged with fear, and I would jump at the slightest provocation. I became skittish and wary of any sudden moves by him. I was careful and always tried to keep the big man in front of me. One day as I turned away from him, he slapped me sharply across my behind. I stepped back, alarmed at what he had done. He stood watching me with an evil grin on his face. The grin faded, and the muddy eyes narrowed when he spoke his voice was low, menacing, the voice of a killer. Venom dripped from every word.

Jailhouse Blues

"Listen, you dumb son of a bitch," said Black Daddy. "You don't have to shy away from me. If I had wanted to, I could have fucked the shit out of you when I first got here. You know who I am and you know what I do."

He moved closer, baring his teeth. His bad breath blistered the air around me. "The only reason I let you keep your asshole was because of your Bible reading and praying reminded me of my Pa!"

He leaned forward. His eyes were boring into mine. His face was almost touching mine.

"Don't get shitty with me, nigger, and don't think it's too late. I might bust your behind wide open or do your mouth first just for the hell of it."

I was dumbfounded. I didn't know the reason for his anger, and I wished that I was a thousand miles away. From that moment, I was back at square one. As the days dragged on, it became harder and harder to resist his advances. If it hadn't been for the Bible and constant prayer, I don't what the outcome would have been. At the beginning of my sentence, I had been counting the days, but the strain of having to cope with fending off Black Daddy made time a relative thing. He was getting more insistent as the days went by. There were times when I thought about just giving up and letting him have his way, but the spirit of Stonewall restrained me from making such a dirty surrender. Jackson had been a fighter, not a gutless quitter who would give in to adversity, and neither was I. I was not going to be Black Daddy's female. He would have to kill me first.

Each day seemed like an eternity. I knew that my time was getting short, but I didn't know the exact date of my release. Black Daddy continued to taunt and threaten me. The only respite that I gained was when he was asleep. His snores were welcome music to my ears. It was not so during his waking hours. He suddenly developed the habit of putting his hands on me and rubbing my behind at the most inopportune moments. It was on a Tuesday evening, and Black Daddy's verbal and physical assault on me continued at a stepped-up pace. That afternoon I was glad when it was time for supper. The jailer was looking at me with a wide grin as he shoved our trays into the cell.

"Well, slick-ass nigger, it looks like the judge took pity on your black ass. They're giving you time off for good behavior. You're gonna be getting out of here tomorrow morning."

It took a moment for the news to sink in. Suddenly I was laughing out loud.

"Hot damn! It's about time, boss man. I ain't had no business here in the first place!" I felt like jumping up and down. "One more night and I'm outta here!"

Black Daddy's face was screwed up in a frown. He walked over to the door of the cell and waited expectantly.

"Ain't got a bit of news for you, big nigger," said the jailer shaking his head. "From what I hear upstairs, boy, they're still trying to hang murder one on your black ass. They still think you killed the nigger that they found in the ditch." Black Daddy grabbed the bars of the cell door in helpless anger. The jailer walked back down the corridor whistling loudly.

I backed away from the cell door and looked at Black Daddy. He was furious. It was then that the realization hit me. I had been so excited at the prospect of getting out of jail until I had completely forgotten my other problem. There was no way on God's green earth that Black Daddy was going to let me leave that cell with my behind intact. He was still scowling as he walked back to his bunk. He put his supper tray on his lap and began to eat. I grabbed my tray and handed it to him. Wordlessly, he took the tray and sat it on the bed beside him. That was nothing new. I had been giving him my food for a while. He would eat what he wanted and leave me the rest. When he had finished eating, he sat the trays on the floor and looked directly at me.

"So, you're getting out tomorrow, are you?" He didn't wait for an answer, but stood up and walked over and faced me. "Listen bitch, don't think you're gonna git away from me. I'm gonna start fucking you jist as soon as the lights go out." He grabbed my collar. "Your cherry belongs to me! I'm gonna ride your rump until daybreak tomorrow morning." He slammed me against the wall of the cell. Trembling with fear, I ducked around him and climbed up into my bunk.

I lay on the bunk shaking violently, knowing that it would soon be time for the lights to go out. There was nothing I could do. Black Daddy would keep his word. I was about to calm down, but the lights blinked once, and suddenly the cellblock was dark. Sweat began to drip from my armpits. I knew that bad things were about to happen. I stiffened and braced myself for the attack that I knew was coming. Out of the darkness I heard a muffled snore. I waited a moment. The snoring became louder, then leveled off with an occasional groan. I eased to the side of the bunk and listened to be sure. I couldn't believe my good luck. Black Daddy was sound asleep. I placed my palms together, looked toward heaven and said, "Thank you Jesus!"

I couldn't remember dropping off to sleep. I wasn't dreaming. It was a nightmare, a giant earthquake that shook the bunk and threw me out of bed and onto the floor. I awakened hurt and confused. A hand was twisting my ankle. I realized that Black Daddy had pulled me from my bunk onto the floor. The pressure on my ankle increased, and Black Daddy growled in the darkness. He was grunting loudly as he tried to pull my shorts down.

"Goddammit, nigger, turn your ass over where I kin git to it!" I was scrambling as hard as I could to get away.

"Turn me loose, Black Daddy! I ain't gonna do nothing with you. Let me go, you fucked up son of a bitch!"

It was no use. I couldn't get away. Black Daddy grabbed my collar, and still holding my ankle, picked me up and threw me on his bunk. He jammed my head against the foot of the bed and held it there. He was breathing hard as he awkwardly leaned over the bed above me. I knew he was fumbling at the front of his trousers. I turned my head just in time. He jerked my head back and growled, "Awright, nigger, here, take it, and if you bite me, I'll break your goddamn neck!"

It was a superhuman effort. I could not have done it without the spirit of Stonewall. As the foul odor came closer, I arched my back and twisted away. My undershirt split, and Black Daddy released his grip on my neck. I freed my ankle from his other hand, scrambled onto the floor and crawled underneath until I reached the far side of the bunk. I plastered myself against the wall of the cell, grabbed the leg of the bunk that was against the wall and held it with all of my might. I knew that it wasn't over. Still grunting, Black Daddy knelt down, reached under the bunk and grabbed my left leg. He jerked furiously, and I screamed with pain.

Suddenly, a beam of light flashed briefly, and a voice cut through the darkness.

"What the fuck's happening in there? What are y'all doing?" The jailer's voice rang hollow as he yelled down the corridor. "Hey y'all, turn on the lights! These niggers in cell five are doing something funny!"

Light flooded the cell block. I could see the feet of the jailer and the deputy as they stood at the door of the cell. Black Daddy released my ankle and jumped up. The jailer sounded really pissed off. "Dammit, I'm gonna ask you again. What the fuck were you and Sawyer doing under that bunk, and why is he still under there?"

"Aw man," said Black Daddy, "ain't nothing for y'all to git upset about. Sawyer dropped his Bible behind the bunk," he snorted. "Then, the dumb-ass nigger got stuck when he crawled under there to get it." I could see his knees as he leaned down as if to look under the bunk. He sounded sincere. "I wuz jist trying to git him out. I ain't lying y'all." He gestured. "Look, I believe the son of a bitch is still stuck under there."

It was quick thinking on Black Daddy's part because the Bible had fallen under the bed during the melee. I grabbed it and slowly crawled from under the bunk. The jailer's face was red with anger.

"I swear to God. Leave it to you goddamn niggers to do some outlandish shit that nobody ever heard of." He scowled down at me. "Nigger, git up offa that floor! I ought to have the judge give you ten days extra jist on general principles."

The jailer was still mumbling to himself as he walked back down the cell block. Black Daddy was furious. As he paced about the cell, his face was contorted with rage. His whole being was boiling with hate and frustration. It didn't bother me at all. It was daylight, the dawn of freedom for me, and if the Lord were willing, and the creek didn't rise, I'd be out of there in no time. It was half an hour later when the jailer and the deputy came back. Walking between them was a thin good-looking young man about my own age. The deputy opened the cell door, shoved the prisoner inside and grinned at Black Daddy.

"Well, big nigger, it looks like you're in luck. Sawyer, here, will be leaving in a few, but I've got you a brand-new playmate."

Black Daddy's eyes narrowed imperceptibly, but he said nothing.

"This here's Lenny Blue," said the deputy. "He's got to do 30 days and some change." He sniggered nastily. "Treat him right, you hear?"

The young prisoner looked sullen. There was the beginning of a sneer on his handsome face. His eyes traveled around the cell and came to rest on the top bunk. He reached up and took the Bible from the bunk and held it toward me.

"Does this book belong to you?" he asked. I responded quickly.

"Nah, it ain't mine. It comes with the turf." I looked directly into his eyes. "It's a good read though. Maybe you ought to check it out." His lips pouted in disdain.

"Nah, fuck it, man. I don't wanna read no shit like that. All I want is to do my time and get back on the street."

"I guess I know what you mean, hoss." The youngster seemed bold, brash and sure of himself. I knew that would change. It was a certainty. Just as sure as God made little green apples, Black Daddy was going to pop him. He would not be as lucky as I had been. His posterior and his mouth would be Black Daddy's exclusive property for at least a month. I had a feeling that neither end would be treated with kindness. I shivered at the thought, a tinge of pity came over me. A moment later it was gone. "Well," I said nonchalantly, "you take it easy greasy 'cause you got a long way to slide. That's the way of the world, some coming and some going. Don't worry sport, you can do it standing on your head. Time ain't nothing but a number."

The jailer looked at me and said angrily, "Awright Sawyer, quit bullshitting and come with me. They'll process you up front."

There was a bounce in my step. Freedom was just yards away. When the paperwork was finished, I bounded through the big double doors and stopped for a moment on the marble steps of the courthouse. I breathed deeply. The air of freedom was sweeter than the smell of honeysuckle flowers. It was a new beginning for me.

The sun shone brightly, and the downtown air carried the slight stench of exhaust fumes, but that too was the smell of freedom. I laughed out loud, and the spirit of Jackson laughed with me. Once again I had triumphed, this time in an arena where I had come to grips with my own sexuality. The size of my penis was a done deal, but there would be no more doubt in my mind. I would be forever small, but I would also be forever masculine. The cunning and wit of the famed general had asserted itself, and it was another decisive battle won by the legendary Stonewall Jackson.

18

Preparation for Redemption

It was the middle of May, 1950, and it was after ten o'clock in the morning. In the swamp, it was already hot. I didn't mind the heat or the mosquitoes because I was in the swamp to do my religious duty as a member in good standing at Mood's Temple Church. Papa's bush axe, rake and a shovel were leaning against a poplar tree a few feet from the stream bed. The bush axe was razor sharp. Papa always kept his tools in good shape.

The little stream meandered swiftly until it reached this spot. Here it swirled lazily with eddies gently brushing its banks. Then the dark water dipped suddenly and rushed down the narrow chasm. At this point, the little creek was at its widest, with a depth of about five feet. This was the place chosen by the pastor to perform the ritual of water baptism for the saved souls who had promised their lives to Christ. I could have asked for help, but this was my swamp, and I wanted to do it alone.

I made a beeline for the church on the first Sunday after I had gotten out of jail. Reverend Elliot, the pastor, was really impressed when I stood up at the end of the service and asked for the prayers of the church to help me to quit my sinful ways.

The congregation rejoiced as I knelt before the altar while the pas-

Preparation for Redemption

tor asked the Lord to give me one more chance. Reverend Elliot was even more impressed when I volunteered to make sure that the site of the baptism was clean and safe for the upcoming service.

My job was to clear the banks of the creek, get rid of the snakes and make the area safe for the candidates for baptism. I had volunteered because it was part of the new direction that my life had taken. I planned to serve the Lord. There would be no more slick suits, no more gangster shirts and loud ties and no hip talk from the side of my mouth. From now on, I was walking the straight and narrow, strictly adhering to the principles upon which Grandpa built his life. It was only fitting that my new direction would begin right here in the swamp. I was a willing candidate for the healing waters. My baptism there would be the turning point, a means to stop my downward slide to oblivion. So much of my life had unfolded there in this tranquil greenness. For me, this was a shrine of sorts, a holy place. The decision to restructure my life had taken a lot of soul searching. It would mean giving up a lot of things that I had become accustomed to, but with strength and fortitude inherited from my fabled ancestor, Stonewall Jackson, I could do it with grace.

It was not going to be easy to clean up the area on this side of the creek for the baptismal ceremony. I would have to cut all of the briars, reeds and overhanging vines so there would be room for the congregation to stand near the water. I would also have to make sure that there was nowhere for cottonmouth moccasins or other poisonous snakes to hide. I had already cut a narrow path leading from the Rose Hill Road to the edge of the stream. I glanced up through the trees. The clear blue of the sky was a reminder of the purity that I was seeking. Peace was mine for the asking. The sun was high, and its bright rays sliced through the foliage. Soon it would get scalding hot in the swamp. I grabbed the bush axe and began to clear the ground near the creek. It was hard work, but it felt good to do the right thing.

I raked the debris into piles near the the edge of the woods. The heat from the sun glued the khaki shirt to my back, and beads of sweat rolled down my forehead. The perspiration burned as it ran down my face and into my eyes. I stopped, fumbled for my handkerchief, and began to wipe my eyes.

At that moment soft, derisive laughter filled the small clearing. I'd know that laughter anywhere. Reluctantly, I turned toward the sound. Fast Fanny, resplendent in her work clothes, walked slowly toward me. Aw man, Satan sure didn't waste any time. He was already starting to obstruct my path, and he knew exactly what obstacles to use. The short pink dress seemed to be stretched tighter than ever about the lushness of her full body. There was a wicked smile on her face.

"Hey, Davy boy! What kind of bird can't fly?" I was angry. My composure and Christian reserve went down the creek.

"Why did you come up here Fanny?" I leaned on the bush axe and looked directly into her eyes. "You know I ain't selling no liquor, and you know I just got out of jail." I waited a moment to let the words sink in. "There is one other thing. I'm changing my ways, so you don't have to come up here shaking your big butt at me. I'm trying to get close to the Lord. The last thing I want is a piece of tail. I don't walk that road any more. You can take that mess you're selling right back to Jones Street. I don't want it! Your customers are waiting for you," I growled. "Sell it by the pound!" Her eyes flashed angrily.

"Why, you pimpish son of a bitch," Fanny bellowed.

She walked slowly toward me. Even in anger her slouchy walk was an open invitation, as raunchy as ever. When our faces were almost touching, she snarled. "Listen punk, I heard you were locked up with Black Daddy. It ain't no wonder that you don't want a woman. After Black Daddy manhandled your ass, you probably just want more of the same."

I was about to reply, but her smell filled my nostrils. The odor of stale liquor and her cheap perfume mingled with the earthy smell of her body. Small droplets of sweat beaded her upper lip. Her careless eroticism created a disturbing scene. Waves of lust engulfed my body. I didn't know if it were my own feelings or the Jackson curse. There were times when it was hard to tell the difference. My senses went wild, and instant desire heated my loins. The forces of darkness was about to win this one hands down. It was no contest. Fanny's tongue came out and slowly began to massage her full lips. It was a gesture meant to upset me, and it did just that. My throat was dry, and my breathing grew ragged. It was a blatant invitation. Dalliance was the name of the game. Reeling, I backed away.

Preparation for Redemption

I was in a quandary. After the stay in jail, I had done a lot of soul searching before deciding to mend my ways. Abstinence was at the top of my list. This situation simply proved me wrong, and I lost the test. My mettle was pliable, especially where Fanny was concerned. She tossed her head and with hips swinging walked to the edge of the clearing and sat on a slight knoll with her back leaning against the base of a small pine. She squirmed a little and then crossed her legs with a careless move that sent the short dress halfway up her thighs. Fanny made a kittenish sound and arched her back. The nipples of her breasts strained against the fabric of the tight pink dress. I could feel myself losing restraint. I knew all was lost when her brown eyes widened and looked into mine. She was sure of herself, and it showed.

"It looks right good, don't it Davy, boy?" She grinned lasciviously. "You want it bad. I know it, and you know it. Before I leave this swamp, there's gonna be some hard loving done." Impatience shrilled her voice.

"Come to Mama, baby!"

Angrily, I turned and walked a few feet up the creek bank to a stand of vines and reeds. I grabbed the bush axe and began to swing it as hard as I could. It was no use. Lust kept pestering me.

Why did Fanny keep messing with me? She had told me over and over again that I wasn't worth a damn in bed. Why did she still want me? She wasn't convinced that I was attempting to change my life. If I refused her offer of sex, she would spread the word that Black Daddy had made a bitch out of me. She already believed I had given in to Black Daddy. I couldn't have that sort of gossip going around the neighborhood. It would ruin what was left of my reputation. I slammed the axe into the pile of brush, then turned to look at Fanny.

Her actions were slow and deliberate. She took a crumpled pack of Luckies and a book of matches from her bosom, kicked a cigarette out, tamped it with her thumb and looked up at me.

"Well, Davy boy, what's it gonna be?" She grinned evilly as she lit the cigarette.

"Are you gonna fuck? Or, are you too used to getting fucked?"

Her eyes narrowed as the smoke from her cigarette drifted slowly upward. I whispered.

"Dear Jesus, oh Lord, please don't let this happen!"

Preparation for Redemption

It was no use. My dedication to Christian service also went up in smoke. I grabbed the axe and turned back to the pile of debris. The axe was in mid-air when Fanny laughed loudly. I turned just as she hiked the dress up and opened her legs as wide as possible. She was wearing nothing underneath. The bush axe came down, barely missing my right foot. I quit. It was the only thing left to do. I stood for a moment, fighting the impulse to be with Fanny. If I didn't make love to her, she would certainly spread the word that I had been Lobo Johnson's bitch. I would never live it down. I walked over and leaned against the giant poplar. As I looked down at Fanny, my groin began to ache, and the heat from wanting her scorched my inner thighs. The feeling was so intense until I decided to go with it just this once and worry later. Maybe the good Lord would forgive one quick slip from the straight and narrow. The pungent odor of her earthiness swirled upward as I knelt beside her.

"Okay Fanny," I said slowly. "Just how much money do you want for a quickie?"

The long lashes fluttered as she looked up at me. Her right hand came up, and she gently ran her fingers through my hair. "Lord, that curly hair of yours is something else." she spoke softly. "It won't be a quickie babycake, and it ain't about money." Her breathing grew hurried. "This is a freebie, hon. I jist want you." I backed away, making one last effort to shun the very appearance of evil. The short distance to Fanny's buxom body was a road paved with good intentions. Unable to resist any longer, I went into Fanny's arms with the sinking feeling that the devil had finally caught up with me. Big loose breasts and wide open legs were beckoning me. There was no confusion. I knew I was in the presence of evil. The prince of darkness, resplendent in all of his wickedness, was in the guise of a trashy, well-built woman with fire and damnation blazing between her hungry thighs. Without any coercion, I willingly went straight to hell.

I lasted just about as long as a snowball in a hot place. It was over before Fanny could utter her familiar scream. I lay there waiting for the tirade that I knew would follow. Instead her arms tightened around me, and her lips nudged my cheek.

"Please Davy, boy, don't move. Stay inside me, it's okay."

Her lips pressed against mine, and after a moment her tongue crept

Preparation for Redemption

into my mouth, timidly at first, then boldly probing as her passion flared. Desire stirred, and my flagging spirits rose like Phoenix from the ashes. The heat from our bodies welded with the steamy wetness of the swamp. Suddenly, Old Jack took over, mounted firmly in the saddle and raring to go. This would not be a skirmish, but a full fledged assault. Lengthy Walker's advice was uppermost in my mind, and Jackson also knew that care and tenderness were the keys to this delicious puzzle. This saga was not going to end with "Wham, bam, thank you ma'am." There were no rabbits in these woods. This would be slow dancing to the muted music of myriad noises in a dense swamp. It could last forever. My satisfaction had come first, and now my goal in life was to please this sensuous woman who had a devil inside her and answered to the name Fast Fanny

It wasn't as hard as I thought it would be. Once I placed Fanny's feelings and desires at the forefront, it was incredibly easy. If a certain move pleased Fanny, I did it more than once, and surprisingly enough her screams were not loud. It was a fact of life. I knew she couldn't help herself. Instead of the usual loudness, there were quiet sighs and moans of gratification. Again and again, I brought her to the brink and then held her tightly as she shuddered with pleasure. When it was finally over, she looked up at me with the heavy lidded eyes of a satisfied woman.

"Davy, boy. You're good. You really are. In fact, when it comes to pure fucking, you're the best I've ever seen." She shook her head slowly. "I don't know what happened to you in jail, but it's been a long time since anybody made me feel like that."

Fanny had made me feel quite good about myself. I kissed her gently. I liked lying there beside her in the quiet solitude of the swamp. She looked quite vulnerable, like a big spoiled child who had just gotten her way. Suddenly, I had an urge to nuzzle the nape of her neck. I did it gently. Her full lips parted, and her big brown eyes looked into mine. She cuddled closer, and her voice was a soft whisper. "David, don't say anything until I finish, please?"

I didn't say anything, just pulled her closer and held her tighter. A tear rolled slowly down her cheek. I wasn't ready for that. Why was she crying? She gave a small sob and choked back the tears.

"Don't laugh David. This is gonna sound crazy as shit," she said. Her voice was barely audible, but it had an intensity that I had never heard before.

"I'm in love with you David. I love you more than I've ever loved anybody."

I was about to tell her everything was okay when she put her fingers to my lips. "No no, let me finish, David. I know that I've done a lot of bad things. I've sold a whole slew of pussy, and I done some other things that I'm not proud of, but I love you, David. I'll quit all that mess if you want me to." She paused. The tears were back. "I'm serious David. Please believe me." Her voice was suddenly husky. "I'm as serious as a heart attack."

I was beginning to care a lot more about Fanny than I cared to admit. I smiled at her revelation.

"What are you doing Fanny, baby? You're not trying to bullshit the bullshitter are you?"

Truth or crap. It was nice to hear such a compliment. Fanny spoke with the voice of experience.

"You're putting me on, babycake, but I don't mind one bit."

Fanny's head came to rest on my bare chest, and her voice was a husky whisper. "David, honey, let me show you just how much I love you." Her mouth gently kissed my nipples and moved slowly about the flesh of my chest and stomach. Her head continued its provocative journey, moving downward inch by inch. One minute there was nothing, and then a moist tenderness engulfed and gripped me with such intensity that my fingers clawed at the damp earth of the swamp floor. I had to bite my lip to keep from screaming. Her skillful manipulations were like nothing I had ever encountered. My spirits soared again and again.

There was no comparison to Fanny's expertise. Jamie June was a bumbling amateur. This was as it should be, a ritual of love performed by the right gender doing the right thing. It was too much. Fulfillment leaped hurdles through my being with the speed of light. A crash of gigantic proportions was about to happen. I tried to pull away but Fanny wouldn't let me. She was firm in her commitment to love me. She made the ultimate sacrifice. I lay still for a moment and for reasons that I didn't understand suddenly remembered the conversation with Ed and Lengthy's tricky answer to my personal question. I had sworn never to do anything like that unless it was absolutely necessary. Lying there in the quiet swamp with Fanny in my arms, I knew that I loved her as much as I had

Preparation for Redemption

ever loved anyone. I loved her more because of the unselfish act that showed without any doubt just how much she loved me. I had to reciprocate. It was not only fair. It was the right thing to do. She moaned softly and trembled slightly as I kissed her full breasts. My head moved slowly down the warm mound of her belly until the coarse hairs tickled my nostrils. There was no hesitation. It was absolutely necessary, a simple gesture worshiping my new love in a manner that would assure her of my love.

It was late afternoon, and we had talked for hours, mostly about our love. I did not know exactly when it became truth, but I was convinced that I was in love with Fast Fanny. She had almost choked me with her tongue before disappearing down the path to the Rose Hill Road. As I watched her figure fade in the distance, I knew that our love would last forever.

Well, so much for Christian endeavor. It hadn't worked. I was alone with my guilt and remorse. I did wonder for a moment about the Jackson curse. Who had been in charge during the recent sweaty encounter? Was it myself or the wanton spirit of Stonewall Jackson? Had his ghost somehow exorcised the same burning lust of a hundred years ago? Was it his idea or mine to worship at her shrine? Maybe Fanny's passion required the two of us to work in unison. I wished there was some way of knowing when Jackson's crazy spirit would show itself. In such a situation, there could be no order in my life, just disorder. I suppose both of us knew that Fanny was truly a daughter of Eros. It was not easy to cool the heat that smoldered in her busy body. A feat of that magnitude deserved accolades of the highest order. It was another triumph for the indomitable Jackson.

I don't know how long I sat there with the axe at my side. Once again I had reneged on my promise to the Lord. I had read somewhere in the Bible that the Lord would forgive a sinner 77 times seven. Here lately I had been pushing my luck, and I wondered just how close I was to that fateful number. Maybe when I got baptized I would ask Reverend Elliot to dunk me a few extra times instead of the usual single immersion. My strange behavior seemed to come in bunches like bananas. Would I ever be free, or would the Jackson curse dog my footsteps forever? Was

Preparation for Redemption

he responsible for all of my problems? I had barely gotten out of jail, and already I was into wrongdoing. I couldn't stop thinking about what had happened between Fanny and myself in the swamp. It was funny how I was always full of remorse after a big screw up. I needed to stop fooling around and address the problem. I longed for the day of my baptism.

19

Baptism, Wet Devil, Dry Devil

After the incident with Fanny, remembrance of her glowing tribute to my sexual prowess made my ego soar to unbelievable heights. The feeling didn't last. Depression set in when I suddenly remembered that in my haste to be with Fanny, I had used nothing to protect myself. One look at Fanny's body, and I had forgotten everything. It was a dumb thing to do because I had been twice bitten by the love bug. Now, I was afraid that I might have caught a venereal disease. Because of Fayetteville being just a stone's throw from Fort Bragg, syphilis and gonorrhea were prevalent all around the county. I swore that if I were all right, I would never again touch a woman without adequate protection. I waited a few days for the axe to fall and nothing happened. After a careful examination of everything involved, I decided that I had not gotten infected. Amen! My faith in Fanny had never wavered. I still loved her, but if it happened again I would certainly use protection. It showed that the good Lord was in His holy temple, and maybe He wasn't too angry with me. Amen again.

Maybe it was my spiritual upbringing, but the question of how to halt my rush to hell and damnation preyed on my soul. It was time for me to be decisive in my actions. Once again, I began to think more and more about returning to the sanctity of the church. Mood's Temple was

Baptism, Wet Devil, Dry Devil

my church of choice. In fact, it was the only church that I had ever attended regularly. But, I had one other thing to do. I needed a church wardrobe, something quite different from the flashy stuff that I usually wore. It would mean that I had to go downtown to Mr. Avon's pressing club, and since my incarceration I stopped going into town unless it was absolutely necessary. It made no sense to give the two colored policeman another whack at me.

It was Saturday morning, and I was back in downtown Fayetteville. This time it was different. There was nothing flamboyant about me. This trip was necessary. It was about change. I was dressed in worn khakis and carried a bundle of suits and shirts to be cleaned and altered at Mr Avon's. His little tailor shop was located in back of the poolroom on Person Street. He was also the Sunday School Superintendent and a deacon at Mood's Temple. He looked up from the steam presser as I entered the door. Mr. Avon was short, brown-skinned and completely bald. He had dedicated his entire life to teaching young people at the church. He smiled as he peered over his brass-rimmed spectacles.

"Good morning Dave boy. How you doing?" The smile broadened. "I haven't seen you for a while." I had known Mr. Avon since I was a small boy. I liked him a lot.

"I'm doing good Mr. Avon, real good." His brow arched a bit, and his eyes narrowed. I knew that he was skeptical of my pat answer. He knew from past experience that urging me to straighten out my life and come back to church was an exercise in futility. I didn't give him a chance to say anything.

"Honest, Mr. Avon, I've been thinking real hard about paying my general claims and renewing my membership. I'm coming back to church for good." I held up the bundle of clothing. "I'm dead serious Mr. Avon. I want you to do my shirts and fix up these suits so that they'll look okay for church. I don't want to look sporty or anything. I just want to serve the Lord."

Mr. Avon looked thoughtful for a moment and then peered into my eyes. When he spoke his voice was solemn.

"David, I hope you are serious. The church needs young people like yourself." There was a glimmer of hope in his eyes, and when he spoke again, his voice was hoarse.

Baptism, Wet Devil, Dry Devil

"Right now would be a good time, David. The congregation is in a transitional phase. Folk are arguing among themselves, and there's a lot of conflict." His voice was somber.

"The church is our staff, David. We've got to support it. Membership has dropped to an all-time low." He shook his head sadly. "Come on back David. The church needs you." I was impressed by the sincerity in his voice.

"Yessir Mr. Avon, I'll be glad to help in any way that I can. Just let me know when to start."

"Well David, I guess the first thing we need to do is to get the area around the church cleaned up." He paused for a moment. "Miz Janey Smith lives right in back of the church, and she has an awful lot of company. I hate to point a finger at anybody, but there's a lot of trash and liquor bottles in back of the church. Folks can't hardly get to the toilets without stumbling over liquor bottles. I would certainly appreciate it if you could clean it up a little bit, especially around the path to the toilets."

When I left the little tailor shop, I felt good. It gave me a warm feeling to know that there was something I could do to help the community. The work that Mr. Avon wanted done was not what I had expected, but I would do it with pride.

It was after three o' clock when I got to the church. I crawled under the church steps and pulled out a rake, shovel and a hoe. The heat was stifling as I walked slowly around to the rear of building. Mr. Avon was right. The back yard of the church was a real mess. The afternoon heat was oppressive, and the air behind the church was filled with the stench from the trash. The church toilets stood side by side with the doors closed. Just behind them stood Miz Janey Smith's outhouse with its door wide open. The odor was sickening. I walked back up the path to the rear of the church and began to rake furiously.

I worked my way down one side of the path and made a pile of trash, bottles and debris between the toilets. I went back and worked the other side of the path and made another pile. I stood for a moment looking at my work.

Suddenly, another odor filled the air, strong, and familiar. It was either shit or hog chitlins. As I looked around to see where the smell was coming from, Miz Janey Smith, Retha Jane's mother, suddenly appeared

Baptism, Wet Devil, Dry Devil

at the back door of her little house. The smell of hog maws and chitlins billowed out of the open door. Chitlins was a delicacy of sorts for most colored folk, but I seldom ate them. I felt that nobody could clean them properly except Mama, and she was dead. Miz Janey's voice knifed through the acrid odors.

"Little David Sawyer, what in the world are you doing? I thought your dainty hands were too good for raking and such." I walked slowly toward her back porch.

"Nah, it ain't like that, Miz Janey. How you making out in all of this heat? I'm just helping out. Mr. Avon asked me to clean up a little bit back here."

My eyes roamed about her buxom body. She was an older version of Retha Jane, quite good-looking in a slovenly kind of way. I peered inside the little shotgun house. It was slovenly too. She smiled good-naturedly.

"You look hot and bothered," she said. "C'mon in for a minute. I got a pitcher of lemonade on the table." She eyed me shrewdly as I hesitated. "C'mon in, David. You don't have to act so skittish. I know Retha Jane's baby ain't yours. That lil' gal is the spitting image of Slick Willie B. I don't know why Retha tried to bullshit you into thinking that you were her baby's daddy." She pointed to the lemonade. "I'll git you a glass, and you kin sit down while I stir these chitlins. They're jist about done."

I poured a glass of lemonade, pulled up a chair and sat near the window. I could still feel the heat from the wood stove. Miz Janey busied herself stirring the chitlins. Sweat streamed down her ample bosom, and her clothing plastered itself to her body. Her large breasts loose and unhindered, jiggled wildly beneath the plain white shift. It was a raw, incredibly earthy scene and a sight that I would not soon forget. Her brown eyes twinkled as she looked over her shoulder at me.

"Davy, boy, I been hearing a lot of stuff about you. All of the women on Jones Street are talking their asses off about you. "Boy, you're something else!"

"I don't know what you mean Miz Janey." I was puzzled. "Who has been talking about me?" I kept a low profile since coming out of jail.

"You mean you don't know." Grinning lasciviously, she left the stove and came over to where I was seated. Her breasts brushed my face as she gently rubbed my head and lifted my chin so that she could look into my eyes.

"Fast Fanny's been telling everybody that you're a regular humdinger between the sheets."

My nostrils tingled. The odor of her body mingled with the smell of hog maws and chitlings was a strange mix, an unlikely aphrodisiac.

The way things were shaping up I was in trouble again. I looked deep into her eyes and decided that Miz Janey wasn't fooling. She was serious. Her full lips parted, and her breath came in short bursts as she leaned down and placed her mouth against my ear. Her lips pursed, and she blew into my ear.

"Yessir Davy, boy. Fanny said you were a dick-slinging fool." She was chuckling softly as her tongue caressed my ear. "C'mon David, tell me, are you a dick-slinging fool?"

Her nimble fingers were suddenly inside my shirt playing with the hairs on my chest. Her voice was hoarse, and her breathing was harsher yet.

"You wanna sling some dick, Davy?"

Her breasts were still pressed against my face. I tried to push her away. It was a half-hearted attempt, and she wasn't about to move.

"Aw c'mon Miz Janey, I ain't got time to mess around."

I grabbed the table and managed to struggle to my feet. At that point, I was as anxious and as upset as she seemed to be, but I was trying not to show it. My face was burning. It felt red hot, and my breathing was nothing to brag about.

"I don't know why Fanny said that all of that stuff, Miz Janey. I can't do nothing!" What was happening here? Silently, I quoted a scripture from the eighth chapter of Romans.

"For to be carnally-minded is death, but to be spiritually-minded is life and peace." It didn't help at all, the devil was in control again.

The Jackson lust surfaced with full force. I was amazed at its intensity. What in the world happened to Jackson's stern Calvinist religiosity? It came and went like a thief in the night. Right then it was nowhere in sight. The old rascal wanted this woman as badly as I did. Resolve to sin no more had suddenly evaporated, just like the steam swirling up from the pot of hog maws and chitlins. The three of us—Miz Janey, Stonewall and I—were caught up in the heat of the moment.

Miz Janey's fingers were still busy. Deftly she undid my belt buckle. I backed away just as her fingers snaked downward. The zipper came open, and as her eyes focused on me, I tried to turn away. She held me tightly, smiling as she looked down at me. She snatched my fly open, completely baring my nakedness.

"C'mon dick slinger, let's see whatcha got!" Grinning wickedly, she looked down at me.

I was angry. I was still embarrassed at anyone seeing my private parts. Frantically, I covered myself with both hands. Miz Janey put her hand under my chin and patted my cheek. She must have sensed how I felt.

"Don't be mad, David, honey. I was just teasing you. I already know about you being kinda small. Fanny told me. It's okay."

All was lost. I decided to get it over with as soon as possible.

"I've got to go to the toilet for a minute, Miz Janey. I'll be right back."

I hurried out of the back door and ran the few feet to the toilet. I closed the door and fumbled in my wallet for the single condom hidden behind my Social Security card. It took a while because I was so excited, and I almost gagged from the smell, but the odor of the chitlins had prepared me for the smell of the toilet. I hurried back into the house. The kitchen was empty. I was inside the bedroom door before I looked toward the bed. Miz Janey's large breasts loomed toward me like watermelons. What a sight. She was lying stark naked on the bed, spread-eagled and sweaty with her hands entwined behind her head. Her long tongue slowly licked her lips, and a cynical smile came and went. Her eyes twinkled as she looked up at me. "Davy, boy, do you see anything that makes you want to sling some dick?"

My throat was dry as a desert. I was trembling as if I had the ague. Stonewall Jackson was in control, and he was well known for striking with lightning speed. It was amazing how quickly he helped me to disrobe. I dived toward the bed and landed squarely on a body worthy of the painter's brush of Rubens, who gloried in bringing buxom beauty to his canvas. The Jackson lust groaned in anticipation as I went helter-skelter into the open arms of Miz Janey Smith. She caught me with ease and held me tight as her passion grew like fire in the wind. The general was in his element. He was a regular tiger in bed.

With a low groan, we came together, trembling. It seemed as if the earth began to move. Here again it was a matter of control. I exercised the teachings of Lengthy Walker to the fullest degree. Caring and concern and making sure that the woman's desires were fulfilled was the key.

Personal satisfaction could come later. Age made no difference. Orgasm after orgasm could be curried like small favors, leading to the height of satiety. I was beginning to be very good at doing nice things for women.

Miz Janey was grunting, groaning and twisting. Again and again, she shuddered violently. Kitten-like moans came from her open mouth. Keeping up with her was a difficult job, but it was something I had to do. I was really getting caught up in my work when the unthinkable happened. She groaned loudly as her legs tightened around my back. Her hips banged against me three times with incredible force. The third time her hips collided with mine the condom burst, and she screamed.

"Lord have mercy, David, hold me! I'm coming again!"

Ohh shit! My sudden naked descent into that heated orifice was an electrifying experience. Fear gripped me. It took every ounce of willpower for me to continue. Excruciating seconds passed, and then my role in the drama was over. I backed away, stood up and tried not to let her know of my concern.

"I've got to run, Miz Janey. Don't be mad. I just remembered something that I have to do. Maybe I'll come back later."

I was almost out of the door when Miz Janey stretched and smiled up at me.

"Fanny was right on the money, Davy, boy. You're a regular pine rooter when it comes to fucking." Her eyelashes fluttered coyly. "You're good Davy, boy, mighty good."

Praises meant nothing. I didn't have time for compliments from a well-satisfied middle-aged woman. The burst condom had put me at risk, and I had to do something about it. It was early evening and still hot when I ran out of the door and into the backyard of the church. Speed was essential. I did stop long enough grab the tools and place them under the back steps of the church. Time was a crucial element in what I had to do. I went around to the front of the church and waited for the traffic on the main highway to clear. I crossed the highway and hurried down the Rose Hill Road. I was almost out of breath when I ran up the steps of Aunt Lizzie's little house. I knocked loudly, stamping my feet in frustration as I heard Aunt Lizzie shuffling to the door. She recognized me at once. The words tumbled out.

"Aunt Lizzie, I'm in an awful hurry. I need a half pint of the strongest liquor you got. It's an emergency I got the money right here!

Her eyes narrowed as she peered up at me over her horn-rimmed glasses.

"What's your problem, boy?" She shook her head knowingly. "I knew you were lying when you said you'd quit messing with liquor." She turned and shuffled toward the bedroom. She came back with a pint bottle. Her eyes squinted as she held it up to the light to determine its contents. Reluctantly, she handed me the bottle and took the $2. "I ought not to sell you a drop, David. You're your own worst enemy, boy." I jumped down from the porch. "Thanks Aunt Lizzie, I appreciate it to the highest."

I hurried around to the back of the house. I looked around to make sure that no one was watching. Then I unzipped my trousers and saturated my pubic area with the hundred proof-plus moonshine. The raw alcohol seared the sensitive flesh of my penis and set my genitals on fire. I was hoping that the moonshine would kill any germs that I might have picked up from Miz Janey.

A week went by, and the moonshine either worked or Miz Janey was free of any venereal disease. But, I was not home free. I developed a terrible itch in my pubic area. I examined my groin and discovered tiny insects imbedded in my pubic hair. I grabbed the bottle containing the last remnants of Aunt Lizzie's corn liquor. I doused myself generously with the contents of the bottle. In a few seconds, I knew that I had made a terrible mistake. It had to have been been Jackson's idea. The wacky, old rascal should have known that the liquor would not kill the crab lice. The strong alcohol simply made them drunk. There is nothing, absolutely nothing more irritating and painful than being attacked by a bunch of drunken crab lice.

Regardless of my religious convictions, the sin of fornication continued to haunt me. The women from Jones Street and others from the Rose Hill Road were quite willing to force themselves upon me. The single women did it openly. The married ones did it covertly, and it made me awfully uncomfortable. It was unnerving as hell to have a woman that I barely knew accost me in broad open daylight.

"You're David Sawyer, ain'tcha? I heard about you. They say that you're a pine rooter from way back." The women were bold as brass. "I've got some pussy for you, if you want it. We can go to your place. You don't need money."

There was something about me that the women didn't know. It was

Baptism, Wet Devil, Dry Devil

a well-kept secret that I jealously guarded. Since the near mishap with Miz Janey Smith and the faulty condom, I had come upon a unique solution to my problem. I knew that the best of all possible worlds was to use nothing at all during the sexual act. Going naked into that delicate moistness was the greatest thrill of all. But, I couldn't help it. I was almost paranoiac about the prospect of catching venereal disease. If one sheath afforded a certain amount of protection, then two condoms together would do twice as much. Anyhow, by using two condoms the girth would be a tad larger, and in my condition every little bit helped. In retrospect, I decided that it was one of Jackson's better ideas. There was one drawback. The sensitivity was lessened, but it would also permit the man to last much longer. It worked quite well for me, and I found that women liked the aspect of love stretched to the breaking point. They liked it immensely.

The urge to engage in promiscuous behavior was overpowering. It seemed as if Stonewall Jackson could not leave women alone.

Retha Jane was my undoing. I still liked her even though she was Slick Willie B's woman and the mother of his child.

Early on a Saturday morning, I opened my eyes, and she was standing over my bed. A mischievous smile was on her face. She was still smiling as she slipped out of the blue dress.

"Good morning David, honey. I was just in the neighborhood, and I decided to bring you a shot of tail."

I came fully awake when she cupped her large breasts in her hands. She leaned over until her breasts were almost touching my face.

"Check these out, David. They're not bad for a girl who just had a baby."

I sat up wide awake. Papa would have had a fit if he saw her there. She giggled and pushed me back.

"It's all right Davy. There ain't nothing to worry about. I passed your Daddy down by the bridge."

The pink panties slithered down past her broad hips and fell to the floor. Impulsively naked, she sat on the bed and looked down at me.

"You're something else, David, honey. You're a real pistol. Fanny can't stop talking about you."

She giggled and began to rub my chest, kneading it gently. She pulled the hair of my chest and licked her tongue out at me. "Listen honey bunch, you ain't the only one who knows how to screw. I've been busy too. I've learned a brand new way to fuck." I had been about to get up, but that statement got my attention. She lay back on the bed and looked up at me. Then, she sat up slowly, reached forward with her right hand and grabbed the big toe of her right foot. She watched my face closely as she grabbed her left big toe with her left hand, then lay back and slowly opened her legs. Her voice was a husky whisper. "David, baby, tell me, what do you think of doing it like this?"

My ego was soaring. In the game of sex, Willie B. was not a bit player. He was huge. To have his woman come looking for me was a star in my crown and no small accomplishment. Retha Jane was vibrant, exciting, and she had a body that would whet the appetite of any male who could breathe. Great day in the morning! Her unique position on the bed presented amazing possibilities.

With this exciting new development it was easy to get completely carried away. I was as eager as she was, but in light of what had happened to me the last time, there was no way that I would do anything to her without using protection. Because of her association with Willie B, she was at risk. Being with her would certainly require the use of two condoms. I got up quickly, went into the kitchen and did what I had to do. I thought for a moment about using three condoms, but Jackson nixed the idea. It would have been ridiculous. A minute later, the two of us were lying on the rumpled bed, locked in a fury of give and take. Suddenly, a harsh voice rumbled, shattering the air around us.

"Goddammit! I knew I would find you here!"

Shock paralyzed my voice. It was Slick Willie B, and he was highly upset. He had the old owl head pistol in his right hand and a straight razor in his left hand. His face was blue-black with rage, and his eyes blazed daggers at Retha Jane.

"Bitch, I been following you ever since you left the house!"

He was waving the gun between the two of us. Finally, the ugly snout of the barrel focused on me.

"Motherfucker, I'm gonna blow your ass away and be through with it! Every time I turn around, you're in my goddamn business!"

Jackson was a prudent commander who had no qualms about a

strategic withdrawal if it were deemed necessary. However, it is a humiliating experience to have to run buck-naked out of your own house. I jumped out of bed, shoved Willie B aside and ran helter-skelter around the corner of the house. Two shots rang out as I took the path that led to the spring. One of the bullets whistled past my ear. I glanced back and saw an equally naked Retha Jane gaining on me. Willie B was not far behind, cursing loudly as he ran. Bouncing breasts meant nothing at this point. I yelled back at Retha Jane.

"Goddammit, Retha Jane, don't follow me. Get your ass away from me! He'll kill us both! For Christ's sake, run in another direction!"

Luck had not deserted me altogether. The vines and briars down in the swamp near the spring gave me a terrible beating, but the Bible asserted with firmness that for the sins that I had committed it was fitting that I be beaten with many stripes. Half an hour later, I came out of the swamp at the rear of Grandpa's farm. The house was a welcome sight, and Aunt Sarah's wash on the clothesline looked even better. Grandpa's corduroy pants were a trifle too short, but they were better than nothing. I was about to walk away when Aunt Sarah suddenly appeared at the back door. Her eyes widened at the sight of me. She recognized Grandpa's pants immediately. "David," said Aunt Sarah, shaking her head in disgust, "there's nothing you kin do to surprise me any more. But, tell me, jist what in tarnation are you doing with your Grandpa's pants, and why were you walking around buck-naked in broad daylight?" I hesitated.

"Aw, I'm okay Aunt Sarah. I ain't crazy or anything like that. A skunk got me down at the spring a few minutes ago. He sprayed me something fierce. I washed up and left my clothes soaking in the creek." I waited, watching her face, hoping that she would believe me. "Honest injun, Aunt Sarah, I'm trying to straighten up my life. I already quit drinking, and I don't chase after women no more." Uncertainty furrowed her brow. "Yes ma'am, Aunt Sarah, I'm going to get reinstated at Mood's Temple Church." She shook her head again and turned abruptly and went back into the house.

I waited for about an hour and then walked slowly up the hill to the house. After all, it was my house. I could come and go as I pleased, just as soon as I made sure that Slick Willie B was nowhere in sight.

Baptism, Wet Devil, Dry Devil

There was no sign of Retha Jane either, which was a good thing. I heaved a sigh of relief and then began to laugh. I kept laughing until the sound reverberated about the small shack. Hot damn! I was home free! There were times when I enjoyed living boldly in the shadow of a legend. Stonewall Jackson had out-maneuvered the enemy again.

Well, that did it for me. I had fornicated with a mother and her daughter, almost gotten myself killed and broken every promise that I had made to myself. From now on, I was through with sin, period. I was going to put Satan behind me and work strictly for the Lord. I was a little perturbed because the spirit of Stonewall with all of his vaunted religiosity wasn't helping me one iota.

Time passed with agonizing slowness. It was two weeks later, and I was still waiting for the atonement that the ritual of baptism would give me. I had finished clearing the brush and cleaned up the banks of the creek the week before.

All was in readiness for the baptismal service. At the previous Sunday's service, I learned that the baptism had been delayed because of internal problems at the church. The elders of the church and the members of the deacon board had discovered that Reverend Elliot had been doing funny with the money in the church treasury. The reverend did not go willingly. He resisted the ouster to the very end. In an unusual move, the matter was referred to the courts. It was an interesting development because Negroes had never done anything like that before. The matter was finally resolved when Reverend Elliot left town in the middle of the night, carrying whatever monies he could scrape together. Church records and ledgers containing minutes of recent church meetings were also missing.

The trustees, deacons and the church fathers were in no hurry. They were not going to snatch up the first jack-leg preacher that came looking for the job. Times had changed, and the church was in step.

With the influx of soldiers at Fort Bragg, Fayetteville was becoming worldly and sophisticated, a thriving community whose nearby cotton and tobacco fields blossomed with a new growth called surburbia.

Negroes were watching world events as avidly as whites. Radios complete with battery pack could be found in the front rooms of little shotgun houses of whites as well as in the rag-tag shacks of Negroes.

For folk accustomed to keeping piles of corncobs in the outhouse for obvious reasons, there was store bought toilet tissue hanging on the wall secured by a clothes hanger. The tissue's softness was constantly touted on the airwaves as a true panacea that could cure all ills. Octagon soap, that mainstay of country folk, was losing its importance. The harsh soap had always been used even in the most intimate areas of hygiene. In this new age, there were newer and better products on the market. In smart circles, the saying was, "If Rinso don't rinse it, and Duz doesn't do it. Fuck it!"

The year was 1950, and the conviction of Alger Hiss, the rise of Joe McCarthy and the war in Korea were heatedly discussed by Negroes and whites. Sometimes the conversation even crossed the color barrier.

For me, it was a time of abstinence. I no longer wore suits styled after Mickey Spillane. I decided to grow a small goatee and began to read everything I could get my hands on. But, salvation was always on my mind as I waited anxiously for the arrival of a new pastor at Mood's Temple. My soul cried out for redemption. I would be all right if I could just get certain parts of my body to behave properly. Mornings were the worst of times.

It was a hot, humid Sunday morning in the middle of July. The sun played peek-a-boo with the shifting clouds, and a soft breeze ruffled the leaves of the trees. I had been in the swamp since early morning to make sure that everything was in readiness for the baptism. This was to be the the day when I would give my body and soul to the Lord. I would go down into the dark waters of the creek a repentant sinner and rise up out of the depths a new creature, cleansed of all my sins, blessed with new birth and ready to serve the Lord. My khaki shirt and pants were damp with perspiration. The green vegetation of the swamp was hanging limp and listless. Beads of sweat dripped from the leaves and branches. The surface of the creek was calm, with none of the waterbugs that usually flitted across its surface. The big mosquitoes, lethargic and lulled by the intense heat, kept mostly to themselves. The swamp insects seemed to sense that this was an occasion devoted entirely to the Lord.

The entire congregation of Mood's Temple was gathered along the Rose Hill Road waiting for word to proceed down the path to the creek

Baptism, Wet Devil, Dry Devil

and begin the baptismal service. Vintage automobiles and even a pair of two-horse wagons lined the roadside by the swamp. The new pastor had been installed, and a rousing revival had been held the week before. The baptism of new members was once again on schedule.

The pastor, a much younger man than Reverend Elliot, was brimming with a restless ambition that had pushed him to the top of his class in Langston College, a divinity school in eastern North Carolina.

His name was Stanford McCoy, and he drove a shiny 1939 Buick. He was good-looking, well-dressed, had a pretty wife and, according to the womenfolk, was a regular firebrand. His sermons were a mixture of old time jump and shout and the calculated speech of a learned scholar. It was said that he had something for everybody and delivered it in words that each could understand. I was duly impressed and determined to have him help me shed my sins in the murky waters of the little creek.

As I stood near the banks of the little stream, the sound of gospel music floated through the tangled thickness of the swamp. The choir was called "The Voices of Mood's Temple." Light and shadows played about their blue and white robes as the choir made its way down the path. Members were singing softly, "Lead me to the water, Lord!" It was wonderful music that sounded majestic against a backdrop created with exquisite detail by the hand of Almighty God. Oh happy day! My mind, my soul and my body were open and awaiting the blessings of the Lord. The sounds grew louder as the congregation joyfully made its way down the small path toward the creek.

As I stood reverently, Reverend McCoy strode up the path toward me with his pretty wife respectfully at his heels. The pastor's wife was staring at me with a quizzical look on her face. I was careful not to look in her direction.

"Well, brother David," asked the minister, "how're we doing? Is everything okay?" His brown eyes narrowed as they searched my face.

"Everything's shaping up real good, Reverend McCoy." I pointed to the open area between the creek and the trees. "The congregation can assemble right over there by those poplar trees. I saw a few cottonmouth moccasins and one copperhead, but I beat the bushes real good and scared them away." I walked a little way along the creek bank until I came to a low place. "You can go in the water right here, Reverend. The water here is about four and a half feet deep. I cleaned up all of the trash and leaves, but there's still some mud and silt on the bottom. It will feel kind of messy to your feet but it won't hurt anything." He nodded his approval. "You did a good job David." He looked toward the congregation. "Well, we'd best get started." He chuckled. "We've got 14 young people to baptize, including yourself."

He walked back along the creek and gestured to the parishioners. "Praise the Lord. The choir will bless us with a song, and then we'll begin the service with a word of prayer from Father Fred Sawyer."

I didn't even know that Grandpa was there. He seldom came to church any more. My eyes roamed about the crowd. Everybody was there: Aunt Sarah, Papa, Uncle Mike, Ed and Louise, Fast Fanny and the whole Jones Street crowd. Aunt Lizzie was there too. I had heard her say on many occasions, "Yes, I sell moonshine, but I'm a God-fearing woman and selling liquor ain't got nothing to do with serving the Lord." Her eyes seemed to follow every move I made. I felt as if all of the folk present were watching me.

I had heard Grandpa pray many times, but in my state of mind it was as if the Lord himself were talking to me. When Grandpa finished praying, there wasn't a dry pair of eyes in the whole swamp. I anxiously waited my turn.

Sister McCoy stayed at the reverend's side as he stepped briskly into the stream. There were seven young girls and six boys to be baptized. The ritual was simple. With the help of his wife, the reverend would lead the candidate into the stream, place his hand over his mouth and look toward the heavens. Then he would shout in a ringing voice, "I baptize you in the name of the Father, Son and Holy Ghost!" With a loud splash, the candidate would be immersed into the cool water.

It was a sacred moment, and this was a holy place. The huge poplars, the reeds, vines and briars were sentinels for the Lord. The swamp was hallowed ground. Finally, it was my turn. The water was muddy by the time I stepped into the stream and stood between the pastor and his wife. "Praise the Lord," said Reverend McCoy. "We greet the prodigal son!" The pastor and his wife held me for a moment as he looked toward the sky. He spoke reverently.

"I baptize you in the name of the Father, Son and Holy Ghost!" I was gently lowered into the cool water. I was under the water for what seemed an eternity. When I finally surfaced, a miracle had happened. I felt clean. My mind was clear, and my whole body felt fresh and new. Even the sight of Sister McCoy's heaving bosom didn't faze me. The white robe plastered to the firm mounds of her breasts made her look quite spiritual. Praise the Lord! I would go and sin no more.

I had been the last of the candidates for baptism or at least the reverend thought so until Fast Fanny walked up the path and into the clearing. She wasn't wearing her usual make-up. Her face looked clean and fresh. She was dressed in a demure white dress with half sleeves, and her short hair was in tightly woven corn rows. She weaved her way through the crowd until she was standing in front of the pastor. There was a look of determination on her face. When she spoke, her voice was loud and clear.

"Excuse me Reverend McCoy." When she was sure that she had his attention, she said firmly, "Reverend McCoy, I know I ain't on your baptizing list. In fact, I ain't been to church in years." Her voice faltered. "I done a lot of bad stuff. Everybody here knows who I am and what I do. But, I've made up my mind that I'm gonna come to Jesus. I need your help. I want you to baptize me."

The whispers of the congregation rose and fell. The onlookers were amazed at this new development. Reverend McCoy clasped his hands, looked to the sky and beamed. "Praise the Lord! Thank you Jesus! Another lost soul is about to come into the fold!" Sister McCoy also had a broad smile on her face.

The pastor reached out and took Fanny's hands.

"Sister, Fanny, of course I'll baptize you, but you'll have to answer these questions first."

The pastor and his wife placed Fanny between them and led her to the edge of the stream. The reverend spoke in his best baptismal voice.

"Sister Fanny, do you believe in your heart and confess with your mouth that Jesus Christ is your Savior?"

"Yessir," said Fanny. "I sure do reverend, with all my heart!"

"We make no judgement of you," the preacher told Fanny. "We follow the Scriptures."

The three of them walked slowly into the muddy water. Fanny

closed her eyes as they went deeper into the stream.

"I baptize you," said the pastor, "in the name of the Father, Son and the Holy Ghost!" He was jubilant as he quickly immersed Fanny in the cool water. She emerged seconds later spitting and shouting. "Sister Fanny," said the pastor, "your baptism is complete! Go and sin no more! We welcome you as a full member of Mood's Temple Church. See the church clerk on Sunday."

Fanny came out of the water and into my arms. Her eyes were clear and without guile as she looked into mine.

"I truly love the Lord David," she said. "And I love you too David. We're gonna be all right, aren't we, honey?"

"The Lord is good, Fanny. We'll be fine, you hear." We stood there for a moment, holding each other tightly. The cool water dripping from our bodies was a sure sign of our redemption. Fanny and I were new creatures, and we were not ashamed. Our sins had been forgiven, and we had been washed in the blood of the Lamb. Life was suddenly a wonderful experience to be shared by the two of us.

We were deeply in love, and it was no wonder that thoughts of marriage and a home for Fanny and myself were suddenly at the forefront of my imagination. We waited until the congregation had left. Then we walked together arm in arm down the little path that led from the banks of the creek to the Rose Hill Road.

20

Jimmy's Back

I had kept the faith. My time was spent thinking good thoughts and trying to restructure my life in the manner according to the teachings of the Apostle Paul. I was no longer suffering from tunnel vision, Now, I could see things other than breasts and buttocks. Since my baptism, all thoughts about sex had taken a back seat. Marriage to Fanny was something about which I seldom thought. I began to really look at the world around me.

On a national level, trouble had been brewing in Korea, and the United States, as a member of the United Nations, was committed to defend South Korea from Communist North Korea. The resurgence of hostilities involving the United States did have one positive effect on Fayetteville and the surrounding community. For the first time since the end of the World War II, there were jobs, real honest-to-goodness jobs.

Men were needed at Fort Bragg to refurbish the military equipment that had been flowing back from overseas after the war. Some of it would be rerouted to Korea for the limited police action by American and U.N. forces. The jobs might not last because according to the President it would only take a few days to settle the conflict.

I was no longer concerned about the military aspect of the situation. The spirit of Stonewall Jackson had not deserted me. I was trying to rid

Jimmy's Back

myself of the spectral image that continued to haunt me. I was convinced that he had become so much a part of me until I had trouble figuring out whether my actions were my own or the wily manipulations of a man who had been dead for over a 100 years. It was time for Jackson to back off and let me live my own life. As a boy, I had often relied on tales of his bravery and daring to see me through many difficult situations. Maybe I had put too much stock in the fact that he was my mother's grandfather. I had to concentrate on the here and now. This was the real world, and I needed a real job. It was necessary. Honest work was essential in my effort to walk closer to the Savior.

On the morning that I applied for a job at Fort Bragg, civilian personnel was crowded with applicants, white, colored and a few Croatan Indians from down near Lumberton. It was a long shot that was made easier to attain. Warm bodies were desperately needed to refurbish the equipment that had been returned from Europe and the Chinese, Burmese and Indian theater of operations. It was also a long shot because Negroes were always the last to be hired in any event. I was totally surprised to receive a letter in the mail a week later. The job was mine if I could pass the physical. I was hired immediately as a painter's helper at Post Ordinance. My job was to sand and mask trucks, jeeps and tanks to be painted with camouflage colors for shipment overseas. Things were heating up in Korea.

Two weeks later at five a.m. Monday morning Papa and I were eating breakfast. I was about to leave for work, and he was getting ready to meet Miz Nellie Smith for their new enterprise. Papa's ministry and religious convictions were on hold for the moment. This time Miz Nellie and Papa were going to plant tobacco. She had talked Papa into using the joint tobacco allotment that had been assigned to Reverend Lonnie Pierce and him when they were sharecropping. Miz Nellie were going to plant the tobacco down in the woods behind her little house. They had cleared an acre of swamp that could not be seen by prying eyes from the road. The idea was to plant, harvest and sell the tobacco on Papa's allotment. I knew it was illegal, and I was sure that it wouldn't work, but Papa had caught so much hell from the world in general, and white folk in particular, until I was hoping that he and Miz Nellie could pull it off.

Papa was in high spirits. How else could he make money and also have the companionship of a woman who resembled his dead wife? He gulped down the last of the grits, sopped his plate clean with the last biscuit and stood up from the table. He looked at me and grinned.

"Well, Dave, I got to get on down to Nellie's place. We've got a lot of work to do."

Suddenly, my brother, Jimmy, was standing in the kitchen door. He was grinning from ear to ear. Papa was astounded. He grabbed Jimmy in a bear hug and picked him clean up off the floor. "Great day in the morning, boy! Where in the world did you come from?"

"I decided to come back home, Papa," said Jimmy. "I'm through with farming." The grin grew wider. It was a pleasant reminder of the past.

"I'm gonna sop up some of that gravy that David's been getting. Folks say it's running free and greasy all up and down the Rose Hill Road."

I looked closely at Jimmy. He was taller than I remembered but not as tall as I. His hair wasn't as curly as mine, but his skin was lighter, and he had the aquiline features peculiar to the Jackson clan. His shoulders were slightly slumped from carrying heavy golf bags. He had started to caddy much too soon over at the golf course. I blamed myself for that one. I had insisted that he accompany me. Jimmy's eyes were laughing as he turned to me.

"How about it big brother? You want to bring me up to date and cut me in on your hustle down in the swamp?"

Papa snorted. "Did you say hustle? Why don't you tell him about your hustle, Dave?" Papa grabbed my arm playfully.

"Go ahead, boy, tell him about ol' slick Dave." I grinned sheepishly.

"Aw man, Papa's full of junk, Jimmy. I quit the hustle, and I just got me a job at Fort Bragg doing honest work. Papa's laughing his ass off because I grabbed a little time in the county jail." Jimmy's eyes widened. I spoke slowly.

"It was no biggie, Jim. I was down on Person Street, and the two bullshit colored policeman arrested me for supposedly littering the street. They also claimed my fly was open and tacked on a charge of indecent exposure." Jimmy was watching me closely. "The whole thing was a bunch of bullshit, Jim. Derrick Carter and his goons couldn't catch me in the swamp, so he had his house niggers set me up. They really hung a bum rap on me." Jim was enjoying himself.

Jimmy's Back

"Well, I declare big brother," he said, "all of that preaching Papa used to lay on us, didn't mean shit to you, did it?"

"Ease up on him a little," said Papa as he reached for his hat. "Dave's been doing real good since he got out of jail. He got baptized the other week, and he's goes to church every Sunday." Papa shook his head with wonder. "Nellie said that she saw him coming from prayer service the other night." He walked toward the door. "It's a plum mystery to me, but it's a good thing if he'll just keep it up." He patted Jimmy's shoulder. "I tell you for a fact, boy, I'm sure glad you're home. I'll see y'all tonight. Maybe we can talk about old times."

Jimmy watched Papa as he walked down the path to the road.

"David," he said, "Papa's sure aged a lot since Mama died." Jimmy turned away from the door, and his eyes met mine. "When Papa walks, he's leaning over more than usual. Papa always did rock from side to side, but now it's getting worse."

I looked at Jimmy's face hoping for a clue as to what he had been doing, or whether or not he still had a problem with alcohol. He had started drinking heavily just after Mama died. Jimmy had been just 14 when he moved in with Mr. Jessop, the farm's owner. Jimmy was a good worker, and he did as much work as a grown man. Mr. Jessop drank a lot and always kept plenty of moonshine for the hired help. I was a little worried because Jimmy simply couldn't hold his liquor.

"What's wrong with you?" Jimmy asked.

"I didn't realize that I had been staring at you," I said.

"You were way off somewhere. Maybe you were talking to angels or something. You want I should say 'Amen.'"

I grinned. It was good to be with Jimmy again. It made me remember just how much I had missed him.

"Nah, I was just trying to figure out what we could do since you're back home. I don't drink liquor no more, and you ain't started fucking yet. Messing around with you might wind up being dull as shit." I looked at my watch. It was time to leave, or I would miss my ride to work.

It was late evening, and Jimmy and I had just finished eating beans and hotdogs for supper. Jimmy reared back from the table and looked intently at me.

Jimmy's Back

"Boy, you are something else! Everybody's been talking to me about you. And from what I've heard about you," said Jimmy, "you're doing enough screwing for both of us. From what they told me, even a case of the bullhead clap didn't slow you down. They're saying that you'll fuck a snake if you can get somebody to hold his head. You don't have to worry about me! I'll get me some tail when I get good and ready."

I knew that was coming. A moment later he was smiling. The old camaraderie was back. I put my arm around his shoulders, "Well, whenever you do get a girlfriend, I hope that you don't fuck like you catch fish." I knew that would irritate him. "I tell you what, Jimmy, ol' buddy. It's kind of late now, but let's go down to the pond and do some fishing. I got a good flashlight, and once we get the poles in place, we can fish as long as we want. What do you say?"

When we reached the pond, the shadows had lengthened into late evening.

"Okay, Mr. Bullshit Fisherman," proclaimed Jimmy, "we'll find out who can catch fish."

We usually dug our bait in the rich dirt under the back kitchen window. That was the spot where Mama used to throw her dishwater. But there was also plenty of earthworms right there in the dark earth near the bank of Slater's pond. When we had enough bait, Jimmy's movements quickened. I could see that he was in a hurry to start fishing.

"C'mon David," he said excitedly. "I want to see if that big ass eel is still in that hole near the spillway. I got a feeling that I'm gonna catch that sucker, tonight!"

It was like old times. We had a full can of big juicy jumping jacks and slow-moving earthworms. We rigged several hooks quickly, using a ball of twine that Papa kept in a shoe box under his bed. We didn't have to worry about fishing poles. We had cut a couple of reeds and small saplings when we first got down in the swamp.

"All right," Jimmy bellowed. "Let's go fishing!"

Slater's Pond was big enough to be called a lake. We were at the southern end of the pond and were going to fish at the mouth of the spillway. It was a good place to fish because the spillway was fairly large and dumped fish along with the pond's overflow into the creek. The swirling waters hesitated for a moment before rushing down the narrow confines of the stream. We stood for a bit watching as the dark water tumbled from the pond into the stream. Just below the spillway was a makeshift bridge of logs with a hand rail. Papa had built the bridge years ago when we had to cross the creek to get to school. Across the bridge and a few feet downstream was another pool of quiet water where Jimmy always fished. It was the same spot that he had almost caught the biggest eel that I had ever seen.

We divided the bait. Jimmy wanted the big jumping jacks because they wiggled more than the sluggish night crawlers. He took the can and tiptoed across the rickety bridge. I placed my worms in a small hole that I dug in the soft earth beside the creek. Jimmy could have his eel. I would be fishing for blue gills and sun perch. Aunt Sarah liked a good mess of fish for breakfast now and then. There were plenty of perch, blue gills and catfish swimming right near the bank on this side of the stream. I gauged the length of the lines to the depth of the stream, then baited both hooks and dropped the lines into the stream a few inches from the creek bank. Seconds later, both poles dipped one after the other. I grabbed the poles, jerked the lines and quickly landed a medium-sized catfish and a small perch.

I broke a small limb from a nearby sapling then carefully slid it through the gills of the fish and laid them on the bank and yelled.

"Hey Jimmy, when you gonna stop bullshitting and start fishing?"

He didn't even look up. He was busily engrossed in baiting his hooks. He placed several of the wriggling jumping jacks on each of the hooks. Finally, he tossed both hooks into the water. His eyes followed the bait as it sank into the murky water.

"Aw c'mon Jimmy, catch a couple of fish. Don't let me make you look bad," I said scornfully. Jimmy said nothing, apparently engrossed in his thoughts.

We sat quietly, each of us peering at the rippling water of the stream. The gathering darkness was hindered only by the crescent of a half moon that shone through trees. Its rays came and went as it reluctantly peeked at us from behind a cloud. It was a time for reflection.

Fanny had been in my thoughts for the last few days. In fact, before Jimmy came home, I had been thinking seriously of marriage. Since Fanny had quit prostitution, I could move in with her and pay all of the household expenses. There would be no need for her to hustle any more. We loved each other, and two people in love should be together. Her past would be just that. I was satisfied that I could live with what she had been.

Both of us had clean slates because we had been washed in the blood of the Lamb. Spirituality flooded my being. Glory be! The soft darkness of the swamp was fertile ground for thoughts of marriage and family.

Suddenly, the line nearest the creek bank jerked and became taut. The pole that Jimmy had secured by burying the butt end into the soft dirt of the bank pulled out of the ground and began sliding through the reeds into the water. Jimmy fell to the ground and grabbed the end of the pole just in time.

"Shit, fire and molasses!" hollered Jimmy. He hung onto the pole with both hands. "I got him! I got me a big one!" It was a big one. If Jimmy hadn't braced himself by jamming his heels against a small stump at the edge of the stream, he would have been pulled into the water. His eyes were filled with glee as he looked across the stream at me. "Dammit, Dave! Don't you come over here! I'll land this rascal myself! It's got be that big ass eel"

"Hold him, Jimmy, I'm coming! I ain't gonna help you! I just want to watch."

I scurried across the bridge. Jimmy was having real problems wrestling with the pole. My hands closed around the pole just above his fingers. The pole bucked and twisted as if it had a life of its own. The waters of the creek churned, dark and crested with foam. Jimmy backed up slowly, keeping the line tight. A huge ugly head appeared briefly at the surface, then disappeared. I said, "Shit, fire and molasses, Jimmy! You got him for sure! Pull the old rascal outta there!"

The thing was pulling Jimmy toward the water, and he was trying to retain his balance among the tightly woven reeds and briars. Jimmy fell, quickly regained his balance and pulled with all his might. The waters of the creek parted, and suddenly the creature was hanging in midair at eye level. We stared in horror. Jimmy screamed. "Great jumping Jehosaphat! What the fuck kind of eel is that?"

The creature was at least four feet long with a white belly and funny-looking dark spots that covered the slimy greenish skin. It had a really strange-looking mouth. There were no jaws, just a big cup-like sucker disk lined with funny-looking teeth. The tongue had serrated edges like a saw. Whatever it was, Jimmy wasn't about to let go. He began to jerk the pole violently. He shouted.

"I want to get the blame thing to the bank."

It surfaced again. The big disk of a mouth was opening and closing eerily. The hook was securely imbedded somewhere deep in its throat.

Jimmy's Back

It was a scary sight. I had never seen anything like it.

Suddenly, the line slashed away from the bank and out into the middle of the stream. It criss-crossed the stream and came to a halt just downstream near some overhanging brush. The only thing that stopped Jimmy from being dragged into the water was a rotted tree stump. He still ended up with one leg in the creek. His face looked grim as he scrambled back onto the bank.

"He ain't done shit," said Jimmy. "I'm gonna git him outta there if it takes all night."

I wanted to tell Jimmy to cut the line and say to hell with it, but knowing Jimmy that wasn't going to happen. His stubbornness was well known to me. He wouldn't quit, and we would probably be there all night, if not longer. I shook my head.

"I don't know Bro whether you will or not. I just remembered something that Papa said about an eel like that. You can't eat the blame thing. He called it a Lamphrey eel. Papa said that he saw one years ago down in the Cape Fear River. He claimed that it kills regular fish by boring a hole in them and sucking their blood."

"That's all the more reason for me to git the sucker outta there," Jimmy said. "You jist leave me the fuck alone. I'll git him."

Oh! oh! Here it comes. I was about to meet the other side of Jimmy, the obstinate, inflexible cussedness that could surface at any time. At times he would be dark, brooding and had a self will that filled me with envy. I might just as well sit back and watch because it wasn't a matter of if Jimmy would land the eel, but how long it would take. His denim shirt was soaked with sweat. I knew he was tired, but I also knew that he wouldn't quit. It seemed as if we had been in the swamp for hours. The shadows of the tall poplars and pines lengthened. The sun disappeared, and darkness invaded the swamp. Jimmy's eyes bulged, and his face was high yellow turned to granite. He was cussing up a blue streak.

"Come on, you slimy motherfucker! Git away from that bank! I'm gonna bring your ass outta there." He was bending and twisting the pole, trying to maneuver the fish away from the submerged roots near the bank.

"Easy Jimmy. Try pulling him straight up. It might work."

"Stop, David! Will you please shut the fuck up and let me do this? You're always trying to tell me what to do. I don't want your help!"

Jimmy's Back

I decided to leave him alone. It came to me. It did not come out of the blue because it was something that I should have realized a long time ago. Jimmy also had his share of the Stonewall heritage. He too was troubled by the quirky behavior that plagued Stonewall Jackson.

Ever since Jimmy was a small boy, his temperament and actions were just like the ones attributed to our great-grandfather. Early on, I had decided never to discuss it with him. I knew Jimmy didn't give a damn about Jackson, and he cared less than a fuck about why he acted the way he did. He was completely oblivious of the heritage, and more than once I wished that I had never heard about the relationship. It was trouble of the worst sort.

The sun had disappeared, and a half moon was rising through the trees when Jimmy pulled the big Lamphrey eel out of the water. I struck matches so that we could get a good look at it. The eel no longer struggled, and there was blood coming out of the disk-shaped mouth.

"I told you I was gonna bring that rascal in," Jimmy boasted. "Ain't nothing gonna stop me when I make up my mind to do something. No sir! I'm a bad motherfucker when I take the notion!"

I said nothing. I was still thinking about Jim and what I knew about Stonewall. "Awright Mr. Lamphrey," Jimmy said to the eel. He took the end of the pole and whacked it across the head. In the same instant, he kicked the big eel back into the water.

"That'll teach the slimy rascal to mess with me." I knew he was grinning at me in the darkness. "Come on Bro, let's go home!"

There was a catfish on each of my lines. They were really too small, so I decided to throw them back. Aunt Sarah liked fish of any kind. She would eat everything including the head and eyes, but she was kind of particular about the size. Jimmy was watching my face as I threw the fish into the water. His eyes probed mine in the darkness. He had a serious look on his face. He led the way as we took the path out of the swamp. When we reached a small clearing, Jimmy paused for a moment. "David, there's something I've been meaning to ask you."

"Sure, baby brother. What do you want to know?"

"Do you remember all of that crazy stuff that you made me do, like playing dead or having me pretend to be a Union soldier, and you were calling yourself 'Stonewall Jackson'?"

It was funny that he should ask. I knew exactly what Jimmy was talking about. "I'll swear, David. You really had me going. I got mighty tired of falling down every time you pointed a stick at me and yelled, 'Stonewall Jackson rides again!'" I knew he was smiling in the darkness.

"Boy, you did some dumb-ass stuff," Jimmy continued. "You were even trying to ride Missy, the cow. She'd throw your butt every time. You didn't have sense enough to know that you ain't supposed to ride a milk cow. You kept calling her 'Little Sorrel.' You said that was the name of Stonewall Jackson's horse. Boy, you were really hung up on that 'Stonewall' shit. I declare, David, I still don't understand what difference it made if Jackson were our kin. Nobody else in the family gives a shit, and a lot of the Jacksons out in 71st township don't even know about it. It's the first time I ever heard of anybody going clean fool about an old white man. From what I heard, he sure didn't care that much for colored folk. Papa said that he had slaves just like the rest of the white folk."

I thought for a moment. Jimmy was the one person in the world that I could be completely honest with.

"I don't know, Jimmy." Recalling the past was easy, but painful. "We were so damned poor, and things were so bad, I was getting tired of that hand-to-mouth shit. Things never got any better. When Aunt Lou and Grandma Jackson told me that we were kin to somebody famous like 'Stonewall' Jackson, I guess I went ape."

Jimmy was watching my face. My answer to his question seemed terribly important to him.

"At first it wasn't too bad, Jimmy. In fact it was fun to make myself believe that I could be like him."

"You sure gave it a heckuva shot," Jimmy said. "Every time I turned around it was something about Jackson. Papa thought you were crazy as shit."

"Nah, Papa knew I wasn't crazy. He was just as excited as I was when I went into the army. I thought everything was falling into place. I was finally getting my chance to be famous. I was already brave. All I needed was a chance to prove it." I thought for a moment. "If I'm lying, I'm flying Jimmy. It wasn't all my fault. Everything was going pretty good. I was moving right along, making rank, plus I was in the field artillery just like Stonewall. If I hadn't got mixed up with the first sergeant's woman, everything would have been all right. She gave me the clap, and I almost got kicked out of the army. I was lucky to get an honorable discharge."

"Yeah, right," responded Jimmy. He turned abruptly and starting walking. "C'mon, let's get back up to the house. I'm getting kind of hungry." He walked ahead of me with his head down. I knew he was thinking about what I had said. As we approached the spring, Jimmy stopped again. "Great day in the morning," he said. There was wonder in his voice. "You been real busy, ain'tcha, Bro?" He laughed softly in the darkness. "Boy, I tell you, you're a shot in the dark, for sure! There you were, way out in Oklahoma, showing your ass and fucking up all over the place. C'mon David, you didn't talk that Stonewall shit, while you were out there, did you?"

I began to laugh louder than Jimmy. This was just like old times. I put my arms around his shoulders and hugged him tightly. Side by side we walked slowly back up the hill. When we reached the house, I paused before going up the steps.

"Tell you what Jimmy, since you're so hungry I'll whip you up a quick pot of grits."

"You'll eat them yourself," he said as we went up the steps and into the kitchen. "I don't want no junk. I want me some real food, like fried chicken, collard greens and biscuits."

I lit the kerosene lamp, cleaned the smutty globe with a piece of newspaper and sat it on the table. I looked at the table. Papa had already come home and cooked dinner. He must have gone down to Miz Nellie's. The kitchen was a mess. There was a plate with two pieces of charred smoked sausage, several pieces of crisp fatback and a half-filled can of pork and beans. Spilled coffee and pork rinds lay beside the plate. Lying on the corner of the table in a puddle of fatback grease was a plain white envelope. Papa had gotten the mail from the mailbox. Jimmy and I saw it at the same time.

Gingerly, I picked up the envelope and looked at the address. It was addressed to James Harvey Sawyer. One glance and I knew exactly what it contained. Jimmy had gotten some important mail from the President of the United States. It was a draft notice. Without a word, I handed it to him.

Jimmy took the envelope, opened it quickly and began to read. Several things happened to Jimmy's face as he read the letter. His eyes widened, and his features screwed up like Papa's always did when there was a problem. His mouth opened, but no words came out. His eyes met mine. There were many things mirrored there, resolve, determination or resignation. I couldn't tell which.

"David," he said, with awe was in his voice, "I've been drafted into the army. I've got to report to the induction center at Fort Bragg on the 17th of September. Holy Moses!"

I didn't say anything. Words refused to come. But, there was one thing that I knew for a certainty, I didn't want my baby brother to go into the army. It wasn't that I was afraid for Jimmy. I knew that he would fare quite well in the brutal atmosphere of a basic training camp. Suppose he had to go to Korea? He might be killed. Death didn't frighten Jimmy at all. I walked around the table and put my arms around his shoulders and hugged him, just for a moment. Jimmy didn't like too much hugging. My voice did not reflect my true feelings. It occurred to me that fate might have a hand in that development. Maybe the powers-that-be had decreed that my brother Jimmy would fulfill the Stonewall legacy.

I said with confidence, "Don't worry about a thing, Bro, you'll be okay. Honest injun, Jimmy. I wouldn't kid you or lead you on. You can do that army shit standing on your head!" I consoled him with confidence.

"Well David," Jimmy said as his eyes traveled slowly around the little shack, "I'll be okay. Like Papa said, 'A man's gotta do what a man's gotta do.'"

21

Jimmy's Blues

"I got a mind to ramble, got a mind to go back home. I got a mind to be a good boy and leave all these women alone. Women off screaming murder, and I ain't never raised my hand. Yes Lord, women off screaming murder, and I ain't never raised my hand!"

Jimmy Rushing was a juke joint entertainer, who wailed the bluesy lament with cotton patch sincerity. The song became my brother Jimmy's personal blues. He loved it with a passion, but he couldn't carry a tune if it were as light as a feather. Jimmy always sang when he was drunk, and he was maudlin, almost in tears, when he sang it after receiving his draft notice in late August. Jimmy was no rambler, but that's the way he felt when he was in his cups and that was most of the time.

Neither patience, sobriety nor patriotism were Jimmy's strong points. He wanted to get his physical examination, be inducted and get it over. He continued to drink heavily. Money to buy whiskey was not needed. All Jimmy had to do was take a leisurely walk down the Rose Hill Road. Aunt Lizzie, Uncle Mike, Ed or Uncle Joe would be only too happy to give him a drink. On the surface, Jimmy was a good drunk, affable, outgoing and easy to be with. But, there was a darker side to Jimmy's drinking. At times, he was strange and withdrawn, surly. Mildy mad would be a good description of his actions. He might have drunk

Jimmy's Blues

himself into poor health before the date for his physical, except for the fact that he was not alone. Two other young men from the neighborhood had also received notice that their country required their services.

They were Kelly Elliot, a tall thin mulatto with a receding chin, who was Aunt Lizzie's grandnephew, and Harold Jones, a short young man with a face like the black comedian, Mantan Moreland. Harold was the son of Mrs. Alma Jones who lived across the field from Grandpa's. It was rumored that Harold Jones might not pass the physical because at 18 he had a heart condition.

Kelly and Jimmy had not really known each other.

Kelly had lived with his mother, Ellie, down in Whiteville. He had been sent to live with Aunt Lizzie when it was discovered that he couldn't keep his hands off the young girls in the neighborhood. The situation soon became intolerable because Kelly had two sisters, Allie, 14, and Ellie, 13. There really wasn't enough room in the little shotgun house for all the children. Propriety, good taste and common sense dictated that Kelly be removed from the house as soon as possible.

Other than that, Kelly was a good boy. There had been only one small incident since he had moved in with Aunt Lizzie. It had been a puzzling occurrence.

The trouble started one morning when Uncle Mike heard a terrible squealing coming from the pen of his huge brood sow that was located just behind the house. Uncle Mike grabbed his shotgun and hurried out to the hog pen, certain that wild dogs were attacking his blue ribbon sow. When Uncle Mike reached the pig pen, he was totally surprised and shocked to find Kelly chasing the sow around the pen in what could be called an extremely compromising position. One look at what Kelly had in his hands as he chased the sow around the pen was enough to convince Uncle Mike that his intentions toward the sow were far less than honorable. Uncle Mike was quite provoked by Kelly's pursuit of his prize sow. He did not inflict bodily harm on Kelly, but he did laugh about it frequently. From Uncle Mike's description of the fray, the sow would have been in trouble had Kelly managed to catch the animal. Word got around about Kelly's unusual liking for four-legged creatures. His image was slightly tarnished, and pointing fingers and giggles followed him for weeks. But, it had nothing to do with keeping him out of the army.

Jimmy's Blues

Maybe the army was where Kelly needed to be. He was raring to go.

Harold Jones was also raring to go. Alma, his mother, and her sister, Tessie, had come back home after living in New York for over 18 years. They had worked the swing shift in a defense plant during the war.

Mrs. Jones was divorced from Jay Jones, who was Harold's father. Tessie was married to a man named Hokey Smith, who had also worked in the defense plant. Hokey adamantly refused to return South with Tessie. So, Alma, Tessie and Harold moved back to the old homestead. Both women had the starved, dried-up look of women who were used to living without men in their lives. Their mother, Miz Suzy, was long dead, and their father, old man Henry Wright, had died the year before. The war was over, times were changing, so it was time to come home.

The three New Yorkers moved into the old ramshackle family house until they could build their new home. With little outside help, and within several months, they put up a three-story structure complete with basement, which was exactly like the row houses in Harlem.

The new house was an unusual sight. Its square facade sitting right in the middle of a corn field was an eye-catcher for sure. The family did enjoy some of the same comforts that they were privy to in New York's Harlem. It had electricity installed, but water was a problem. It had to be carried from the same spring that Uncle Joe used. An outdoor toilet was built and placed a few yards behind the rear of the house. It would do fine for now, and besides they had used an outhouse before.

Mrs. Jones's next purchase of note was a shiny black 1939 Buick with a spare tire on each side of the engine. The huge white-walled tires on the automobile was a sure sign of success. The former New Yorkers were soon the talk of the neighborhood. Mrs Alma, Tessie and Harold were all set to do some good living, Harlem-style.

Besides, the prestige of driving the big Buick, Harold had one other accomplishment to his credit. He had sung and danced more than once on the "Ted Mack Amateur Hour." Harold was a born entertainer who liked attention. He would sing and dance in a New York minute.

The three potential soldiers became thick as thieves while waiting for the date of their physical examinations. Our little shack became their meeting place. I took their exuberance and enthusiasm with a grain of salt because I had been there. As a veteran, even though I had done no fighting and had not even been out of the states, I was qualified to tell them of the rigors of military life. They did not listen to me. Their lack of concern did not really bother me. My own problems continued to mount with one unusual situation after another.

In the Bible, the Holy spirit said on more than one occasion, "I will never leave you." It was becoming increasingly evident that the spirit of Jackson felt the same way about me.

Most of the time, I was caught off guard. Jackson's errant spirit asserted itself if and when it so desired, and the consequences of its visit always played havoc to my being on a vast scale.

I saw no hint of trouble that Friday night as I was walking home from church. Fanny and I had sat through a wonderful service. I was cleansed and rejuvenated, filled with new faith in the goodness of the Lord. Mr. Avon must have noticed it too because he pulled me aside in the vestibule as we were about to leave. "David, the elders of the church are very impressed with you," he said. "They appreciate the work you are doing with the Sunday School and how you relate to the young folk. They are looking at you in a very positive light, David. Keep up the good work." I was glowing with pride.

"I'm really trying this time, Mr. Avon. I promise you. I won't fall off the wagon this time. The good Lord has really been looking out for me."

The thrill of sanctity was soon dampened by Fanny's expression of love. It started as soon as we left the churchyard. Most of the parishioners had left except a few stragglers. When we were out of earshot, her arms tightened around my neck, and her lips sought mine. I backed away.

"Quit Fanny. You know we can't do this, just leaving church and all."

"I can't help it David," she admitted. "I just stay hot all of the time."

I could tell that she was still excited. I wondered if the service had affected her in that manner. I felt her body tremble. "I know we promised the Lord not to screw until we get married. But, he won't mind if we get one little piece. After all, we are gonna get married," she pleaded. She sounded sure of herself. Her lips covered mine, and her tongue began to do exciting things inside my mouth. Her tongue seemed reptilian, searching and seeking as it snaked in and out. The heat of her body seared me with longing, and the temptation to go home with Fanny was an over-

Jimmy's Blues

powering force. In desperation, I prayed.

"Help me Jesus!"

With a superhuman effort, I managed to walk away. The good Lord must have been in my corner. I felt good about being able to resist the temptation of Fanny's pleading offer of togetherness. The sound of her voice rang in my ears, and my body still tingled, smarting from the scorching heat of her embrace. I ran across the Raleigh Road and hurried down the Rose Hill Road. I was almost past Aunt Lizzie's little house when Miz Nellie, Papa's lady friend, came out of the door, walked up the path and fell in step beside me.

"Howdy Miz Nellie," I said. "How're you doing tonight?"

In the dim light of the moon, it was difficult to see her face. She smelled of alcohol, and it was easy to tell that she had been drinking heavily.

"How come Papa's not with you? Did he go home already?"

Miz Nellie grunted but didn't answer. Even when she was drinking, her placid face was serene with a studied blankness that portrayed nothing. It was okay. I could understand Papa courting Miz Nellie. I knew that he would be drawn to a woman who somehow reminded both of us of Mama.

"Your Pa's all right David. He's at my place," Miz Nellie said. "I jist decided to walk down to Aunt Lizzie's and git me a little taste." She laughed softly to herself. "Your Pa's pretty good in the sack, but earlier tonight I laid one tough titty on the old boy. He'll sleep all night."

"Yes ma'am Miz Nellie. I'm sure glad that you and Papa are getting along good." She sidled up to me until we were touching as we walked.

"How is everything going with the tobacco crop, Miz Nellie?"

The stench of Aunt Lizzie's liquor on her breath was overpowering. Aunt Lizzie sold good moonshine, but something awful had happened to it after it passed Miz Nellie's lips. I turned my head away. It was evident that I needed to change the subject quickly. I had just come from church, and I didn't like the way this conversation was going at all.

"The tobacco patch is doing right well. We're tending almost an acre. Your Daddy and I are gonna make us some real money come harvest time."

I started to mention the aspect and the consequences of trying to hide an illegal acre of tobacco in the deep woods, but I thought better of it. We were passing Courtney's dairy and walking down the long hill when she stumbled against me in the darkness. It was a moment before

257

Jimmy's Blues

she righted herself. When she spoke again, there was a sneer in her voice.

"What about you Davy, boy? Are you still trying to diddle every woman in Cumberland County?"

She stumbled again. That time she took my arm and held it tightly. It was a precarious situation. We were beginning to bob and weave, and several times we almost fell into the ditch. She began to giggle crazily, and her right hand fumbled for my crotch.

"Lemme see whatcha got, Davy, boy?"

I backed away from her groping fingers. I wished she would stop acting like that. She was insistent.

"I wonder why everybody's keeps on talking about you, Davy, boy. Are you as good as your Daddy? Can you roll like your old man?"

"I ain't thinking about nothing like that Miz Nellie. I just left prayer meeting. I'm trying to live by faith, and I can't do it if you keep messing with me." She was trying to lead me in a direction that I did not want to go. Miz Nellie was trying to take a simple walk up a country road and turn it into something nasty. I wanted no part of it. Her language and her insinuations were making me nervous.

Suddenly without any warning, she stumbled again and stepped on my foot. We both fell backward into the ditch. She landed belly down, right on top of me. The weight of Miz Nellie's heavy body was pressing me deep into the mud of the ditch. Instead of trying to get up, she began to laugh like crazy. She grabbed my shoulders. "Did you enjoy the trip, Davy, boy?" she asked in a mocking voice. She began to squirm and move her big behind until it was situated astride my middle.

"You know what I think David," she said softly. "I think that since we're down here in a fucking position, we might as well fuck."

She began a slow grind, forcing her buttocks against me. She started making jerky movements that mashed my body even deeper into the mud of the ditch. It was quite uncomfortable.

"Get offa me Miz Nellie. It's cold and wet down here!" I demanded. I tried to get up. "I ain't gonna do nothing with you!" I squirmed again. It was no use. "C'mon Miz Nellie, get offa me. Papa would have a blue fit and kick my ass from here to breakfast if he thought I were down here like this with you. Will you please move, Miz Nellie?" Her voice grew harsh and demanding.

"We're gonna fuck tonight Davy, boy. You're either gonna do it to me, or I'm gonna tell your Daddy that you fucked me. It will be the same difference. You might as well make the best of a good situation." Miz Nellie loomed above me like an avenging angel. She fumbled under her dress for a moment, shifted her position slightly and from that point on her every move was coitus, biting and as sharp as a razor's edge. She ripped my pants open, breaking the zipper in the process, then clumsily pulled them down around my knees. I shuddered as the coldness of the muddy ditch enveloped my backside, and in the same moment, I felt the warm loose flesh of her thighs. In the corridors of my mind, I begged the spirit of Stonewall Jackson to cease and desist. In tormented silence, I cried out, "For God's sake, Jackson. Don't make me get hard. Papa will kill me!"

There had been no foreplay, and my plea to the long dead general went unanswered. I hated the erect hardness that was suddenly a part of me. It got worse. I grew as rigid as the rock hard times of 1932. The spirit of Jackson went ape. We were both crazed with desire. As always, Jackson's leadership was superb. He guided me inside her, pushing upward again and again. The initial coming together was a harsh brutal occurrence. Our movements were jerky and uncontrolled, with frequent stops and starts, almost like jump-starting an automobile. It began with a sigh from Miz Nellie and a sudden thrust from me that caused her to gasp with pain. Soon, I was off and running at full speed. To be as brutal as possible was exactly what I intended. I wanted to cause her discomfort, and I wanted her to feel the hurt that I felt. I was ashamed and didn't like what I was doing. I didn't like it at all. She was Papa's woman, and she had no business making me do such a thing. My brutality didn't help matters. She seemed to enjoy my furious assault on her body. The only thing my roughness did was to increase the intensity of her desire.

I didn't make the decision. Stonewall made it for me. He whispered a harsh command, "Go for broke!" I dug my heels into the side of the ditch bank, arched my back and went to work. Even the wet muddy confines of the ditch did not hinder me from putting into play all that I knew about satisfying a woman. Miz Nellie was not finicky. In fact, she was a glutton for the sort of punishment that I was inflicting, enjoying it immensely and eagerly taking everything I had to offer. I was generous to a fault. The rhythm of our coupling synchronized and became a slow sloppy grind. Good feelings ebbed and flowed between us like the mud and water in the ditch. When it was finally over, a feeling of comic relief washed over me. I was wet, muddy and angry at myself for the whole sorry business.

Miz Nellie was not angry. She was pleased as punch. She had huffed and puffed with complete abandon, liking every nuance of my ferocious assault. Even after it was over, she kept mouthing a variety of grunts and groans. It seemed that her breath had mellowed somewhat during the tirade. It was bearable now. She leaned down, and her lips brushed my cheeks.

"You are good, Davy boy, a real pine rooter. You're almost as good as your Daddy. Next time, I'm gonna let you kiss you know where. I wonder if you're any good at that. Your Daddy does it for me. I don't even have to ask him. He does it right often."

That was probably true, but I really didn't need to know Papa's business. I walked away without a word. There was nothing to say. My sin was even greater because Miz Nellie reminded me of Mama. I started to walk faster, anxious to get away from the scene of my most recent debacle. The familiar curves of the Rose Hill Road stretched wide ahead of me in the moonlit darkness, but I was still lost, foundering in a wilderness of guilt and broken promises.

It was almost eleven o' clock when I walked up the steps and into the little shack. All three of the soon-to-be soldiers were seated at the kitchen table. There was a half empty pint bottle of moonshine sitting on the table. Jimmy reached for the bottle and poured himself a double shot. All eyes widened as they searched my face. Jimmy was the first to speak.

"Damn, brother, what in the world happened to you?"

Kelly began to laugh, "I swear David, you look fucked up, like somebody might have kicked your ass and threw you in a mudhole." Harold's eyes rolled, and his big mouth opened wide with laughter.

"C'mon David, tell us what you been doing to look like that. I'm from New York City, and I need to know."

It was time for some jive-ass talk delivered staccato-style from the side of my mouth.

"I don't know what y'all so excited about. The Kid's been out there doing what comes naturally."

The fast talk and the bullshit were expected. Their faces relaxed, and they waited to see what else I was going to say. "I'm the sneezing weasel, and I been doing some deep ditch fucking, something y'all know nothing about. It don't matter where or when as long as you get the job done. They call me the healer." I wasn't about to call names. I had

Jimmy's Blues

already been caught in that trap.

"Yeah, right," said Kelly. There was a wide grin on his homely face. "The only fucking you been doing is fucking up. "I heard that you promised the Lord, several responsible white folk and a few religious niggers that you were gonna do something productive with your life. From what I can see, you ain't done shit."

"You sure do put a lot of stock in a piece of ass," said Jimmy. He shook his head slowly. "I don't know about you Bro. There's other important things in the world. I'm thinking far away places with strange-sounding names." He looked over at Kelly and Harold. "How about it y'all? What's your take on this mess?"

"I don't know," Harold admitted. He bit his big bottom lip as he always did when he was trying to think. He smiled. He reminded me of Mantan Moreland. In fact, he looked a little bit like the comedian.

"David's full of shit, but I ain't thinking about that." His brow furrowed. "I'm beginning to like the idea of going into the army. It might even be better than New York City, and there's hardly anything that can top the Big Apple." He stood up, grabbed the cane-bottomed chair that he was sitting in and placed it in the center of the floor. He did a quick heel and toe that ended with a flourish. Harold could really tap dance, and like I said, he would cut a rug in a New York minute. He twirled the chair once and put it back at the table. "I forgot to tell y'all," Harold said with a wide grin on his face, "Mom's gonna give the three of us a going away party on Friday night before we leave the following Monday." He smirked as he looked over at me. "By the way, she said we could invite old slick ass Dave."

It was Friday night, not just any Friday night, but the night of the going-away party that Mrs. Alma was giving for her son, Harold, my brother Jimmy and Kelly, Aunt Lizzie's nephew. It was also prayer meeting time at Mood's Temple Church. Since the night that Mr. Avon told me about the nice things the church elders were saying about me, I had become more dedicated than ever before. My soon-to-be bride, Fanny, would always accompany me. Her sincerity about serving the Lord was genuine. The only fly in the ointment was her insistence that the Lord wouldn't mind if we strayed into the bushes across the road and got a quick piece. Once again as we left the church, I held her tightly and yielded not to temptation. My lips brushed hers, and I said gently, "Don't worry Fanny, we'll be married before you know it. Just hang on, and don't stop loving me, you hear? The longer we wait, the better it will be."

"The waiting is hard, David, real hard," said Fanny. There was desperation in her voice. "It wouldn't be so bad David, but you know I quit hustling 'cause I don't want nobody but you. It's jist that my money is kinda short, and I've got to do something. Let's make it soon. All you have to do after we get married is jist move in with me." It was a moment before I realized that she was crying. "Marry me David, marry me please!"

"Don't worry Fanny, we'll be okay. The Lord is on our side."

I left her standing there wiping away her tears. I walked slowly across the highway and down the Rose Hill Road. I started thinking about a home and marriage. Maybe Fanny was right. Marriage would serve me in good stead. I would no longer be celibate, and since we truly loved each other, maybe we could raise a family and live like folks. My spirits soared, and my steps quickened, barely touching the sand and dust of the road bed.

Aunt Lizzie's little house was ablaze with lights, which was a sure sign that business was good. I wished her well and kept walking. I was way past the bridge and almost around the curve when I heard the faint sounds of music. It was coming from the direction of Uncle Joe's cabin. I suddenly realized that the music was coming from Mrs. Alma's house. The sounds that I heard were party music, a special going-away treat for the soon-to-be soldier boys. I surmised that Harold, Kelly and my brother Jimmy were having a blast, living it up before giving their all for their country. A celebration was fitting for such brave young men.

I left the road and took the path that led up a small hill and into the field where Mrs. Alma's Harlem-style house dominated the landscape. I figured there was no harm in stopping for a little while. My religious convictions would be in no danger. All I had to do was sit quietly and watch the fond farewells and tearful goodbys. Women always cried during times like these.

The music grew louder as I approached the house. There was no mistaking it for anything else. It was the down and dirty blues, New York-style. I walked along the path until I came to the front door. I hesitated for a moment, enjoying the clear mournful wail of a trumpet solo. It was night music designed for anybody who had ever had the blues and especially for lovers and other fools. I walked up the one flight of brand-new brick steps and knocked on the door.

Mrs. Tessie opened the door. Her thin face wore just enough make-up to be in vogue, and her hair was coiffed uptown style. The man-starved look was still there, but her smile indicated that sustenance was in sight.

"Well, if it ain't Little David Sawyer. C'mon in you handsome devil! It's party time!" I smiled and took her out-stretched hand.

"I know what you mean, Mrs. Tessie," I said gracefully. "I know exactly what you mean! It was mighty nice of y'all to invite me." I stood there for a moment and looked around me. It was a strange feeling, as if I had somehow changed worlds. One minute I was walking through a corn field and a split second later I was standing in the big city atmosphere of a house in middle class Harlem. The living room floor was plush carpet, and the heavy drapes were New York drapes. The walls were covered with pictures depicting New York scenes, and the furniture was vintage Harlem. It was as if the whole house had been uprooted from 125th Street and replanted in Cumberland County.

"C'mon you sweet rascal, everybody's down in the basement," Mrs Tessie held onto my hand and said coyly. "There's plenty of room to dance and clown around. I ain't about to let y'all country niggers mess up my house."

She led me down a temporary stairway and into a furnished basement that stretched the length of the house. The lighting was subdued, reflecting equally on the happy faces of the seated party goers and the dancers milling around the room. "I'm gonna cut you loose," said Mrs. Tessie. "I got things to do."

I looked around the crowded room. It seemed as if everybody in the neighborhood was there.

There, were Aunt Sarah, her daughters, Baby, the youngest, and Ruth, who wore her usual blank far away look. Miz Snoog was decked out in a big red dress and wearing redder rouge and purple lipstick. Jody Peet, the back door man, was dressed in faded overalls. Jody did not have to dress fancy for a party. All the women who knew Jody also knew that clothes did not make a man. The gardening skills and plowing abil-

Jimmy's Blues

ity of the back door man was well-known. Louise was wearing a short flapper dress seated demurely beside Ed and as beautiful as ever. Ed looked bored. He was really not at ease in such a setting. Seated on the other side were three school friends of Mrs. Alma and Mrs. Tessie that I didn't know and a very pretty light-skinned girl named Maggie, who was the daughter of one of the women. Harold, Jimmy and Kelly were seated together in a corner at the far side of the room. They were glumly watching the dancers.

I walked over to the other corner of the room and sat in a tattered maroon chair. My intention was to be seen and not heard. Parties like this generated togetherness, and all I wanted to do was to sit quietly and listen to some good music. Mrs. Alma had been standing by the floor model record player. She put a record on the turntable, and the throaty voice of Bessie Smith floated across the room. It was time to do some tight holding and slow dragging, swaying to the mournful wail of big Bessie, the queen of the blues. Couples moved quickly to the center of the floor. Miz Snoog tripped gaily onto the floor with the big red dress twirling around her huge body. She was large enough to be a couple or maybe a threesome, but her dancing was as effortless as a member of the royal ballet company. Suddenly she threw back her head and began to sing with Bessie Smith. Her big voice blended beautifully with Bessie's mournful wail. "Trouble in mind I'm blue, but I won't be blue always, 'cause the sun's gonna shine in my back door some day."

Her singing got the attention of everybody in the room. I looked over to the far corner where Kelly, Harold and Jimmy were seated. Harold and Jimmy were sitting quietly, but Kelly's agitation was plainly evident. He was leaning forward in his seat, and his mouth was wide open. His eyes were focused on Miz Snoog, and he made gurgling noises as he gripped the chair with both hands. Suddenly he jumped up and began to follow Miz Snoog around the room. Kelly was pursuing Miz Snoog with the same determination that he had exhibited in Uncle Mike's hog pen. It was a situation with amazing similarities. The only difference was that this time Kelly had nothing in his hands and unlike the sow, Miz Snoog allowed herself to be caught. She stopped, turned toward him, and they came together with a big, squishy bump. There was a wide grin on Kelly's face. He was in that special heaven reserved for 18-year-olds who still retained their innocence.

Kelly began posturing, twisting and flaunting his manhood as if it were a baton. Miz Snoog was not daunted by his actions. She loved every minute of it. Every now and then she would stop dancing, reach down with both hands and pull up her huge belly. With the overhang reduced, the prudent act allowed Kelly and herself to achieve a closeness that I didn't think was possible. It was a wonderful exhibition of togetherness. It was really a sight to see.

It was turning out to be a great party, things were picking up, New York-style. The sound of tinkling glasses being filled with good wine from an expensive decanter mixed with the syrupy voice of Billy Eckstine. The song was soothing and caressing, deftly creating the sounds of uptown Harlem on a Saturday night.

Mrs. Alma was grinning girlishly as she walked over to Jody Peet and pulled him to his feet. She went into Jody's arms as if she belonged there.

Billy Eckstine crooned softly, "I cover the waterfront. I'm watching the sea." Mrs Alma snuggled her head on Jody's shoulder, and her large breasts rested comfortably against his broad chest. Everybody in the room knew that a risk had been taken by Mrs. Alma, and they also knew that dancing with the back door man was just a prelude of things to come.

Louise knew exactly what was going on, and she was mad as hell. Her eyes flashed fire at the sight of Jody and Mrs. Alma dancing cheek to cheek and body to body. Ed was watching Louise with a perplexed look on his face. He didn't have the slightest idea of the intrigue that was fostered by the intimacy on the dance floor, and he didn't know why Louise was so angry. But, this was a party, and like the crowded streets of New York City, close quarters were the rule rather than the exception. Here in the soft light of the basement, nearness was a part of the charm transplanted from the naked city. I became uneasy. I wasn't sure about Louise. I didn't know what she was capable of doing. This was not shaping up to my liking. I remembered the fracas at the juke joint. I scrunched my chair farther back into the corner. If this party were going to blow, it wasn't going to be my fault.

It was Harold's turn. He minced onto the dance floor with the experienced walk of a professional dancer. The pretty light-skinned girl pirouetted gracefully and joined him. They began to dance ballroom style.

Jimmy's Blues

Maggie reminded me of Lila. She was just as pretty and just as precocious with a willowy beauty all her own. There was a wide grin on Harold's face as they moved effortlessly about the floor.

Jimmy was seated in the same corner where he had been all night. He hadn't drunk any of the wine. He had his own private stock, moonshine of uncertain proof nestled in his back pocket. I knew he was high. In fact, he was almost drunk.

Mrs. Tessie walked over, placed her hands on her hips and said loudly, "Get up boy."

She said in a teasing tone of voice: "We're gonna dance!" The glum look left Jimmy's face, but he didn't move. Mrs. Tessie pulled up Jimmy and dragged him to the center of the dance floor. Jimmy just stood there weaving and bobbing. Mrs. Tessie placed her hands on Jimmy's backside, pulled him to her and began grinding her hips against him. Jimmy wasn't dancing. He just stood there as Mrs. Tessie scrubbed her thin body against his pelvis.

There was a determined look on Jimmy's face as he held on for dear life. The ballad ended, but that didn't stop Mrs. Tessie's desperate search for togetherness with Jimmy's pelvis. And at that point Jimmy didn't want to stop either. There was a silly grin on his face, and it was crystal clear that another 18-year-old was in that special heaven reserved for virgins. I wondered how long it would be before Jimmy got his first piece.

For a moment, the dimly-lit basement was as quiet and empty as a deserted street in the borrough of Queens. Mrs. Alma, too, had been reluctant to leave the arms of the back door man. She finally tore herself away and went over to the record player. Her taste in music was exceptional because the next record was Lionel Hampton's "Hamp's boogie woogie." The hard driving beat of the xylophone rang throughout the basement, and the joint went hog wild. Everybody rushed to get on the dance floor. Ruth, who had been sitting quietly with her eyes darting to and fro, surprised everyone by jumping to her feet and doing a sizzling rendition of the "Shim Sham Shimmy." Baby joined her and added her flashing legs to the swaying swinging malaise on the dance floor. Ruth stopped dancing as suddenly as she had begun. The darting eyes were bright and busy, looking at everything and seeing nothing.

"'Cuse me Mr. Pistol, I didn't know you were loaded," she said plaintively. She threw her head back and demented laughter filled the room. "Does anybody want a piece of tail?" Nobody was offended, and nobody got excited. Ruth's madness was well-known to everyone at the party. "Has anybody got a cigarette? I sure do want me a cigarette. Shit, fire and molasses!"

One monkey didn't stop the show. It was time to boogie down. I looked up in complete amazement. Aunt Sarah had left her seat and joined the dancers on the busy floor. She stood in the center of the floor, placed both hands on her hips and started to do a messy little dance called "The Drag Nasty." I was shocked at what she was doing with the lower half of her body. Aw man, her slinky movements were just as suggestive as they could be. It must have been some sort of signal.

The joint began to really jump. The transplanted big city folk and their cohorts were no longer in the basement. They were on cloud nine. In fact, they were not even in the middle of a corn field. They were doing the boogie woogie up in Harlem. It was perfectly all right because they were in a New York state of mind.

The record ended, and the usual lull followed as the dancers went back to their seats. I leaned back and closed my eyes to clear my head of wrongful thoughts. When I opened them, I was looking into the face of an angel. Maggie had left Harold and walked over to where I was seated. Her lithe body was angelic too, with a tiny waist and hips that were more than just a suggestion of intimacy. She looked down at me.

"You're David Sawyer, ain'tcha? I heard a lot of stuff about you."

Here it was again. I wondered if I would ever live it down. Her lips were pursed in a half smile, but the big brown eyes weren't smiling at all.

"They said you were bad news. Are you really bad news, David Sawyer?"

I said vehemently, "I don't know what you're talking about, girl. I'm a churchperson, and I try to live my life in a God-fearing way." I decided to change the subject. "I saw you and Harold dancing. Y'all make a nice couple." She looked across the room at Harold, and her pretty face tightened a bit. I didn't know what that was about. "Y'all seem pretty close. Are you gonna get married before he goes into the army? Or, maybe you're gonna be a good girl and wait for him?"

"Ohh, Harold's okay. In fact, he's really a nice boy. We ain't got no

Jimmy's Blues

plans for marriage or anything like that." She seemed glad to talk to someone about Harold and herself. "I don't know why I'm telling you this, but a girl has to think about a lot of things when it comes to marriage and stuff like that." She paused for a moment as if lost in thought. "It's just that Harold's got a really dark complexion. He's just too black. It's not his fault. He's also got a funny-looking head. It's long and shaped like a peanut." She sounded adamant. "I really like him. It might sound crazy, but I have to think about what our children would look like." The issue of skin color was alive and well. I had almost forgotten what an important part it played in every aspect of life.

I was about to answer Maggie when a commotion over near the basement steps got my immediate attention. It was Mrs. Tessie and Jimmy. She was trying to drag the unresisting Jimmy up the steps of the basement. At first I thought she was pulling him up by his belt buckle, but a closer look told me I was dead wrong. It was evident from the very nature of the grip that she had on Jimmy that he was going to be deeply involved in ending the man-starved condition of Mrs. Tessie Smith. I couldn't help but feel that Jimmy's first piece was going to come about much sooner than I had anticipated. What a nice thing to happen to my brother. It would make a wonderful going-away present. It took awhile, but the two of them finally made it to the top of the stairs. I glanced at my watch and turned to Maggie to continue our conversation.

"I have to go, now," said Maggie. "Harold will get his ass on his shoulder if I keep talking to you." She shook her head pensively. "Nobody trusts you, David, nobody at all. I wonder why?"

She turned and walked slowly across the room. There was another commotion at the basement stairs. It was Jimmy and Mrs. Tessie coming back down the steps. If Mrs. Tessie had not been holding Jimmy's arm, he would have fallen for sure. I looked at my watch again. It had been just four and a half minutes since the two of them had gone upstairs to work on the starvation problem. They were absolutely right. Time does fly when you're having fun. Mrs. Tessie did look kind of sleepy-eyed. Her movements at that point were very deliberate, calm and serene. From that distance, I couldn't tell what was happening with Jimmy. His whole body looked kind of limp, and there was a sheepish grin on his face. There was one thing that I was doubly sure of. His innocence was shot to pieces.

Jimmy's Blues

There was never a dull moment in the Big Apple. It was a typical New York night. Something was always happening. There was a loud bump somewhere upstairs and then a series of bumps over at the basement steps. Somebody had fallen head over heels down the steps. I craned my neck to see who had fallen and how badly the person was hurt. I knew it was a woman. She managed to regain her footing and grabbed the hand rail.

Ohh, shit! What crazy rotten luck. It was none other than Papa's lady friend, Miz Nellie. She looked groggily around at the gaping New Yorkers and said angrily, "What the fuck y'all looking at?" Her resemblance to Mama faded from my mind. Mama would never say anything like that.

I scrunched down as far as I could in the old chair. I did not want to be confronted by Miz Nellie. I prayed quickly. "Dear Jesus, don't let the old bag see me. She'll start something sure as shooting!"

The Lord was probably busy with something else because Miz Nellie weaved her way through the crowd, came across the room and stood right above me.

"Well," she said with a nasty grin, "if it ain't Little David Sawyer, the pine rooter!" The basement got deathly quiet. New Yorkers knew when it was time to listen. Miz Nellie's loud voice rang out in the silence.

"Are you over that piece of tail I laid on you in the ditch the other night?"

I sat there, not knowing what to do. I had to do something. She was getting angrier by the minute. Miz Nellie's eyes flashed, and her rasping voice grew even louder.

"Don't you ignore me, you pine rooting son of a bitch!"

I jumped up, brushed past her and ran across the room toward the stairway. Half way across the room, I bumped into Aunt Sarah, almost knocking her down. She righted herself, grabbed both my arms and hollered out.

"Fool, that's your daddy's woman. Good Lord in heaven, boy, you ought to be ashamed of yourself! I thought you had quit that mess. You're still whore-hopping everything in sight. You won't stop at nothing, will you?"

I didn't answer Aunt Sarah. There was nothing to say. I pulled away from her and ran up the steps two at the time. I walked out of the door

Jimmy's Blues

and into the night. In the darkness, the corn field looked like a long lost friend. I had left the dim night lights of New York City in complete disgrace.

Well, that the way things happen. Some make it, and some don't. I was glad to get out of there. There were eight million stories about life in the naked city. Mine was an event of no consequence.

22

Rice with or without Gravy

It was Saturday morning, the day after the party, and I was on my way down to the spring to get two buckets of water. The house was bone dry, and we needed water for washing or cooking. Memories of the New York scene were fresh in my mind, as I walked slowly down the path to the spring. New York's Harlem was a nice place to visit, but I wouldn't want to live there.

I wasn't really curious about what happened after my abrupt departure from the party. I knew that Jimmy had gotten his first glimpse into the grown up world of sex, and I supposed that Kelly had big fun. Miz Snoog was certainly big enough. I didn't know about Harold, but my feeling was that he and Maggie were not going to become a couple.

Jimmy was still sleeping. He was curled up on the little cot in a fetal position, and there was a half smile on his face. There was spittle in the corner of his mouth, but not because of last night. Jimmy drooled a bit anyhow when things were going well. I could understand how he must have felt. Going into the army and losing his innocence at the hands of an older woman was manly stuff. For Jimmy, life had taken on all the aspects of a good thing.

I was a bit proud of myself because I had made it through the party without any lascivious thoughts or any craving to do bad things. The

Rice with or without Gravy

Lord was good. Now it was time to go on to other things.

My job at Post Ordnance was coming along just fine. The government's policy of separation of the races worked as well in the civilian sector of Fort Bragg as it had in the military.

The complex of ordnance shops where the civilians worked was in the main post area near the bus station. Negroes and whites managed to work together with a minimum of friction. The paint shop where I worked did olive drab, lusterless and camouflage painting on all of the army vehicles. It was located at the far end of the complex near the maintenance shop. There were five Negroes, four whites and one Hispanic working there. The Negro workers were careful to use their own toilet facilities and not the one's assigned to the white employees. The two drinking fountains located in the front of the paint shop near the foreman's office did not cause any problems. They were not labeled "White" and "Colored," but by tacit agreement the whites used one and the Negroes used the other one. A Puerto Rican painter of indeterminate race used whatever facility he wanted, and nothing was said.

Demand for workers had increased since the start of the Korean police action. I personally felt that it was anything but a police action. To me, it looked like a full-scale war, but what did I know about the present administration's business? But, the government had done the right thing by giving ordnance workers a blanket raise of ten cents. As a painter's helper, I was making 87 cents an hour. It was a lot of money, and it was honest pay, something unusual for me. I had it all. My religious integrity was intact, and I had a good job.

It was a good feeling to know that I was doing something of which Jackson would approve. It was even better because once again my mind turned to thoughts of a home and family. My feelings would give me strength to wait patiently for the sanctity of marriage. It would have to be soon because Jackson would overlook no opportunity to play tricks on me. He knew that I always slept on my back, and he also knew that I would be erect, especially in the mornings. Being half asleep, it was easy for him to goad me into quickly turning over to lie on my belly. The result was a really painful awakening. The general was not known for his humor, but I could have sworn that I heard his eerie laughter echoing about the little room.

Rice with or without Gravy

There was one other thing. Since Jimmy was going away, I wanted to spend as much time with him as possible. I hurried down the hill. The path to the spring took a sudden dip and then wandered through the little ravine to the spot where the spring nestled in a small grotto. The Autumn sunlight filtering through the trees made the water look crystal clear. I filled the two buckets carefully and gingerly made my way back up the hill.

When I reached the crest of the hill, I stopped and looked over at the blue smoke spiraling up from the chimney of Miz Snoog's little shack. The little house sat cozily, almost obscured in a clump of trees near the swamp. As I watched, the back door of the little shack opened, and Kelly and Miz Snoog were standing there. The sunlight shone brightly on their faces as they kissed passionately. Even from that great distance, it looked like a ritual that proclaimed undying devotion. Now, it was evident that the closeness exhibited by the two of them the night before was a good thing. I was glad that love at last had found them. I thought of Bessie Smith's sultry voice and imagined how it would sound wafting through the morning air. "Trouble in mind I'm blue, but I won't be blue always. The sun's gonna shine in my back door some day!"

Kelly held Miz Snoog tenderly for a moment, then kissed her again and reluctantly walked away.

When I got back to the house, Jimmy was still asleep. After putting the buckets on the kitchen table, I went to the door of the tiny bedroom and looked down at Jimmy. He was still asleep, lying on the little army cot. The silly half smile was still on his face. I was curious about what happened between Jimmy and Mrs Tessie at the party, but I would never ask Jimmy. Our relationship was not of that nature. However, I was sure of one thing. There had been no oral involvement, not even a kiss. Jimmy was quite fastidious in that regard, and I was wholly responsible.

I grinned as I remembered the incident that changed Jimmy's eating habits forever. It was late evening several years ago, and we had been down in the swamp to get the cow. On the way back, we stopped at Grandma's. It was past supper time, and the family had eaten, but there were plenty of leftovers.

Supper was ham and collard greens seasoned just right, with big chunks of corn bread sprinkled with pork cracklings. We were out on the

Rice with or without Gravy

front porch eating like there was no tomorrow when Jimmy looked down at his plate.

"Man, this mess is just right! Mama never put no rice in her collard greens."

I looked down at my plate and saw tiny white objects in the chunks of ham. Grandma had fixed supper, but because of her bad eyesight she hadn't noticed the damage done by blow flies as the ham hung from the rafters in the smoke house. There were a lot of maggots imbedded deep in the chunks of ham. I made sure Jimmy wasn't looking, then quickly emptied my mouth of food and threw it down beside the porch. I forced myself not to upchuck and looked over at Jimmy. He was doing some serious eating. I waited until his plate was almost empty before I gave him the bad news. I said, "Jimmy, stop! Don't eat no more of that stuff. I saw worms in that ham and some in the collard greens too!"

Jimmy looked down at his plate, and his face turned ashen. He threw the contents of his plate to the ground, stumbled out of the yard and ran up the path toward the house. He was spitting ham, collard greens and corn in every direction. As I watched his figure grow smaller in the distance, I was thinking that maybe I should have told him sooner about the blow fly eggs. The worms did look like cooked rice. It was a dirty trick, and there were still times when I felt a tad of remorse. I'm not sure Jimmy ever forgave me for that one. From that moment on, Jimmy was very careful about anything having to do with his mouth.

I looked down at him. He was snoring softly, and as I watched, he turned fitfully toward the wall of the little shack. From the angelic look on his face, I figured he was still having sweet dreams about Mrs. Tessie and last night. I yelled in his ear. "Awright, you would-be soldier, you might as well get used to getting up off your butt! It's chow time!"

Jimmy groaned once and sat up blinking rapidly. He rubbed his eyes until they focused and then scowled angrily at me. "Damn, David, why did you wake me up?" He rolled over to the side of the bed and sat with his head in his hands.

"Aw, man, you just screwed me up good. I was in the middle of a real good dream." He thought for a minute, and then a look of pure wonder furrowed his brow. His mouth opened, and his bottom lip sagged.

"Great day in the morning," Jimmy said, as he suddenly remembered. "I got me a piece of tail last night!" I decided to play it noncommittal.

Rice with or without Gravy

"I'm happy for you, Bro. I saw you and Mrs. Tessie trying to grind each other to pieces on the dance floor. You didn't think anyone was watching, but I saw y'all sneaking upstairs. I figured something was gonna happen 'cause she had a strangle hold on your dick. It's a wonder she didn't hurt you, pulling you up the steps like that."

"She bit me too," Jimmy said ruefully. He rubbed his crotch and shook his head slowly. "I'm telling you for a fact David, I couldn't believe all of the stuff that she did to me. I had no idea that screwing was like that." He was still shaking his head. "It's a mess, I tell you."

"Well little brother, it looks like you've finally grown up, and according to my watch it took you all of four and a half minutes. Did you kiss her on the mouth?"

Ohh ohh! Jimmy's memory was working overtime. His face twisted up like he had tasted something sour. His mouth opened, but no words came out. He gagged loudly and begin to spit like crazy. I knew that the mention of anything oral would upset Jimmy terribly. When he was finally able to talk, he whispered.

"We were doing jist fine David, until she put her tongue in my mouth. Good grief!"

I knew exactly how he felt. For Jimmy, rice was nothing compared to somebody trying to put their tongue in his mouth. "It was just plain nastiness. I don't know where her mouth had been before me, but I knew where it had just come from. Mrs Tessie was on top of me, bouncing up and down like a jack hammer. I didn't want to stop because it felt so good. When I tried to get up, the old huzzy turned the two of us over and locked her skinny legs around my back in a death grip." Jimmy looked toward the ceiling. "Great day in the morning, David! It seemed as if I could feel every bone in her body. Aw man, it was all I could do to keep my mouth out of her way. I don't like that kissing stuff." Jimmy looked up at me and grinned "I tell you for a fact Bro, except for the kissing part, when you put it all together, that screwing is right on the money! I see why you keep acting so crazy. When I get in the army, I'm going to get me a whole bunch of tail, but I ain't gonna make no fool out of myself. It's a mess, I tell you!"

Jimmy's words brought back memories of the party and the entrance of Miz Nellie. She should have been home with Papa, instead of falling

Rice with or without Gravy

down the basement steps and then taking the spite out on me. It was a good thing that I left when I did because she probably would have told everybody what happened that night in the ditch. I turned to Jimmy.

"Hey, What's going on with Papa? He hardly ever comes home any more. That crazy-ass Miz Nellie must have him hogtied down at her place. He sure picked a humdinger that time. What do you think about her?"

"I don't really know," said Jimmy slowly as if weighing each word. "Papa must be crazy about her because he let her talk him into planting a whole acre of tobacco in the swamp behind her house. He can't be thinking straight. Why else would he try to use the preacher's tobacco allotment to sell tobacco that he and Miz Nellie raised in the swamp?" Jimmy shook his head. "They're gonna catch the two of them sure as shooting." Jimmy's brow furrowed, which always happened when he was confronted by a real problem. "I jist hope he don't wind up in jail. It ain't gonna work, David. If Papa were in his right mind, he would never think of doing such a dumb thing."

Jimmy was absolutely right. I felt sorry for Papa. As hard as he had tried over the years, nothing ever really worked for him. His carefully-thought-out schemes usually fell apart at the last minute. He was basically a good man, and he had somehow provided for Mama and the four of us over the years. There were times when we had nothing to eat, but we were never really starving. He always managed somehow to take care of the family. One of the things that really bothered Papa was the fact that he was never able to get a pump put down at the house. There was certainly water flowing under ground, but he was never able to get enough money to buy piping and dig deep enough to find water. After Mama's death, digging a well for water lost its importance. With Mama out of the picture, Papa no longer considered it necessary, but hope burned eternal in Papa's breast, and he moved on to other unfortunate endeavors.

Speak of the devil, I looked around, and there stood Papa in the front door with a bleary-eyed Miz Nellie peering over his shoulder at Jimmy and myself.

"Morning boys," said Papa with a grin. "How you boys making out?" He looked over at Jimmy seated on the bed. "I figured I'd better stop by and see my youngest, especially since he'll be leaving for the army on

Monday." There was concern in his voice. "How you making out Jimbo?" I hadn't heard Papa call Jimmy by his baby name for a long time.

"I'm doing real good, Papa," Jimmy said with conviction. "I'm ready to go, and I'm willing to do whatever they want me to do. Dave did it, and I know I can do it too. It ain't no big thing."

I declare," said Miz Nellie, "it seems like yistiddy when little Jimmy was in diapers, and now he's about to jine the army. I tell you for a fact Noah, time really flies when you're having fun."

I glanced at Miz Nellie. She was weaving and bobbing on the steps behind Papa. If I didn't do something quick, she was going to fall as sure as shooting. I said quickly, "Y'all come on in and set a spell. I was just fixing breakfast for Jimmy and myself. He's having grits, fatback and eggs. There's chicken, rice and some greens from yesterday, and it's a plenty for everybody."

I pulled two chairs from under the table and made room for Miz Nellie and Papa to sit. As soon as Jimmy's plate was ready, he grabbed it from my hands and headed for the door. He looked back at Papa and Miz Nellie. "Y'all help yourselves. I'm gonna go out and sit on the steps. I like eating outdoors. I'll be doing a lot of eating in the field when I go in the army." I knew exactly where Jimmy was coming from. He hated rice with a passion, and he couldn't stand being in the same room with it, whether smothered in gravy or not. It was still rice.

I warmed the leftovers quickly and sat plates of steaming chicken and rice in front of Papa and Miz Nellie. The minute I sat down Papa said the blessing.

"Dear Lord, we thank you for what we are about to receive, and bless the dear hand that provided it, Amen."

Nothing had changed. Papa had always been mighty particular about thanking the Lord before eating, and his reverence made me think of his calling to the ministry. I wondered idly how Papa balanced the shack job he was doing with Miz Nelly with his religious convictions as a minister of the Gospel. I decided to leave that one alone and began eating with gusto. I was trying, but there was no way I could keep up with Papa or Miz Nellie. They were wizards at cleaning a plate. I was about to give it the old college try when things took a nasty turn. I felt something pressing against my groin, gently at first, and then pressure

Rice with or without Gravy

that grew more insistent with each moment. I couldn't believe what was happening to me. Maybe it was some sort of a joke.

I had been eating hurriedly, but I stopped in alarm and leaned away from the table. Miz Nellie's eyes were slits of evil as she looked at me with a wicked smile on her loose face. It was a moment before I realized that it was her leg stretched under the table and her foot massaging my genital area. Papa had no idea of what was happening or any hint of the sleazy stuff that was going on under the table. He was busy gulping down the chicken, rice and greens. I got up abruptly, angry at Miz Nellie for doing such a thing. I was also angry at myself and wished to heaven that the episode in the ditch had never happened. For some reason, she wanted to get me in trouble with Papa. I hurried out the door and walked to where Jimmy was just finishing his plate. I couldn't help but wonder, why didn't Miz Nellie leave me alone?

23

Physical Education

I was reluctant to leave the table because I wanted to talk to Papa. I hadn't seen him for a while, and I wanted to know how he was getting along. Miz Nellie's trashy actions had prevented that from happening. In a way, it was a good thing because it made me stay on track and do the right thing by continuing to shun the very appearance of evil. The devil was right on my trail and gaining ground. In the guise of Miz Nellie Smith's slouchy sleaze, wrong-doing was alive and well. My crotch was still tingling from the not-so-gentle massaging by the clumsy foot of Papa's main squeeze. More than once I wished that the night in the ditch had never happened. I had to get away from there. Miz Nellie was getting increasingly bold. I didn't know to what lengths she would go to embarrass and humiliate me. The last thing I wanted was for Papa to figure out why she kept on pestering me.

I needed a leisurely walk in the woods to clear my head. I took a deep breath of the crisp September air and walked slowly out to the Rose Hill Road. There were no automobiles in sight, and except for the chirping of a few last minute insects, there were no sounds to mar the serenity that surrounded me. I took to the woods immediately and walked along the road, gradually moving deeper into the brush. The brightness of the morning sun filtered through the branches of the tall oak and pine and

Physical Education

caressed me fondly. Good thoughts of marriage and a home came gently into focus. Thinking about my rosy future caused my steps to quicken out of pure joy. Since my betrothed and I were both saved, we could do as the Lord intended and rear our children in a spiritual atmosphere that would be acceptable to the Almighty and Most High God. I was elated, transformed by the beauty of the morning and reveling in the feeling that the Holy Ghost Himself was walking with me.

I felt a sublime closeness as I slowly made my way toward the bridge over the little creek crossing. Just ahead of me was the path that led down the hill from Mrs. Alma's place. I paused, completely immersed in the solitude of the moment. I parted the brush and walked out into the path. Out of nowhere came a soft, sweet voice that interrupted the silence.

"Good morning, Mr. David Jonathan Sawyer. What are you up to?"

What a pleasant surprise. Maggie, Harold's pretty girl friend from last night, stepped carefully out of a small stand of trees beside the path and stood before me.

"Don't look so startled," David, she said with a grin. "Mama and I spent the night at Mrs. Alma's. Since Harold will be leaving soon, Mama thought we should have some time together."

She moved closer until we were just inches apart. I stared in awe. In the harsh light of day, her subtle beauty was more pronounced, easily surpassing the way she looked in last night's New York setting. Her skin had a translucent quality, and her patrician features were barely Negroid. She was a beautiful mulatto, high yaller in every since of the word. The simple print dress hugged her supple frame like white on rice. My eyes roamed about her young body unashamedly. If she had been Caucasian, I could have been charged and sent to jail for reckless eyeballing. This was no Satan's imp or devil in disguise standing in the path before me. If ever there were an angel, surely this was one of the first order. My composure slowly returned.

"Hey girl, it's good to see you again." I was thinking that Harold was one lucky dude.

I looked into her eyes, and it was suddenly clear to me that something was wrong. I hadn't noticed it before, but Maggie's cheeks were tear-stained, and her eyes were puffy and reddened as if she had been crying. A wave of sympathy engulfed me. Impulsively, I took her hands in mine. "Aw c'mon girl. Don't feel like that. It ain't like he's going overseas next week. He's just going for basic training, and anyhow he might take his training right out at Fort Bragg."

"It ain't that David," she paused, pursing her full lips. "I don't really know why I'm crying. I guess it's because I don't know for sure whether I love him or not." She leaned against me sobbing quietly. All at once the words came pouring out. "We stayed in the basement most of the night." The long lashes fluttered as her eyes looked down, and her lips quivered uncontrollably. "David, we made love twice, and it wasn't at all like I thought it would be." For a moment, she seemed lost in thought. When she spoke again, her voice was a ragged whisper. "Good Lord, David, there's got to be more to love than that. I felt cheated." She grimaced. "It was awful."

I didn't know what to tell her. Twisted feelings and jumbled emotions in others were something I knew very little about. I had enough problems of my own dealing with the Jackson thing. I did feel sorry for her though and wished that I could help. Maggie's agitation increased, and I became more concerned.

"Come here," I said softly. "It's gonna be all right. Don't cry."

Without hesitating, she came into my arms. I held her for a moment and tried to calm her. As it always happened, when I least expected intervention, the spirit of Stonewall stirred inside me. The general had always been sympathetic to beautiful women, especially those that reminded him of the dusky senoritas of old Mexico. It figured because my great-grandmother, Mary Walker, had also been a victim of his lust.

It was a few minutes later, and we were sitting at the base of a small poplar on a slight knoll above the path. I was still holding her even though she had regained her composure. She seemed very much at ease. Our faces were almost touching as she looked up into my eyes. "I feel a little bit better now." There was a teasing smile on her face. "Tell me about you, David Jonathan Sawyer." Her eyes were pleading. I could tell that she was serious. "Is it true what they say about you, David? C'mon, tell me about yourself. Are you as good as they claim you are?"

"Ain't nothing to me, girl. What you see is what you get. Don't listen to all of that junk about how good I am. I quit all of that stuff. I'm walking with the Lord on the right track and trying to do the right thing." There

Physical Education

was a quizzical expression on her face, as if she didn't believe me. I said, "Honest injun, I ain't kidding. Besides, I'm getting married pretty soon."

She snuggled closer and placed her hand on my thigh. "I still don't believe you, David." Her hand slowly moved and began to gently caress my thigh. "Why don't you show me a teeny bit of what you can do?"

I shook my head frantically. No siree Bob. No way was I going to get caught in that trap. Harold was my friend, and she was his girl, and I still had my vow of celibacy to think about. The movement of her hand was insistent, probing my inner thigh.

I don't know the exact moment the devil invaded our privacy, but suddenly he was there, and the smell of brimstone filled the air. It was incredibly easy for the Prince of Darkness, a touch here and a touch there coupled with a gentle caress followed by nuzzling her slender neck freed her mind of all inhibitions. The spirit of Stonewall surged to the forefront, leering wickedly as he welcomed that denizen of the doomed. Between the devil and Thomas Jackson, Maggie and I had about as much chance to remain chaste as a snowball down under.

With her arms wrapped around my neck, Maggie lay back against the trunk of the small poplar. Fiercely, she pulled me down until I was lying beside her on the cool bed of leaves beneath the tree. The dance was about to begin. With Maggie's help, the prince warmed to his task. His was a labor of love. He didn't undress her completely. In seconds flat, the skirt of her dress was hiked above her hips, and the top was down around her navel. It was neither the devil nor Stonewall who helped Maggie to make the next move. I hardly recognized my own voice. It was guttural and harsh with want. "Maggie, sweetheart, turn around and lay with your head downhill. It'll be better for both of us. C'mon now!"

The smell of brimstone grew stronger, but now it was mixed with the stench of betrayal. My actions were not my own. It was the general's turn to do mischief. It was Jackson himself who initiated the oral worship. In my right mind, I would never have done such a thing. Maggie went berserk. She was scratching and clawing at my head and shoulders with complete abandon. The devil inside me was ravishing Maggie's body. Our expertise was making her hungry and as mean as a junkyard dog. With blue eyes flashing, the general goaded me on. He was in his element, and he gloried in making Maggie cry for more. My role in that sordid affair was a simple one. I changed my position and moved between her legs. Soon I began thrust after thrust with agonizing slowness. My slightest effort made her groan with pleasure. "Ohh, oohh," said Maggie. "Whew! whew! ohh Lordy me!" We were dancing with the devil to a forest flamenco that Harold, even though he was a good dancer, could not do. Our bodies entwined and writhed to the sound of unholy music played by the evil one himself.

Well, hello guilt. How are you doing? You just made it with your friend's best girl. Do you feel any remorse at all? You are one dirty bastard. You didn't even have the decency to wait until he was out of sight. What were you trying to prove? Answers to those questions were not expected or needed. They were salve to assuage the swelling of wrongdoing. Guilt was my companion all the way back up the hill. From force of habit, I still walked in the woods beside the road. My thoughts were with Maggie. She had asked me to leave her there beside the path.

"I'm okay David, honest," Maggie had insisted. "I've never had anything like this happen to me, and I need to be by myself." She sounded amazed, and her eyes widened as she looked up at me. "Good Lord in heaven, it was wonderful!" She shook her head slowly. "I know it sounds crazy, David, but Harold is just too big. You're much better than he could ever be." She smiled up at me. "You go ahead now. There are things I have to sort out about Harold and myself."

I walked away thinking that it was a half-assed compliment, and I didn't know whether I liked it or not. As I rounded the curve just below the house, I heard voices. It was Papa and Miz Nellie walking slowly down the road. I stood quietly for a moment and let them pass. When I reached the house, Jimmy was still there. He was in the little bedroom rummaging through an old burlap bag. He stopped for a moment and looked up at me.

"Listen, David, this is some stuff of mine that I need to save. I'm gonna put it under Papa's bed. Don't let nobody mess with it or throw it out." I nodded. I knew exactly what Jimmy had in the bag. It was his fishing tackle, an old aviator's cap, an old cap and a ball pistol that Papa had given him a long time ago. Jimmy was serious about his personal stuff. "By the way, David," he said slowly with a trace of concern in his voice, "I don't know what to tell you, but you're gonna have to do something about Miz Nellie." He frowned. "The old bag's gone clean off her rocker. All she could talk about was you. I'm telling you for a fact, David, you better get her straightened out before Papa gets wind of all the bullshit she's spreading around the neighborhood."

"I'll swear Jimmy, I don't know what to do. The old bitch just won't leave me alone." I didn't want to admit it, but I was really concerned about the loose way that Miz Nellie talked about me. It was as if she wanted to get me in trouble with Papa. Aw man, I just thought of something. What if Fanny found out about that night in the ditch? I would be in real trouble. She had been acting possessive ever since we decided to get married. I had been giving her money for expenses so that she wouldn't have to sell her body, but that only made it worse. Fanny felt that I was her property, and she was quick to show anger toward any woman that looked twice at me. I had to put an end to Miz Nellie's ranting about me.

Jimmy tied the burlap bag, leaned down and pushed it under Papa's bed. When he straightened up, there was a crooked smile on his face. "I tell you for a fact, Bro, I'm certainly gonna give the army my best shot." His face was suddenly solemn. "I'm gonna try my best not to fuck up like you did. I think I'm gonna do a pretty good job for Uncle Sam."

"Listen old buddy," I said with conviction, "I wish you all the luck in the world." I meant every word. Maybe Jimmy would do better than I. Maybe he would fulfill the Stonewall legacy. After all, the blood of Jackson twice removed flowed through his veins as well. I didn't begrudge Jimmy's chance for his moment in the sun. He was my brother.

The long-awaited Monday came with a vengeance. They called it Stormy Monday, and I wondered idly, would Tuesday be just as bad? The gray dawn ushered in rain that had been gathering impetus all night. Now, the cold wetness was a slow, steady downpour. It was a day when men of mettle such as Harold, Kelly and Jimmy would get a chance to prove their worth. The three of them would not meet their destiny without saying good-by.

The meeting place for the fond farewell had been determined ahead of time. All three young men were to leave from the little shack at precisely 6 a.m. Harold, Maggie, Mrs. Alma and Mrs. Tessie arrived in the big black Buick promptly at 5:30 am. A few minutes later Miz Snoog, who was soaking wet with the big, flowered dress plastered to her body, came out of the woods behind the house and walked into the yard. Kelly, dripping wet, suddenly appeared out of nowhere. It was a motley crew that Jimmy and I greeted on that rainy day in late September.

"C'mon in, y'all," Jimmy said. I was mortified. With the rain pouring down outside, it was hard not to invite them inside. The little shack was a complete mess: dirty dishes littered the kitchen table and discarded clothing and trash were all over the floor. The lone kerosene lamp in the center of the table was the cleanest thing in the house. I had no idea they would have any reason to come into the house. Nobody seemed to mind the filth. The occasion was much too important to worry about a dirty house.

As they converged around kitchen table, Mrs. Alma was the first to speak. "Well y'all," she said with a touch of sadness in her voice, "we're here to see our boys off to war. We've only got a little time, so I think we should say a quick prayer." Her eyes traveled around the table and came to a rest on Mrs. Tessie who was standing beside Jimmy. "Tessie, give us one of your earnest prayers, but make it short."

"Awright y'all," Mrs. Tessie said abruptly, "everybody join hands, and we'll take it to the Lord."

The small group moved about the table jockeying for positions. Harold was already holding Maggie possessively with his arm around her shoulder. I was standing between Mrs. Alma and Maggie. She was looking up at Harold when she squeezed my hand hard enough to make me wince. I didn't squeeze back or give Maggie any indication at all. I wanted no familiarity on the solemn occasion. Jimmy looked a wee bit uncomfortable as he grabbed Mrs. Tessie's hand. Kelly was just inside the door, and Miz Snoog didn't quite make it inside. Her large behind was still outside in the rain. But, her hand was inside, and Kelly grabbed it with love. When everybody had joined hands, Mrs. Tessie began to pray. Her voice was choked with emotion and sincerity. "Gracious Lord we are gathered here to see our boys off to war. We ask you to go with Harold, Kelly and Jimmy. Be a light unto their path and make their enemies your footstool. Bring them back home safely, Lord."

She was suddenly overcome with emotion, and tears began streaming

Physical Education

down her face. She placed her arm around Jimmy's shoulders and said fervently, "One other thing Lord, please deliver a special blessing to Little Jimmy Sawyer, and bring him back home to me as quick as possible. We ask this in the name of the Lord Jesus. Amen!"

It was a solemn occasion. Miz Snoog had a death grip on Kelly's arm and undying love was in her eyes as she looked up at her departing warrior.

"You be a good boy, Kelly, honey. Your chubby baby will be right here waiting for you." She smiled coyly. "That is, unless you send for me first. I'd go anywhere to be with you, honey."

"You got that right, baby cake," said Kelly with a wide grin. "Don't you worry your pretty head about me fooling around, 'cause ain't no woman like the one I got." I could believe that without question Miz Snoog was special in her own sweet way.

It seemed that love was all over the place. I was waiting for Harold and Maggie to declare their commitment to each other. They were looking into each other's eyes, completely oblivious of what was happening around them. They said nothing to each other. I guessed that their love needed no trite words of assurance. It was deeper than that.

Jimmy, who was still standing beside Mrs. Tessie, did encounter one minor problem. Without a warning of any sort, Mrs. Tessie put her arms around Jimmy's neck and kissed him squarely on the mouth, boring her tongue between his teeth. His face was contorted, and his eyes rolled backward. He stood helpless as her tongue lingered in his mouth. Ohh ohh, my goodness. I wished that hadn't happened. If my thinking were correct, Jimmy was about to spit all over the place, on anything and everything in sight. Surprisingly, Jimmy didn't spit. He just gulped once, and his face turned a funny shade of gray. His face slowly returned to normal, and I could tell that the urge to spit was gone. Jimmy would be okay.

Dawn arrived fully, with its garments still wet from the persistent downpour. It was time for the fledgling warriors to meet their destiny. Harold, Maggie and Mrs. Alma got into the front seat of the Buick. Kelly, Mrs. Tessie and Jimmy got into the rear seat. Oblivious of the rain, Miz Snoog stood in the doorway watching her beloved. I stood behind her looking over her shoulder at the moving scenario. Miz Snoog had shed her tears and said her last good-by. She was well aware that there was no room for her in the Buick.

I didn't need a ride either. My regular rider, a taciturn Croatan Indian from Lumberton, would come along promptly at five minutes of seven.

Mrs. Alma was going to drive the boys out to the reception center. It would give Harold and Maggie a little more time to talk about their future. From what I could see from the doorway, they were still gazing soulfully into each other's eyes. There were two small incidents of no consequence that broke the monotony. Jimmy suddenly opened the rear window, leaned out and began gagging and spitting up like crazy. In fact, he almost upchucked on Jody Peet who just happened to be walking up the path. A pretty smile, utterly disarming, lit up Mrs. Alma's face when she saw Jody.

Unmindful of the rain, Mrs. Alma leaned out of the window. "Why Jody, you are a sight for sore eyes," her voice trilled. "I ain't got time to talk right now. I've got to get Harold and the boys out to Fort Bragg. They're taking their physicals to go into the army." Jody stood quietly waiting for Mrs. Alma to continue. "But, there is one thing, the latch on my back door is loose. I wonder if you can come by and fix it for me? It shouldn't take much. The door is brand-new." I could understand her feelings about the door. Life had to go on, even while Harold was away in the service of his country.

Jody's charm was always with him, even on rainy Mondays. He said politely. "Yes ma'am, Mrs. Alma. I'll fix it for you whenever you want." She nodded her head, and the Buick moved slowly out of the yard toward the Rose Hill Road. I knew that Mrs. Alma was sure that her door would be as good as new. After all, Jody was the back door man.

Time flies even if you're not having fun. It had been a dreary day at work, with a lot of rush orders. The police action in Korea was heating up, and men and ordnance were sorely needed in the areas of the peninsula that were controlled by the Allies. Running in and out of the paint shop in the cold rain to bring in trucks and jeeps did not make my job any easier. I was dead tired that afternoon when I walked up the path from the Rose Hill Road and entered the little shack. I was in for a rude awakening. The last thing in the world that I expected to see was Jimmy

Physical Education

sitting at the kitchen table. There was a quart of cloudy moonshine sitting at his elbow, and his eyes were bloodshot. I should have known something was wrong because Jimmy was drinking Pegleg Pete's bad liquor and that was something highly unusual for Jimmy. He would walk extra miles for good, clear drinking, moonshine.

"Jimmy," I said with alarm, "what in the world's going on? Why are you home, and why are you drinking Pegleg Pete's sorry-ass rotgut? He won't even drink that shit himself. That crap has got enough Clorox in it to wash a tub of clothes. You ought not do that to yourself"

He shook his head sadly. "I dunno Dave," he answered. He looked as if he were about to cry. "Everything's all fucked up. Harold and Kelly passed their physical examinations, but I didn't pass mine." For a moment he was at a loss for words. Then he said slowly, "The examination was going real good. I passed the eye exam. My hearing and my blood pressure were fine, and the doctor said my heart sounded okay. Then he started a pelvic examination and after that he started probing my groin and messing with my dick." Jimmy rubbed away a tear from his left eye. Another fell from his right eye and landed on the front of his shirt." His voice was ragged and hoarse. "I was doing real good, David, until he examined my nut sack." His eyes were averted now, and the tears were coming faster." The next words came even faster, blurted out in complete despair. "He said my nut sack had only one nut inside it."

I was dumbfounded. "Great day in the morning, Jimmy! What in the world did he mean? I ain't never heard of no shit like that. Did he say why?"

"Well," said Jimmy with a tremor in his voice, "he said that I had another testicle, but it was buried in the tissue in the left side of my groin. He showed me the condition in his medical book. It's called an undescended left testicle." Jimmy was quick to add, "It don't hurt none, and he said I could still make babies. The only problem was that unless I got an operation, the testicle would atrophy, and I would lose it altogether." For the first time Jimmy looked me squarely in the eye. "The army would give me the operation, and I could still go in service, but I told him hell no. I know I kin fuck, and I know I can get babies. I'm going to leave that nut right where it is, and if I lose it, I just lose it and to hell with the whole thing."

God damn Stonewall Jackson to hell! He wasn't satisfied with fucking up my life with an undersized dick. He did even worse to my little brother. The bastard gave him a single nut in the right place and a half-assed promise of another nut if he would take an operation. The dirty old son of a bitch was somewhere laughing at the two of us. Instead of his own troops doing it, I wished that I could have been the one who shot the old rascal.

    I wondered about old Aunt Easter, the drunken midwife who had delivered Jimmy and myself. According to Jimmy's doctor, she could easily have corrected Jimmy's problem at birth. She did circumcise him, but she even botched that simple procedure. The foreskin of Jimmy's penis was ragged and uneven like the petals of some strange flower. Maybe the reason I never noticed the other problem with his testicle was because Jimmy was terribly self-conscious, and I tried never to stare and embarrass him about it. I also wondered why the old whiskey-soaked mid-wife hadn't circumcised me. Maybe she thought I was so small that I needed everything available to me. Even with that thought in mind, I still blamed the quirky, wildly eccentric Stonewall Jackson. He was the villain of the piece. I wondered if Jimmy knew that the culprit responsible for the debacle was his great-grandfather and that his own actions were guided by the vagrant whims of a man who had been dead for over a 100 years.

24

Papa, a Squirrel And I

I was concerned about Jimy's situation, but there was nothing I could do. Besides, I had my own problems. I had to do something about the guilt I continued to feel from the interlude with Maggie. If I had been Catholic, I would have immediately gone to confession. As it turned out, I had to choose between Mr. Avon and Reverend Elliot. I desperately needed some counseling about the loose way I was handling my vow of celibacy. I did not want to embark on the sea of matrimony in a leaky ship. Help was in the offing.

I was a Christian and a Methodist. There were Methodist solutions to my problem.

On Sunday after church, I finally got up enough nerve to do something about my concerns. I had decided to talk to Reverend Elliot because he was nearer my own age. Besides, he and his wife seemed to be an ideal couple who really exemplified the way a marriage should be. I recalled how heavenly the two of them looked standing with me during my baptism ceremony. The devil was still stalking me, even in the sanctity of the church. All I could think about was how the white silk robe had looked plastered against the full breasts of my pastor's wife. I began to think as I walked down the aisle to the small door of his office.

"Check yourself David. It's getting worse. You're out of control."

The pastor didn't feel that way. He seemed genuinely glad to see me. After the first knock, he said, "Cmon in David. Pull up a chair, and let's talk a bit." The smile on his young face put me completely at ease. His bespectacled brown eyes bored into mine. "What did you want to talk about? Is everything okay?"

His demeanor gave me courage, so I decided to be honest and straight forward about myself.

"No, it ain't Reverend. I've got a real problem." The words rushed out of my mouth. "You know Fanny and I are gonna get married, and I've been trying to keep myself straight and not fornicate. It's a difficult thing to do. I kinda slipped up a couple of weeks ago and got a piece of tail. The girl wasn't Fanny, so I guess that made it even worse. In fact, it was the girlfriend of a close friend. I asked the Lord to forgive me, but I guess even He gets tired of having to do the same thing over and over again." I was about to mention Miz Nellie, but I decided to let sleeping dogs lie. There's just so much forgiveness to go around.

The soothing voice of Reverend Elliot droned on reassuring me that the Lord still loved me. Finally his admonitions were over, and as I was about to leave, he said firmly:

"David, you're going to be fine, and I'm looking forward to your wedding. I'll get Sister Elliot to help Fanny put it together." He smiled graciously. "You behave yourself, now. Go, and sin no more." I felt good. It was as if Jesus himself were talking to me.

I left the church and hurried down Jones Street to Fanny's little house. I paused when I reached her yard and marveled at how neat and fastidious she kept her little place. A straw broom was leaning against the porch. Evidently, she had just swept the yard since coming from church. She came into my arms as soon as she opened the door.

"I didn't mean to leave you, honey," she said. "But I had had just about enough church for one day." She was bubbling over with curiosity. "Did you see the preacher?" She grabbed my arm and guided me to the small couch near the door. As always, the little shotgun house was spotless. When we were seated, she said breathlessly. "What did y'all talk about? Is he gonna marry us? Don't keep me waiting, David, tell me?"

"Yes, yes, yes," I said as I hugged her tightly. "He's gonna marry us any time we're ready. And guess what? Sister Elliot is gonna help you plan the wedding. How about them apples?"

"Ohh David, thank the Lord!" Her arms went around my neck, and she kissed me squarely on the mouth. The kiss turned sexual immediately. The heat of her hungry mouth evaporated my spiritual thoughts, leaving a vacuum that was quickly filled by lust. Regardless of the way Fanny made me feel, I had no intention of giving in. Besides, I had just come from church. I was about to pull away when she grabbed my left hand and placed it at the juncture of her thighs. Her legs opened, then closed tightly around my hand.

"I know what we promised the Lord, David, and I know we can't do nothing nasty. I just want you to touch me for a minute."

She opened her legs and jammed my hand firmly at the juncture of her thighs. Her voice quivered. "Please, honey, help me a little bit. It won't be a sin."

Fanny didn't wait for my help. Her breath came in short gasps as she grabbed my wrist with both hands and began to wriggle and squirm. I was not going to be a party to her sinful ways, but my left hand did not agree. It joined the fracas wholeheartedly. I could tell by the frenzied look on Fanny's face that her scheme was working. My right hand was lying idle on my lap. I knew that Jackson despised idleness, so I quickly unzipped my pants and gave it a chore. I knew then that the devil had not let up on my case. He had followed me from church. Fanny stifled a scream, and the whole affair ended in a shuddering fleeting moment. When the trembling subsided, it left me wondering. Had we committed fornication? Certainly, the end result was the same. Did we, or didn't we? I was in a quandary trying to figure it out. Finally, I decided it was too close to call, and I hoped the Lord felt the same way.

Glory, glory, glory, the Lord was merciful, and His goodness was everywhere. I felt like doing the "Huckle Buck." Everything was beautiful.

My marriage to Fanny was scheduled for the second week in October, and my brother Jimmy was no longer upset about not being accepted by the army. He had gotten a job as a grease monkey at Fort Bragg. The shop was right next to the paint shop. Papa and Miz Nellie were also riding high. They were all set to harvest their illicit tobacco crop. Bright leaf tobacco prices were at a record high in all the nearby markets. The golden leaf was a good wholesome thing. It could be smoked, chewed or dipped with no after-effects. The habit-forming and constant craving that it caused was part of its charm.

The best laid plans of Papa and Miz Nellie were suddenly interrupted by a small single engine plane on loan to the North Carolina Department of Agriculture. The pilot and his passenger were flying low early one morning to map the general area of the Rose Hill Road for zoning purposes. It was just Papa's misfortune that they spotted the acre of prime tobacco growing smack dab in the middle of the swamp. It was an unusual sight, and they lost no time in reporting their discovery to the bureau. Neither Papa nor Miz Nellie went to jail, but it took all of the persuasive powers of Charlie McBride, a lawyer who had been Papa's company commander at Camp Greene in South Carolina. It was a stroke of good fortune that Mr. McBride had friends in the Department of Agriculture. He managed to keep Papa from going to jail and possibly from doing time in a chain gang on the county roads. It was only natural that Papa would be quite upset when I saw him a few days after the incident.

It was Saturday morning and Papa, Jimmy and I were at the kitchen table. We had spent most of the previous day together. Papa had been behaving strangely. His narrow eyes kept darting to and fro, never staying on any object for more than a second. His plate of fatback, greens and potatoes sat untouched, and the coffee I had poured for him was already cold. There was a funny twitch to the muscles of his jaw, and I smelled the faint odor of alcohol. I had never known Papa to take a drink for any reason. The smell of whiskey was not on Jimmy's breath. He had been on the wagon since failing the army physical.

"Why don't you eat a bite, Papa?" asked Jimmy with a slight frown. Papa usually ate everything in sight and asked for more.

"I ain't hungry," Papa answered. Irritation was evident in his voice. "I ain't gonna eat nothing until your Ma gets back." His eyes were darting up, down and around the room. "I don't know what's keeping Mary. She should have been back."

Ohh! ohh! Papa was in worse shape than I could have imagined. There had been occasional lapses when he spoke of Mama as if she were alive, but never in that manner. I didn't like the out-of-kilter matter-of-fact way he was acting, and I was especially concerned about what was happening with his eyes.

Mama's death and the failure of everything he tried to do had forced Papa's mind into deep trouble. Because of my heritage, I was no stranger to the the thin line between sanity and insanity. It was easy to see that Papa's mental anguish had pushed him to the edge. My heart went out to him because I knew first-hand about teetering on the the brink of lunacy. It was an everyday occurrence with Jackson and myself. We were accustomed to being in the throes of disordered intellect. It was a feat that we managed with the style and grace of a trapeze artist.

I looked at Jimmy, and he looked back, shaking his head sadly. I got up abruptly and pushed my chair under the table.

"I'm getting outta here. I'll dig y'all later." I placed my hand on Papa's shoulders. "You take care Papa, and everything's gonna be okay, you hear? It's Saturday, and I've got a lot of things to do." I didn't like seeing Papa at his worst. The alcohol was something new, and I was worried because it certainly wouldn't help his state of mind.

I walked out into the crisp morning air and immediately felt better. On that morning, the Rose Hill Road was like a very good painting, complete with the red, brown and yellows of Autumn. I was going to enjoy its beauty all the way down to the quiet neatness of Fanny's little house. We had to make wedding plans.

I had my own plans. A brand-new bed was the first thing I was going to buy. I wanted no reminder of Fanny's past. We would be living at her place for the time being, and this would be a new beginning for both of us. Shortly after we did that crazy hand jive, Fanny and I decided not to see each other for a couple of weeks. The risk of sinning was just too great. And anyhow, we had a lifetime of loving and caring to share.

The trickling water of the creek reminded me that I was crossing the bridge. I kept walking with my head down, completely absorbed in thoughts of marriage. A shadow suddenly appeared on the ground in front of me. I looked up and to my dismay I was staring into the bloodshot eyes and slack face of Miz Nellie Smith. The beauty of the Autumn evening quickly faded. The last dollop went along with the big gob of snuff that Miz Nellie spit into the ditch beside the road.

Miz Nellie staggered a bit, and then moved closer until she was right in front of me. Her broad face was an angry mask, and her voice was a study in nastiness. "Well, if it ain't Little David Sawyer. You been kinda ducking me, ain't you, boy?" She was rocking back and forth, barely able to maintain her balance. "Fancy running into you like this," she chortled. "I'm looking for your old sorry-assed daddy. Have you seen Noah lately?"

"Yes ma'am, Miz Nellie, he's up at the house, but I think he's kinda sick. It might be better if you left him alone for a little while."

"You got that right, boy. There's something wrong. I don't know what's happening with the old fool. He walked out of the house this morning without saying a word." Her face screwed up in thought. "Ever since the government plowed our tobacco under, he's been acting strange as shit. I tell you for a fact, boy, he'd better get hisself together."

"Yes ma'am, Miz Nellie," I said as I tried to maneuver around her wide frame. "I'll be sure to tell him next time I run into him."

She grabbed my arm roughly, grinning widely through a mist of snuff spit. "It ain't no big thing, Little David. You'll do jest fine." She started pulling me toward the bushes beside the road. "We got some unfinished business, Davy boy. Let's fuck!"

Great day in the morning! She was after me again! There would be no repeat performance in this neck of the Rose Hill Road. I jerked away from Miz Nellie, stumbled into the ditch and scampered up the slippery slope and fled into the swamp. I didn't look back because I was afraid of what I would see. There was no telling just how determined Miz Nellie was, so I went deep into the morass of briars and vines until I came to the creek. The safety of the swamp cuddled me like an animal nuzzling its young. I needed time to think.

It was late evening, and shadows were stretching their long arms across the road when I came out of the swamp. There was still time to see my beloved Fanny. I hadn't told her I was coming, and she would be pleasantly surprised to see me. My spirits were sky high as I hurried down the road.

I stopped walking for a moment and listened intently. Someone was calling my name. As I listened, the voice was suddenly louder. I looked back up the road and saw a figure running toward me. It was Jimmy, and he was shouting, "Hey David, wait up, I've got to talk to you!" He was completely out of breath when he reached me. The veins in his neck were standing out like small ropes, and his eyes were wide with worry.

When he finally got his wind back, it was still a moment before he could speak.

"David, for God's sake, get away from here! Miz Nellie was up to the house, and she told Papa a bunch of lies about you. She told him that you had been fucking her all Summer, and you wouldn't leave her alone."

Jimmy looked like he was about to cry. "I'm serious David. Papa's got that old double-barrelled shotgun and some double ought buckshot shells. He's looking for you, David, and he's mad as hell."

I was dumb-founded. It had never occurred to me that Miz Nellie would lie to Papa out of pure spite. If Papa were as mad as Jimmy said, I was really in a mess. I looked at Jimmy. He was plainly worried. I didn't know what to do. The safest place I could think of was Grandpa's. I turned to Jimmy and said calmly, trying desperately to hide my fear, "I'm going up to Grandpa's. Maybe Papa won't do nothing bad at the old home place."

"For God's sake, David, be careful," begged Jimmy. "I ain't never seen Papa acting like he's doing now." His agitation increased. "I'm going down and tell Uncle Mike. He might be able to talk some sense into Papa." He started walking rapidly down the road, and then he stopped briefly and said over his shoulder, "You'd better get a move on, David. There will be hell to pay if he catches up with you."

I turned and started walking back up the road. I had to take the chance that I would reach the path that led up the hill to Grandpa's place before I ran into Papa. My heart stopped racing when I spotted the path just ahead of me. I thought I had it made, but Papa suddenly stepped out of the bushes beside the path. My heart did a flip-flop, and my breathing stopped altogether. Good grief! It was worse than I thought. Papa didn't look like Papa. His face was contorted into a malevolent leer, and his little eyes were red with rage. He stood looking at me without saying a word. The old shotgun was cradled in the crook of his arm, and his eyes never left my face. Finally he said in a dirty, rasping voice, "You're the devil, ain'tcha, boy."

The barrel of the shotgun rose slowly until it was pointed at my middle. "They say you can't kill the devil," said Papa. "Let's see if a load of double ought buckshot will make a dent in old Satan's ass." This was it. There was no doubt in my mind. Papa was certainly going to kill me, and Stonewall Jackson would die a second time.

It was irony at its worst. Jackson's death had been at the hands of his own troops. My death was about to come at the hands of my own flesh and blood. I stood there looking at Papa. There was nothing to say, and I was not going to beg. I accepted the fact that my life was going to end at that moment. I was resigned to my fate. For no special reason visions of a squirrel came to mind. It was almost laughable. I was about to die, and all I could think about was a squirrel.

It happened on a snowy morning in December when I was about eight years old. There was no food in the house except some grits and a piece of dried fatback. "Noah," said Mama plaintively, "there ain't nothing decent in the house to eat. I sure would like to have a nice fat squirrel for breakfast. Please Noah, run down to the spring and get one for me." Mama's eyes were shining at the thought. "I could pot boil the little rascal and then simmer it down in onions and make some gravy."

"Okay Hon," said Papa. "I'll run down the hill and bring you back a squirrel." He walked over to the corner by the door and got the shotgun. Then, he reached up and took a shell from the box on the shelf above the icebox.

As he was going out the door, I called out to him. "Hey Papa, why are you taking just one shell with you?"

He grinned broadly. "Your Ma didn't want but one squirrel, boy. Y'all sit tight. I'll be back in a hot minute." He was still grinning as he walked around the corner of the house. Mama got her squirrel, and I gained new respect for Papa.

Reluctantly, my mind returned to the death scene. I was horrified as the Grim Reaper slowly raised his scythe. Two loud explosions ripped through the late afternoon silence. I couldn't understand why I wasn't lying in the dirt at Papa's feet covered with blood. Instead, I was still standing and that didn't make a lick of sense. I looked down because I felt a stinging sensation in my left foot. The ground around my feet had been skewered with buckshot. The cuffs of my pants were ragged with holes. And both shoes were shredded on the outside, and blood was seeping from the sole of my left foot. Papa's eyes were still boring into mine as he slowly lowered the gun, broke it down and removed the shells. He turned as if in a daze and walked slowly back into the brush.

My right foot was okay except the shoe was ruined, but my left foot was bleeding badly. I started to walk down the road toward the junction.

If I could make it to Fanny's little house I would be all right. The pain was sharp and biting, and the blood sloshed inside my shoe with a sucking sound. The sight of blood didn't bother me. Jackson was never concerned by the sight of his own blood. I began to feel woozy after I passed Aunt Lizzie's little house. By the time I crossed the main highway and entered Jones street, I was dizzy and reeling with pain. I somehow managed to make it to Fanny's yard.

I stood looking down at the blood seeping from my foot. Fanny would be pissed at blood in her spotless yard. The yard was not in its usual spotless condition. There were a lot of footsteps leading in and out of the yard. I couldn't understand it. I took a deep breath and made my way carefully up on the porch.

I was about to knock when an ear-splitting scream came from the house.

"Ow, ooh, ooh, shit, shit, shit!" The screaming lasted for a full minute, and then there was silence. Fanny's screams were not implications. They were a fact of life that I had to accept. Sadly I turned and limped slowly back down the steps. Even though wounded, Jackson was stalwart in defeat. Sharp, searing emotions as real as the dizziness and loss of blood made it extremely difficult for me to maintain my balance, but somehow I made it across the main road and down the hill to Aunt Lizzie's little house.

I tried to walk up the steps, but I fell flat on the floor with my face against the door jam. Somewhere from a great distance, I heard Aunt Lizzie's voice. "Good Lord, boy! What have you done this time?"

Consciousness came and went as I lay there. I remember saying, "Aunt Lizzie, I'm kinda sick. My feet hurt, and I think I've got a touch of the colic."

The good Lord was with me, and Thomas Jonathan Jackson did not die a second time. There were other battles to fight, and the spirit of Stonewall would not leave me. The old rascal was having too much fun. There was no need to blame Fanny for being a screaming backslider. The clean, swept yard was simply an anomaly. Perfection is a fleeting thing that does not linger. I forgave Fanny whole-heartedly. I would still love her but from a great distance.

Epilogue

I would return to my swamp like a wounded lion seeking the cool marshes of the deep jungle. The soft, dark earth of the bottomland would mother me and be a healing balm to my injured flesh and spirit. But, there would be more to this tawdry tale of ghostly-driven wantonness and unbridled lust. There were many things I had to know and do. Would I continue to wander through a twisted maze of failed ambitions and flawed relationships? Or, would my weak faith strengthen enough so I would not have to resort to trickery and deceit to achieve my goals? Would the elusive dream of safe passage ever become a reality?

The final volume of this trilogy will properly address these disturbing questions. Enough of this morbid speculation, maybe simplicity is the key. It might be a simple matter of taking a little bit and making it go a long way. I was convinced that time would march on, and soon the spirit of Stonewall and me would emerge from the verdant greenness of the swamp, ready to take on all comers, barring none. We would relish the thought of taunting the world at large. With eyes flashing scorn at insurmountable odds, we would go forth and do battle. And, once again the North and South will witness the indomitable skill and prowess of the mighty "Stonewall" Jackson.

Appendix

The following are documents and photographs that support my claim to the Stonewall legacy.

> Stonewall Jackson was not a youthful saint; he was fond of horse races and had his full share of the hot blood and indiscretions of youth. It is known and not denied by those conversant with the facts that he was the father of an illegitimate child. Maj. Jed Hotchkiss (May 14, 1895) informed me that this was well known to Jackson's military family among whom the matter was frequently discussed. When a cadet at West Point and on a visit to his home, he seduced a young girl at or near Beverly and the result was a child, which Jackson acknowledged and to which he frequently made presents and sent money. The late Asher Harman also confirmed this and had knowledge of the fact before the war. Dr. Dabney, when hunting material for his life of Jackson, was horrified to learn this fact and utterly refused to believe it.
>
> > Note in the holograph of Gen. Ezra Ayers Carman, filed in an "Antietam Studies" file box, folder marked "Jackson's Division." Antietam Battlefield Commission Papers, RG 92, National Archives. (One of eleven boxes not described in the directory at RG 92.)

Weathered by time, this copy of the Winchester Portrait of Stonewall Jackson bought by Mary Walker and passed down through the Sawyer family now resides in the author's Baltimore home. (Photography by C.B. Nieberding.)

The author, 1945

This print of young Jackson is from a small book by Ralph Happel called "The Last Days of Jackson."

Isaiah Jackson, son of Stonewall Jackson and Mary Walker

Death certificate of Isaiah Jackson, December 1, 1918.

Death certificate of Mary Sawyer, the author's mother.

Thomas J. "Stonewall" Jackson, photographed at Winchester, Virginia, in 1862. National Archives. Print courtesy of the Museum of the Confederacy, Richmond.

The similarity between the Jackson photography and my own is certainly a family likeness and not a coincidence by any stretch of the imagination. You are the product of those who came before you. The third volume of this work will explore in depth the strange uncontrollable forces unleashed by the Jackson heritage and how they affected my life.

The estate papers of Thomas Jonathan Jackson

ESTATE APPRAISAL - June 5, 1863   THOMAS J. JACKSON

ORDER	ITEM AND VALUATION	ACCESSION NO.	ROOM PLACEMENT	OTHER
	Map of County of Rockbridge ($5.00)			
1	Rag Carpet ($35.00)			
4	Remnants (rag carpet) ($5.00)			
3	Remnants (Scotch Carpets) ($20.00)			
1	Scotch Carpet ($50.00)			
1	Scotch Carpet ($90.00)			
3	Pieces of bocking ($6.00)			
1	Piano Cover ($5.00)			
1	Oum Door mat ($3.00)			
1	" " ($.50)			
(	CommodeBedsteade ($5.00)			
7	Pillows (?) ($20.00)			
3	Bolsters ($10.00)			
1	Trunke Strape ($.75)			
1	Parlor Curtain ($10.00)			
1	Oiled Table Cover ($1.00)			
1	Pair Transparent Blinds (5.10)			
1	Green Sofa ($10.00)			
1	Mahogany Sofa ($60.00)			
1	Pair of Muslin Curtains ($4.00)			
1	CLOCK ($15.00)			

ESTATE APPRAISAL __(Page 2)

NUMBER	ITEM AND VALUATION	ACCESSION NUMBER	ROOM PLACEMENT	OTHER
1	Rosewood Bureau (70.00)			
1	Rosewood Bureau ($50.00)			
1	Lamp ($5.00)			
1	Lamp ($1.00)			
2	Looking Glasses ($6.00)			
1	Looking Glasses ($.50)			
1	Passage Lamp ($6.00)			
1	Centre table ($30.00)			
1	Extension Table ($15.00)			
1	Sett casters ($25.00)			
1	sett china ($25.00)			
2	waiters ($5.00)			
1	desk ($6.00)			
1	Negro woman Hetty aged 40 years ($1,120.00)			
1	Negro girl Emma ($600.00)			
1	Negro man Cyrus 21 years ($2,000.00)			
1	Negro man George 19 years ($2,000.00)			
1	Wardrobe ($10.00)			

ESTATE APPRAISAL - Page 3

NUMBER	ITEM AND VALUATION	ACCESSION NUMBER	ROOM PLACEMENT	OTHER
1	Marble top wash stand ($10.00)			
2	Marble top wash stand ($10.00)			
1	Hair mattress ($20.00)			
2	other mattresses ($20.00)			
1	chamber sett ($8.00)			
1	hat rack ($10.00)			
1	tin slop bowl and foot tub ($5.00)			
1	spittoon ($.50)			
40 yards	matting ($40.00)			
1	library ($210.00)			
1	fire screen ($2.50)			
1	rosewood bedsted ($25.00)			
1	lot jars ($8.00)			
1	varnish brush ($.50.00)			
1	lot Queensware, pitchers etc. ($80.00)			
6	mahogany chairs ($50.00)			
1	mahogany arm chair ($25.00)			
4	strawbottomed chairs ($8.00)			
	canebottomed chairs ($20.00)			

ESTATE APPRAISAL page 4

NUMBER	ITEM AND VALUATION	ACCESSION NO.	ROOM PLACEMENT	OTHER
2	rocking chairs ($5.00)			
1	bedstead ($30.00)			
1	side table (marble top) ($20.00)			
1	set shovel, tongs, etc. ($5.00)			
1	small table ($3.00)			
1	parlor carpet ($100.00)			
2	paper blinds ($1.50)			
1	bathing tub and apparatus ($12.00)			
1	coffee mill ($4.00)			
1	hominy mill ($3.00)			
1	hand saw ($3.00)			
	gallon and quart measure ($1.00)			
1	_____ pot ($1.50)			
2	horse collars ($6.00)			
1	_____ iron ($1.00)			
2 pair	andirons, shovel and tongs ($2.50)			
1	spade ($1.50)			
1	auger ($1.50)			
1	m------ing scythe ($4.00)			

134

	ITEM AND VALUATION	ACCESSION NO.	ROOM PLACEMENT	OTHER
1	grass cradle ($8.00)			
1	chisel ($.50)			
1	Jack plane ($1.25)			
1	jug ($2.00)			
1	Pr. olde gears ($.50)			
1	passage oiled carpet ($25.00)			
	fork and rake ($1.50)			
2	parlor stoves ($30.00)			
1	sheet iron _____ ($10.00)			
11	jars and crocks ($6.00)			
1	trowel ($10.00)			
1	churn ($3.00)			
1	ice cream freezer ($5.00)			
1	_____ ($6.00)			
1	sifter ($1.50)			
12	barrells, lime, seeds, clover, etc. ($10.00)			
	tin pans ($1.50)			
2	_____ (2.00)			
1	manure fork ($2.00)			
2	buckets ($1.50)			

ESTATE APPRAISAL page 6

SAWYER

NUMBER	ITEM AND VALUATION	ACCESSION NO.	ROOM PLACEMENT	OTHER
2	sheets of zinc ($10.00)			
1	cooking stove ($50.00)			
1	plough and harrow ($18.00)			
2	Kitchen tables ($1.50)			
1	bay mare ($450.00)			
1	sorrell horse, not present, supposed to be worth $500.00.			